JIM THOMPSON

▼

SLEEP
WITH
THE
DEVIL

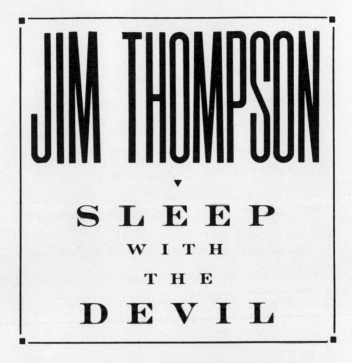

JIM THOMPSON

▼

SLEEP
WITH
THE
DEVIL

MICHAEL J. McCAULEY

THE MYSTERIOUS PRESS
New York · Tokyo · Sweden · Milan
Published by Warner Books

 A Time Warner Company

Mysterious Press books are published by
Warner Books, Inc., 666 Fifth Avenue, New York, NY 10103.

A Time Warner Company

The Mysterious Press name and logo are trademarks of Warner Books, Inc.

Printed in the United States of America
First printing: April 1991
10 9 8 7 6 5 4 3 2 1

Library of Congress Cataloging-in-Publication Data

McCauley, Michael J.
    Jim Thompson : sleep with the devil / by Michael J. McCauley.
      p.   cm.
    Includes bibliographical references and index.
    ISBN 0-89296-392-1
    1. Thompson, Jim, 1906–1977—Biography. 2. Novelists,
American—20th century—Biography. I. Title.
PS3539.H6733Z78   1991
813'.54—dc20
[B]   90-50548
                                        CIP

Book design by Giorgetta Bell McRee

Poem in epigraph is © 1988 Dying Art Ltd, reproduced by kind permission.
Extracts from Jim Thompson's work are used with
permission from Alberta Hesse Thompson.

For Sue

This place is Hell to me
With the Devil in my bed
And the Devil in this bottle
And the Devil in my head
I'll meet you in Heaven again
If you wear that dress again
(I'll have one more drink, my friend)
Where my heart is kept on ice
And prayers burst into flames
Prayers on fire.

—Nick Cave

JIM THOMPSON

SLEEP
WITH
THE
DEVIL

INTRODUCTION

Jim Thompson wrote twenty-nine published novels, dozens of short stories, two of Stanley Kubrick's best films, and thousands of manuscript pages before dying in obscurity in Los Angeles in 1977. Although his lifelong dreams of recognition and fame never were realized while he lived, Jim Thompson did become something of a trend in America in the late 1980s—nearly all of Thompson's novels were reprinted and subsequently optioned for films. Hollywood offered adaptations of Thompson novels *The Grifters* (1990) and *After Dark, My Sweet* (1990); but it was independent film director Maggie Greenwald who finally brought a true Thompson vision to the screen in her adaptation of *The Kill-Off* (1990). Countless admirers, from Stephen King to Sean Penn, logged in with praise for Thompson's work. In a curiously fitting irony, dead more than a decade, Jim Thompson had finally made it big.

Jim Thompson's growing stature as a popular culture figure was matched by his rising literary reputation—critics raved about his "nihilistic" writing, while favorably comparing him to not only fellow crime writers Dashiell Hammett, Raymond Chandler, James M. Cain, and Horace McCoy but also to Dostoevsky, Nabokov, Sophocles, Swift, and Céline. In France, where Thompson had long been considered one of the most important American writers of the twentieth century, his novels were the basis for two films, the Academy Award–nominated *Coup de Torchon* (1981) and Alain Corneau's *Série Noire* (1979).

Reviewers, having little to go on but the novels, often speculated that Jim Thompson was similar to the monsters he depicted so convincingly—gaining vengeance with a pen instead of a gun. And the few available facts, which sketched Jim Thompson as a banal and boring family man, only fueled more lurid speculation, since most of Thompson's killer psychopaths seethe behind similarly bland public masks.

Despite Thompson's 1980s "comeback," both he and his work continue to be as misunderstood today as when he was alive. The sensational elements that define his novels, and the rumors about his life, only further obscure the truth of Jim Thompson and his work. The "real" Jim Thompson, and the purpose of his writings, still lies waiting to be recovered.

While preparing a collection of Jim Thompson's short stories and previously unpublished writing, I met many of his family and friends, obtained some preliminary facts about his life, and set out to write this biography.

Yet later many key facts proved either unfindable or unavailable; the Thompson family offers a bland version of Jim's life and character from which they refuse to waver, despite any outside evidence to the contrary. Though initially discouraging, this dearth of information about Thompson's domestic life later proved paradoxically appropriate and illuminating.

While his life story may be compelling, the real interest in Thompson's life stems from the brilliant novels written in, around, and through it. Thompson's reputation deservedly rests on the crime novels *The Killer Inside Me, A Hell of a Woman, Savage Night, Pop. 1280,* and *The Getaway,* but the key to his fiction lies in the earlier, more mainstream novels *Now and on Earth* and *Heed the Thunder,* where Thompson circumscribed the parameters of his world and established the themes that would run through all his later efforts.

In his first two novels, Thompson's characters, doomed by heredity and circumstance, fight their fates in an effort to recover a lost world or discover a lost part of their selves; later protagonists are so unsure of their worlds and their selves that there seems nothing left to recover. Thompson was always writing about the same basic condition, whether on a macro or a micro scale: unknowable dualities and unbridgeable gaps—false and true, illusion and reality, good and evil, conscious and unconscious, cause and effect. Often the environment and the self become so intertwined they are indistinguishable—and the evil world and the evil inhabitant become one. More than just hollowed-out psychotics, Lou Ford, Dolly Dillon, and Carl Bigelow are manifestations of the central plight of the Thompson world.

And it's not surprising to discover that Jim Thompson was constantly writing about himself, and his own life. Thompson did resemble his psychotic narrators, but not in the sensational, lurid way one might initially expect. The least likely books prove to be "autobiographical" in the most unusual ways. Many passages strikingly portray Jim Thompson or a loved one, or illuminate his inner thoughts and feelings.

Although Jim Thompson may now be mentioned in the same breath as crime novel giants Hammett, Chandler, and Cain, that often seems just an attempt to further pigeonhole (and dismiss) this crucial American writer. Thompson's fiction may be *noir*—but it springs whole from his unique vision of America and the plight of its inhabitants. His use of crime novel conventions, like his narrators' put-on masks, are most often just useful disguises and misdirection for the terrible horror lurking underneath. Jim Thompson wrote powerful, subversive novels of a truth that could not be told in other ways.

Ultimately, Jim Thompson's novels place the unsuspecting reader right in the middle of a battle to recover identity, to retain sanity, to discover truth, in a world where the odds are stacked; we will come to know how this is actually a good description of Jim Thompson's personal struggle.

Jim Thompson: Sleep with the Devil is the story of a lost writer, a lost man, a lost soul.

The preparation, research, and writing of this book have taken a longer amount of time than I care to think about, but along the way I have benefited from the assistance of many people and institutions. Some were strangers when I began this project, and I now number them among my friends; others were good friends when I began it and still are.

Special thanks to Craig and Patty Graham, Arnold Hano, John Simon, Leith Adams, Bill Malloy, Blaine Campbell, and Richard Curtis; and to the whole Thompson family: Alberta Thompson, Sharon Thompson Reed and Jim Reed, Patricia Thompson Miller and Max Miller, Michael Thompson, and all the grandchildren. And an extra bit of thanks to Sharon and Jim Reed for all their help with the photographs for the book.

Jim Thompson's two sisters, Freddie Thompson Townsend and Maxine Thompson Kouba, passed away during the preparation of this biography. Both of these great ladies were of immeasurable assistance, and I consider myself lucky to have known them. Many times they both told me how much a biography of "Jimmie" would have meant to him—I think it was their way of saying how much it meant to them. I hope this book measures up to their, and perhaps Jim's, expectations.

Thanks also to Lucille Boomer Parsley, Jerry Bick, Patrick Goldstein, Jeremy Townsend, Maria Pagan, Val Almenderez, Dennis McMillan, Guadalupe Cabral, Marguerite Grant; and the staffs of the Library of Congress, the National Archives, Widener Library at Harvard University, the UCLA Research Library, the University of Nebraska, and the San Diego Public Library.

And thanks to my parents, Margaret and Tom McCauley, to Phyllis Jacobson, and especially to my wife, Sue, whom I can only begin to thank by dedicating this effort to her.

PROLOGUE: ONE-MINUS

■

You ringed me in with my failures, and each action of mine that was unlike yours you snatched up and laid on top of this ring. And in time I was walled in with nothing but failure to look at . . . And I began to think perhaps I was wrong, perhaps the things I thought right were wrong and the wrong right, and I began to lose something called character.

Now and on Earth, **1942**

Late in the winter of 1941, Jim Thompson moved from Oklahoma City to a three-bedroom apartment in San Diego with his wife, three children, his sister Freddie, and his mother, Birdie. Ten months before, Thompson had obtained a one-year fellowship from the Rockefeller Foundation through the University of North Carolina to research and write a book on the building trades. He had spent most of the year "living high" and doing only desultory research; the book was nowhere near completion. He hoped moving to San Diego would somehow motivate him to finish the job.

Thompson should have been motivated enough by other circumstances. He had resigned from the best job he had ever held, the directorship of the Oklahoma Writers' Project, in late 1939. The federally funded state Writers' Projects, part of the Works Progress Administration, were among the more successful of Roosevelt's New Deal Depression fighters—providing jobs for countless out-of-work writers. Thompson's three-year stint with the Project had resulted in the publication of two remarkable short stories, "Time Without End" and "The End of the Book." The latter was excerpted from his first novel, *Always to Be Blessed,* for which Viking Press paid him a $250 advance but never published. Thompson wrote hundreds of unpublished, uncredited manuscript pages for the Writers' Project, in addition to those published in *Tulsa: A Guide to the Oil Capital, The Oklahoma State Guide Book,* and *A Labor History of Oklahoma,* before resigning in a controversy over the politically volatile labor history. Some last-minute string-pulling before resigning landed Thompson the fellowship from the Rockefeller Foundation. Now, with his year nearly up, he needed to deliver a book or face the likely prospect that he was not going to make his living as a professional writer.

Not that that scenario really was anything new. Jim Thompson had struggled through the previous twenty years in the oddest assortment of bad jobs, from hotel doorman (eighty-four hours a week, no breaks) to vaudevillian actor/comedian, from golf caddy to collection agent. He wrote through it all in his brief spare time, but hadn't truly made a living writing until the WPA job. He noted in later years: "I've never wanted to do anything but write for as far back as I can remember, and most of the time I've managed just about anything else."

There was even more compelling personal pressure on Thompson to finish the book. His father, James Sherman Thompson, was in failing health back in Oklahoma, in a nursing home of sorts run by an old friend, William Stoors. Thompson and the family had tricked Pop into going there one day and had left him behind, crying and feeling betrayed. Jim Thompson knew in his heart there was no way they could take care of the old man out in San Diego, but he grimly promised himself that he would send for his ailing father as soon as he was settled on the West Coast and a few dollars ahead. Of course, his financial outlook would be considerably brighter if and when he finished the building trades book.

Unfortunately, Thompson was "written out"—the years of churning out prose for the WPA had taken their toll, and he was unable to complete the building trades tome. When his request for a renewal of the fellowship was turned down, he searched San Diego for work, and secured a menial day laborer job at Ryan Aeronautical, a local aircraft factory.

The Thompson family spent one of its bleakest summers in 1941. Thompson was torn up by his failure to complete the building trades book, but more upset by his resultant inability to rescue his despondent father. Thompson worked twelve-hour days at the aircraft factory, slept and drank cheap wine the rest of the time. His meager earnings barely met expenses; at the rate he was going, he'd never be able to send for his father. He pondered his own future, knowing he had let everybody, but especially Pop, down once again.

James Sherman Thompson and his son Jim never understood one another. They couldn't have been more disparate in personality or interests. James Sherman Thompson was convivial, funny—a man who loved people and made friends easily. Jim had been a brooding, quiet boy, uneasy with people and himself. Nothing was more important to James Sherman than a trip to New York to see the Yankees; Jim had no interest in sports, spectator or otherwise. They never felt the easy camaraderie of shared experience.

Worse, Jim always considered his father a "big man," and suffered in his shadow. He spent most of his young adult life trying to prove his own worth to Pop, but he never received the recognition or approval that he craved. The elder Thompson constantly pointed out Jimmie's shortcomings, to such devastating effect that Jimmie eventually ceased (at least consciously) trying to live up to his father's expectations.

At one point in the early 1920s James Sherman Thompson was a millionaire, but through a combination of dry oil wells and bad deals he lost nearly all the money within a few years. The final blow came in 1925 on a wildcat well that both the elder Thompson and his young son worked on in Big Spring, Texas. The well came in a gusher, but the Thompsons had mortgaged away nearly all their interest in it; everybody got rich but them, and James Sherman Thompson never recovered. He retreated behind a mask of mock joviality, a semblance of his former "true" personality. As his daughter Maxine recalled, James Sherman Thompson was "a broken man in many ways."

Father and son eventually made a peace of sorts out in the barren West Texas oil fields when James Sherman Thompson encouraged Jim to attend college. Still, Jim's adolescence had instilled deep inside him the lingering belief he could never be the man his father had been. Frighteningly enough, ultimate success had eluded his father, and the weight of failure had subsequently crushed the old man's spirit—what then did the future hold for Jim?

As the summer of 1941 drew to a close, Jim believed that getting his father out of that nursing home was probably his last chance to prove himself. He aimed to fulfill his dream of being a writer and rescue his father at the same time. But judging from the desperate, garbled notes the postman delivered daily from Oklahoma City, Jim Thompson had to move fast.

What happened next was undoubtedly the turning point in Jim Thompson's life, both professionally and personally. The most controversial and shadowy episode in a life lived in the margins of society, it is an appropriate prologue to Thompson's story because it informs all that occurred before and affected all that came after. Since there is no single factual version upon which to rely, Thompson's own fictionalized accounts (the source of most of the disputed and sensational "facts") are presented first, followed by the recollections of Jim's sisters, Maxine and Freddie, his wife, Alberta, and daughters, Sharon and Patricia, his good friend Arnold Hano, and the few documents still extant.

Sometime during the fall of 1941, Jim Thompson decided to leave San Diego and go to New York in search of a writing job. He considered it the only way to make enough money quickly enough to get his father out of the rest home before it was too late.

Thompson wrote in his second volume of tall-tale "autobiography," 1954's *Roughneck:*

> I managed to labor out two short detective stories. With the slender proceeds from these, my wife and children returned to Nebraska for a visit and I caught a bus for New York. . . . We arrived in Oklahoma City the third day out, and I laid over there a day to see Pop. He could not believe it was I when I first walked in on him. The seven long, lonely months must have seemed like years to him, and I think he had begun to feel we had abandoned him.
>
> I made him understand the truth: that his remaining here was due to circumstances beyond our control.
>
> "Well, it's all over now," he said. "You just help me get my things together, and I'll clear out of here right now."
>
> "Pop," I said. "I—"
>
> "Well?" He looked at me. "You're going to take me away, aren't you? That's why you've come back?"
>
> I hesitated. Then, I said, yes, that was why. "But I can't go with you, Pop. I'm on my way to New York."
>
> "Oh?" He frowned troubledly. "Well, I guess I could travel by myself if—"
>
> "I've got a swell job there," I lied. "Give me a— Well, just give me a month and I can send you to California by stateroom. Get you a nurse if you need one. But the best I can do now is a bus ticket."
>
> "I don't know," he said dubiously. "I'm afraid the doctor . . . I'm afraid I couldn't . . ." He sat back down on the bed. "You're sure, Jimmie? If I wait another month, you'll—"
>
> "That's a promise. And I never break a promise."

Jim Thompson continued on, arriving in New York (by this account) in November 1941. He then convinced Modern Age, a small publishing house, to stake him to a hotel room, paper, and a typewriter for a few weeks. At the end of that time he promised to deliver a finished novel. According to *Roughneck,* he finished the book in three weeks. After a two-week period while he recovered from alcoholic exhaustion in Bellevue and the publishers sent the manuscript out to be read by established writers Richard Wright and Louis Bromfield, Modern Age accepted it:

> I started across town toward my rooming house, worrying again— continuing to worry. It was a day short of five weeks, since I had left

Oklahoma. Not much over a month, to be sure, but to an old man, a lonely old man who secretly feared that he might be forsaken . . .

I reached Fifth Avenue. Instead of crossing it, I suddenly turned and headed uptown. Surely the publisher would be able to make his decision by this time. By God, he simply *had* to.

Well, he had.

He walked me into his office, his arm around my shoulders. "Got some good reports from Louis and Dick. They're going to fix us up with blurbs to put on the cover. . . . Now, I do feel that quite a few revisions are necessary. There are a couple of chapters I'd like to see excised, and new ones substituted. But—"

"Oh," I said, pretty drearily. "Then it'll still be quite a while before—"

"What? Oh, no, we'll pay you for it right now. We're definitely accepting it. Incidentally, when you get this one out of the way, we'll be glad to— Yes?"

The receptionist was standing in the doorway. She murmured an apology, held out a yellow Western Union envelope. "This came in yesterday, Mr. Thompson. I tried to reach you by phone, but—"

"It must be from my mother," I said. "I wasn't sure how long I'd be at that rooming house, so I told her to—to—"

I ripped the envelope open.

I stared down at the message.

Blindly. Stricken motionless.

"Bad news?" The publisher's hushed voice.

"My father," I said. "He died two days ago."

The "facts" of his father's death and the writing of Thompson's first published novel as depicted in *Roughneck* are not in dispute. The Thompson family agree that Jim went to New York to obtain a writing job, stopped to see Pop on his way across the country, and that Pop died while Jim was in New York (but the dates don't coincide, as we'll see). It was what Thompson wrote about his father's death in a chapter added to the novel he wrote in New York, *Now and on Earth,* that upset everyone so much, and conveyed Jim Thompson's own distress.

Now and on Earth is a thinly veiled autobiographical novel, the story of James Dillon, self-confessed "hack writer and aircraft flunkey of San Diego, California." Put upon by his family, tortured by his co-workers, and haunted by his inability to write, Dillon drinks and broods his way through the days. Those surrounding him are depicted with a brutal, depressing realism; the resultant portrait of American day-to-day family life is often truer and bleaker than anything in *The Killer Inside Me.* What it implies about Jim Thompson's attitude toward life and his family will be explored in later chapters. Here, we are concerned with the story of

James Sherman Thompson's death; Jim Thompson opened Chapter Eighteen of *Now and on Earth* with this "obituary":

> William Sherman Dillon, well-known inmate of the H—— Sanitarium, and former millionaire oil-man, politician, and attorney, died at his residence early Sunday morning after gorging himself on the excelsior from his mattress. At his bedside was his wife, who had to be, his daughter Margaret, who didn't know any better, and several imbeciles who wanted to taste the excelsior themselves. While the will has not yet been probated, it is understood that the entire estate, consisting of unpaid bills and a heritage of lunacy, is to go to Mr. Dillon's son, James Grant Dillon, prominent hack writer and aircraft flunkey of San Diego, California.

The rest of the chapter contains a wrenching "dialogue" between dead father and living son, as Jim Thompson wrestles with resentments and misunderstandings then too late to purge and resolve.

In later years, when Thompson would drink and tell tales of his life to friends like Lion Books editor Arnold Hano, inevitably he would lament that his father didn't have enough faith in him to hang on for a few more days. Evidently, Thompson's fictional embellishment of his father's death—suicide by way of the mattress stuffing—had become the truth in his own mind—or come to impart a terrible truth.

Arnold Hano repeated Jim Thompson's oral version of James Sherman Thompson's "suicide" in an obituary Hano wrote for the *Los Angeles Times Book Review* at the time of Thompson's death in April 1977:

> Back in 1941, his father had been in an asylum in Okalahoma City, begging Jim to get him out. Jim needed money to get him out, so he said to his father, "Give me a month, and I'll raise the money." His father brightened, because Jim never went back on his word. Jim took a bus to New York City and went door to door to the publishing houses, asking for money for a hotel room, a rented typewriter, and meals so he could write a novel. Finally, at Modern Age, they took a chance, and in ten days he wrote a novel. But things being what they are in publishing, it was a month plus one day before Jim got his advance. The same day, a telegram arrived. His father had committed suicide, ripping the excelsior out of his mattress and stuffing it down his throat.
>
> When Jim would drink he would sometimes cry and say, "Why couldn't he have waited another day? Didn't he trust me?"

The surviving members of the Thompson family were outraged by Hano's allegations. Jim Thompson's younger sister Freddie wrote in a letter published in the *Times*:

My sister and I want to thank Arnold Hano for writing the beautiful tribute to our brother, Jim Thompson (Book Review, May 1). It was a fine tribute to a wonderful man and we appreciate the warmth and understanding Hano had for Jim.

Our family, however, would like to clear up one statement which was incorrect. Our father was staying in a nursing home in Oklahoma City at the time of his death—the cause of death was pneumonia, according to the attending physician, not suicide as stated in the article.

On behalf of my family, we would greatly appreciate this correction being printed.

> Winifred Thompson Townsend
> Beverly Hills

When initially questioned about their father's death, Freddie Thompson Townsend and Maxine Thompson Kouba seemed genuinely puzzled about the origin of the suicide story. They maintained that Pop died of natural causes, with his wife, Birdie, by his side. Freddie's recollection:

> Before Pop died Jimmie went to see him and found him looking so desolate. . . . All of us were broke, it was just at the beginning of the war.
>
> We were planning to bring him out as soon as we found the right situation for him—he had become almost senile. He was a big fat man—Jimmie got there to see him on his way cross-country to write *Now and on Earth*—and found him thin and miserable. Jimmie wrote back and said we've got to get him out of there. This place was run by Bill Stoors, an old friend from better days—it was a nursing home—and at the time we left him there. We'd get letters from him that were full of half-finished sentences—little garbled notes—wondering when he could come.
>
> When he died Jimmie said he died of a broken heart, that's what killed him. Mother got there just before he died.
>
> There are all sorts of stories about him eating the mattress—not true. Mother got there just as he was dying. It was pneumonia.

Thompson's wife, Alberta, and daughters, Sharon Thompson Reed and Patricia Thompson Miller, agree with Maxine and Freddie, and are equally upset about the rumors surrounding Jim's father's death. When told most of the confusion and rumors stem from her father's own writing, Sharon Reed responded adamantly:

> Anybody that takes *Now and on Earth* as a biography doesn't have a brain! If you had known my dad, you would say there's no way this man could have written these things. My dad was nothing like his writings, and

everybody that knew him knows that. To take a chapter or a line or phrase out of any of my dad's books and to say "Well he wrote it, so it must be true" is ludicrous.

Indeed, the available documents concerning James Sherman Thompson's death don't match up with Jim Thompson's fictionalized accounts in *Roughneck* or *Now and on Earth*. James S. Thompson died on October 1, 1941, and was buried in Oklahoma City on the third. His wife, Birdie, paid a total of $75.80 for a burial plot and bronze marker. She paid $45.80 immediately and carried a note for the balance, which was paid up in May of 1942. The death certificate lists pneumonia as the cause of death.

Jim Thompson wrote in *Roughneck* that he arrived in New York City in early November 1941. But Alberta Thompson recalls that her husband was there when James Sherman Thompson died (October 1); therefore Jim Thompson must have arrived in New York much earlier, in late September. Thompson must have finished at least some of *Now and on Earth* before Pop died on October 1, yet Alberta remembers he was still in New York on December 7, when the Japanese bombed Pearl Harbor.

Most likely Thompson wrote the novel in September, and completed his draft around the time his father died on October 1. Modern Age then accepted the book, and Thompson wrote a few new chapters, including Chapter Eighteen (about "his" father's death).

Thompson finally left New York for San Diego just after the bombing of Pearl Harbor, looking forward to the spring 1942 publication of his first novel. Rather then ten days or two weeks, the writing of *Now and on Earth* probably entailed an initial burst of about three weeks, and some later additions and rewriting over two months.

In any case, Jim Thompson suffered through the death of his father alone in a cheap New York hotel room, with only his typewriter and whiskey for comfort. His inability to rescue his father confirmed in him the nagging suspicion that his father had been right—he was a failure, not the man that his father had been. Jim Thompson may have glimpsed his own future in that hotel room in New York City—mourning not only the loss of his father but also the loss of himself. The product of his solitary mourning, *Now and on Earth* is a painfully realistic and depressing document of psychic pain.

The publication of *Now and on Earth* in 1942 launched Thompson on a real, if wildly unsteady, career as a writer. He completed thirty more novels, many of which seem driven by his need to purge himself of relentless personal demons. No one has read *The Killer Inside Me,* or *Savage Night,* or *A Hell of a Woman* without wondering about the personal hell of the man who conceived them. Certainly Thompson's conviction that he let his father down—or worse, that his father had no faith in him—is a big part of the hell he carried with him every day.

Arnold Hano:

> I suspect it is Jim's relationship to his father that is much more of a causal factor than anything else. It comes up in *Now and on Earth,* putting the father in the nut house. When Jim was drunk, he'd cry a little bit and say, why didn't he wait, he knew I was going to show up. Why did he have to kill himself. Alberta swears that the old man never killed himself. Everybody swears he didn't kill himself.
>
> But in Jim's mind, perhaps deluded mind, he believed he killed himself. He didn't wait and, also, he did it to get back at Jim. He did this so Jim would be carrying this burden of grief all his life. Now I don't know to what degree it happened, or that Jim had chosen to make it so important in his own life, or Jim was just being maudlin when he was drunk.
>
> But I suspect there's an awful lot of the relationship between Jim and his father that you see in the novels. The anger, the quiet murdering that goes on, is Jim getting back.

The many dry facts of Jim Thompson's life—his endless assortment of bad jobs, his years with the WPA, his newspaper and true-crime reporting, his steady production of novels in the early 1950s, his roller-coaster years in Hollywood, his death as a forgotten man—don't add up to the tortured visionary of hell that was Jim Thompson, writer. We should not expect them to. Jim Thompson's demons were kept dark inside him, and brought into the light only in his writing.

The sometimes meager, often contradictory facts of his life resemble that roadside sign in *The Killer Inside Me*—"Warning: Hitchhikers May Be Escaped Lunatics!"—hinting at the horror, yet in the end merely informational. The dark truth lies in the novels; Arnold Hano's belief that Thompson's relationship with his father had a profound effect on the novels rings true.

In the fall of 1941, as America prepared for war, Jim Thompson had fulfilled his dream of becoming a published novelist, but had failed to rescue (and therefore prove himself to) his father. Success invariably tempered by failure would echo through the rest of Jim Thompson's life, more a perverse self-fulfilling prophecy than persistent bad fate or bad luck. Thompson believed he was not the man his father had been, and never could be. For the rest of his life, Jim Thompson made sure not to "succeed" more than his father had—to do so would have amounted to the final betrayal.

Deep down, Jim Thompson rendered himself incapable of success—but he sought it anyway, like some sort of all-American Sisyphus. In his best novels, Thompson portrayed the madness and death inherent in the persistent pursuit of the American dream by those who are predestined and preprogrammed to fail. Every Thompson protagonist, from James Dillon of *Now and on Earth* to Allen Smith of *Child of Rage*, is doomed because of circumstance, heredity, fate, and personality. All of Jim Thompson's novels are autobiographical in this most telling, frightening, and enlightening way.

James Sherman Thompson did not commit suicide in any active manner, never mind asphyxiating himself on mattress ticking. He was an old man, at least slightly deranged, who felt forgotten and betrayed. In the end he gave up hope and died, allowing himself to waste away. James Sherman Thompson decided he had nothing left to live for; he stopped eating, ultimately becoming so emaciated that he succumbed to pneumonia. To Jim Thompson, that amounted to suicide; he wrote it up as an active, rather than passive, suicide in *Now and on Earth* both to dramatize the death and reveal the endlessly aching sore it left on his own soul.

And when Jim Thompson himself decided, decades later, that a series of strokes had rendered his own life pointless, he made a final gesture of loyalty and homage to his father.

Jim Thompson stopped eating, wasted away, and died.

As James Sherman Thompson had done.

SOMETHING LIKE LIFE

■

I laughed then. This was something like life. This was
life. Where else was there anything like the oil towns?
I asked Martin, and he told me.

"Character at Iraan," 1930

ONE

James Myers "Jim" Thompson always liked to shock new acquaintances with the news that he was born in jail. It was literally true. He was born in the second-floor living quarters above the jail in Anadarko, Caddo County, of the Oklahoma Territory on September 27, 1906. His father, James Sherman Thompson, was at the time the sheriff of Caddo County; Oklahoma statehood was still a year away. Jim's mother, Birdie Myers Thompson, was a schoolteacher.

James Sherman Thompson was one of the six children of Harriet and Sherman Thompson. He had sisters, Amy, Christie, and Otie, and twin brothers Arthur and Elmer. His father had been with William Tecumseh Sherman and the Union Army on their devastating March to the Sea. Born in Illinois, on September 16, 1870, James Sherman Thompson set out for territorial Oklahoma just before the turn of the century. His uncle, Harry Thompson, was Chief United States Marshal in El Reno, an important city in the territory. James Sherman served for a short time as Harry Thompson's deputy. The ambitious young Thompson then moved south to Anadarko, where he was elected county sheriff for three consecutive terms.

In 1903 James Thompson married Birdie Myers, some six years his junior. Birdie's father, another soldier who had fought for the Union, had moved from Iowa to the valley town of Burwell, Nebraska, when his family was young. Birdie and James had their first child, Maxine, in 1904, and James Myers "Jimmie" Thompson followed two years later.

When statehood came in 1907, James Sherman Thompson ran for Congress as a Republican and was soundly defeated when his chief opponent, Democrat Scott Ferris, capitalized on Thompson's middle name, and the fact that his father had joined in General Sherman's destructive march. It probably would have done James Sherman Thompson no good to explain he was named after his father, not the general. In any case, that *was* his name and James Sherman Thompson was too proud a man ever to apologize or explain.

Oklahoma was full of displaced Southerners with long memories; the final vote tally for the first race in the fifth congressional district of the state of Oklahoma was 31,026 for Scott Ferris and 19,149 for James S. Thompson (55.7 percent to 34.4 percent). Thompson didn't just lose the election, he also lost most of his friends and associates—and did some damage to his illustrious Uncle Harry up north. He turned in his sheriff's badge a short time later and set off for Texas and Mexico.

Birdie and her two young children traveled back to Burwell, Nebraska, and lived with her folks. Maxine Thompson Kouba has almost no recollection of this time in her life; Jim Thompson hints in his fiction that Maxine suffered a shock that left her without a clear memory of her childhood. In any case, the best insight about this time is to be gained from Thompson's fictionalization of the period of his second novel, *Heed the Thunder*.

The greatest influence on young Jim Thompson during the time spent in Burwell was undoubtedly his Grandfather Myers, a wizened, wise old patriarch who was later fictionalized as Lincoln Fargo in *Heed the Thunder* (one of the most important characters in the Thompson canon). Pa taught the young boy, among other things, to drink hot toddies, chew tobacco, and have a generally sour outlook on things. In 1953's *Bad Boy,* Thompson's first volume of tall-tale "autobiography," he calls Pa Myers "the most profane, acid-tongued, harsh, kind, delightful man I ever knew."

Jim Thompson was also greatly impressed by his Uncle Bob, a displaced Englishman who had married Birdie's only sister. Uncle Bob was a great fan of the satirists, and introduced the young boy to the work of Jonathan Swift. The subversive power of Swift's writing made a lasting impression on the young Jim.

It is unknown exactly what James Sherman Thompson was doing during this time, or how long Birdie and the children had to stay in Burwell, but Thompson had reunited with his family in Oklahoma City by the time Jimmie was eight years old, in 1914. James Sherman Thompson, after a long and unsuccessful adventure drilling for oil in Mexico, had obtained degrees in accounting and law from correspondence courses. He then passed the state bar examination, and set up a private practice in Oklahoma City.

Jim Thompson had grown from toddler to an eight-year-old boy with only a vague memory of his father, and the time that was lost due to circumstance never was recovered. Jimmie, a gangly, awkward child, felt ill at ease under his father's eye, and the boy's quiet, introverted personality puzzled the boisterous James Sherman Thompson.

Evidently James Sherman Thompson remained confused by his introspective young son; Jim Thompson's younger sister Freddie Thompson Townsend recalled: "He never understood Jimmie, at least Jimmie felt that he didn't. Jimmie never watched a ballgame, or knew who was doing what—he had no interest. My father would break his neck to take the train to New York for the World Series. He could not understand where this boy came from, who blinked his eyes a lot and was shy, withdrawn." Added Maxine: "Jimmie was devoted to Pop, but they were not that close in those ways."

James S. Thompson's law practice soon proved a mild success, and the family lived comfortably for a time. In 1916 James Sherman began to dabble once again in oil well drilling, with predictably mixed results. He was away from home often, speculating on wildcat wells in Oklahoma and Texas; Birdie and the children again made frequent visits to her family in Nebraska. By all accounts, James S. Thompson was too trusting a man, assuming everyone was as honorable as he. Thompson often sealed contracts with just a handshake—a lawyer should have known better. He was always on the verge of drilling the big well that would make his fortune, and never on secure financial ground.

Now back in Oklahoma City, Birdie spent a particularly hard winter in 1916–17 with Maxine, Jimmie, and her newborn daughter, Winifred. Her legs had failed her during the pregnancy, and she was bedridden most of the time. Jim Thompson later fictionalized this hopeless winter, with Pop out in the oil fields, and not enough to eat at home, in his first novel. It is possible that this excerpt from *Now and on Earth* is an exaggeration:

Well, Margaret and I went down to the drugstore after a jar of malted milk, and on the way back a group of the neighborhood hoodlums chased us. And Margaret dropped the bottle. It was all wrapped up in that tough brown paper, and we didn't know it was broken until Mom unwrapped it.

No, she didn't scold or spank us . . . she just sat there among the pillows, and something terrible happened to her face. And then she placed one starved hand over her eyes and her shoulders trembled and she cried.

I think an artist must have been peeking in the window that night, for years later I saw a painting of Mom. A painting of a woman in a torn grown, tangled black hair and thin hand concealing her face but not hiding—oh, Jesus, no! not hiding but pointing at—wretchedness and pain and hopelessness that were unspeakable. It was called *Despair*.

James Sherman Thompson returned home late that winter with a bag full of cash and presents for everyone: his latest well had come in. But a combination of bad luck and bad judgment conspired to keep the oil business a roller-coaster ride. As Maxine Thompson Kouba recalls: "Out of every four jobs, he'd make money on two, on the third break even, and on the fourth he'd go broke. We later asked Mom why we didn't put any of the money away. She didn't know why."

Eventually James S. Thompson, who had somehow kept his law and accountancy practice going throughout his oil field adventures, was offered a job auditing the holdings of a local multimillionaire, Jake Hamon. According to Jim Thompson in *Bad Boy,* and confirmed by Maxine Thompson Kouba's memory, Hamon taught Pop some much-needed business sense. In addition to being the victim of oil field swindles, the affable James S. Thompson was given to undercharging for his legal services and forgiving large debts owed him. Hamon put a stop to those practices.

As a result, 1918 and 1919 were better times for James Sherman Thompson and his family. He finally was able to give up what was now a hated law practice and speculate full-time on oil wells and investment deals. Under Hamon's tutelage, Thompson structured deals that couldn't lose—at least not everything at once. When Thompson moved his family to Fort Worth, Texas, in the late summer of 1919, he was a millionaire. Thompson had also risen to some prominence in political circles; he was a guest aboard Warren G. Harding's campaign train in 1920.

The only drawback to the situation was that Thompson was almost never at home. And when he was at home, he had become an eccentric and demanding presence to teenager Jim Thompson. The jaunty prose of *Bad Boy* does little to hide Jim Thompson's adolescent resentment of Pop, when Pop begins to take a more active interest in the boy's upbringing:

> I was a rich man's son, he pointed out, and someday I would inherit great wealth. I must be made into a proper custodian for it—sane, sober, considerate. I should not be allowed to become one of those ill-mannered, irresponsible wastrels, who behave as though they had been put on earth solely to enjoy themselves.
>
> No error in my deportment was too tiny for Pop to spot and criticize. No flaw in my appearance was too small. From the time I arose until the time I retired, I was subjected to a steady stream of criticism about the way I dressed, walked, talked, stood, ate, sat, and so on into infinity—all with that most maddening of assurances that it was for my "own good."

James S. Thompson encouraged what he considered Maxine's inherent musical talent; she was given expensive violin and piano lessons. Jimmie was expected to work and do well in school; he coveted the musical lessons and was jealous of his sister. Among the jobs provided young Jimmie by his father were plumber's helper, auto mechanic's helper, and, for a short time, the boy's own milk business—James Sherman bought him the cows. Jimmie was not enthralled by any of the work.

Finally young Jim Thompson found a job he liked, as a caddy at the Glen Garden Country Club in Fort Worth; predictably, James Sherman Thompson did not approve, thinking the job beneath a rich man's son and of little practical value.

Jim Thompson always claimed he sold his first short story at the age of fifteen. He probably did, but there is no record of it. He was living at the time in Fort Worth, attending high school and caddying on weekends. According to *Bad Boy* he had "sold fillers to the pulp periodicals and brief humorous squibs to such magazines as *Judge*."

Judge was a humor magazine similar in format to England's *Punch;* each issue contained dozens of uncredited jokes, gags, and small inserts. The crime pulps of the day featured similarly uncredited filler. A perusal of the magazines of the time, including *True Detective*, turned up no Jim Thompson bylines, or any uncredited work that was undoubtedly his.

In any case, Thompson cited some previously published writings when he applied for a job at the *Fort Worth Press* in 1922. His sisters both recall him working at the paper for a time, but Thompson's version of events is all we have. From *Bad Boy:*

> . . . with the returns from the magazines so small I tackled a new outlet. I gathered up the invoices from my free-lance checks and exhibited them to the editor of the Forth Worth *Press,* modestly suggesting that in me there was at least the making of a star reporter.
>
> . . . I reported on the job at four in the afternoon (at eight a.m. on Saturdays) and remained as long as I was needed. For my principal duties as copy boy, phone-answerer, coffee procurer and occasional typist, I was paid four dollars a week. For the unimportant stories I was allowed to cover, I was paid three dollars a column—to the extent that they were used in the paper.
>
> Due to their very nature, my stories were usually left out of the paper or appeared in such boiled-down form that the cash rewards were infinitesimal. About all I could count on was my four dollars salary—which just about paid my expenses.

From the *Press* he moved on to *Western World,* a local trade journal. Again from *Bad Boy:*

. . . I found brief employment on *Western World*, an oil and mining weekly. . . . I did a little of everything, from addressing envelopes for the subscription department to reading copy to running errands to rewriting brief items.

It wasn't until later in the decade, after Thompson's three-year stay out on the oil fields of far West Texas, that he published work that would survive for posterity.

After the newspaper jobs Thompson worked for a short time in a burlesque house, although he evidently hung out there more than he actually "worked." None of his jobs had paid very much, and now pay was becoming increasingly important; James Sherman Thompson's fortune was steadily eroding from a string of bad deals and dry holes. As Thompson later wrote: "Pop's luck went sour from the day he set foot in Texas." Soon Jim acquired a lucrative job as a nightshift bellboy at the Texas Hotel.

James Sherman Thompson had never approved of his son's caddying or burlesque house activities, but he was particularly aghast at the prospect of his son providing women and booze to hotel guests. Since the family by now needed the money Jimmie made, James Sherman could not argue. Jimmie knew how his father felt about the bellboy job, but perceived it as another denial of the approval he craved. He figured nothing he could do could measure up to his father's expectations.

Bringing home the much-needed rolls of bills from the bellboy job was little solace to Jimmie. Still, he took no joy in the fact that his father's fortune was slipping away. For a glimpse of Jim Thompson's view of things during this time, we can turn to *A Penny in the Dust*, an incomplete novel sample that he wrote years later. In this passage, the young Thompson surrogate is wrestling with the facts of a world turned upside down:

> Pop had not lived as I had to—when he was a boy or at any other time. In Pop's world, wrong and right were clearly defined; if you did wrong you were bad, and if you did right you were good. In the world I occupied, or my particular part of that world, almost the opposite prevailed. And I lived in constant despair and confusion.
>
> I had been assured, almost from the time I was born, that I had never done and was unwilling or unable to do what Pop had selflessly, cheerfully, and easily done when he was my age.
>
> Growing older and bigger, though regretfully little smarter, having learned little from a nonage of sinning and error, an occasional doing of right entitled me to no praise. It was no more than I should do. Others had done a great deal more and gotten a doggone lot less . . .

Getting a ninety five in geometry was fine, but getting a hundred was axiomatically finer. Working hard and going to school was fine. But it would have been finer if I had already graduated, as had many boys, including Pop, at my age. It would have been finer if I had already advanced myself along the path of fame and fortune, as had Julius Caesar, Abraham Lincoln, and Pop at my age.

Most of the time, I was almost unbearable to me. At age seventeen, I was a failure and damned to even greater ignominy than I had previously endured.

The roots of Jim Thompson's most important obsessions are reflected in the above passage. Thompson's novels take place in a world where good and evil are slippery concepts; personal motivations nearly unknowable. An all-consuming drive to live up to a personal or cultural concept of success—in that inverted world—fuels almost all of Thompson's novels.

Jim Thompson, looking back years later, realizes he never solved this problem in his own life. Again from *A Penny in the Dust:*

Sulkily, feeling very sorry for my seventeen-year-old self, I brooded over the ill-fate which endlessly bestrode my skinny shoulders. Wondering why anyone who always tried so hard to do the correct and proper thing invariably wound up by achieving the opposite. And now, decades later, still beset by this hideous attribute, I continue to wonder and as fruitlessly.

The bellboy job was murder on Jim Thompson's health—very nearly literally. He worked the graveyard shift, 11:00 P.M. to 7:00 A.M., seven days a week, and attended Fort Worth Polytechnic High School full-time. He soon was drinking and smoking to excess, and became well skilled in providing the guests of the hotel with bootleg booze and prostitutes. He made a lot of money, but his father never let him forget *how* it was made, and Jim Thompson felt ashamed. From *Now and on Earth:*

Have a drink? Have a cigarette? Aw, go on. Little drink never hurt anyone. Remember I told you that once before? Remember that Sunday morning when I fell down on the front porch and almost bit a hole in the planks, and you carried me into the bathroom, eyes filled with disgust. Yeah, I knew what you thought of me. I never got so drunk that I didn't.

The once boisterous and confident James S. Thompson had become quiet and confused. No longer was Pop dispensing wisdom for his son. From *Bad Boy:*

I . . . . asked him to come to breakfast with me.

He did so, rather coolly. He had been cool and formal with me for some time. At first he had argued sternly against my going to work at the hotel. Then, his affairs went from bad to worse, and my earnings were necessary for the maintenance of the family. Pop's attitude changed. He no longer argued.

It seemed to him, I suppose, that I had usurped his position in the family. I could not help it, perhaps, nor could he, but the fact remained. I was my own man. So be it.

We were like polite strangers to one another, rather than father and son.

Jim Thompson graduated from Polytechnic High School in Fort Worth in June of 1925. His sisters recall that he then took sick and collapsed. But they do not remember exactly what was wrong with him, beyond the general collapse. For that there is *Bad Boy,* with what might be an overstatement of his ill health:

I hadn't been home an hour when the good feeling rushed from me like water rushing down a drain. Then, after a long moment of absolute emptiness, my heart stuttered and raced, beating faster and faster until one beat overlapped the other. Blood gushed from my mouth and I fell to the floor in convulsions.

Doctors came, although I was unaware of their presence. They administered to me wonderingly. I was eighteen years old, and I had a complete nervous collapse, pulmonary tuberculosis and delirium tremens.

Jim Thompson's physical collapse was triggered by too much drinking, smoking, and working; spiritually the young man had suffered a collapse of another kind. A particularly bitter eighteen-year-old, he felt wronged by almost every event and circumstance of his life. He had no friends at school; he felt ill at ease among the Texans, and hid his native intelligence from them. It was the same story at the hotel. And at home, although his father had lost a lot of his off-putting, boisterous joviality due to his financial problems, Jim still found him unapproachable. As a defense mechanism, Jim Thompson did the outside world one better, becoming a resentful young man who had had enough of trying to get along with others. From *Bad Boy:*

A photograph of the period reveals me as a thin, neat, solemn-faced young man, surprisingly innocuous-looking at first glance. It is only when you look more closely that you see the watchfully narrowed eyes, the stiffness of the lips, the expression that wavers cautiously between smile and frown. I looked like I hoped for the best, but expected the worst. I looked like I had done just about all I was going to do to get along and others had better start getting along with me.

When Thompson had recovered sufficiently from his collapse, he decided to set out into the oil fields. His health was miserable; it was a surprise that he had lived. Perhaps the West Texas air would cure his tuberculosis, and good hard work build up his strength again. He knew he had to go.

James Sherman Thompson was by now living on days of past glory, but he could never give up hope of another big well coming in. He set off for West Texas also, and he and his son met up in the town of Big Spring in the fall of 1925. The elder Thompson was certain there was a fortune in oil bubbling under the desolate soil of Big Spring, and he and Jimmie set out to prove it. Jim Thompson told what he called "a middling true" version of what happened next himself, in his 1965 novel *Texas by the Tail:*

You see, Big Spring *was* a cattle town not so many years ago. Just another wide place in a dusty road. A town like any other such town, built around the traditional courthouse square; its streets drifting with dust, its iron-awninged buildings baking under the incredible heat of summer, ice-painted with the North Pole blasts of winter.

That was how it looked when the two wildcatters first saw it—like the ass-end of Far Nowhere. The town, for its part, looked upon them with little more favor. The town had seen wildcatters—prospectors for oil—before, and this pair just didn't fit the picture.

There was first of all their drilling rig; a cable-tool rig, naturally, since the rotary had not then been perfected. It was one of those big Star-30 machines, a so-called "portable" rig which occupied two railroad flatcars with its accessory equipment. None of the harum-scarum wildcatter breed had ever owned such a rig—an outfit worth a not-so-small fortune. And these two were the last people in the world who should have owned it.

They were a middling-old man and his son. The father wore the unmistakable stamp of defeat, a man who had drilled one dry hole too many. The kid looked mean and snotty and very sick, and he was all three and then some.

Into the rig and the job it had to do, the old man had sunk his home, his furniture, his insurance policies; every nickel he could beg and borrow. That still left a hell of a hump to get over, for an outfit and a job like this, so the kid had kicked in for it. The kid was a loner, he'd been one almost since the time he was old enough to walk. Some things had begun to happen to him about then that shouldn't happen to kids, and maybe they could have been avoided and maybe they couldn't have. But it was all the same to him. He didn't ask for excuses, he didn't give any. As far as he was concerned, the world was a shitpot with a barbed-wire handle and the further he could kick it the better he liked it. As far as he was concerned, he had plenty owing to him. And he was hell on wheels at collecting.

He was now nineteen years old. He was suffering from tuberculosis, bleeding ulcers, and chronic alcoholism.

Rig hands, drillers and tooldressers, accompanied the old man and his son. Huge tractors were hitched onto the rig, and it was hauled eighteen miles out of town to the drill site. They had no road to haul it over, of course. A road had to be made, straight out across the tumbling prairie, up hills and over streams, through hub-high mud and sand.

It took a lot of money. They were in over their ears before they were ever rigged up. They started to drill, and the hole went down a hundred and twenty-five feet—and every inch of it was a high-priced waste of money. For the driller hadn't known his stuff, and he'd got a crooked hole. And you can't set casing in a crooked hole. You can't—when you're using cable tools—go down very far before your drill bit and stern drag on the side.

Wildcats are always Jonahs. You're in unexplored territory, and you never know what you're going to get into until you've already got into it and it's too damned late. This particular wildcatter had enough hard luck for a hundred wells.

The boiler blew up. The rig caught on fire. The mast snapped. The tools were lost in the hole a dozen times. The drill cable bucked and whipped, cleanly slicing off a tooldresser's head.

The kid announced that he had gone his limit; he had nothing left but his ass and his pants and they both had holes in them. His father said that they would manage some way, and he took over the financing from then on.

The well finally got drilled. It wasn't a gusher but it was a very respectable producer. Diffidently, the old man asked his son what plans he had for the future.

"You mean what do I want to be when I grow up?" the kid said sarcastically. "What's it to you, anyway? When were you ever interested in what I wanted to do?"

"Son, son . . ." the old man shook his head sadly. "Have I really been that bad?"

"Oh, hell, I guess not. But I'm just not much on talking about things. You talk about what you're going to do, you never get it done."

The father guessed that it was probably a slam at him. He had, possibly, always indulged too much in talk. "I suppose," he said timidly, "you've been counting on having a lot of money?"

The kid said, why not? They'd brought in a good well, and they had hundreds of offsetting acres under lease. Conservatively, they were worth several million dollars. "But I'll settle for a hundred and eighty-two thousand. I won't live long enough to spend any more than that."

"A hundred and eighty-two—Why that particular figure, son?"

"I've been keeping a little black book since I was seven years old. There are one hundred and eighty-two names in it, one for every rotten bastard who's given me a hard time. I've shopped around, and I can get them bumped off for an average price of one thousand dollars."

"Son—" The father shook his head, aghast. "What happened to you? How can you even think of such things?"

"Thinking about it is all that's kept me alive," the kid said. "I can die happy knowing that I'm taking all those bastards to hell with me."

The father decided that it was a good time to give his son the word. The kid listened with a kind of gloomy satisfaction, as one accustomed to seeing his dreams washed down the john.

"So we don't own anything, huh? You hocked it all to get the well drilled."

"I'm sorry, yes."

"What about the rig and the tools?"

"All gone. The trucks, our car, everything."

"Goddam," the kid said. "Those one hundred and eighty-two bastards could be dead right now for what this well cost!"

He had a right to be pretty damn sore about it, he felt, but somehow he couldn't be. Somehow, he wanted to howl with laughter, because when you thought about it, you know, it was really funny as hell.

He started to take a drink, and then decided that he didn't want any. He lighted a cigarette, noting wonderingly that he no longer had ulcers pains. He coughed and spat in his handkerchief, and there was no blood in the spit.

"My God," he told his father, and there was awe in his voice. "I'm afraid I'm going to live!"

He and the old man walked out of town together; they couldn't afford anything but the ankle express. With the discovery of oil, Big Spring was already burgeoning into a city. The old man turned and looked back at it from its outskirts, and there was pride in his defeated eyes.

"We did that, son," he said. "You and I. We caused a city to bloom in the wilderness. We've made history."

"We should have stood in bed," the kid said. But then he laughed and gave the old man an affectionate slap on the back. For his physical health was not all that had improved during the past two years.

Out there on the prairies where time had stood still for endless eons, out there where nature loomed large and man was small, he had gotten a new perspective on himself. And his once all-consuming problems had shrunk in size, and he had grown proportionately in the only way that growing matters. Out there he had discovered that a man could be much less and much more than the sum of his moments, and that what had been done could be undone by enduring.

Arm in arm, he and the old man went down the road together, not into the sunset for that was behind them, but into the dawn or where the dawn would have been if it had been that time of day. They went down the road together, the old man and his kid, the kid became a man, and he got rid of the book with the one hundred and eighty-two names, getting rid of a lot else along with it. And it was the last book he ever compiled of that kind.

It is likely, of course, that the list of 182 people who wronged him was just Jim Thompson's literalization of the many resentments and grudges he held over his childhood and adolescence.

In any case, the drilling of the Big Spring well marked a new beginning for Jim Thompson but the beginning of the end for James S. Thompson. Maxine and Freddie recall that Pop never really hit bottom spiritually until the Big Spring well fiasco. Maxine Thompson Kouba:

> Pop drilled that first deep well in Big Spring, Texas—it was 5,800 feet down. But he had some kind of bad contract—anyway, they became millionaires and he didn't come out of it all that well. That was the beginning of the end.
>
> My own theory was that Pop couldn't face in his own mind, finally, not quite making it and losing everything. So instead of being depressed, sitting around and being depressed, he took the other route. He was cheerful, happy, content—but underneath, a broken man in many ways. He just didn't show it.

Jim Thompson noted his father's response to failure well, and used a cheery, joking persona to mask the "broken" spirit of many of his later fictional characters—most notably Lou Ford of *The Killer Inside Me*. More important, Thompson eventually adopted his father's stoic, sacrificial stance, suffering alone behind a mask of his own.

Jim Thompson remained out on the oil fields nearly two more years, returning to Fort Worth around Thanksgiving of 1928. He had worked building the pipeline from Iraan to the Gulf of Mexico, and held just about every other job available out on the fields. Though he nearly died several times, from accidents or plain exhaustion, Thompson returned from the fields a swarthy, muscular giant, standing six feet four inches and weighing 240 pounds. His adolescent gawkiness was long gone, and his continuing shyness now had some confidence behind it.

Thompson later fictionalized his oil field adventures in *Bad Boy, Roughneck,* and *South of Heaven*, but what he learned most from his adventures were the facts of a true-life inverted world and the way he felt about them.

Jim Thompson watched a lot of men die due to the working conditions, and the men that weren't killed were barely living; it was more like existing. Thompson saw the cruel workings of capitalism at its simplest and most arbitrary. The common employer's attitude out on the fields was the men didn't have to work these killer jobs, they could choose to starve to death instead.

Thompson developed a deep bond with the victims of the system—not only those who lost their lives, but also those who lost their hope, their pride, even their identity. Thompson meditated on the big lie of capitalism as manifested in its most deadly form—the split souls of psychotic, doomed pursuers of the American Dream. Soon rich and poor, appearance and reality, right and wrong, good and evil seemed to Thompson not so much polar opposites as a matter of power and perspective, on both a societal and a personal scale.

Out on the West Texas fields Jim Thompson developed a lifelong affinity for the marginal victims of American society; quite fitting, since the terminally frustrated ambitions of America's losers only echoed, on another level, Thompson's own allegiance to failure. Out on the oil fields, Thompson discovered both some sort of peace and what he wanted to do with his life. He would write the stories of America's doomed—implicitly criticizing and hoping to change the conditions that rendered them so. To what degree he knew he was actually writing his own story, we'll never know.

At least unconsciously, Thompson recognized his brethren; hopefully the discovery that his "condition" was shared was some solace. From the widespread death and hopelessness of the West Texas oil fields, young Jim Thompson paradoxically drew new life and new hope. He had set out for the oil fields a dying, sickly boy and returned reborn, a healthy and hopeful man—and a writer with a purpose.

Jim Thompson had written a few stories out on the West Texas oil fields, and they eventually found their way to a friendly editor at *Texas Monthly,* who published them in 1929. The title of February 1929's "Oil Field Vignettes" speaks for itself; Thompson presents three short sketches of men he met or heard about while working in the fields. Slight and undeveloped, they are put across with a dry wit and realism that would mark Thompson's writing style throughout his career.

The vignettes are studies of three men whom the world has made eccentric, and whom the world then goes on to punish for being the way they are. "Jake Fanner," a well driller, asks only some peace and quiet from his co-workers; naturally, he is saddled with the most garrulous of companions. But Jake never stops hoping for a suitably quiet co-worker, and after weeks on a job with a man where not a word is spoken, he dares to dream he's finally found heaven.

Eventually a dangerous but funny accident involving some mules elicits an amazed comment from the formerly silent tool-dresser. Jake is crestfallen: "once again his dream was shattered, his faith misplaced. Then with the fury of a disillusioned man he yelled up at the tooly, 'Get outta here, you blankety-blanked son of a phonograph. You talk too damn much!' "

"Big Hole Ben" can never see an oil well to completion. As soon as the drill bits drop below a certain size, he moves on to another job. When lean times hit, this eccentricity makes it nearly impossible for Ben to land a job. He decides to drill his own wildcat well, determined not to give up until the smallest drill bit is used.

Ben becomes more and more nervous as each successively smaller bit is fitted to the drill. He has terrible premonitions of doom; he controls himself with rotgut whiskey. Just when it seems Ben has overcome his phobia and his wildcat well will make him a rich man, he is killed while peering into the hole: "a four pound nut sped down the ninety feet from the top and caught Ben slantwise on the head. Ben's brains were knocked out of his mouth right along with his tobacco, and they must have fallen down the hole, for they never found either."

The fate of "Baldy Sealbridge" is to be saddled with an amazing succession of unfaithful and murderous wives. Yet he approaches each new marriage with hopeful innocence, having learned nothing from past experience.

Time passes, and the narrator hears reports of Baldy's latest close calls: "his wife had accidentally chipped glass into the pancake batter . . . he married a snake charmer and one of the lady's pythons had swallowed him. . . ."

When finally we meet up with Baldy again, he's crying by the side of the road, having been booted out of his own house by his wife's lover:

"It's all right, kid," I said, "I wouldn't let them hurt my feelings."
He arose groaning. And by his next words I knew that Baldy's spirit was forever tanned to life's barbs. Nature had gone a little too far with him. There was resolve in his figure; resolve quickly altered by pain.
"It—it ain't my feelings," he whimpered. "It's the seat of my pants!"

Texas Monthly followed "Oil Field Vignettes" with a similar collection, "Thieves of the Field," four months later in June 1929. It tells three tales of con men and crooks who employ various colorful methods to steal the pipe needed to drill an oil well. Neither as moralistic nor as bleak as its predecessor, it does evoke the lawless, predatory nature of the oil field and its denizens.

Though far from a mature, polished work, it would be a mistake to consider "Oil Field Vignettes" little more than three tall tales. The protagonists' manias and obsessions, and the circumstances that act upon them as a consequence, circumscribe the boundaries and set the rules of a particular world. Nature makes these men as they are, and then sets about destroying them for it. Jake loses his dream, Baldy loses his hope, Ben loses his life.

Later Jim Thompson protagonists, malformed mutations though they are, seek their destiny in the uncaring world that made them so. Characters determined to be true to themselves even when their dark selves seem unknowable, and their dark fates unavoidable, later would narrate the important Thompson novels *Savage Night, A Hell of a Woman*, and *The Killer Inside Me*. One key reason Thompson (and his readers) can understand the actions of a Jake Fanner or a Lou Ford is there seems no way out for these men.

Thompson would continue to let his characters play the cards they've been dealt, subverting the all-American belief that it is every man's right to fulfill his dream and destiny. Jim Thompson just happened to record the dreams and destiny of America's truly "free"—the free-floating psychotics that seem the inevitable by-products of the modern age. And he infused each of his characters with his own personal experience of success and failure. In doing so Thompson told more about the human condition than many people wanted to know.

Upon Jim Thompson's return from the oil fields, he reacquired his bellboy job at the Texas Hotel. The editor at the *Texas Monthly* soon advised him to stop wasting his talent, and to go to college. Thompson's sister Maxine was already attending classes at the university in Lincoln, Nebraska, where she had just married a young man, Russell Boomer, whose father was a professor at the Agricultural College at the University of Nebraska.

The Boomers were old acquaintances of Birdie's family, and had been more than happy to take Maxine in as a boarder. Before she married Russell, Maxine shared a room with Lucille Boomer, the only girl among five children. The family was musically inclined; they would sit at night and have impromptu recitals: Maxine on the violin, Lucille on the flute, her parents on harpsichord and piano.

Eventually, Jim Thompson struck up a letter-writing relationship with Lucille, who had become Maxine's best friend. Lucille Boomer Parsley recalled "Jimmie," and a summer with Maxine:

> Jimmie was a very intuitive, sensitive person, I felt that when I first read his letters . . . there was something unusual about how he wrote. A rather quiet person, alone in many ways.

Maxine had come to live with my family while she went to the University of Nebraska. She was quite a fine violinist. So her family were willing to allow her to leave Texas and come to the university if she could stay with us—they had known my dad, who was a college professor—and we were happy to allow her to come to our home. So Maxine and I were roommates during that time, and then she was married to my brother Russell.

In the summer of 1929 I went out on Chitaqua—I played the flute and Maxine played the violin—in this group that traveled all over the Midwest. A town a day. It was called the Summer Shows of 1929, and I was engaged to go out on it through a man who had come to the university—I was a sophomore. I tried out and he hired me, then he was looking for the rest of a little group, so I suggested Maxine. By that time she was my sister-in-law, though they hadn't been married very long.

It was going to be rough for her to leave Russell behind for the summer, but she took the job and we went out on tour that summer. There were seven girls in the group, and we played things like "Bells of St. Mary's," "Melancholy Baby"—we had a very fine vocalist and dancer. When summer ended I went back to school, and Maxine went back to her husband.

In the meantime, Jim Thompson had decided to enroll at the University of Nebraska that fall. James S. Thompson was encouraging, though the loss of Jimmie's income from his bellhop job would leave the family almost without support. It was decided that Birdie and Freddie, now a beautiful young teenager, would go live in Burwell once again.

Jim Thompson was worried about Pop being left alone in Texas, but Pop shrugged it off, telling him not to worry. The elder Thompson, still dreaming of the big well, was going to head out into the fields once again. Jimmie protested, but there was no arguing with his father—the plans were set.

Thompson had to leave Fort Worth earlier than planned because of a bootlegging scam at the Texas Hotel where he was hopping bells. As usual, the only full account we have of it is from Thompson's fictionalized writing. According to his undoubtedly dramatized version, he was approached by some syndicate boys to wholesale bootleg whiskey inside the Texas Hotel. They put pressure on Thompson, and he couldn't say no. He did, however, plan to swindle them.

The syndicate would deliver a certain number of cases a week, and demand payment a week later with the new delivery. They understood Thompson didn't have money up front. Thompson kept selling more and more cases each week, until he asked for double his allotment, or twenty cases, the week a convention was at the hotel.

The bootleggers were a little nervous, but understood his reasons for asking for so much booze. Or they thought they understood. Thompson was planning to sell all the whiskey in a few days, and skip town long before payment was due.

He successfully smuggled all the cases into an empty room at the hotel, and went home to sleep before his shift that night. He knew he couldn't leave the hotel once he started selling until the cases were all gone and he was ready to leave town. He was a little worried about the bootleggers demanding early payment, a little worried about other bellboys or the hotel detectives discovering the whiskey, and a little worried about federal Prohibition agents.

Birdie woke him from sleep in the middle of the afternoon; federal agents had found the whiskey—all five cases.

Thompson was puzzled—five cases? but there had been twenty—then it hit him. The federal agents, and probably the hotel manager and detective, had kept the rest. They'd likely been aware of his operation for some time, and had waited to knock it over at an opportune moment. Worse, his syndicate suppliers would now expect payment for the fifteen cases he supposedly had sold. Thompson had to get out of town, and fast. He packed up Birdie and Freddie, and by evening was headed out of town to Nebraska. Pop stood on the doorstep of the house waving goodbye, and got the hell out of town himself.

Jim Thompson never forgot the sacrifice his father was making for him, or the spirit in which he was making it. There were a lot of things the two of them wished to say to each other, but somehow couldn't. From *Now and on Earth*, the "conversation" between the narrator and his dead father:

> It must have been hell, Pop. To have been a big man, to have been something—
>
> *Yes, and may you never know that hell, Jimmie. Because I love you, now. I hoped you would die out there on the pipeline. I had taken your money because I thought I would shame you by taking it, and you had shamed me instead. I thought you were mean, rotten to the core; a dirty blob of scum that floated by virtue of its own filth. You came back and I sank even further within myself——*
>
> I wanted to talk to you, Pop. I wanted to tell you about the stories.
>
> *I know that now; I never understood you, and I could not take time for understanding. There were so many things to do, and— But you came back. It started all over again. Then you came to me and told me about the magazine, about going to school . . .*

And you made me, Pop. You stood there before the empty house with the locked doors and without a penny in your pocket—damned little anyway—and there was a smile on your face as we drove off.

Yes, we understood each other then. Twenty years too late. It was not your fault or mine. Circumstances had made us different and we were too long in adjusting ourselves . . .

"Circumstances had made us different"—a central theme of Thompson's later writing is the maddening impossibility of truly understanding another human being—especially if you cannot yet fathom yourself.

Winifred "Freddie" Thompson Townsend, who accompanied Jim and Birdie on the long, dusty ride to Lincoln, corroborates the bootlegging story to some degree: "We had to get out of town quickly, Jimmie's bootlegging had blown up in his face in some way."

Birdie and Freddie traveled on to Burwell, Nebraska, where they took up residence with the Myers family. Jim headed to Lincoln, looking forward to meeting finally the recipient of so many of his letters, Lucille Boomer.

Lucille recalls:

Well, I think perhaps I fell a little bit in love with him immediately—I think it was more having had the letters before that did it—feeling as if I knew him before I met him.

We had a very warm relationship—not like you talk about relationships today—that lasted a good two or three years, with many little upsets in between.

It wasn't casual—just somebody I dated—it was a little warmer than that during the time that I knew Jimmie.

Thompson enrolled in the University of Nebraska in September of 1929. He was affiliated with the school of animal husbandry and agriculture, a seemingly bizarre major for a prospective professional writer. In *Bad Boy,* he ascribes this to the fact that he was pledged to a fraternity, Alpha Gamma Rho, in which all the brothers were agriculture majors; they insisted that Jim be the same. In any case, Thompson did take English and writing classes as well.

He lived with Maxine and Russell Boomer in a small apartment above a drugstore. As was fast becoming a lifelong habit, Thompson worked his way through an assortment of hideous jobs during the school year 1929–30, including stints as the lone night guard at a funeral parlor, a film projectionist, a dime-a-dance dancer, and "batch man" at a bakery.

Thompson placed two stories and a poem in the *Prairie Schooner,* the university's literary magazine. The poem, "A Road and a Memory," appeared in the Winter 1930 issue of the quarterly; and the first of the stories, "Character at Iraan," in Spring 1930.

The poem is an awkward student's work in form, yet is undeniably heartfelt and compelling:

> *I can still see that homely, grass-grown trail*
> *That clung so closely to the shambling fence:*
> *Sand-swept, ruts filled with every gale;*
> *A helpless prey to all the elements.*
> *A shower would make those soft black tracks a mire*
> *That sucked at wagon wheels and made the horses sweat;*
> *The sun would turn them into flinty fire*
> *That burnt and tore each unshod foot they met.*
> *In winter, with the grass and sand-burs dead,*
> *I walked the bellying center of the trail*
> *And filled the gopher holes that might have led*
> *To broken legs when moon and stars should fail.*
>
> *Each morning found me plodding down that road to school.*
> *The evening sun was low on my return.*
> *And every roadward thing construed itself into a tool*
> *To make my hot resentment deeper burn.*
> *Those tortuous ruts were like two treacherous bars*
> *So spaced to show an eye-deceiving gape*
> *So while one ever struggled for the stars*
> *They hugged too close for actual escape.*
>
> *Escape: tell me the meaning of the word:*
> *Produce the man who's touched a star, for me.*
> *Escape is something for a bird;*
> *A star is good to hang upon a tree.*
> *Not long, however, lags the flesh behind the mind.*
> *I left the road, the ruts, the hole, the dust.*
> *And sought a symbol of another kind*
> *To mark reward for labor, right and just.*
> *. . . and twenty years have trickled through my hand.*
> *The hand is soft; it's white, preserved and clean.*
> *As unlined, vacant as the wind-brushed sand;*
> *As meaningless, as—mean.*
> *The road? Why yes, the road is there.*
> *And now it seems the road will always be;*
> *Not white, not soft, nor fair,*
> *But hard and straight as strange eternity.*

Again young Jim Thompson works the theme of an uncaring world, which inexorably erodes its inhabitants' souls. He does not expect better in the next world (if there is a next world), for our fate will be found upon the earth: "Escape is something for a bird." The inert road is the only thing eternal.

The short story "Character at Iraan" is a personal reminiscence of his time out on the oil fields. Slim, a young oil field worker, narrates his last days in West Texas. Homesick without admitting it to himself, he has become a steady drinker. One night he goes too far, and collapses after drinking a couple of bottles of white (actually green) lightning. He nearly dies; in fact, he narrates his own "death" in a passage that at least formally signals what was to come in later Thompson works:

> There was the feeling that a belt was being tightened on my chest. Ted kept bathing my head in cold water and that seemed to make my chest worse.
>
> Martin asked me if I couldn't eat some soup or something. Then Ted asked me. I didn't answer either although I heard them perfectly. I just lay there and looked at them. Ted leaned over me and looked into my eyes. I looked back into his at the little picture in the pupils. Then Ted passed his hand back and forth in front of my face. It came very close, so close that I could see a faint little cross in his hand joining the life- and heart-line.
>
> I wished I could have seen how Martin was taking all this hocus pocus, but he had stepped out of my view, and the desire was not strong enough to move the eye nerve. And while I wondered I heard Martin scream.
>
> He's dead! Oh, Christ—he's dead!

Thompson's later novels are full of references to the living dead. From Joe Wilmot's "They can't hang me, I've been dead a long, long time" that concludes his narration of *Nothing More Than Murder,* to Dolly Dillon's observation in *A Hell of a Woman* that he feels like "a mechanical man with the batteries run down," the vital signs of Thompson's protagonists seem to have flatlined long ago; the death of their souls manifesting itself physically.

Since our narrator has gone on to write this memoir, "Character at Iraan" also features the first instance of "death" and rebirth. An apparent "resurrection" recurs among the "dead" narrators of *The Killer Inside Me, A Hell of a Woman, Savage Night.* This might seem just an awkwardness of the crime genre if it were not for the more surprising and identifiable elements of Christ's death and resurrection in *After Dark, My Sweet, Pop. 1280,* and *Child of Rage.*

Thompson's last appearance in the *Prairie Schooner* was Fall

1931's "Gentlemen of the Jungle," another set of three satirical sketches, this time of hoboes. Although shorter and more economical than the sketches that appeared in *Texas Monthly,* they offer no new themes or techniques.

Judging from all the evidence, Thompson and Lucille Boomer had fallen deeply in love. They would take long drives at night, or just sit together on the porch swing, talking. The usually reserved Thompson opened his heart to her and told her his dreams and aspirations.

Lucille's father liked Jim quite a bit. Recalls Maxine: "My father-in-law at the time, Professor Boomer, thought Jimmie was a second Walt Whitman—admired him, liked him, just crazy about him."

Professor Boomer died in 1930, and Jim Thompson lost his biggest (perhaps only) fan among Lucille's kin. Her brothers were naturally watchful of all her suitors; as she remembers: "I was the only girl, with four brothers—I had a surveillance that you wouldn't believe."

Mrs. Boomer, by Lucille's account, did not share her late husband's enthusiasm for Jim Thompson:

> My mother wouldn't have been very happy if I decided to marry Jim. He was living in a world of his own—a writer, a dreamer—you know mothers are apt to think of their daughter's future—and what he might amount to or not amount to—well, he wasn't one of her favorites of my friends.
>
> My mother was concerned about how deeply we both felt at the time—and it was true.

Still, their courtship continued for nearly a year and a half.

> We'd go to the movies—I was in a sorority, and Jimmie pledged a fraternity—we'd go to the dances. We spent many, many nights in my parents' home—Maxine would play violin, et cetera. A lot of time was spent in our own home.

But Jim Thompson eventually lost Lucille Boomer to Walter Larson, a student at the dental collage. Presumably a dentist was more what Mrs. Boomer had in mind for Lucille's future. Lucille recalls:

> We were married in Nebraska before he graduated from dental college, with a big church wedding, on Valentine's Day, February 14, 1931. My four brothers were ushers. Walter Larson was a fine, fine, person—and as different from Jimmie as night and day.

Adds Maxine:

> Mrs. Boomer liked Jimmie, but disapproved a little bit because she wanted Lucille to go with somebody that had a lot of money. Jimmie always blamed her for breaking them up. And Lucille blamed her too.
> Lucille married Walter, the one her mother wanted her to marry all along, and whom she didn't like—well, she liked him but she liked Jimmie better. She and Jimmie really liked each other.

While Maxine was at the wedding, Jim Thompson was not. According to Lucille they never saw each other again.

The newly married Larsons moved from Lincoln, Nebraska, to West Hartford, Connecticut, a year later, at the height of the Depression. Dr. Larson practiced there the rest of his life, with Lucille by his side. Lucille eventually lost track of Maxine and Jim, especially after Russell and Maxine later were divorced.

When contacted for this book, Lucille Boomer Larson Parsley (Walter Larson died in the 1960s and Lucille subsequently remarried) was completely unaware that Jim Thompson had actually gone on to some success as a writer. Yet when told that Thompson later wrote a now-lost novel whose lead female was probably a fictionalization based on her, she offered the title immediately: *Always to Be Blessed*. She said that book was written for her, or about her. But then Mrs. Parsley was rather embarrassed and at a loss to explain how she knew about it.

The only extant portion of *Always to Be Blessed* is the final chapter, which was published when Jim Thompson was a member of the Writers' Project in Oklahoma, under the title "The End of the Book." Lucille Parsley could not recall whether she had ever read the complete novel, or how she came to know that it was written about her. When asked if Jim or Maxine Thompson ever contacted her in later years, she was adamant that they did not. She had never heard about Jim Thompson after she moved to Connecticut in 1932; yet the novel was not completed until at least 1933, if not 1937.

How Lucille came up with the title of the novel Jim Thompson wrote for her remains a mystery. Thompson's fictionalization of an affair with Lucille after they both were married (contained in *Now and on Earth*) would go a long way toward explaining things, if it actually occurred.

Jim Thompson wrote about Lucille Boomer after their breakup, in *Now and on Earth* and elsewhere. Like his many written and oral versions of his father's death, these passages are dramatizations of deeply held memories, thoughts, and emotions. While not literally true (at least unconfirmed as such) these fictional passages may reveal more of what happened to Jim Thompson at the time, and its lasting effect upon his life, to a greater degree than any other available facts or recollections.

Lucille Boomer's statement that *Always to Be Blessed* was written for her, about her, is probably on the mark. Lester Cummings of "The End of the Book" is a savage, insane murderer, with a consciousness that has been split in two by some unknown trauma. He kills the father of a migrant family he meets along the roadside, and then turns to the daughter, mistaking her for his lost love. In his last moments, he tears the clothes from the girl and hallucinates the happy times spent with Lois.

Lois is the name Jim Thompson used for a character unquestionably based on Lucille in *Now and on Earth*.

Unless the manuscript of *Always to Be Blessed* is found someday, we'll never know whether Lester's memories of better days with Lois actually occurred within the action of the novel or are a madman's delusions. It is known that Jim Thompson never lived the scenes of domestic happiness with Lucille that are depicted in "The End of the Book." Frighteningly, an interpretation of this story as "autobiography" requires Jim Thompson to assume the role of Lester Cummings; Cummings's mutated exterior and foul actions become literalizations of Jim Thompson's wounded interior and poisonous thoughts.

Whatever forces turn Cummings into a mad murderer in the lost chapters of *Always to Be Blessed* that preceded "The End of the Book," it is clearly implied that his life with Lois would have or did keep him sane. From "The End of the Book," as Cummings imagines he has found Lois:

> *Ah, God! It is Lois. Kneel down by her. Kiss her lips, her breasts, take her into your arms. Hold her against your shoulder. That is good, isn't it? Just to hold her and protect her; let her sleep while you stand guard. All these days, these months, these years, and now you are together again. It was a long time but is past now. Remember the last day of school when you walked home together? Remember the night you drove your new car around to her house? Remember the lane with the tall elms, the elms dripping diamonds of sunshine from their leaves, the robins teetering on the fence wire, the grass singing in the wind? Ah, God! and the little apartment over the drugstore. The smell of hot coffee on a cold morning. Hands ruffling your hair, probing your ribs, tickling you into wakefulness. Remember the days when you lived for the nights, the nights with Lois asleep on the lounge while you sat at the kitchen table poring over your correspondence course in accounting. Remember the kindly gloom of the streetlight drifting through your window, drawing your struggling shadows upon the wall until*

you laughed at your own antics. And went to sleep. Remember rising on your elbow to look at her; the slow, instinctive opening of her eyes, those serene brown eyes, round and shadowed with love and happiness . . . Ah, God! Do not speak! Let me give back what has been taken from you.

Jim Thompson may have been able to give Lois back to the deranged Lester Cummings as hallucination in his writing, but he himself never regained Lucille Boomer in real life. Again seeking approval and validation, this time from a woman and not his father, Thompson was once more rejected. The dramatization of "The End of the Book" only hints at the permanent scars left on Thompson by his failed romance.

Russell Boomer felt bad about how things turned out; he thought himself at least partially to blame for setting Jim and Lucille up in the first place. It was obvious how hard Jim Thompson had been hit by Lucille's marriage, and Russell tried to cheer him by setting up dates with other girls.

A few weeks after Lucille's wedding, in early March 1931, Jim Thompson stood on the front steps of a house, waiting patiently for the blind date with which Russell had set him up for the fraternity dance. Alberta Hesse Thompson recalls:

> It was a blind date, set up by his brother-in-law, Russell Boomer. He called me, Jimmie was living at their house in Lincoln, Nebraska—I had known Russell for years—he called and said, Alberta, would you like to go out on a date with my brother-in-law to a fraternity dance? I said "Oh, I don't think so . . ." "Oh, come on he really needs a date, he just broke up with a girl."
>
> So I asked my mother if was okay if I went dancing—I had given up dancing for Lent—I didn't give up dates but I gave up dancing. Mother was a good sport, and she said yes, go ahead and go.
>
> Next thing I knew it was a couple of nights later. Jimmie showed up at the front door, all by himself, and we stood and looked at each other for a minute. We went to the dance, had a wonderful time, and he said, "I'll call you."

Jim Thompson fictionalized the differing experiences of picking up Alberta Hesse and Lucille Boomer for a date in *Now and on Earth*, where Lucille Boomer is known as Lois, and Thompson's wife, Alberta, as Roberta:

> The first time I called at Roberta's house she and her mother were in the kitchen. Roberta let me in and whispered I'll be right with you, honey; and

then she went back into the kitchen and I could hear her and her mother talking in low voices. I wanted to smoke, but I couldn't find an ashtray; I looked around for something to read and there wasn't anything. Not a newspaper, not a book or a magazine of any kind. I began to get nervous. I wondered what in the name of God they were talking about, whether the old lady was trying to talk her out of going out with me. Lois' mother hadn't been exactly fond of me either, and her father, who was in the School of Economics at the college, felt that Lois needed someone a little more stable. But it hadn't been like this. . . .

There:

"My dear boy! Aren't you just frozen? Lois will be right down. She's had such a cold today; barely able to drag herself around. I don't suppose I could persuade you two to spend the evening here? The doctor and I are going out, and—goodness gracious! You're sneezing! Aren't you afraid that Lois will catch—?"

"It's nothing serious," I'd say. "Just t.b."

"Oh . . . now, you're teasing me, aren't you? By the way, I've a book you must take with you when you go. Dear, dear Willa! I do know you'll enjoy her. What sacrifices she must have made! What a lonely life she must have led!"

"Willa? Which Willa do you mean?"

"Why, Miss Cather!"

"Oh. I thought you were talking about the other one."

"Which—what other—is there another—?"

Then the doctor, chuckling: "Martha, Martha! . . . By the way, Jim. I've just received my copy of the *Prairie Schooner*. Your story is very well done. Too bad there isn't some money in that sort of thing. Too bad."

That's the way it had been at Lois' house. They didn't hide in the kitchen there. They seated you in a room with a baby grand and more books than a branch library, and then they pelted you with words until your hide became so sore that you began to shout and snarl even before you were touched, until you made such a fool and a boor of yourself that you could never go back.

But at Roberta's:

I got up and began to pace the floor, and finally, call it eavesdropping if you will, I stopped where I could hear:

"Why Mother! You don't mean it!"

"Yessir, that's just what she did! She took a little cornmeal and beat it up with some canned milk and water, and she dipped the bread in that. And it made the finest French toast you ever saw!"

I thought, well for the love of—But it went on and on . . .

I'm not blaming anyone, unless it's myself. Not Roberta. I've only been telling you about Roberta, not blaming her. She couldn't have been any different, under the circumstances, just as Jo couldn't have been any different, or I couldn't have been any different. Abe Lincoln could have, but I couldn't. Maybe he couldn't. . . .

This is a rather savage fictionalization of events, both self-lacerating and lashing out at the Roberta and Lois characters. For instance, the narrator implies that Lois's father did not like him, while Maxine states that Mr. Boomer was a great fan of Jim's. Thompson seems to have been projecting his own feelings of inadequacy in regard to the relatively upper-class, well-educated Boomer clan.

Alberta Hesse Thompson finishes her recollection of her whirlwind courtship with Jim Thompson:

> Two weeks went by after that dance, and he didn't call, and I said to heck with him. Two weeks after that he called me, and we went together ever since, and finally got married that September.
> We ran away and got married. The job I had at the time, I knew I would lose it if anyone knew I got married. We were married in Marysville, Kansas, on September 16, 1931. As we came down the walk they started whistling "Here Comes the Bride." Then we went over and had an ice cream sundae, and went back to Lincoln where they were having a fall fashion show, and that night we saw *American Tragedy* by Theodore Dreiser. And he went to his house, and I went to mine.

Jim and Alberta Thompson had to keep their marriage a secret for some time. Alberta was a telephone operator, and there was a rule at the phone company that no married women were allowed to keep a job. Also, Alberta's family were strict Catholics, who would not recognize Jim and Alberta's marriage by a justice of the peace.

The couple's secret was discovered when nosy neighbors spied Jim and Alberta together at Maxine and Russell's house while Maxine and Russell were away. Their marriage became more public upon their marrying in the Catholic Church on April 6, 1932, when Alberta was already four months pregnant.

Alberta Hesse's parents, a policeman and a housewife, were less than thrilled with their new son-in-law. Not unlike the Boomers, they thought Jim Thompson would likely be a decidedly unsteady breadwinner—times were hard enough without relying on something as seemingly unessential as writing. Of course, they were right in a way: the times ahead were to be very rough, but not only for writers, for everyone. The Depression was just starting to hit.

Daughter Sharon Thompson Reed prompted Alberta on the subject of Mrs. Hesse's prejudices:

Sharon: "My grandmother did not like my father."

Alberta: "She liked him to a certain degree."

Sharon: "He wasn't good enough—you know how some mothers are."

Alberta: "I'd hate to tell you what she said. My mother was a very refined woman, but when it came to that she was not."

So Jim Thompson married Alberta Hesse some six months after losing Lucille Boomer to Walter Larson. The couple had three children by the end of the 1930s, and remained married forty-six years, the rest of Thompson's life.

Alberta Thompson does not give the impression that she ever truly shared or recognized her husband's inner life. Though clearly they understood and loved one another on some level—and shared a lifetime of good times and bad times—there was a part of Jim Thompson that either was shut off from her, or that she now refuses to discuss. The former seems more likely.

Young Jim Thompson thought the one woman with whom he was able to "be himself" was Lucille Boomer, and his loss of her was devastating. In *Now and on Earth,* the narrator tries to convince himself that things would not have been much different if he had married Lois:

> And, no, it would have been the same story with a different twist with Lois. We found that out the hard way.
>
> One day, after she was married and I was married, we met on the streets of Lincoln. And I undressed her with my eyes and she me with hers. And nothing mattered but that we should be together again. We drove to Marysville, Kansas, and registered at a hotel. We even wrote letters—unmailed, fortunately—explaining why we had had to do what we had done. Then the physical reunion, and after that, talk, lying there together in the dusk. She had it all planned. She had a sorority sister whose husband owned a big advertising agency in Des Moines, and he was a perfectly gorgeous person. If I would just be nice to him—
>
> "What do you mean, nice? I've never spit in anyone's face yet."
>
> "Well, that's what I mean, dear. You say so many things that are misunderstood. They give people the wrong impression of you. They think that—"
>
> "—that I've been in some pretty nasty places. Well, I have been. And anyone who doesn't like it can lump it."
>
> "Please, dear. I think it's marvelous the way you've worked to make something of yourself—"
>
> "—with so little success, is that what you mean? Well, what do you want me to do? Never mind—I'll tell you. . . . 'Ooh, my dear Mrs. Bunghole, what a delightful blend of pee—excuse me, tea! And what are your beagles

doing this season, Mrs. Bunghole? Beagling? Why how gorgeously odd! Do tell me—' "

"Now you're becoming impossible!"

"Perhaps I always was."

"Perhaps."

We went back to Lincoln that same night.

Five years later I would have admitted, in the security I had then, that she was not superficial, and she would have conceded that the common streak in me was no broader than it needed to be. And each would have borrowed from the other, and profited by it.

Thompson wrote this in 1941, when he had been married to Alberta Hesse for over a decade. Among other subtleties, he cruelly sets Lois and James Dillon's affair in a hotel room in Marysville, Kansas, the very city in which Jim Thompson married Alberta in September of 1931.

The huge chip on James Dillon's shoulder over Lois's upper-class family seems to be not just a sign of inadequacy—but the one self-imposed insurmountable hurdle that ensures a failed romance. Rather than succeed, Dillon draws failure from deep within himself. We can guess Jim Thompson did much the same.

Jim Thompson, of course, could never know what his life might have been like with Lucille Boomer by his side—he could only speculate, as here, hoping that it might not have turned out better. That maddening hope, that nagging possibility of happiness, was of course just another bit of endless torture as Thompson continued establishing his lifelong pattern: denying himself full success not only in his writing career, but in his personal life and marriage as well.

Despite rumors of later affairs, there is absolutely no evidence that Thompson engaged in any, and his good friend Arnold Hano is certain that if Thompson did fall for a woman, it would have been strictly from afar and never consummated.

Of course, Jim Thompson's fiction is full of sadomasochistic beatings and sexual abuse of women, and it is tempting to try to trace it back to his own life. There seems no real-life incident from which this recurring theme and obsession clearly stems. Lucille Boomer and Alberta Hesse were it—there are no other women to be found in Thompson's life. So to the extent that violent sexual passages in his books may be autobiographical, there are only these two women from which to choose.

Perhaps the violent sexuality of the books represents sublimated urges, as do the violence and murders. Yet many of Thompson's fictional sadomasochistic relationships are consential and mutually enjoyed—if we can believe Lou Ford, for instance, both Amy Stanton and Joyce Lakeland enjoy being beaten. So perhaps some of Thompson's own sexual experiences were finding their way onto the pages of his books.

Upon reflection, pain coupled with pleasure seems to be the key autobiographical element of the novels' sexual relationships, and the sadomasochism a literalization of a purely psychic state. Witness this excerpt from *Now and on Earth,* as James Dillon makes love with his wife Roberta:

> I had seen her that way five thousand times, and now I saw her again. Saw her for the first time. And I felt the insane unaccountable hunger for her that I always had. Always, and always will.
>
> And then I was in heaven and hell at the same time. There was a time when I could drown myself in this ecstasy, and blot out what was to follow. But now the epigamic urgings travel beyond their periphery, kneading painfully against my heart and lungs and brain. A cloud surrounds me, a black mist, and I am smothered. And the horrors that are to come crowd close, observing, and I feel lewd and ashamed.
>
> There is no beauty in it. It is ugly, despicable. For days I will be tortured, haunted, feeble, inarticulate.

An ugly view of sex, yes, but perhaps an unsurprising one for a man who always believed polar opposites—like pleasure and pain—went hand in hand, and who never enjoyed anything without regretting it as well.

Jim Thompson most resembled the characters of his crime novels in the way he kept an important part of himself hidden, even from his closest family and friends. While still young he never felt comfortable divulging certain inner thoughts and attitudes, and began watching the world from behind a quiet, affable mask.

The later, more permanent donning of that mask was secured by what Jim Thompson considered rejection of his true self by two of the most important figures in his young life—his father, and his first love, Lucille Boomer.

TWO

According to his wife, Jim Thompson continued to attend classes during the winter of 1931–32, although records show he was no longer officially enrolled at the University of Nebraska. In fact, the university credits Thompson only with the classes he took in the fall-winter term of 1929–30. In any case, by late 1932 Thompson's formal education was at an end; he had a newborn baby daughter—Patricia—and a wife to provide for, and the Depression was taking a devastating toll on Nebraska, Oklahoma, and Texas.

Always on the lookout for new sources of income, Jim Thompson hatched a scheme with Maxine's husband, Russell Boomer. They went about town convincing various merchants to place discount coupons in a booklet that Thompson and Boomer intended to print up and sell for five cents a piece.

Alberta recalls:

> Jimmie and Russell originated the idea of coupon books—everybody was so hard up—they printed up coupons and sold them—you got something free, or a little off. He didn't do much writing those years, he worked for a department store, as a collector—he hated it, and felt sorry for the poor people.
>
> Jimmy finally had to leave school after our first daughter, Patricia, was born on September 9, 1932. He and Pop left for Oklahoma City in October, looking for work, odd jobs.

Alberta and infant Patricia joined up with Birdie and Freddie Thompson in Burwell, Nebraska, where they spent the winter with the Myerses. On January 12, 1933, sixty-three-year-old James Sherman Thompson wrote to his wife from Oklahoma City, describing both the difficulties of drilling for oil without money, and the day-to-day realities of Depression life:

Dear Birdie:

Got your letter this morning. I will endeavor to answer all the questions that have come up since my last letter. Jimmie, I suppose, has covered most of them. Have been trying to get a block of acreage in south texas, drilled for an interest. It is in Bee county, about one hundred miles southwest of Houston. I have a contract in connection with another party. We have a derrick on the ground. About four miles west of us is another well drilling. It will be finished in about two weeks. They have agreed to move the rotary drilling tools over on our lease and they will take acreage for the rent and moving. In addition to that, we can get casing for acreage. With this much help we can drill the well for about $3,000.00. This structure is known as the Oaks Anti-cline; the Shell, Sun, and Humble companies have acreage in and around our block. I can figure out for myself and Jimmie who has a half interest with me, about four hundred acres; if we can make the deals I think we will make.

I went down to see Jake Hamon at Ardmore about helping out on the deal, but he was out of town. I wrote Charlie Wheatley at San Antone, and got an invitation from him to come and see him while in San Antone. I also put the proposition to Bill Mapes. I think we have a chance, especially if I can get as much as a ten dollar bill ahead—I think we have a good chance to put it over. I will try to sell about half the acreage and keep about half.

The relief work stopped here about a month ago for lack of funds from Washington. It started up about a week ago, and I have been going down and getting in line about five o'clock in the morning; but as there are 23,000 idle and only jobs for about one-fourth that many it is almost impossible to get a place. Otis Smith announced yesterday that all men who had worked previously need not come to the relief station but could remain at the addresses [and] that they would have messengers call at their homes when they want them. This will save a whole lot of unnecessary trouble. It will only be two dollars a day for five days per month. In addition to this we have lines out for many other things. Unemployment is increasing as it always does in the first two months of the year, but I am looking for a pickup in the latter part of February.

Regarding the accounting note don't let it worry you for you have nothing they could attach. All of your property is fully exempt. If I can put this deal over, I mean by this: the drilling of the well or the sale of the acreage, will send for you and Freddie immediately. This would probably also include Alberta. We fully realize the hardship that has been worked on you. This has been no picnic here either; but we are trying to cut our way through it just the same.

We cashed your check, but when we get one from Pa (it hasn't showed up yet) we will send that amount back to you. Tell Bilderback that I believe he put a curse on my Chicago Cubs. I thought of him the other day as I sat by the radio and heard the outcome of southern California and Pittsburgh. Tell Bill and Virgil that I often think of the good times we had in their home.

Tell Freddie to get some text books and put in a little time each day with them. As soon as we possibly can we must start her on the road to completing her education.

The Catholic minister who married Jimmie and Alberta was severely burned at the rectory in Lincoln the first of the week. Some others who were present were also burned.

Give my regards to mother. Tell her I wish I was up there where I could read to her of evenings. Tell Freddie to write and we will write again as soon as we hear from Pa. Sending papers.

> Love,
> Jim

James Sherman Thompson never "put over" the hoped-for oil well deal, and he and Jimmie eventually had to separate. Jim Thompson worked various oil field and relief jobs for more than two years. Little is known abut this time period; Thompson compresses the time in *Roughneck;* Alberta remembers he was taken in one winter by an old friend of Pop's in Oklahoma City, and while there he wrote drafts of two novels, likely *Always to Be Blessed* and *Nothing More Than Murder*. From *Roughneck:*

> I have many sharp memories of that winter in Oklahoma City. Of writing two novels and selling neither. Of selling three hundred thousand words of trade journal material and collecting on less than a tenth of it. Of distributing circulars at ten cents an hour, and digging sewer ditches at nothing per.

Some men Thompson met on the sewer ditch job led him back out into the oil fields for the spring and early summer of 1934; Alberta Thompson recalls that she, Patricia, Birdie, Freddie, and Pop reunited with Jim in Fort Worth late in the summer of 1934. Thompson landed a job as doorman at the familiar Texas Hotel, but the job was worse than his previous bellboy stints: he manned the door seven days a week, twelve hours a day, with no relief and no breaks.

Such work hours and conditions left him no time to resume his writing career; he wanted to write true-crime stories for the pulp periodicals. According to later self-penned biographical sketches, he had been contributing steadily to oil and mining weeklies and other trade journals. There's no record of this work, although it probably did occur; likely

these articles would have nothing to offer of biographical interest, if they
do still exist. Thompson's only presently unearthed appearance in print
from this time was in *Bandwagon,* "The Magazine of the Southwest,"
which published Thompson's "Arnold's Revenge" in February 1935. A
short story broken into humorous cliffhanger episodes, "Arnold's Revenge" apparently was a parody of the radio and movie serials of the day.
(See photos.)

Eventually Thompson employed the help of his younger sister and
mother in writing true-crime stories. Freddie recalled that she and Birdie
would research past murders, and Jim would write them up into the
correct format. Freddie also reveals another reason Jim Thompson didn't
do the research:

> I used to help with the true detective stories—Jimmie was very
> sensitive . . . he couldn't stand to read anything in the paper that was a
> horror story . . . the murder, things that happen. He was also on the shy
> side . . . hated to go and do the interviews. I loved that part. My mother
> and I would go out to the state capitol and go through the morgues, follow
> a newspaper story through from the killing and on to make sure there was
> a conclusion—a conviction.
>
> They did some rather colorful murders . . . My mother would go
> endlessly through the clippings taking notes. Then I went to the town where
> it took place with my nine dollar Jiffy camera and looked up the people
> involved; usually it had been years before. I tried to make sure everybody
> was still in jail, but very often in Oklahoma after ten years they had been
> released (that's another story . . . I almost got into trouble . . .). I
> interviewed the sheriff who would take me to the scene of the crime.
> Sometimes Alberta would go along, and I'd make her lie down on the
> ground and pose as a corpse. Mostly crimes of passion . . . and not at all
> like he wrote in later years.
>
> Then we'd come back and narrate the story to Jimmie and he'd write it
> up. I remember walking in on him one evening—he was sitting in the
> kitchen typing, deep into something, and he nearly jumped out of his shoes.
> He'd get so nervous and upset, hearing these things, but he needed the
> money.

It might seem odd that the author of *The Killer Inside Me* was so
shaken by tales of murder, but everyone that knew him agrees that
Thompson actually was like that.

Thompson seemed to have had almost no filter or distancing ability
when it came to violence—he was always terribly affected by it. Every
day we hear stories of violence and death, note them but do not dwell on
them unless something has happened to someone close to us. Thompson

evidently reacted to every act of violence he heard about as if it had occurred to someone he knew personally.

Upon reflection, this character trait seems to hold the answer to exactly why his novels seem so violent. There's more murder and violence in almost any other crime novel one might pick up, but they lack Thompson's powerful, obsessive mix of fascination and revulsion. One feels every punch and kick to Amy Stanton's body in *The Killer Inside Me*—not in the service of some over-the-top, lurid exercise in pulp writing, but because Thompson imparts exactly what it must be like to kill, and be killed.

If Jim Thompson himself seemed to have no "sanitary distance" from the violence of the world, his novels offer the flip side of sanitized violence. You read *The Killer Inside Me* and come away feeling unclean, like you just murdered Amy Stanton or Joyce Lakeland yourself. This from the man who was aghast at secondhand tales of true-life murder.

Of the dozens of true-crime magazines of the time, only McFadden Publications' *True Detective* and *Master Detective* were collected and preserved by any American library, and these only by the Library of Congress. Though Jim Thompson undoubtedly sold stories to other crime magazines during this time, they are impossible to unearth via conventional research methods. One such story, "The Illicit Lovers and the Walking Corpse," was kept over the years by Alberta Thompson because it featured the picture of her posing as a murder victim which Freddie remembers taking. The story appeared in *Daring Detective* sometime around 1935. The other two extant examples of Thompson's true-crime stories of the period are "The Strange Death of Eugene Kling" and "Ditch of Doom," from 1935 and 1936.

The format and content demanded by the true-crime magazines were quite strict. The crime had to have a satisfying outcome: that is, the criminals must have been caught, tried, and sentenced. Usually the tale was told through the eyes of the investigating officer or prosecuting attorney. The format left little room for Thompson's developing authorial voice; in particular, "Illicit Lovers" and "Kling" don't offer much to distinguish them as the work of Jim Thompson.

In "The Strange Death of Eugene Kling," which appeared in the November 1935 issue of *True Detective*, a young hobo sets out to solve the murder of a friend. He chases the murderers cross-country via freight train, pondering the possible motive for the killing of Eugene Kling. He finds the motive a common one: money. Trouble was, Kling had no money. The criminals had killed him for a pair of dice and a pocket comb.

The title of "The Illicit Lovers and the Walking Corpse" is the most intriguing thing about it; what seems a supernatural mystery turns out to be a murder scheme involving mistaken identity. Thompson lays out the tale carefully, keeping up the suspense for as long as possible. The story was accompanied by a fuzzy snapshot that was supposed to be the victim dead in the woods—the snapshot of Alberta Thompson, facedown in a pile of leaves.

Only "Ditch of Doom: The Crimson Horror of the Keechi Hills," from the April 1936 issue of *Master Detective*, hints at Jim Thompson's later narrating style and thematic obsessions. The tale concerns Uncle Billy Royce, an old man who has spent fifty years digging up acre after acre of his own land, searching for the buried treasure of the James and Dalton gangs. He knows it's there; Frank and Jesse said it was, and they wouldn't lie to a member of their own gang.

Long ago written off by the town as a harmless eccentric, Uncle Billy is questioned about the disappearance of his latest wife. He tells a wild tale of her running off to New Mexico with a Dutchman in a seven-passenger car. Soon blood is found in his kitchen, and after repeated questioning by the sheriff, Uncle Billy breaks down: his wife had found the treasure, and she wouldn't give him any. He killed her with a shovel and buried her beneath the chicken coop.

Uncle Billy can't relate his story coherently; he continues to babble about the Dutchman. With slowly dawning horror, the narrator (the sheriff) recalls several of Uncle Billy's housekeepers who disappeared after a few days work, never to be seen again . . . and the abandoned car in Billy's barn, supposedly left behind by overnight visitors years ago. Grimly, the sheriff realizes that Billy has murdered many times before. He looks about Billy's farmland, full of ditches dug in search of the treasure. All of them devoid of treasure . . . but many filled with the bodies of Billy's victims.

"Ditch of Doom" is narrated in both the third and the first person; seemingly an awkwardness of the genre, Thompson puts it to good use here. He opens with a narration of the murder, as "heard" by Uncle Billy. It's atmospheric, ominous—and a total hallucination:

> He shot the rusted bolt of the door and pulled it open. Again, standing on the little porch, he listened. Again, he heard the owl's echoing cry.
> That, and other sounds.
> The soft shuffle of a spade. Digging. The quiet click of a pick, striking its way through the rocky shale. And . . .
> The grisly crunching of an axe: the terrified pleading of a woman—choking, groaning.

We are *inside* the warped mind of Uncle Billy Royce, perceiving his "reality." This wouldn't be, of course, the last time Jim Thompson trapped his readers inside a deranged murderer's mind.

Arnold's Revenge

By Jim Thompson

A short--short-short-short novel by the author of "Concessions of a Husband"

Part One

Trouble Brewing

FIRST, the door-bell rang. Marcia looked at Arnold. He gestured with his revolver.

"Come in," she called.

The outer door opened, and feet walked and scraped uncertainly in the hallway. Arnold gestured again.

"In here," said Marcia.

There was a moment of silence then, like the silence a thunderbolt undergoes when deciding between a prize bull and a rotten tree. Marcia felt tense, but strong. That had always been the way with Marcia; she had great tensile strength. The door opened.

"Come right on in and make yourself at home," said Arnold cordially. "Before I blow hell out of you." *(To be continued.) Who has Arnold threatened to blow hell out of? Yes, yes, the man at the door, of course! But who is the man? Is it someone Marcia knows? If not, what is he doing there? If so, ditto. Be sure to read the next episode on page 18 of this swiftly moving novel of today.*

ARNOLD'S REVENGE
Part Two
Harve Bannister and Marcia Are Caught In A Web of Circumstances

HARVE BANNISTER, in the doorway, felt a warm Niagara of perspiration cascading down the back of his neck. At least, it seemed to him that it must be cascading.

"Before I blow hell out of you," repeated Arnold, transposing, "come right on in and make yourself at home."

He nodded approvingly as Bannister wobbled into a chair.

"You've come to see my wife, I suppose?"

"W-why—"

"I'll blow hell out of you if you lie to me!"

"W-why—yes. I came to see her."

"You've been here before when I was gone?"

"W-why—"

"I'll blow—"

"Yes!" *(To be continued.) Who is this—oh, all right, all right! But what's going to happen next, if you're so smart? Save yourself a headache and read the next exciting episode on page 19.*

ARNOLD'S REVENGE
Part Three
Harve Bannister and Marcia Are Still Caught In A Web of Circumstances.

ARNOLD sat down in a corner easy-chair and pulled out the reading lamp. Lifting the shade, he focused the rays on the lounge where Marcia half-reclined, her white face angrily enigmatic under the improvised spotlight.

"*Tableau!*" His voice was a trifle insane. "Come on, you rat-eared, back-belted mess of slumgullion, make yourself at home!"

"Y-you mean me?" quavered Bannister.

"You're the only rat-eared, back-belted mess of slumgullion here, aren't you?"

"I—I believe so," said Bannister, eyeing the revolver.

"Well?"

"I'm perfectly at home, thank you."

"If," Arnold warned him solemnly, "you lie to me again I'll blow hell out of you . . . I said make yourself at home. Get over there with *her*. Act as though I wasn't here. Kiss her. Make love to her. But do a good job of it, or I'll bl—" *(To be continued.) Can you guess what Arnold is about to say? Ah-ah—mustn't say it! You cannot afford to miss a single line of the next exciting episode on page 24.*

ARNOLD'S REVENGE

Part Four

Harve Bannister Confesses

TWO figures, male and female, clasped upon the lounge. Merely clasped. Arnold shook his head.

"No life. No feeling. Let's see how you kiss. And keep in mind that I'm not supposed to be here."

Harve Bannister stared deep into the black pools of Marcia's eyes. There were questions in them; questions but no fear. Then their lips met and there was a long, pleasant silence.

"Let's have a little action," growled Arnold, peevishly. "Marcia, don't be so particular about your dress. I'm not supposed to be here, you know. Young man, will you take your coat off or will I have to blow hell out of you?"

Bannister arose with alacrity, and shucked off his coat. A hard oblong object fell out of a pocket. Arnold leaped to his feet, his eyes glowing.

"What's that?"

"One of our brushes," explained Bannister, with pride, for he was a proud man. "My sample case is out in the hall. I've been here several times before, but your wife wouldn't let me in." *(To be continued.) Now, do you want to read the next and final exciting episode on page 26 or not? Yes, or no. We're not going to tease you.*

ARNOLD'S REVENGE

Part Five

After Troubled Seas

BRANDISHING his gun, Arnold fled the room, a wild cry on his lips.

Marcia's first words to Harve Bannister were pregnant with meaning.

"When," she whispered, "you are through with the toothpaste, do you always replace the cap on the tube?"

"Never," he replied. "I always drop it down the drain."

"Darling!" cried Marcia. And threw her arms around him.

She stayed there a long time, reveling in this new love. Only when the shot rang out upstairs, did displeasure cloud her eyes. "Well," she was on the point of saying, "Arnold has finally succeeded in blowing hell out of something."

But she did not say it. There was something so unspoiled—something that needed sheltering about Bannister. It would be like a slap in the face to confront him with any further crudity.

"Just Arnold," she whispered again. "Just Arnold—clearing his head."

THE END

* * *

Thompson moved the family up to Oklahoma City in the late winter of 1936, having finally quit the doorman job at the Texas Hotel, which he maintained left him with permanent kidney damage due to his inability to leave his post to relieve himself. According to *Roughneck,* and confirmed by his wife's memory, Thompson had been assigned to write a long article on a heroic small town Oklahoma sheriff by one of the true-crime magazines. He soon churned out what he claimed were "forty thousand words of the best detective story I had ever written." He had been promised $2,000 upon completion and publication.

Thompson drove out to the sheriff's town for the requisite photos to accompany his story, only to find the sheriff in custody in his own jail. It turned out the hero was actually the leader of an interstate auto theft ring. Thompson's story was worthless.

Once again nearly broke and looking for work to support the family, Thompson received a tip from a friendly newspaper writer. From *Roughneck:*

"If you're not too particular about money, I may be able to put you next to another job."

I said that I would be grateful for anything at all, for the time being. He told me where the prospective job was, and my face fell again.

"Writers' project? But that's relief work, isn't it? I'm not a relief client."

"They have a few non-relief people—men who really know writing and editing. Sort of supervisors, you know, for the non-professionals. One of the fellows who got laid off here is over there now."

"Well," I said dubiously, "I suppose it won't hurt to look into it."

Thompson was appointed as a non-relief worker on the Oklahoma Writers' Project on April 1, 1936. His salary was about $60 per month.

The man who hired Jim Thompson was William Cunningham, the state director of the Federal Writers' Project. A native Oklahoman writer who had recently published a novel, *The Green Corn Rebellion,* Cunningham had been appointed state director upon formation of the project in November 1935. He had since been struggling to get some work out of the drunks, loafers, and illiterates that had qualified as "relief-writers" according to the Works Progress Administration.

Jim Thompson was put on the payroll as a non-relief professional, whose task it was to oversee the relief writers' work. The only people on the project who had previously "made livings" as writers, Thompson and Cunningham respected each other and became fast friends. In September 1936, Cunningham wrote Federal Project Administrator Henry G. Alsberg about filling a job vacancy:

Royden J. Dangerfield, a teacher at the University of Oklahoma, has been on our coordinating project for a couple of months and has prepared articles on Government, Education, Social Development and the like. He has left the state however, so we have a vacancy.

I had planned to get another university man in his place, but it is hard to find a competent man willing to work 100 hours for $75. One of our own workers has displayed considerable competence. He is Jim Thompson, now on the operating project as professional, non-relief. He has been writing Tours and now is re-organizing and rewriting the Introductory Essays. He is a professional writer (wood-pulps), about 32 years of age, is quiet and commands a great deal of respect on the project.

I should like to put him on the coordinating project at about $125 per month, full time, as Guide Book Editor. He has wide, general interests and a better grasp of things than has anyone else on the project. . . .

Another reason I should like to get Thompson into a position like this is that he, of all those I know about, would be best qualified to take over the job of state director in case I should be struck by lightning. The stormy season is approaching.

Jim Thompson was subsequently appointed Guide Book Editor by Washington, and received a substantial increase in salary. The Guide Book, part history and part tourism promotion, was the chief task to be undertaken by the Project; every state was preparing one.

Besides Cunningham, Jim was friendly with Ned DeWitt, who organized some of the Oklahoma WPA writers into a local chapter of the American Writers Union. No sooner had writers formed the chapter when five members of the Writers' Project in St. Louis were fired because of organizing activity. Dozens of letters were sent off to Washington by protesting fellow writers. Thompson's was the most eloquent:

Oklahoma City, Oklahoma,
November 2, 1936.

Mr. Henry Alsberg,
Director,
FEDERAL WRITERS PROJECT,
Washington, D.C.

Dear Sir:

I wish to protest against the recent outrage in St. Louis which for sheer tyranny and the usurpation of human rights has not been equaled since the Homestead strike.

As I understand it, six union writers there were dismissed from the Writers Project because of some very reasonable requests which they made to the project director; another cause for their dismissal, I understand, was their attempt to organize their fellow writers and thus improve the working standards.

Who is this martinet who violates the cardinal principles of human liberty? Why does she stop with sic-ing the police on the picketeers? Why doesn't she equip herself with thugs and tear gas and completely annihilate these villains who have the base temerity to "ask for more." Why doesn't she show herself for what she is—a disciple of Bergdoff, Pinkerton, and William Randolph Hearst?

I cannot believe that when you know of the true state of affairs in St. Louis you will allow it to continue. I feel sure that you will have these writers reinstated, and at the same time familiarize the director with the rights of employees to organize. To adopt any other course—to allow the wrong to go unrighted—would strike a severe blow at the labor movement, and render "free speech" an empty phrase.

Sincerely,

Jim Thompson

Member:
Writers Project Union, Oklahoma City,
American Writers Union

The protest letters caused a noticeable stir among the politicians and officials of Oklahoma City; a project member with a grudge voiced the general opinion when he branded DeWitt, Thompson, and the rest of the union members "commies" for supporting their union brothers in Missouri.

Things got so out of hand that the FBI eventually sent out an agent to investigate charges of un-American activity on the Oklahoma Project. A bemused William Cunningham wrote back to Alsberg after the G-man's visit:

As you may know the Writers Project here has been rather thoroughly investigated by the F.B.I. The matter is unimportant but I thought perhaps you should know about it.

Several months ago some of the people on the project decided to organize a Writers Project Union. I told them what the WPA regulations are regarding organizations and attended the meetings for a while, helping the Union frame its constitution. At the second meeting of the Union opposition developed and I soon learned what the trouble was. One worker on the project had been active in an unemployed organization several years ago; another worker on the project had tried to join this organization, so the story goes, and had been refused membership because officers of the organization were convinced that he was selling information to the police.

I have no personal knowledge of this incident and so cannot vouch for it. The first worker was active in forming the project union; the second opposed it very vigorously, tying up one meeting completely by parliamentary maneuvers. The latter worker resigned from the union but the enmity continued.

At that time a complaint was made secretly that four persons among those most active in the union were not doing any work on the Guide. This complaint went to the State office, then to Washington, and about two weeks ago the G-man appeared. His name is Van Doren . . . He interviewed the four workers accused. . . . Fortunately the four persons investigated were among the dozen most useful persons on the project. As I told the G-man at the time, we have had on the project persons so incompetent or so unstable nervously that they have been of no use whatever, but we have kept them on simply because they had no means otherwise to feed themselves. These latter took no part in union activities and so were above suspicion.

Van Doren said after his investigation that the charges were absurd and that he would turn in a very favorable report. . . .

The project workers enjoyed the sensation of being investigated by G-men, but otherwise all is quiet.

The charges of Communism on the project never quite disappeared and later would prove instrumental in Jim Thompson's resignation as director.

At home, Jim Thompson enjoyed one of the more peaceful stretches of his marriage. The small family moved into a series of apartments in Oklahoma City, each a little better than the previous as Thompson's salary increased. Alberta gave birth to a second daughter, Sharon, on Christmas Day, 1936, and a son, Michael, on May 17, 1938. Money was still a problem, though; Thompson supplemented his salary by selling an occasional true-crime story to the pulp magazines, and writing a few articles for local newspapers.

Thompson wrote a story for the editorial page of left-wing newspaper *Oklahoma Labor*: "A Night With Sally," chronicling his stay with the Salvation Army one night in Omaha, appeared in the September 17, 1936, issue. According to Alberta Thompson, the Salvation Army remained Jim Thompson's favorite charity.

Things went smoothly at the Writers' Project through the winter and spring of 1936–37. By June, Cunningham and his small staff of competent workers considered themselves well along in the writing of the State Guide. As budget cuts from Washington threatened Thompson's job, Cunningham wrote:

James M. Thompson—editor—the most capable writer on the project— has a wife and two children and a father who he has to support—could be certified if the WPA ever actually considers certification of non-relief people already on the project. This has been promised us so long that we are very skeptical as to any immediate action.

Cunningham took an extended vacation during the summer of 1937 due to his wife's ill health. Thompson took over as acting director during this time, and apparently handled the day-to-day operations well enough.

James Sherman, Birdie, and Freddie had moved back to Oklahoma City that spring of 1937, and all three found work of some kind. Pop held a janitorial job only briefly. From *Roughneck:*

> It was menial and monotonous. He could not, willing as he was, give it the necessary attention. He became increasingly absent-minded, retreating into the memories of better days, and his employers fired him.
>
> Poor as the job had been, its loss was a severe blow to Pop's morale. He felt useless and cast aside, and his distress saddened and worried me as nothing else could.

Pop's retreat into better yesterdays was the inspiration for Thompson's short story "Time Without End," one of four works written by Writers' Project members that comprised a pamphlet titled *The Economy of Scarcity: Some Human Footnotes,* published by Cooperative Books of Norman, Oklahoma, in 1939. A series of pamphlets issued monthly, Cooperative Books was the brainchild of Winifred Johnston, a professor at the University of Oklahoma. From her editor's note: "Cooperative Books is an attempt at a new kind of institution, cooperative in nature and cultural in its ends." *Economy of Scarcity* was the third pamphlet issued; the other authors were Welborn Hope, Daniel M. Garrison, and Ned DeWitt.

From the "Book and Its Authors" page:

> *Some Human Footnotes* presents the reverse side of that glamorous world of penthouses, furs, and shining cars which the movies give us. But for a complete reflection of the economy of scarcity this picture also is needed.
>
> The authors all belong to the Federal Writers' Project of Oklahoma. The collection is assembled from their offtime creative work.

> Jim Thompson, born in Anadarko, Oklahoma, attended school in Oklahoma, Texas, and Nebraska. He began writing for pay at the age of fifteen and "worked at other jobs considerably earlier." At various times he has been hotel worker, plumber's helper, truck driver, pipeliner (Iran to the Gulf), roustabout and harvest-hand through the Middle West. He is a

contributor to more than twenty trade, class and technical journals, to little magazines such as *Prairie Schooner* and *Texas Monthly,* and to almost the entire field of slick-paper detective magazines. Since April, 1938, he has been director of the Federal Writers' Project of Oklahoma.

"Time Without End" is the carefully constructed story of Mr. Joseph Mazinky, an increasingly senile old man no longer sure of himself or his interpretation of present reality, who seeks refuge in memories of a safer and surer past. Though he lives alone, he takes his meals with his son Joe's family, one day absently managing to offend both Joe's child and wife. Joe, who has no money to spare, gives his father two dollars to live on for the next few days until he can straighten things out with his family. Knowing his father's growing absentmindedness, Joe warns him to keep track of the money and how he spends it. Slightly offended, Mr. Mazinky begins his long walk back home.

Immediately he forgets everything except the hunger pangs in his stomach; he stops at a Chinese restaurant for ham and eggs:

> Although the check was twice as large as the one he ordinarily received at the beanery he did not argue about it, first because he had more than enough to pay it, and, second, because of his unwavering belief in his propensity for error. Daily, a dozen or more times—depending on the number of his actions and speeches—it was borne home to him that he was unfailingly fallible. The act of putting on his trousers or a simple remark about the weather burgeoned with possibilities for the ludicrous. Naturally, he did not cherish this capacity for being wrong, and, insofar as he could, he limited its manifestations. . . .
>
> He enjoyed a few moments of self-confidence and well-being on the way to the hotel. Then, like a cloud of locusts the day's sins descended upon him.
>
> Joe. He had lied to Joe about losing the money. He had told Myra that he didn't like the water. He hadn't taken little Myra any candy. . . .

In a fit of remorse Mr. Mazinky proceeds inside a drugstore, where the clerk sells him an expensive box of chocolates for nearly the rest of the money Joe had given him. By the time he makes it to his hotel (with the assistance of a friendly policeman), he has forgotten all about the candy. He asks the porter to bring some ice water up to his room, and tips him with the last of his change:

> He was so weary, after the three flights, that he flopped down on the bed without turning on the fan. Then, prodded by his memory, he got to his feet again. He had forgot something, something very important. The porter

came in without knocking, and placed the pitcher of water on the dresser. Sullenly, he started out.

"Wait a minute," said Mr. Mazinky. "I guess I ain't given you nothing in a long time, have I?"

"Nosuh. You sure hasn't."

"Well"—Mr. Mazinky produced two dimes and two pennies--"here's a little present for you."

"Thank you, Mistah Mazinky. Anything you need, now, you jus'—"

"I will. You go on."

Mr. Mazinky closed the door.

That wasn't it; it was something else. Frowning, he turned on the fan and took a long drink of ice water . . . Something about Joe, maybe. Or Joe's wife . . . He sat down.

On the box of candy.

Absent-mindedly, he shifted his weight a little and retrieved it . . . Maybe it was about buttoning his shirt straight, or looking out for the wagons, or . . . There was chocolate on his thumb. He licked it . . . Maybe it was . . .

Staring down at the broken cover of the box, he slowly completed its destruction. He ate a piece of the candy, then another, and another. He inched forward on the bed until he was within reaching distance of the water.

The fan sang in a tone above tonelessness—*like the little wheel on the cream separator.* And in the alley below the garbage cans rattled as . . .

As Pa rinsed out the milk pails.

Firmly, the tether of the past tightened, drawing Mr. Mazinky away from the frightening crevices of the present.

So the story ends. The past is both a refuge and a trap for Mr. Mazinky; his memories of happier times, along with periodic memory loss, prevent him from functioning fully in the world.

Thompson was eager to show off his writing skill in "Time Without End"—the prose style is straightforward, but more high-flown than in his later work. Up to then Thompson had had little opportunity to write fiction: this was only the third published short story by a man who had considered himself a writer since the age of fifteen, eighteen years before. The use of italics for Mr. Mazinky's hallucinations of the past would become a trademark device in the later novels.

Jim Thompson claimed to have written two novels during the winter of 1932. One of them eventually evolved into his third published novel, 1949's *Nothing More Than Murder.* The other almost became his first published novel, *Always to Be Blessed,* the last chapter of which, "The End of the Book," was published as a short story in Viking's 1937 collection of Writers' Project material, *American Stuff: An Anthology of Prose and Verse by Members of the WPA Writers' Project.*

Already discussed in the previous chapter in connection with Lucille Boomer, "The End of the Book" concerns the last moments on earth of Lester Cummings, a man who has become, quite literally, a monster. He awakes in a metal toolhouse, finding a rat just inches from his face. What follows is one of Thompson's most grotesque passages, as Lester first dazes the rat with his fist, then bites its head off. The rat's death is narrated from its point of view.

Lester wipes his mouth, realizes he's thirsty, and goes outside to let the rain beat down his throat. He reminisces and hallucinates and begins to walk through rows of cotton. He meets up with a family of tenant farmers who are driving a beat-up car down the washed-out road. They honk the horn to get him to move out of the way.

At this point in the story, the narrative splits into italic and roman type, not unlike the last three pages of 1954's *A Hell of a Woman*. Here, the italics signal Lester's inner dialogue; the roman the "objective" reality of the story.

The father of the family leaps from the car with a curse and approaches Lester:

"God damn yuh! Will yuh get outta the road an' let me by? Are yuh deef?"

"This man has snuff dripping from his lips. His son, the slantjawed stripling with the jack-handle in his hand, would do you harm. And look at those two crones in the back seat, their faces the color of dirty leather beneath their sunbonnets . . . Well?"

"They are in my way . . ."

"Of course. Reason enough for killing them. Then, look at the snuff and sunbonnets."

"I thought you had left me."

"I could not see you tormented . . . snuff, and sunbonnets; people getting in your way."

"What shall I do?"

"There is a knife in your pocket. You can open it with one hand. Quickly. His throat. That will stop the snuff from dripping."

"Paw! Get away from him! That's the . . . help!"

"Yuh—yuh. I didn't do . . . God . . ."

"I knew the boy would run. You will not have to worry about him. Take your time now. The women cannot move. Up on the running board . . ."

Lester proceeds to the car with the two women inside; the young daughter catches his eyes. He convinces himself it is his lost love Lois, despite the evidence before his eyes:

" . . . *This looks like Lois!*"

"*It . . . it is Lois!*"

"*I would not be too sure. Remember how you were fooled before. Lift her out of the car. Lay her there on the ground. That dress is rotten; it will tear easily. Now, do you still think it is Lois?*"

"*I should not be doing this.*"

"*Ah, God! It is Lois. Kneel down by her. Kiss her lips, her breasts, take her into your arms. Hold her against your shoulder. That is good, isn't it? Just to hold her and protect her; let her sleep while you stand guard. All these days, these months, these years, and now you are together again. It was a long time but it is past now. Remember the last day of school when you walked home together? Remember the night you drove your new car around to her house? Remember the lane with the tall elms, the elms dripping diamonds of sunshine from their leaves, the robins teetering on the fence wire, the grass singing in the wind? Ah, God! and the little apartment over the drugstore. The smell of hot coffee on a cold morning. Hands ruffling your hair, probing your ribs, tickling you into wakefulness. Remember the days when you lived for the nights, the nights with Lois asleep on the lounge while you sat at the kitchen table poring over your correspondence course in accounting. Remember the kindly gloom of the streetlight drifting through your window, drawing your struggling shadows upon the wall until you laughed at your own antics. And went to sleep. Remember rising on your elbow to look at her; the slow, instinctive opening of her eyes, those serene brown eyes, round and shadowed with love and happiness . . . Ah, God! Do not speak! Let me give back what has been taken from you. Her nose is not flat and negroid as you see it; her hair is not a stringy mass of wool, green with dirt at the roots; her breasts are not brown with sun and rust. She is clean, clean and pure as you remembered her . . .*"

Eventually Lester tries to run away with the girl, but some men come upon the scene and shoot him down. As he lies dying, he imagines he makes it back home with his lost love.

The rest of *Always to Be Blessed* seems lost forever; one aches to know exactly what turned Lester Cummings into the murderous animal of the final chapter. Evidently, the loss of his love Lois has driven him mad; in the last few moments of his life, when he imagines he has found her again, he escapes from reality into memories of happy yesterdays. At one time a happy man living with his love, some terrible fall from innocence has turned Lester into a monster.

Both "Time Without End" and "The End of the Book" consider the past a happier, more innocent time, now gone forever. Thompson would continue to work the idea of a better world irrevocably lost into most of his later novels, either as pretext or subtext. He presented his most schematic and economical take on lost innocence in his short novel, *This World, Then the Fireworks*.

Since the past was not an option, the search for a way to live in a godless, uncaring, industrial world was a common theme in 1930s fiction, from Hemingway and Fitzgerald to the proletariat writers like Thompson's boss, William Cunningham. Having evolved from Naturalist predecessors Emile Zola and Frank Norris, these writers most often filled the vacuum of a valueless, godless present with moral/political codes of individual conduct.

Jim Thompson wasn't chiefly interested in establishing a new society; he was obsessed with chronicling the vacuum and its victims. The seeds of Thompson's later brilliant work were sown in his early naturalist efforts, where he depicts a world and a people where nothing will ever go right, or be right, for anyone. This empty world was the petri dish upon which many mutated cultures grew, like the horrible Lester Cummings. When Thompson later shifted the focus of his writing to the interior workings of these monsters, he found his niche.

In a typically stoic response, Thompson accepted his plagued world as a given, mourning only briefly for the better, innocent world lost. He mapped the journeys of its diseased inhabitants through the barren terrain of madness and death. When Thompson's mappings eventually brought him (and his readers) closer to finding the devil than finding a god, surely Thompson wasn't surprised.

Viking was impressed enough by "The End of the Book" that it offered a contract for the rest of *Always to Be Blessed,* scheduling its publication for the fall of 1938. The book was never published; the contract, still in Viking's files, gives no reason for the cancellation. Alberta Thompson recalls her husband's working on the manuscript, and thinks he finished it, but does not know any more than that. The complete manuscript of *Always to Be Blessed* seems forever lost.

In September of 1937, William Cunningham voluntarily went on a part-time basis at the Project so he could take care of Sally, his ailing wife. Jim Thompson assumed chief editorial responsibility, receiving a salary increase to $150 a month.

Mrs. Cunningham's health worsened over the Oklahoma winter, and on February 11, 1938, William Cunningham wrote to Alsberg in Washington resigning the directorship and requesting a transfer out of state:

Mrs. Cunningham has to leave Oklahoma because of an allergic condition. It is impossible to discover the exact cause, but the dirt storms seem to have something to do with it . . . it happens only in Oklahoma and no relief is possible here.

And so I want to leave also. If there is anything to do in New York . . . I should like to have it. If not I shall go to New York and wait for private industry to absorb me—to use a quaint WPAism.

There is only one person here who can take my place. You remember Jim Thompson as one of the contributors to "American Stuff." Viking is bringing out his first novel, Always to be Blessed, next fall. He has been guide book editor on the project for a long time and is now in charge of the University of Oklahoma Guide. He wrote, or rewrote, most of the introductory essays. . . .

My suggestion is that Jim and I come to Washington March 1, and you can give him the once-over. If he seems okay he could take my place March 15. I have not discussed this matter with anyone here and shall not do so until I hear from you.

Alsberg was amenable to Cunningham's request. Thompson and Cunningham visited Washington, D.C., on March 3, and Alsberg offered a surprised Cunningham a position as his assistant in the federal office. Alsberg wrote to his superior, Lawrence Morris, recommending William Cunningham as Assistant to the Director, and:

I am also recommending that Mr. James M. Thompson, Guide Book Editor on the Oklahoma Project, be appointed to succeed Mr. Cunningham as Oklahoma Director. Mr. Thompson joined the Oklahoma Writers' project in April, 1936, as a non-relief, security wage worker. He soon demonstrated his ability as a writer and editor and was made Guide Book Editor at a salary of $125 per month. When Mr. Cunningham went on the part-time basis in September, 1937, Mr. Thompson was given almost full responsibility for all editorial work, and his salary was increased to $150 per month. His work has been satisfactory and I am confident that he will handle the work very well. Moreover, there is no other person available who is qualified by ability and experience to do the work. Mr. Thompson is a writer and his first novel Always to Be Blessed will be published by Viking Press in the fall.

We believe that Mr. Thompson should receive $2300 per annum as State Director for Oklahoma.

Jim Thompson effectively took over the directorship on March 15, 1938, upon his return from Washington. Immediately Thompson wrote requesting that Cunningham (his "new" boss) and Alsberg fill his old position of Guide Book editor: "with Ned DeWitt, because it is essential that we have at least one full time writer, as I cannot have as much time to devote to writing as I had in the past." DeWitt was made editor, at $125 a month, effective April 1.

"Solving Oklahoma's Twin Slayings," which appeared in *Master Detective* in March of 1938, when Thompson and William Cunningham were in Washington, D.C., is a routine account of the investigation of two 1934 Oklahoma City murders in which spouses were the chief suspects; a "ragged negro" turns out to be the murderer of both victims.

Only in the overwritten yet powerful preamble to the story do we find a hint of Thompson's voice and concerns:

> Nature had banked a billion dollars under the ground; banked it in the black liquid currency of oil. And in tapping that treasure man had spent millions on towering derricks, hissing boilers, and sinuous miles of pipe. But on the people who lived there, on the outskirts of the world's greatest oil field, both Nature and man had skimped. Poverty-stricken, wretched, they clung to a miserable existence. On the crest of this wave of wealth they starved. And, as is always the case where great wealth is contrasted with deplorable poverty, the evil overshadowed the good. Death loves such places.

Thompson once again circumscribes the parameters of his hopeless world that breeds death. More explicitly political than the viewpoint in earlier works, Thompson blames the uncaring rich and powerful for the conditions under which the poor are forced to live. That the rewards to be had in a successful fulfillment of the "American Dream" are laid in front of those who are unable even to dream it, let alone attain it, is at the root of the crime and madness of Thompson's world—a *sine qua non* of all Thompson's later fiction.

Thompson's next order of business at the Project, in addition to the ongoing researching and writing of the State Guide, was publication of the Tulsa city guide, sponsored by the Federation of Women's Clubs of Oklahoma. Financial sponsorship was necessary for all WPA publications, for although the government funded research and writing, publication funds had to be obtained independently. A resultant procedural nightmare became a minor annoyance on the Tulsa guide, and the root of Thompson's later problems with the State Guide and Labor History.

Procedure required that manuscripts deemed ready for publication be sent to Washington for final editing and approval. But a deadline for printing and binding of the Tulsa guide set by the sponsoring women's group left no time for the manuscript to be sent in for federal perusal. Jim sent the manuscript to the printer and to Washington at the same time, and hoped for the best.

William Cunningham covered for Thompson in Washington, and since there was nothing controversial about the guide, there were no further ramifications. Cunningham warned in a friendly note to Thompson that "We have short-circuited the Tulsa guide very much. . . . I realize . . . the rush was no fault of the Oklahoma Project. Hereafter, things will have to be planned well in advance."

Cunningham also bid Thompson farewell and good luck in that letter; he was leaving the federal office soon for destinations unknown:

> Sally and I have only a couple of weeks more here in Washington and then—don't lose your temper—we will be jerking poor little fish out of a mountain stream while you guys have a stream of perspiration running down your periphery.
>
> Sincerely yours,
> William Cunningham

Thompson had lost a valuable friend in the federal office, one he could have used in the ensuing problems over the writing of a labor history of the state. On May 17, 1938, Senator Josh Lee of Oklahoma wrote to Regional WPA Director, Dean Brimhall:

> Friends of mine in Oklahoma have advised me that a project for the writing of the history of the labor movement in the State of Texas has been approved by the Texas Works Progress Administration. They have suggested that a similar project for Oklahoma would be worthwhile.
>
> I shall appreciate your investigating the possibility of such a project and advising me.

The letter made its way down to Alsberg, who forwarded it to Thompson, with mildly enthusiastic memos by Brimhall and Alsberg attached.

According to *Roughneck*, Thompson considered the labor history a dangerous undertaking. He knew the strong opinions held on both sides of the labor issue; he feared that the inevitable pressures applied by these vested interests would leave him stuck in the middle of a political land mine. Still, a truthful version of the progress and the problems of labor in Oklahoma appealed to him, and he wrote back to Washington requesting permission to put DeWitt on preliminary research. Alsberg gave him the go-ahead, and Thompson went in search of a potential sponsor.

Thompson wrote a progress report to Alsberg on June 22:

WORKS PROGRESS ADMINISTRATION
FOR OKLAHOMA
RON STEPHENS, ADMINISTRATOR

431 WEST MAIN

OKLAHOMA CITY, OKLAHOMA

June 22, 1938

Henry G. Alsberg, Director
Federal Writers' Project
1734 New York Avenue, NW.
Washington, D. C.

Dear Mr. Alsberg:

After hearing from you about the writing of a labor history of Oklahoma, I was called to the State Office by Mr. E. M. Fry, deputy WPA administrator, on the same matter. He is very much interested in seeing this work done, and, at his suggestion, we have been looking into the matter of sponsorship.

The State Commissioner of Labor will include an item in his budget to publish the book, and Governor Marland will recommend the expenditure. The commissioner also will appoint a committee of consultants, give us access to his files, and, in short, help us in compiling the material in any way that he can. The one difficulty is that his budget will not be submitted to the legislature until after January 1, and it is possible that it might not be approved. In any event, the book could not go to press before some time in February.

Shall we undertake the writing of this labor history under these conditions? It is something that all of us, here, would like to work on, and something that needs to be done. We contemplate a book of about 40,000 words, to be given away or sold at cost.

May we hear from you soon about this?

Very truly yours,

RON STEPHENS, STATE ADMINISTRATOR

James M. Thompson, STATE DIRECTOR

Federal Writers' Project, Oklahoma

Two weeks later, the State Commissioner of Labor, W. A. Pat Murphy, wrote to Alsberg:

About three weeks ago I had a conference with Jim Thompson, Director of the Writers' Project for Oklahoma, and several other persons concerning the writing of a labor history of the state. As a result of the discussion I agreed to sponsor the book and sign the necessary application for permission to publish.

My department has no funds to pay for the printing of the volume at this time, but I am asking for $1,000.00 in my next year's budget to take care of the expense. There is a possibility that this item would not be approved; in that event, I would be relieved of any responsibility in the matter.

Alsberg knew that publication depended on the budget committee of the legislature, and he would not know one way or the other until funds were apportioned in January. He decided to give the project the go-ahead anyway. Thompson forwarded a completed application for permission to publish on August 29. It was signed by Murphy, who had amended it to read, "The sponsor will assume full responsibility for both the cost of publication and distribution of the published work, *only* in the event that the expenditure is approved by the legislature."

There the matter stayed until January, when the legislature predictably turned down the request for the money. Murphy then formed a "publication committee" made up of various union leaders to raise the money for publication. This got Thompson the needed money, but it also got him a roomful of editors and censors. As he wrote in *Roughneck:*

> . . . any unfavorable mention of a union was invariably "a goddamned lie" and "that guy sittin over there" (the leader of an opposition union) should be compelled to admit it. As for me, I was charged with everything from stupidity to personal prejudice to taking pay from the National Association of Manufacturers.

Thompson and his writing crew continued research on the labor history and the Guide throughout the fall and early winter of 1938. Both *Tulsa: A Guide to the Oil Capital,* a twenty-five-cent booklet of seventy-nine pages in an edition of 5,000 copies, and *A Calendar of Annual Events in Oklahoma,* a giveaway of thirty-six pages in an edition of 15,000, were published. The Project had also gained a few more competent writers; chief among these was a young roustabout named Louis LaMoor—later to become L'Amour.

L'Amour, DeWitt, and other writers were frequently invited over to the Thompson house for dinner and late-night discussions. Alberta Thompson recalls L'Amour doing little talking, for he was constantly raiding her refrigerator. As much as she disapproved of L'Amour, she was less fond of DeWitt, and Jimmie's other "intellectual" friends, who hounded Jim to officially join the Communist Party.

Freddie Townsend maintains that Thompson eventually did join the Party:

> Jimmie briefly belonged to the Communist Party in Oklahoma, those people were really, really smart and liked him . . . he didn't realize he

could get himself into trouble . . . he just enjoyed talking to people on his
level. . . . Later, when he became intimidated to be more into it . . . we
left San Diego. Later he was always a little afraid [it would hurt him], but
it never came out."

As for Louis L'Amour, he stayed just a few months on the project;
Alberta's opinion of him leaves her marveling at his later success. She
maintains that "Jimmie had to fire him," but there is no record of that.

Meanwhile, trouble was brewing again among the less talented
"writers" on the project. An assortment of derelicts, drunks, and con
men, they brooked no correction or supervision of any kind. Rumors
resurfaced that the Project was run by Communists, and that you had to
join the Party to be treated well. These rumors were all too readily
believed by one Jemima Ellen Wolgamuth, a relief writer of some small
talent who, upon finding out that William Cunningham was no longer in
the federal office, wrote a letter to Henry Alsberg, citing disorganization
and Communism on the Project. An excerpt of her letter:

> Dear Sir:
>   . . . I am one of the editors on the Oklahoma Writers' Project. I have
> no personal ax to grind; I am a candidate for no higher position than the one
> I hold; but I do want, with all my heart, to see our set-up ORGANIZED and
> made as fine and productive as are the Music and the Arts Projects here in
> the City. . . .
>   . . . Perhaps, no single person is to blame for the work's never having
> been properly organized. When I first heard of the projected scheme, the
> aim of it was to furnish employment to those who had once made their
> living by writing but could no longer do so on account of the depression.
> According to that criterion, Jim Thompson, the present State Director, is
> the one on the pay role [sic] at present who could qualify. . . .
>   . . . Mr. Cunningham [had] the authority to classify the clients and
> decide the salary they should receive. Some typists, he called reporters
> though they never did anything but type; some reporters he called editors
> though they never did anything but collect material, and nothing could be
> done about it. We hear it preached that in America men do not have to act
> like mice, but the non-communists on the Writers' Project in this State have
> been MICE under the sway of the Communists in power. And I must say
> that if ever I had been inclined to join the Communist Party, what I have
> observed here at first hand would have wholly disinclined me. For taking
> a high-sounding name has done nothing to eliminate the human desire to
> grab and grab and hold, dominate and suppress.
>   When Mr. Cunningham was our Director, Mrs. Zoe Tilghman was State
> Supervisor. So cruel and overbearing was she that whether we liked his

politics we were driven to our Director for refuge—and we must all say for him that he was always kind in manner. But his parting act was a cruel joke on us all—and an insult to our intelligence, for he arranged for Ned DeWitt to slip into Mrs. Tilghman's place. Now Ned could not pass a senior high school test in English if his life depended upon it. He has no vocabulary, no remote idea of sentence, paragraph, or theme construction. For example, in one sentence of fifteen words that I proof read, he had used the word canyon five times—one-third of the sentence. Yet he ranks second in importance now on the Project and has assumed just as high-handed a manner as Mrs. Tilghman ever used.

If the Project were formed of real writers as I visualize it—and many such have applied and been turned down—I greatly doubt that I would feel that I belong. As it is I acknowledge only Jim my superior in the writing game. Other projects that are attracting favorable comment have highly accredited professors from State Universities or schools in the important positions. Why cannot we have as good supervision as they have?

Personally, I am very fond of Jim Thompson; he has heavy responsibilities; I would desire to do him no slightest harm. He is not a leader, too gentle to be dominating, and often is not very well. One feels sorry for him and dislikes going to him with complaints that would cause him pain. However, on occasion, when complaints have been taken to him, he has not always been just. When the reporters found fault that the communist in their midst was getting an editor's pay, he said, "Well, I will have her earn it by being your boss." Knowing, as he does, how unhappy we have all been at having Ned over us, he recently gave him a higher sounding title and increased his pay! We need someone who can *take it* and give impartial justice. There is no one on the Writers' who has the training and prestige that Mrs. Nan Sheets has on the Arts' Project and Dean Richardson has on the Music Project. Then they have, to boot, professors on leave of absence to help them.

If I had money I would come to Washington to try to see you, but if I had money I would not be on Relief.

Very respectfully,
J. Ellen Wolgamuth

Alsberg evidently ignored Ms. Wolgamuth's letter, though it could not have helped Thompson's cause later, when trouble hit over the labor history.

By early spring 1939, Thompson thought the State Guide sufficiently near completion to warrant a more active search for a sponsor to absorb the publication costs. Savoie Lottinville of the University of Oklahoma Press expressed a preliminary interest in March of 1939. Thompson met with Mr. Lottinville in mid-April, and wrote the following letter to Alsberg on April 25:

WORKS PROGRESS ADMINISTRATION
FOR OKLAHOMA

RON STEPHENS, ADMINISTRATOR

520 WEST MAIN

OKLAHOMA CITY, OKLAHOMA

307 Municipal Auditorium

April 25, 1939

Henry G. Alsberg, Director
Federal Writers' Project
1734 New York Avenue, N.W.
Washington, D. C.

Subject: Guide Book sponsorship
and Publisher

Dear Mr. Alsberg:

Following your instructions of April 18th, I saw Mr. Savoie Lottinville of
the University Press. He is interested in publishing the Oklahoma State Guide;
but, as you probably know, the future of the press is very much in doubt
because of the economy drive of the present legislature. At best they are not
going to have very much money to work with. Mr. Lottinville suggested, if
they decided to accept the manuscript, a first edition of 2,000 copies. An issue
this small, of course, will make the cost price per volume rather high.

It will take him about three weeks to secure reports from his readers and
decide whether or not the guide is something they would like to publish. If
the reports are favorable, we will then proceed, working together, to see
what can be obtained in the way of a subsidy. It is somewhat difficult, in
this State at least, to obtain cash commitments for a volume that has no
publisher and no definite date of publication.

Do you recall that the Press turned down the Guide Book in 1937? They
objected, at the time, to the five-year copyright clause, the fact that the
book to be permanently valuable would have to be revised frequently, and
that the manuscript could not be released to them unconditionally. No doubt
these difficulties can be ironed out if the report on the book is favorable.

Mr. Lottinville asked me whether or not the University could be both
sponsor and publisher of the volume. I do not believe this question has arisen
before and I was forced to tell him I didn't know. I would appreciate it if you
will advise me in the matter.

Mr. James W. Moffitt, secretary of the State Historical Society, is in
favor of sponsoring the Guide Book but is unable to act until he confers
with the president and other officials of the society. He has promised to give
me a report on their decision within a few days. I don't believe there is any
doubt about their sponsoring it.

As I mentioned in my letter of March 25th, it will be almost impossible to obtain a subsidy from any State agency under the present political set-up. Can you suggest any way in which we can make subsidization attractive to some private concern—such as the Phillips Petroleum company? They spend a great deal of money on advertising and if we could offer them something aside from indirect benefits it might be possible to interest them substantially.

> Very truly yours,
>
> *RON STEPHENS,* STATE ADMINISTRATOR
> WORKS PROGRESS ADMINISTRATION
>
> *James M. Thompson,* STATE DIRECTOR
>
> Federal Writers' Project, Oklahoma

Thompson was afraid the State Guide could potentially end up in the same position as the labor history: at the mercy of the state legislature's appropriations. Alsberg advised Thompson that they might be able to offer a substantial discount for purchase of a large amount of Guides by a single private enterprise, like Phillips Petroleum, but no other accommodation could be made. They would have to hope Lottinville could convince the university to sponsor the Guide. In the meantime, Alsberg instructed Jim to inquire if the State Historical Society would be interested in sponsorship in case the university fell through.

The WPA was undergoing a massive restructuring that year, and many projects were falling from federal to state control. Due to the prevailing Oklahoma political climate, and the growing misconception that the project was communistic (evidently enhanced by the labor history), Thompson was sure that when the state took over control of the project on September 1 he would be out of a job. He had several weeks of paid vacation due to him, and was afraid he'd lose them (and more important, the pay) in the shuffle. Thompson wrote a resignation letter to Alsberg on the twentieth of July:

> Written from: 1921½ West Seventh,
>   Oklahoma City, Oklahoma.

Mr. Henry G. Alsberg, Director
Federal Writers' Project,
Washington, D.C.

Dear Mr. Alsberg:

As you probably know, our project becomes State-wide, instead of Federal, on September 1st.

For several reasons, I do not believe I could fit into the State-wide set-up so I am submitting my resignation to become effective the first of

September. Since I have accumulated considerable annual leave, I will submit my resignation to the State office on July 24th—this coming Monday—and will take no active part in project affairs after that date.

I am writing you for two reasons. First, to let you know that I have enjoyed working with you, and that I am sorry I cannot continue to do so. Second, to ask if, perhaps, you could find work elsewhere for my administrative employees. Mr. DeWitt, whom you already have met, will go out of office when I do. You already are familiar with the fine work he has done, and my own recommendation is unnecessary. Miss Clara Stockton, my administrative secretary, is a highly efficient and personable young woman, who, in all likelihood, will find herself out of a job shortly after I am out of mine. Mr. Craig Vollmer, my chief editor, is a man with twenty years experience in newspaper and magazine work; he has a number of dependents; and he will, like the others, be separated from the payroll September 1st.

I do not know whether these people would care to leave the State; but, if they did, could you effect their transfer?

I would like to know, also, whether or not there is anything I can do for you here before I leave.

If you care to write me, you should do so immediately, so that the letter will reach me by or before Monday.

Jim Thompson

Alsberg wired Thompson to suspend any action until Lyle Saxon, the regional director, could visit Oklahoma and assess the situation. Alsberg feared that if Thompson and DeWitt left, the State Guide would be rendered months, if not years, behind schedule. Saxon arrived in Oklahoma on July 25, 1939. He wrote this summary letter back to the national director a few weeks later:

WORKS PROJECTS ADMINISTRATION
OF LOUISIANA

803 CANAL BANK BUILDING

JAMES H. CRUTCHER   NEW ORLEANS   RAYMOND 9711
ADMINISTRATOR

624 Canal Bank Bldg.,
New Orleans, La.,
August 19, 1939.

Subject: Oklahoma Project

Mr. J. D. Newsom,
National Director,
Federal Writers' Project
Washington, D.C.

Dear Mr. Newsom:

On July 25 I accompanied Mrs. Leo G. Spofford, Chief Regional

Supervisor of the Division of Professional and Service Projects, and her assistant, Mr. George Hazleton, to Oklahoma, arriving at midnight. On July 26 Mrs. Spofford, Mr. Hazleton, and I conferred with Mr. Ron Stephens, State Administrator for Oklahoma, and Miss Eula B. Fullerton, Director of Division of Professional and Service Projects of Oklahoma.

Mr. Henry Alsberg, National Director of the Federal Writers' Project, had telephoned, asking me to go at once to Oklahoma as he had received the resignation of Mr. James M. Thompson, State Director of the Federal Writers' Project. Mr. Thompson stated in his letter to Mr. Alsberg (a copy of which will be found in your office, I am sure) that he and his assistant, Mr. DeWitt, were resigning their positions as of September 1, 1939, and that they expected to begin taking their annual leave on July 24. Mrs. Spofford then called Mr. Stephens on the telephone and made arrangements that Mr. Thompson and Mr. DeWitt remain until we got there.

In our first meeting with Mr. Stephens, Mrs. Spofford, and Miss Fullerton, Mr. Stephens expressed his desire that the Writers' Project in Oklahoma continue after September 1. He stated that he would do everything in his power to see that this project continued and will assist in getting sponsorship. In this Mrs. Spofford and Miss Fullerton agreed. Mr. Stephens stated that he knew little about the workings of the Writers' Project, and that he only desired that the Writers' Project work in close cooperation with the other W.P.A. projects in the State.

That afternoon I spent with Mr. Thompson and Mr. DeWitt, who agreed to remain on their jobs and expressed themselves as being willing to cooperate with Mr. Stephens and with the other projects. Apparently all previous troubles were ironed out, and I was most hopeful that the Oklahoma project would continue to function as before.

The only thing which worried me was this: Mr. Thompson told me that a labor history of Oklahoma had been taken to the printers that day and that the printing had begun. He had the approval of the national office for this he told me. I am quite sure that Mr. Thompson and Mr. DeWitt and their assistants had worked long and hard on this labor history, and insofar as I know (I haven't seen the manuscript) it is not of a controversial nature. It has been approved, I understand, by the various labor organizations which were sponsoring it.

A difficulty immediately presented itself. Neither Mr. Stephens nor Miss Fullerton believed it advisable that such a book be printed unless someone in their own organization had read it. As Mr. Stephens pointed out, if some criticism followed he would be held responsible. He said that he did not anticipate trouble, but that he wanted assurance that this book would not upset his organization and undo the work he had done. I then went back to see Mr. Thompson and we agreed to give a carbon copy of the labor history to Miss Fullerton so that it might be read by Mr. Stephens or his representative. Again apparently the situation was cleared.

The next day I went with Mr. Thompson and Mr. DeWitt to the University of Oklahoma at Norman, where I talked with the president of the school, his assistant, and with the head of the University of Oklahoma Press. They seemed entirely willing to cooperate and said that it was highly probable that the university would take on the sponsorship of the Writers' Project, after certain matters were cleared up. He wished to make some sort of an examination into the workings of the Writers' Project, he said. There had been some accusations as to Communism on the Writers' Project in the past, he said, and while he did not believe there was any truth in these accusations he felt that the university should not sponsor the Writers' Project until he was able to assure himself that no future trouble would ensue. The head of the University Press seemed to feel that everything would be all right, and that it was probable that the University Press would print the Oklahoma State Guide. While all this was tentative, the whole tone of the meeting was so cordial and so friendly that I felt Mr. Thompson and Mr. DeWitt would have no further trouble. That was the situation when I left Oklahoma for New Orleans.

Shortly after my return, and while I was still waiting for news that the university had sponsored the project, Miss Fullerton communicated with Mrs. Leo G. Spofford in our regional office and told her that the labor history was being printed and that Mr. Stephens had not yet given his approval. Fearing that a serious situation might arise, I communicated with Mr. Alsberg and asked that he communicate with Miss Fullerton direct and with Mr. Thompson. Miss Fullerton then wrote that Mr. Alsberg had telephoned to her and Mr. Thompson to hold up the labor history until further approval. Mr. Alsberg, Mr. Stephens, Mrs. Spofford, and the others concerned with the future of the Writers' Project, felt that the publication of the labor history would keep the University of Oklahoma from sponsoring the project. As I understand it, there was no desire to destroy the labor history but to postpone its publication until the matter of sponsorship was settled. On August 9 I received a letter from Miss Fullerton, a copy of which is attached to this report.

So the matter stands. The University of Oklahoma will not sponsor the Writers' Project at present. Mr. Ron Stephens believes that the University of Oklahoma is the only logical sponsor. He has decided to let the Writers' Project lapse on September 1, with the idea of submitting a new 301 sometime in the near future, and reorganizing another project in order that their guide may be completed, approved, and printed, as soon as the arguments of the labor history are settled satisfactorily. I have received a carbon copy of a letter from Mr. Thompson in which he states that the complete guide book manuscript has been sent to the Washington office.

Very truly yours,

Lyle Saxon
REGIONAL SUPERVISOR
Federal Writers' Project

LS/sb
Enc.

On the thirty-first of August, Thompson wrote to Saxon:

[Like you], I was also under the impression when you were here that Mr. Stephens, Miss Fullerton, and I had agreed on some form of procedure for getting the project sponsored. Like you, apparently, I was mistaken. I was reliably informed yesterday that it had been decided by the state office, the regional office, and the national office, almost three weeks ago to let the project die. I was also informed that the three had agreed to reopen the project after a month or so—but not under my direction.

Now let me clarify my position on this Labor History. As you had told me to do, I submitted the manuscript to the state office for approval by their labor department. After reading half of the manuscript—the whole thing could have been read by anyone in forty-five minutes—I was notified that the rest could not be ready for approximately two weeks. I then went to Miss Fullerton and asked her if she would not read it, as, obviously, we were very short on time. It was at this time that she advised me that the project could not be sponsored on account of the book. Subsequently, Mr. Alsberg called me and said to hold up the labor history. When I asked Miss Fullerton if the project could be sponsored if we junked the labor history, she told me she was not sure it could be. I asked her just what revisions we would have to make in our program to obtain a sponsor and she said she would have to discuss the matter with Mr. Stephens. I heard nothing more about it. This consistent attempt to make me appear stubborn and uncooperative, and the cause of the project's cessation, has not been justified.

Certain statements have been made about me at the state office which I cannot help but resent. One is that I have insisted on going off on tangents when I should have been working on the Guidebook—the tangent being the labor history. I went to work on this labor history in the first place at the instigation of the state office. Miss Fullerton has the documentary proof of this in her files.

It has also been stated that we have made a mess of the Guidebook. There is just one person responsible for the quality of the work in this office, and I am that person. If a mess has been made of the Guidebook, it has not happened here. Needless to say, since I have been totally dependent for a good many years on free-lance writing, it is a very serious matter with me to have anyone cast any reflection on my work.

Following your instructions, I tried to get in touch with Mrs. Spofford yesterday. Miss Fullerton advised me that Mrs. Spofford was in conference and would call me if she finished in time.

Thompson was in a no-win situation. His resignation became official when the Project lapsed from federal to state control on the first of September, and, without an official state sponsor, ceased to exist. The galley proofs of the labor history finally were read by Lyle Saxon, Eula Fullerton, and Ron Stephens in early September, and printing and binding proceeded.

Still, the governor and the board of overseers of the University of Oklahoma were quite unhappy with the very publication of the history, and would take no interest in reviving the Writers' Project until sufficient time passed to make it clear that they, as new sponsors, had had nothing to do with the labor history. Leo Spofford wrote the WPA Washington office on September 6, 1939:

> During the last week I visited Oklahoma, and . . . had occasion to go into the subject of the Writers' Project again with Mr. Stephens and Miss Fullerton. . . .
> We have not been successful in finding a sponsor for the new statewide Writers' Project due to the . . . controversy over the printing of the labor history. I had a note today from Miss Fullerton in which she states that the Governor has expressed a desire to sponsor a statewide project, so I am very sure that in the near future either the University of Oklahoma or the Governor will sponsor this project and we will be able to finish the Oklahoma Guide and the other books which are now being written.
> I do not believe we will be able to secure sponsorship with the Director of the Federal Writers' Project [Thompson] and his assistant [DeWitt] as supervisors since both the Governor and the University of Oklahoma have stated that they will not sponsor this project with these two supervisors directing the project. We shall keep you informed as to the progress on this project.

Thus Jim Thompson's career as a government worker came to an end. For once he had saved up enough money to get him over the months until he secured steady work. He sent off a couple of true-crime stories he had been preparing in his spare time, and received a few dollars for them.

McFadden Publications printed three Thompson true-crime stories in 1939, all recounting murder investigations in Oklahoma. The "Frozen Footprints" help the actual murderer, a decorated war veteran, nearly succeed in framing a pair of grifters; "The Secret in the Clay" is the victim's body, without which the sheriff would not have had a case; and the ". . . Clue of the Kicking Horse" is that the horse did not kick at all; this leads the sheriff to the real method and real slayer of a local farmer.

As anonymously written as these true-crime efforts were, Thompson did receive at least "as told to" credit for them. The same cannot be said of his output with the Writers' Project, where all efforts were credited to the group.

He was probably just as happy not to have his name solely on the first two publications of the Project. *Tulsa: A Guide to the Oil Capital* and *A Calendar of Annual Events in Oklahoma* were basically guides intended to promote tourism; just who the federal government thought would be visiting one of the hardest-hit areas of the Depression, during the Depression, remains a mystery.

After producing these two bland tomes, the writer inside Thompson probably leapt at the chance to produce *A Labor History of Oklahoma*, despite the delicate subject matter. One need only read his introduction to "Solving Oklahoma's Twin Slayings" (see page 68) to know how he felt about the living to be made as worker in the local oil fields; the workers' story needed to be told.

A straightforward history of the labor movement in territorial and later the state of Oklahoma, 1939's *A Labor History of Oklahoma* chronicles the struggles of the coal miners, oil field, and farm workers from the 1870s up until the present day. The most compelling chapter concerns the 1894 strike by the coal miners' Knights of Labor against the Choctaw Coal and Railway Company, triggered when the company announced a 25 percent cut in daily wages. Citing a law that prohibits the residency in the territory of unemployed men and families, the company tried to have all strikers driven from the territory. Subsequently, the company requested government troops to drive out the thousands of militant miners. The *Labor History* quotes from the *Daily Oklahoman* of June 21, 1894:

Details of the horrible state of affairs which exists in the mining region of the Indian Territory have been brought to this city by the evicted miners. The stories of oppression, hardship and cruelty to themselves, their wives and children by deputy marshals and federal troops are similar to those which sometimes come from Siberia. Many of the men were thrown bodily from their homes, their wives and children beaten and abused, and their furniture and household effects destroyed, after which they were loaded into boxcars like cattle and shipped out of the Territory. The stories told of brutality by the men from the Hartshorne district are revolting to the extreme. August Smith, one of the Hartshorne miners, says troops came to his house and arrested him. They would not allow him to put on his shoes and coat, and refused to let the family eat breakfast. The soldiers threw out his furniture into a wagon and then asked Smith's wife if she wanted to go. "No," she said. "I have worked for this home and if I leave it you will have to shoot me." Smith said, "The house was built by me and belongs to me, though I have no legal title to it. The Commander ordered the privates to put my wife and five children out . . . four or five seized her and dragged her to the wagon and threw her headforemost into it. We were then carted to the station and put into a boxcar with dozens of others." Most of the miners and their families were thrown out in a driving rain and no time was given them to dress or eat breakfast. In one instance a family of four was evicted near Alderson. The wife of the minor was struck over the head with a Winchester and severely maltreated by the soldiers. The woman was enceinte at the time, and while being carted to the station gave premature birth to a dead child. She is in critical condition and may die.

Thus fearing a massacre themselves, the company arranged with the government for a massacre of the workers.

Eventually management was forced to settle when it found it could not successfully drive out the miners, or replace them with cheaper workers. The Knights negotiated a 20 percent reduction in the proposed wage cut, and a lowering of the exorbitant rent and prices of the company homes and stores.

So the stories go throughout the *Labor History;* the odds more than stacked against them, many workers died fighting for small economic gains. Ostensibly objective, the tone of the *Labor History* is decidedly antimanagement, and often implicitly endorses anarchy rather than organization. Still, Thompson probably would have avoided the resulting furor over the book, which cost him his job, if he had not included this account of the then-current strike against the Mid-Continent Refinery:

Many issues, arising over a period of years and never settled satisfactorily, resulted in a strike at the Mid-Continent Refinery—Oklahoma's largest. Among the more important factors in the dispute were questions involving wages, seniority rights, the check-off, and liberalization of the company's vacation policy. Negotiations began in the latter part of October and ended—with a strike—on December 22, 1938.

The National Guard was sent into the strike zone on December 24th, and the 800-acre refinery grounds as well as a considerable surrounding area, were placed under military law. Machine Guns were placed atop some of the low brick buildings three blocks removed from the boundaries of the plant, making picketing virtually impossible. The union then began a picketing campaign against retail outlets of company products.

As the strongest branch of the CIO in Oklahoma, the Oil Workers could not lose the strike without irreparably damaging the movement of which they were a part. At the same time, defeat for Mid-Continent meant strengthening the CIO which had long been anathema to the entire employer group. These were the real issues in the struggle; the matters of seniority, wages, and vacations were not in themselves important. Both sides . . . refused to make concessions, and conferences instigated by the NLRB and Governors Marland and Philips were ineffective. The indictment of 140 strikers on conspiracy charges on April 22 was bitterly assailed by the unionists, but did not result in any weakening of morale. In May

1939 a satisfactory settlement of the strike seemed as far off as it had ever been.

Paralleling earlier government action, like that in the 1894 strike, the calling in of the National Guard and indictment of strikers were further examples of government's persistent and continuing alignment with big business against the workers. Such "radical" reporting of currently topical facts only confirmed the rumors for many Oklahoma politicians: the Writers' Project was a bunch of Communists.

A Labor History of Oklahoma provides more insight about Jim Thompson's life and fiction than one might initially expect. Like his true-crime stories, it reminds us that in the hopeless futures and hopeless pasts of dead-end jobs in dead-end towns grows a terrible evil. Thompson firmly believed that the system spawned killers as naturally as it spawned millionaires.

Enough was being written about the existential problems of the wealthy; Jim Thompson would continue to chronicle the lives of *his people,* the victimized victimizers who could fulfill only an inversion of the American Dream.

In early 1940, Thompson officially received a one-year fellowship grant-in-aid from the Rockefeller Foundation, through the University of North Carolina Press. Ironically, the impressiveness of the *Labor History* and a strong recommendation from Alsberg got Thompson the grant. He was to undertake a study of the building trades in America.

As for *The Oklahoma State Guide,* it was eventually published in December of 1941, under the directorship of renowned Oklahoma folklorist Angie Debo. The last of the State Guides to be published, it had been thoroughly rewritten by the new editors and staff, and was sponsored by the University of Oklahoma Press. By the time it reached the bookstalls, Thompson was in New York finishing up his first published novel, *Now and on Earth.*

He spent the summer of 1940 trying to research the building trades in Oklahoma; he found he couldn't concentrate and got little work done. Instead he convinced his sister Freddie to run for state congress; he promised to write her campaign speeches. Freddie recalls:

> Jimmie wanted me to run for Sheriff, and Pop said, oh, no that was ridiculous. Well . . . what about state senate? So we had one of the most fun summers. Jimmie wrote the most wonderful speeches for me—I just laid 'em in the aisles at the town halls. His speeches were spellbinding, telling things the rest of them never even heard of.
> One night we had a few drinks in the Oklahoma City outskirts—with

country people—and Jimmie wanted to introduce me so they'd feel comfortable about me. So he got up on a table and talked about how I'd slopped hogs, and all these dreadful things.

I ran third in a three-way race, but the incumbent lost, so we were happy. I spent $325 on my campaign.

When winter settled over Oklahoma City, and Thompson was having no more success in getting his research and writing done, he borrowed a car from old friend Bob Woods, the head of the Communist Party in Oklahoma. The car needed to be driven out to the West Coast, so Thompson packed up his family and set off for San Diego, hoping the muse might favor him there.

As has already been described, they had to leave James Sherman Thompson in a rest home, tricking him into going there one day. From *Now and on Earth,* Thompson's fictionalization of the event:

Remember how easy it was? Come on, Pop, we'll have a bottle of beer and go for a little ride. Pop didn't suspect. He'd never think his own family would do a thing like that to him. You had to? Of course you did. And they'll have to. And you won't know until it's too late—like Pop did.

Remember the startled look on his face as you sidled out the door? Remember how he knocked upon the panels? Knocked; then pounded? Clawed? Remember his hoarse voice following you down the hall? The quavering and cadenced tones—"Frankie, Jimmie, Mom, are you there? Mom, Frankie, Jimmie, are you coming back?" And then he began to cry—to cry like Jo might. Or Mack or Shannon.

Or you.

Early in 1941 Jim Thompson and family got their first glimpse of the Pacific Ocean and the promised land upon which its peaceful waves washed ashore. Ostensibly another family in a long line of migrating Okies, they did not fit the Steinbeckian mold. Thompson was torn up by his betrayal of Pop, and still could not complete the book on the building trades. When he was turned down for an extension of his grant, he figured his dreams of being a "real writer" were dashed.

He took the job at Ryan Aeronautical aircraft factory, and worked there in various capacities during the spring and summer. When fall came, he'd had enough of the dead-end job.

Jim Thompson sent his family back to Nebraska to stay with Alberta's family for a time, and set off for New York. Now at age thirty-five, halfway through his own life story, Thompson was about to write the final chapter of the saga of James Sherman Thompson, and the first effort by Jim Thompson, novelist.

THREE

The Thompson family reunited in San Diego in January of 1942. Things settled into a familiar pattern at home, and although "Jimmie" was going to be the author of a published novel come June, the family still had to eat. Thompson obtained a job as the night timekeeper at Solar Aircraft, where Alberta had been hired as a switchboard operator.

The best publicity surrounding the June publication of *Now and on Earth* appeared in the *San Diego Journal* on Saturday, June 6, 1942. The interview with Thompson and the resultant article is interesting not only for its unsurprising omission of James Sherman Thompson's story, but for the embellishments and invention of other "facts." The headline read "Novel Climaxes Privations of Solar Worker":

> The drab garb of an aircraft worker often hides a personality of startling contrasts, and, to look at Jim Thompson, 35, at his job as a timekeeper in Solar Aircraft Co.'s finish fitting department, you would not guess that he's a novelist who has just crashed "Who's Who."
>
> The aircrafter saw drama in the problems of a war worker's family and transposed it to paper in the recently published novel, "Now and on Earth."

Share of Troubles

> "The things we live for seem always far off in the future," he commented today. "We are promised pie in the sky when we die or a brotherhood of man 20 years from now. What I wanted to depict in this book was the struggle to settle our problems now on earth."
>
> As head of a family with three children, Patricia, 10; Sharon, 6 and Michael, 4, Thompson has had his share of the earth's troubles, not

the least of which were circumstances surrounding the writing of his novel.

Forced From University

The depression forced him to leave the University of Nebraska in 1931 after two years' study of agricultural journalism. Extensive writing for the trade press yielded small financial returns. Stranded in Oklahoma City by collapse of a detective magazine, for which he was writing a series Thompson (who, by the way, is a native Oklahoman), got a job with the WPA Writers' project at $75 a month in 1936, and gradually worked his way up to the state director's position, which he held from 1938 to 1939.

Fellowship Awarded

A labor history of Oklahoma attracted attention of the Rockefeller Foundation, which awarded him an $1800 fellowship, through the University of North Carolina Press, to perform research on the building industry.

He arrived in San Diego in January, 1941, at the tag end of his research. When the expected extension of the fellowship failed to materialize, Thompson, again stranded, applied to the U.S. employment service and landed a job as a stock clerk in a local aircraft plant, where he worked seven months.

Publicity Job Missed

He heard of an opportunity to nab a $21-a-day publicity job with a government bureau engaged in writing radio dramas for broadcast to occupied countries, so he tossed the aircraft work overboard and rushed to New York. The position, of course, was filled when he arrived there, almost flat broke. Meanwhile, his wife and youngsters had gone to Nebraska to await results of Thompson's latest venture.

"I decided the quickest way to get some ready money was to write a book," he explained. "I wrote 15,000 words in four days and submitted it to a publisher to learn if he was interested enough for me to continue."

Publisher Stakes Project

While awaiting the publisher's reaction, Thompson spent a couple of rainy nights on a Central Park bench. When he finally received an appointment, he was informed by the publisher that, although he was interested, he wasn't quite sure whether the book would sell.

"I can write the remaining 60,000 words in two weeks," Thompson said. "Give me a typewriter and $30 to stake me, and it ought to be a good bet, even if you lose."

The publisher accepted, and, for two hectic weeks, Thompson, locked in a cheap hotel room, wrote furiously and ate and slept little. He delivered the manuscript on schedule and was taken to Bellevue hospital, suffering extreme nervous exhaustion. When he left his hospital bed, Thompson went to the publisher.

Civil War Era Eyed

"Where have you been?" the book merchant asked. "We're taking your novel and will contract for your next two books."

Back in San Diego and residing with his family at 2601 Nye St., Linda Vista, Thompson is toying with the idea of a Civil War novel as his next literary attempt. "Most of the Civil War books I've seen have dealt with the southern viewpoint," he declared. "I'd like to write one with a northern locale."

Living to be Earned

As an authentic source of material, he has letters and other documents left by his paternal and maternal grandfathers, both of whom marched with Sherman to the sea.

Meanwhile, there's a living to be earned, and Thompson, on his return to San Diego early this year, obtained his present job at Solar.

An obscure timekeeper among thousands of aircraft workers, he's considered important enough to land in the May, 1942, supplement to "Who's Who."

Now and on Earth is fictionalized autobiography, the story of a summer in San Diego with the "Dillon" clan, as narrated by Jim Dillon, former Writers' Project director, now suffering from a massive case of writer's block and working as a day laborer in a local aircraft factory. Dillon's problems are endless; the hopelessness of his life, and his family's, and their inability to change themselves or their situation makes *Now and on Earth* an unrelenting, depressing account of how too many lives are lived.

Chapters One, Two, and Three concern Jim Dillon's return home from his first day of work at the aircraft factory. He is welcomed first by his nine-year-old daughter Jo, and then his mother, who doesn't seem to hear his account of what his job at the factory entailed: "Then I lost my temper and told her what I really had done. When I finished she said, 'That's nice,' and I knew she hadn't heard a word."

He meets his wife, Roberta, and their two younger children, Mack and Shannon, at the bus stop as he returns from the supermarket with food for dinner. After dinner and an argument with Roberta about his new job and money, Dillon sits down alone to a bottle of wine. His sister Frankie arrives home, and they discuss the latest letter from their father, in a

'Who's Who' Crashed by Timekeeper

Jim Thompson, Solar Aircraft Co. timekeeper, is author of a novel that has just landed him in "Who's Who."

Photo of Thompson that accompanied the article in the San Diego Journal *about* Now and on Earth.

sanatorium back in Oklahoma. Finally we learn what his first day at work was like, as Frankie and Jim sit sociably drinking together.

Tormented by the fate of his father, Jim begins to wonder what will become of the rest of his family, including himself:

> I thought about Pop. Now what the hell will we do, I thought. I thought about Roberta, about Mom. About the kids growing up around me. Growing up amidst this turmoil, these hatreds, this—well, why quibble—insanity. I thought and my stomach tightened into a little ball; my guts crawled up around my lung and my vision went black.
>
> I took a drink and chased it with wine.
>
> I thought about the time I sold a thousand dollars' worth of stories in a month. I thought about the day I became a director for the Writers' Project. I thought about the fellowship I'd gotten from the foundation—one of the two fellowships available for the whole country. I thought about the letters I'd gotten from a dozen different publishers—"The finest thing we have ever read." "Swell stuff, Dillon; keep it coming." "We are paying you our top rate . . ."
>
> I said to myself, So what? Were you ever happy? Did you ever have any peace? And I had to answer, Why no, for Christ's sake; you've always been in hell. You've just slipped deeper. And you're going to keep on because you're your father. Your father without his endurance. They'll have you in a place in another year or two. Don't you remember how your father went? Like you. Exactly like you. Irritable. Erratic. Dull. Then—well, you know. Ha, ha. You're damned right you know.

In Chapters Four and Five Dillon introduces the workers at the aircraft factory. His boss is Moon, an experienced man whom the company can't afford to lose; he spends most of his time hurling apple cores at the factory guards. Gross is the parts inventory man; sullen, with a chip on his shoulder, he immediately tries to get Dillon in trouble. Murphy seems to be of Mexican, rather than Irish descent; Busken and Vail are a nasty pair of practical jokers. At the end of his third day Dillon returns home covered in glue he used to assemble some boxes:

> When I got home that night, Roberta took me into the bathroom and soaked and scrubbed me. She cried real tears. And after supper she was still so sorry for me that we went over to Balboa Park and sat until we were sure that everyone had gone to bed.
>
> We came home. Everything was quiet. I went into the kitchen and got a drink of water, and I heard her drawing the shades and slipping a chair under the doorknob. I waited a minute before I went in. I left the kitchen light on. Roberta knows how she looks, and she likes a little light. She is the only woman I have ever known who did.

I went in. She had put the pillows from the divan upon the floor, and was lying upon them and her slack suit was by her side. She looked up at me and smiled and cupped her breasts in her hands. And she was more white, more beautiful and maddening than I had ever seen her.

I had seen her that way five thousand times, and now I saw her again. Saw her for the first time. And I felt the insane unaccountable hunger for her that I always had. Always, and always will.

And then I was in heaven and in hell at the same time.

In Chapters Six and Seven Dillon has to stave off the landlady's demand for rent, because he doesn't get paid when expected. Frankie arrives home with her Portuguese fisherman boyfriend, towing a sixty-pound tuna. The family has its first good meal in weeks.

The good feeling doesn't last long, however. Roberta refuses to allow Jo to go to the library with her dad after she uses some large vocabulary at the dinner table:

"No, you may not go out afterwards! You'll go to bed. I'm getting tired of you gadding around all hours of the night."

"Mama mean to Jo," Mack observed wisely.

Roberta whirled and slapped him, and his fat face puckered and he bawled. Shannon's eyes flickered dangerously. She will beat the stuffing out of Mack herself, but it infuriates her to see anyone else touch him. She slid under the table. Roberta knew what was coming, and she tried to kick her chair back; she even kicked Shannon. But, of course, that wouldn't stop her. In a split second Shannon had buried her teeth in Roberta's leg.

Dillon takes over Gross's bookkeeping job in Chapter Eight, and explains to us he got the car in which he drove out to San Diego from a former friend in the Communist Party. He knows it was a dangerous thing to do, but hopes no one ever finds out about it, especially at work.

Chapters Nine, Ten, and Eleven deal with Dillon's progress at the plant, where he begins to untangle the puzzle of the inventory books. At the end of Chapter Eleven, his high-strung toddler daughter Shannon takes ill, and he recalls how Roberta had tried everything to abort her, but nothing worked. He knows Shannon has always felt unwanted, and feels a terrible guilt, and rage:

For, oh Christ, as she lies here in my arms, exhausted but afraid to sleep, living on hatred, even the thought that we did not want her makes me feel like a criminal. And I am not. And Roberta is not . . . Six in all, we had dreamed of; and a big white house with a deep lawn and many bedrooms and a pantry that was always full. We wanted them, but we wanted that, too. Not for ourselves, but for them. We wanted it because we knew what it would mean if we didn't have it. I knew how I was, and Roberta knew how she was. And we knew how it would be: As it had been with us.

We did want her. Goddammit, I say we did! We want her now. I was crazy to say that we didn't or hadn't. But we are getting tired, and we are so cramped, and there are so many things to be done.

In Chapter Twelve a letter from Jim's sister Marge back east (about her coming out to San Diego, and Pop's condition) triggers memories of Jim's childhood, when Marge was always favored. He writes of his high school days, and a bellboy job, his time out on the oil fields, and his uneasy relationship with Pop.

Chapter Thirteen concerns progress at the plant, where Jim becomes better friends with Moon and Murphy, while continuing to untangle the inventory records. In Chapter Fourteen a lewd imitation of Roberta by Jo sparks a wild fight that brings Shannon back to life:

Jo got behind me and kept moving me around as Roberta fought to get at her. And Roberta seemed to think I was holding her off, which I suppose I was, and she started slapping me and kicking me on the shins . . . And—well, I do think it was about the worst brawl we have ever had.

Then Shannon took a hand. Yes, Shannon. She wasn't listless any more. Far from it.

Before I knew what was happening, I'd been hit about sixteen solid punches in the groin. I think Jo caught it next—a slashing bite on the rump—but I can't be sure, because she and Roberta, who'd had her corns stamped on, yelled at the same time. And then Shannon started going around us like a cooper around a barrel.

"You goddam mama. You goddam Jo. You goddam daddy. Beat the hell outta you. Fix you all. Beat the—" . . .

We got worn out . . .

It is hideous when you think about it. A child . . . sick without this insanity which is driving [her] insane. Lost and bewildered when it was withdrawn. Living in a malarial swamp and not daring to leave it . . . I think, perhaps, if we could catch them now, change their environment by gentle stages if necessary, something could be done. But we cannot do that.

Nothing is settled, you see. We have spent something tonight that we can never replace—that I, I know, cannot replace—and we have solved nothing. It is futile to hope that we ever will. One of us—I think any one of us—alone, might solve something. But he would have to be alone, be far away. If we were away, where the poisons in us could not be refreshed and restored daily, there might be a chance.

The rest of the chapter is a flashback to Jim's courtship of Roberta and his other flame, Lois. He explains how things would have been different, yet the same, if he had married Lois (see pages 45–46).

Chapter Fifteen is an account of Dillon's typical day, from start to finish, including ruminations on the city of San Diego, and why aircraft workers swear so much. Gross is constantly trying to sabotage Jim's work, Moon is lazy and no help, and Murphy means well but reverses his numbers and figures. Moon arranges for a double date with Jim, Roberta, and Frankie.

Chapter Sixteen details the evening with Moon, who brings four pounds of pork chops, and bottles of whiskey, sherry, and gin to the Dillons' for supper. Afterward the four of them drive to Tijuana, despite Jim's resentment over Moon's money and gifts.

Eventually Jim is having a good time, after his own fashion:

> I was drunk—not staggering drunk, I never stagger; but totally irresponsible. Roberta, who doesn't have much capacity, was tipsy. It'd been two or three years since I'd seen her enjoy herself so much. It's been that long since we could really cut loose without scrimping for a month afterwards. Tonight we didn't have to worry about money.
>
> Well, but money couldn't bring us back those two or three years.

Moon and Frankie in the meantime have disappeared, and when Jim and Roberta find them they head home. But trouble at the border ties them up for hours, and it's five in the morning before they're back at the Dillon house. Jim knows he must go to work, the family needs the money. He takes some pills (seemingly amphetamines) to get him through the day; they do so with disastrous results. He insults most of his co-workers, offending Murphy so much that he loses his habitual ride home with him.

Chapter Seventeen details Memorial Day weekend and its consequences. The family goes to the beach, leaving Jim home; they return with painful sunburns. Jim then tells us that the doctor had been out to examine him, after he coughs up blood at the dinner table. The doctor reported back a few days later:

> Pretty disgusted, he was, I gathered. There wasn't any lung infection; the old scars were healed. There wasn't anything at all wrong with me except that I smoked and drank too much, didn't sleep enough, and didn't eat the right things.
>
> When the folks gave it to me with a lot of "you see, Jimmie" and "I told you so," I thought they were trying to kid me. It was so goddamned funny. I laughed until I got another coughing fit, and everyone said, "Oh Jimmie

thinks he's so smart! He knows more then the doctor does." And I finally stopped laughing. They really were sincere. They didn't understand.

Next Jim has a fight with Roberta when she gets up to go to Sunday Mass at five in the morning; later that day the Portuguese fishermen stop by and eat all their food. That night the family is convinced Shannon has run away or drowned down at the bay; it turns out that Jo forged a note to the local druggist, whom Shannon had befriended, asking him to take care of her for a while. Jim muses on this, after Shannon is found safe:

I didn't think it was funny . . . Jo wouldn't feel any different toward Shannon tomorrow than she did tonight. She wanted to get away from Shannon, and she couldn't; so she was trying to get Shannon away from her. And it was pretty obvious she didn't care how she did it. As obvious as the fact that Shannon wasn't going to change or make herself any less detestable to Jo.

Mounting pressure at home, and at work, where his installation of a new inventory system is nearly complete, leads Jim to another collapse that ends the chapter. He receives a letter from the Foundation, asking him to write like he did three years ago:

"All they want me to do," I said, "is write like that. Write like I did then. That's all."
And I got down on the floor and rolled.
The doctor came and went and I didn't know about it. I only know that I went to sleep. When I woke up, I began pumping Roberta as to what he'd said, and I couldn't get much out of her for a while except that "he asked all about you and everything."
"He didn't mention anything about three months of absolute rest, did he?" I said.
"Well, he did, but when I told him—"
"I know."
"I don't want you to work so hard, Jimmie. I don't know what I can do about it, though."
"I know you don't," I said. "Have you got the whisky yet?"
"What whisky?"
"The whisky he told you to let me have."
"I didn't know what kind—he did say you mustn't drink too much, Jimmie."
"What about cigarettes?"
"You mustn't smoke too many of them either."
"That's damned good advice," I said. "I'll have to remember it."
"I hope you will, honey. He said if you'd just keep quiet, and not worry,

and not get excited about things. And eat more. And not smoke and drink so much, and—"

"Why, then I'd be all right."

"Uh-huh. You will mind him, won't you, honey? You'll do it for my sake?"

I nodded. I couldn't laugh any more, and I was too tired to get up and beat her.

Chapter Eighteen begins with the obituary of William Sherman Dillon, as written by Jim. The rest of the chapter is an interior monologue/"conversation" between Jim and his dead father, as Jim tries to come to terms with his father's fate, and what it means for his own eventual fate. Highly enlightening about Jim Thompson and his feelings for his own father, in *Now and on Earth* it explains, to the degree it can be explained, how Jim Dillon came to be in the mess he is in, and why he sees no way out. He perceives his father to have been a "bigger" man than he, with more potential, and even his father died a broken man, alone and without hope. What chance is there for him?

There is no time for Dillon's self-pity, as the next family crisis arrives quickly; in Chapter Nineteen Frankie is pregnant by Moon, and they must raise money for an abortion. The family meeting held to come up with some sort of plan dissolves into the usual petty bickering; then they decide that Jim should write a story to get the money. When Jim argues that he isn't capable of writing a story, his mother cites Jack London, which really sets him off:

"I didn't mean anything," said Mom. "I was just saying—"

"You didn't read your Jack London far enough. He began slipping off the deep end when he was thirty. Well I'm thirty-five. Thirty-five, can you understand that? And I've written three times as much as London wrote. I—"

"Let's skip it," said Frankie.

"You skip it! Skip through fifteen million words for the Writers' Project. Skip through half a million for the foundation. Skip through the back numbers of five strings of magazines. Skip through forty, fifty, yes, seventy-five thousand words a week, week after week, for the trade journals. Skip through thirty-six hours of radio continuity. . . ."

"Please Jimmie". . . .

"What did it get me? Shall I tell you? You're damned right I shall. It got me a ragged ass and beans three times a week. It got me haircuts in barber colleges. It got me piles that you could stack washers on. It got me a lung that isn't even bad enough to kill me. It got me in a dump with six strangers. It got me in jail for forty-eight hours a week and a lunatic asylum on

Sunday. It got me whisky, yes, and cigarettes, yes, and a woman to sleep with, yes. It got me twenty-five thousand reminders ten million times a day that nothing I'd done meant anything. It got me this, this extraordinarily valuable, this priceless piece of information that I'm not . . ."

I opened my eyes and said, "Jack London."

It's finally decided that first a doctor must be found in order to know how much it will cost to get the job done, and that Moon should be asked to come up with some of the money.

Chapter Twenty finishes the night, with Jim apologizing to Roberta, and thinking back on Frankie's childhood, "how she had got to be like this." Then Jim gets up in the middle of the night, and sits in the bathroom pondering a story he'd read by Robert "Henlein." It's about a lunatic who thinks the whole world's against him, and he tells his psychiatrist about it. Then comes the final scene:

The man's wife, his employer, his college teachers, and a host of other demons—yes, demons—are in conclave. There *is* a plot.

He's getting on to us, says the wife. I think he's going to run away again. What'll we do this time?

Let him go, says the psychiatrist. We'll get him back. We always get 'em back.

I guess I don't tell the thing very well. But if you read it, it'll stick in your mind for days.

Perhaps Jim Dillon doesn't tell us this story very well. But Jim Thompson, in his first novel, depicted the paranoid, put-upon thinking that given free reign inside protagonists of later novels would lead to psychic hell and murder. Jim Dillon, Jim Thompson's alter ego, is here the literary forefather of Dolly Dillon, Nick Corey, Lou Ford, and Charlie "Little" Bigger.

The chapter concludes when Roberta, burning with desire, drags Jim back into the bedroom:

And there was a Fury upon me; sobbing, mad with impatience, shivering with heat: an angel-Fury with cream-yellow thighs, who had made herself over, and who would never be able to unmake herself. A Frankenstein monster with silky lashes and a white smile, with breasts that turned outward with their fullness . . .

I don't think I had realized until then how impossibly hopeless it all was.

In Chapter Twenty-one, Jim confronts Moon about Frankie, and Moon is more decent than he expects about it. Moon is, however, suspicious that Jim is after his job, else why is he working so hard? Jim has no answer for him, except that he does not see himself working in the plant forever. This leads to Jim's planning some way out, like leaving his family and living apart. He considers the impact it would have on each of them.

He then learns that Mom has been calling Moon at the plant, threatening him about Frankie's situation. When Jim returns home that night, Mom tells him his sister Marge is probably coming out for a visit.

Chapter Twenty-two is a series of reminiscences, about a scheme to get Pop back on his feet (it failed), about how he ended up in the School of Agriculture at the University of Nebraska, about just missing getting rich from an inside tip on the stock market. This is all presented as further evidence of the plot against Jim.

The next chapter sets up the final action. Jim has a serious falling out with Moon over Frankie's abortion and Jim's impressive new inventory system, which has shown Moon up with his superiors. Then Jim arrives home to find Marge waiting for him on the doorstep; she promptly gets him in trouble with Mom. Jim finally finishes a story he's been laboring over, and Marge accompanies him down to the post office to mail it off to the magazine publisher. In an attempt to cheer her up, Jim takes her into a nearby bar, where Gross rescues them from an embarrassing situation with the waitress. Gross then dances a few times with Marge, and Jim notices Marge is gabbing pretty steadily. When Gross later drops them off, he learns what about:

> Then I saw that Gross had stopped the car and was rolling down the window. I hesitated, thinking he had something to say. He did have.
> "Good night, Comrade," he called.
> And his mean cackle floated back to us as he raced away.

Marge has told Gross that Jim obtained the car in which he drove to San Diego from an old friend, the head of the Communist Party in Oklahoma.

Chapter Twenty-four takes place the next day at the plant, where Jim faces the consequences of what Gross has learned. Busken and Vail team up to torture him, but Jim turns the tables by beating them with a broom. Then Gross arrives and Jim hits him with a two-pound sack of bolts; the guards take Jim away.

In Chapter Twenty-five Jim is grilled by Reynolds, an FBI agent, about his involvement with the Communist Party. Jim's stellar record at the plant only fuels the suspicions about him: if he's never worked around planes before, why is he doing so well? Each piece of "evidence" could point two ways, depending on how one wants to see it; eventually Moon is called in to give his opinion of Jim:

> "I can talk all right," said Moon. "It'd been a lot better for Dilly if he'd let things slide. Everyone would have liked him better. Wouldn't do it, though, so here he is."
>
> "I see," said Reynolds. "Now you've had the chance to observe Dillon very closely . . . Was there ever anything in connection with his work that seemed suspicious?"
>
> Moon studied the remainder of the apple. He tossed it into the cuspidor. Thoughtfully he stared at the floor.
>
> "Well—I don't know. I don't know whether you'd call it suspicious or not."
>
> The FBI man leaned forward. "Explain exactly what you mean."
>
> "Well—I used to think he was going to blow the place up."
>
> "Blow it up!"
>
> "Uh-huh. Used to sit on that stool so long without going to the toilet I was afraid he was going to explode all over us."
>
> There was a dead silence.

Reynolds thanks Moon, barely able to keep a straight face. He then shakes Jim's hand, and offers some sort of apology. Baldwin, the plant supervisor, offers Jim Moon's job: Moon has joined the navy.

At the conclusion of the novel, Jim meets Moon on his way home that night, and thanks him for saving him from the feds. Moon shrugs it off, saying he owed him one because of Frankie. Then Jim tells Moon, and us, that he turned down the job offer, and quit his job.

The somewhat hopeful ending of *Now and on Earth* does little to alter the relentlessly depressing view of the novel. Jim Dillon's problems are unchanged, and unchangeable.

Now and on Earth made no great splash upon publication, but it did garner some respectable reviews. *The New Yorker* called it "an outspoken hard-luck story laid in San Diego. Pop is crazy, Mom has varicose veins, the two girls are loose but good-natured, and Jim, the son, has to support all of them and his own wife and kids too. . . . A first-rate character study, and some family quarrels right out of James Farrell." *The New Republic* noted "an understanding of human character both penetrating and sympathetic, and a sharp contemporary flavor that mark the author as a writer worth watching." The novel was turned down by Warner Brothers as a basis for a movie in June of 1942; a review in the local *San Diego Union*, under the headline "S.D. Aircraft Worker Hero of Doleful Novel," summed up why Hollywood shied away:

The book is not a happy one. It is, indeed, a downright morbid one. Nothing ever goes right with any of them. Nothing ever will go right with any of them. But always, as if just out of habit, they keep piling more troubles upon themselves. And then they keep wondering why everybody is always so against them, including others of their own kind. . . .

The author is a strong storyteller, an amazing workman with little family details. Just for relief, though, I could have stood a little happiness, if merely for a moment, if not a whole paragraph.

Readers looking for an escape from the realities of World War II weren't likely to rush out to buy a novel in which typical American family life, which the troops were fighting for over in Europe and Asia, was depicted as a stifling, torturous psychic prison.

Still, upon publication of *Now and on Earth,* Jim Thompson's pen finally had emerged from the wasted heartland of America. In future years he would write the story of the marginal people of a corrupting, uncaring world, those who by some joke of creation are unable to do anything but fulfill a debased inversion of the American dream. The first-hand and second-hand experiences of the first half of Thompson's life had confirmed him in this bleak worldview.

Thompson remained forever haunted by the Depression, when America's collective dreams of success were murderously dashed; Thompson remained forever haunted by his own father's slow descent into failure and death, and his inability to save him; and Thompson remained forever haunted by the loss of Lucille Boomer to another man, a loss that could have been avoided only if he renounced his own dream of writing, and pursued a less financially uncertain occupation.

Jim Thompson continued to confront the nightmare of "his people," those with a relentless desire for all-out success, coupled with an ability only for all-out failure. The grim realities of Jim Dillon's hopeless life in *Now and on Earth* leave him only one small step from murder; when Jim Thompson followed later protagonists down the deceptively easy path to homicide, his first-person narrative technique evolved into a new literary form, one uniquely suited to the depiction of madness and death.

In *Now and on Earth,* Thompson gave voice to the beliefs, obsessions, and delusions that had marked the first thirty-five years of his life. He would continue to write out both personal and societal demons, producing a uniformly haunting but fiercely iconoclastic body of work in the second half of his life.

A body of work growing in pertinence and importance, as the twentieth century in America nears its bloody close, and the psychotics of the Thompson world become more and more common in our own.

THE CROOKED CUE

∎

Yeah, I reckon that's all unless our kind gets another chance in the Next Place. Our Kind. Us people.

All of us that started the game with a crooked cue, that wanted so much and got so little, that meant so good and did so bad. All us folks. Me and Joyce Lakeland, and Johnnie Pappas and Bob Maples and big ol' Elmer Conway and little ol' Amy Stanton. All of us.

All of us.

The Killer Inside Me, 1952

FOUR

Upon publication of *Now and on Earth,* Jim Thompson, at the age of thirty-five, had achieved his over-twenty-year goal of being a *writer,* in the eyes of the world and, more important, in the eyes of himself. With one published novel, and a contract from Modern Age for his next, he might dare to hope there would soon be no need to work any more dead-end jobs. He was a novelist.

Higher hopes made the failures and disappointments that lay ahead all the more telling. The 1940s would turn out no less rocky than the 1930s, and Thompson's drinking, a periodic refuge from problems up to now, would become a problem in itself, ceaselessly tormenting and nearly disabling him for the next decade.

In 1950, Jim Thompson wrote a confessional entitled "An Alcoholic Looks at Himself," in which he chronicled the events of the previous ten years of his life. A self-demeaning fictionalization, every altered fact or distorted take makes Thompson look *worse.* Reeking more of failure and self-loathing than of alcohol, "An Alcoholic Looks at Himself" is Thompson's own view of his internal struggles throughout the previous decade. Unfortunately, it's about the only inside view available of Thompson's activities during the time.

Jim Thompson considered the 1940s a time of dark frustration in terms of both his personal affairs and his writing. He left behind the fewest clues of his day-to-day activity during this time, and his family is reluctant to speak of it in detail, making it one of the darkest periods of this biography. There are rumors that he spent most of the time in alcoholic asylums, as Thompson himself told his friend Arnold Hano.

Certainly the specter of alcohol hangs across this decade, the few good times and the many bad.

Yet by 1950, Thompson emerged battered, beaten, and depressed from the years of drinking and failure with two more published novels under his belt. Although *Heed the Thunder* and *Nothing More Than Murder* were Jim Thompson's farewell to hardcovers, in them he pioneered the themes and forms of the bleak paperback crime novels of the early 1950s that have become his chief legacy.

Now and on Earth had been such thinly disguised nonfiction that every family member, who had eagerly anticipated reading the book, was angry with Thompson when they saw how he had used them as characters in the novel. Even now, mentioning the novel to Alberta Thompson only garners a stern shaking of her head. Recalled Freddie Thompson Townsend:

> When we all jumped him about *Now and on Earth,* he said he didn't mean anything, "I was changing the characters." But he hit us close enough, so that friends recognized us. . . .
> He referred to Mom as wearing a soiled wrapper, she said, "Jimmie, never in my life . . ."
> And Alberta was ready to divorce him for what he said about her.
> Rather than struggle for characters, he used us all. We all were in it.
> We were horrified. We'd say, Jimmie, where did you hear those words? Jimmie, a quiet, gentle man. You couldn't believe it. Some of the things were so horrible.

Perhaps to escape some of the domestic furor, Thompson immediately set to work on his next book, a rewriting of the "crime novel" manuscript which he had first written in 1932. Evidently he never returned to *Always to Be Blessed*, the other novel he began that winter nine years previous and the source of "The End of the Book." Alberta Thompson recalls that he finished *Always,* although it never saw publication after Viking declined it in 1937.

Thompson toiled nights as the timekeeper at Solar Aircraft, attempting to write during the day. He arranged with his editor at Modern Age, David Zablodowsky, for periodic small advances in return for submission of chapters. This was proceeding smoothly until one day a telegram arrived from Zablodowsky, regretfully informing Thompson that Modern Age had gone out of business. Most of the publishing house's principals had been drafted into the army.

Thompson's manuscript of a James M. Cain–like murder thriller was returned to him. It remained an unlucky novel, and he rewrote it many times until it was published in 1948 as his third novel, *Nothing More Than Murder*.

Thompson remained a timekeeper at Solar for nearly two years. The family recalls him writing true-crime stories in addition to working on novels during the early 1940s, but none were published by McFadden, and so they are virtually unfindable, if they exist.

Thompson's sister Maxine had come out to San Diego just before James Sherman Thompson's death. Maxine had left her husband Russell Boomer, who was constantly sleeping with other women. Freddie, who was working on the switchboard at Solar Aircraft along with Alberta, and Maxine soon got a house of their own. Birdie Thompson later joined her daughters in the small neat house in La Jolla. After obtaining a thirty-day divorce in Texas, Maxine was remarried early in 1944 to a local Marine named Joe Kouba.

In April 1944, Jim Thompson joined the Marines himself; and Maxine, never previously renowned for her diligence, took over the Solar timekeeper position. It is unclear whether Thompson volunteered or was drafted into the service, but his family thought him crazy to attempt a Marine boot camp at the age of thirty-seven. Recalled Maxine:

> Then he joined the Marine Corps, which scared us all to death, while my husband Joe was overseas. . . . We went to boot camp after two weeks, and he had lost about thirty pounds, his hair was shaved. They had to let him out. Everybody liked him, the drill sergeant was crazy about Jimmie. He ended up in the infirmary with rheumatic fever.

Adds Alberta Thompson:

> His sergeant called me and told me I should be very proud of him; he'd never seen a man who tried to get through boot camp as hard as Jimmie. He made it through the boot camp, but was given a medical discharge . . . rheumatic fever.

And from "An Alcoholic Looks at Himself," Jim Thompson's typically caustic, self-lacerating version:

> An alcoholic can be just as patriotic as the next guy. One foggy April night I and twenty other recruits tramped through the gates of the San Diego Marine Base. . . .
>
> I rated even lower in the esteem of the drill instructor than did the other "people" (whose rating was minus zero). For he knew, or said he did, what the harried induction center doctors had overlooked:

My tendency to tire easily and my extreme nervousness were due to just one thing, he said. I was a drunk as surely as he had ever seen one. I was a sot, who, being no longer able to beg a living in the civilian world, was now attempting to get free board and room from the Marine Corps.

Well, the Corps knew how to handle such people. They broke them out.

The life of a Marine "boot" is enough to make a strong man weep. I mean that literally. But as weeks dragged by and the drill instructor had time to learn, for example, that I was more than twice the age of the average boot, he showed signs of relenting and made gestures of friendliness.

But I would have none of either. He had set the pace. Now let him carry on.

The end came one morning near the end of my training period, when victory was almost within my grasp. Unable to walk, to raise my arms or bend my body, I was loaded into an ambulance and taken to the hospital.

I was moved from ward to ward while the doctors puzzled over my alarming pulse, my bruised and battered body with its tortured muscles and swollen joints. I finally landed in the heart ward, where my ailments were officially attributed to rheumatic fever. . . .

I had failed miserably, where I believed I should have succeeded.

Records show Jim Thompson was enrolled in the Marine Corps on April 13, 1944, and was released on a medical discharge twelve weeks later.

Thompson spent most of that summer recuperating at home. The family somehow survived on Alberta's salary from her job as chief switchboard operator at Solar. By this time, all three Thompson women, Freddie, Maxine, and Alberta, were working the switchboard at Solar. To no one's surprise, Maxine had been less than a success as a timekeeper.

Birdie Myers Thompson was in failing health, and she died early in 1945 of natural causes. Sharon Thompson Reed, who was eight years old at the time, recalls not only how upset her father was but, even more vividly, the concern her father had for her.

Alberta was raising all three children in the Catholic Church; although Jim Thompson did not believe, he did not object. In fact, he encouraged their faith. When Birdie grew seriously ill, Sharon lit a candle for her at church, believing that her grandmother would not then be taken away from her. When Birdie subsequently died, Sharon was devastated. She remembers overhearing her father telling Alberta that he hoped Birdie's death did not shake Sharon's faith in Catholicism.

Evidently Thompson thought it was good to believe in something as fiercely as did little Sharon and the rest of his family; perhaps he did not want to see the child become as disillusioned as he.

* * *

Thompson continued working on the manuscript of *Nothing More Than Murder* during the fall of 1944, and sent it off to his literary agent in New York. When he received no favorable response, he boarded a train and set off for the East Coast in January of 1945. Arriving, by his own account, drunk at his agent's doorstep with yet another version of the manuscript, he was turned away with advice to sober up and straighten out.

Thompson then campaigned the publishing houses on his own, as he had done four years before for *Now and on Earth*. No one expressed interest in the "murder mystery," but his pitch for a historical novel fell on receptive ears at Greenberg, a small publisher. Once again staked to a tiny advance, Thompson lived on cigarettes and whiskey and churned out *Heed the Thunder* in a hotel room in New York in about eight weeks.

Greenberg paid him $800 for the novel and contracted for another, the second in a proposed trilogy of which *Heed the Thunder* was the first. *Heed the Thunder* was scheduled to be published in January 1946, about the time the second novel was due.

When he returned home from yet another triumphant trip to New York, Thompson worked at various odd jobs, including the buying of gold door-to-door. He also began selling true-crime stories to McFadden once again; "The Dark Stair" was published in *Master Detective* in June 1946.

"The Dark Stair" is most remarkable for the plot device upon which it turns, which was reused by Thompson in *Nothing More Than Murder*. Set in a small town movie theater, the murderer is driven to his act because he's caught in a clever money-losing lease by his victim. Since Thompson had been working on the novel long before the true-crime story, the use of the same plot device in *Nothing More Than Murder* indicates one of two things: the novel was substantially rewritten or this true-crime story's plot is an unbelievable coincidence.

"The Dark Stair" was probably read by a lot more people than Thompson's next appearance in print, *Heed the Thunder*. Although it failed to find a wide readership, in *Heed the Thunder* Thompson abandoned the claustrophobic, manic first-person narration of *Now and on Earth,* offering instead a more panoramic vision of then-uncharted territory of the Thompson world.

Heed the Thunder, in some ways the least characteristic but most important of Jim Thompson's novels, is a sweeping look at a way of life and a people that vanished in the early twentieth century. Based on his own childhood experiences in his mother's hometown of Burwell, Nebraska, *Heed the Thunder* is set in the valley town of Verdon, where

First edition of Heed the Thunder, 1946.

the Fargo clan is the largest and most powerful family. Young Robert Dillon and his mother Edie Fargo Dillon return to her parents' house after Edie accepts that her husband likely has abandoned her and is unlikely to return. The action of the novel takes place while Robert Dillon grows from an annoying young boy of six to early manhood. The lives of all the Fargo clan and their family and friends are chronicled in *Heed the Thunder,* which clearly owes a debt in theme if not in structure to another study in small town grotesquery, Sherwood Anderson's *Winesburg, Ohio.*

Though the characters Robert and Edie Dillon are based on Jim and Birdie Thompson, it is impossible to say how many of the events in *Heed the Thunder* are autobiographical in a factual sense. Many of the known facts of young Jim Thompson's stay in Burwell, Nebraska, have been changed or omitted in the novel, chief among these being the absence of any character corresponding to Jim's sister Maxine.

Heed the Thunder opens with Edie Dillon and her son Robert arriving in Verdon via the evening train. Edie has dressed Robert like a child to avoid paying full fare; the resultant argument with the conductor over the boy's age reveals both her desperation and her quiet resolve.

Lincoln Fargo, Edie's father and patriarch of the whole Fargo clan, is a man who has seen and done everything, having marched with the Union Army during the Civil War, and been a stonemason, riverboat owner, saloonkeeper, and night rider. He homesteaded in Verdon, with his wife, Pearl, sons, Sherman and Grant, and daughters, Edie and Myrtle.

A series of anecdotes enumerates all the things Lincoln no longer has use for, including war, the ministry, lawyers, dentists, and drunks. Finally the old man laughs, as he catches the truth:

> It was strange, shocking, the number of things he no longer cared about, could no longer trust. He had seen and had all that was within his power to see and have. He knew the total, the absolute lines of his periphery. Nothing could be added. There was now only the process of taking away. He wondered if it was like that with everyone, and he decided that it must be. And he wondered how they felt, and reasoned that they must feel about as he. That was all there was to life: a gift that was slowly taken away from you. An Indian gift. You started out with a handful of something and ended up with a handful of nothing. The best things were taken away from you last when you needed them worst. When you were at the bottom of the pot, when there was no longer reason for life, then you died. It was probably a good thing.
>
> He had no use for life. Very little, at any rate.
>
> He was pretty well stripped, but it had been a good long game and the amusement was worth something. It wasn't so much the loss as the losing

he minded. If there were some way of calling the thing a draw, he would
have pulled back his chair willingly enough.

He supposed he was living on pride. Will power.

He wondered how long it would be before he had no use for that.

He decided that it would not be very long.

Lincoln's view of life as a gift taken slowly from you, its enjoyment
ever decreasing, cannot be far from Jim Thompson's own. A theme that
runs through most of the later novels, Thompson literalized the idea of
diminishing life in the form of the diminutive consumptive hit man,
Charlie "Little" Bigger, in 1954's *Savage Night*. Here, Lincoln Fargo,
wisdom and experience personified, believes he has lost rather than
accumulated precious things through the course of life. By the end of the
novel Lincoln's pride, the one thing not yet taken from him, will be gone
too, and with it the sole reason for existence.

Lincoln has only disgust for his youngest son Grant's put-on mannerisms, constant demands for money, and refusal to work. For the
thousandth time they discuss Grant's unemployment: Grant was trained as
a typesetter, but refuses to learn to use the new Linotype machines.

Lincoln sees right through Grant, on this and a more important subject;
Grant is courting Bella Barkley, the town banker's daughter. Grant
protests they are just friends, but Lincoln reminds him of a crucial fact:

> "Bella is your cousin, your own mother's sister's child. You couldn't
> marry her."
>
> "I hadn't—I don't plan on marrying her."
>
> "Well, you couldn't," Link repeated. "It might be a pretty good thing for
> you to keep in mind."
>
> "Pa . . . for God's sake!" Grant made a wry mouth, flipped away his
> cigarette, and stepped off the porch. As he strode stiffly down the walk to
> the gate, he was injured innocence personified, a young man too proud and
> pure to bandy ugly words or harbor evil thoughts. But inside he was
> frightened, cursing . . . Did the old man know anything, or was he just
> guessing? Damn him to hell, anyway! Damn this whole stinking town.

Grant stops in a saloon for a badly needed drink. Lost in reverie, he
doesn't notice his brother Sherman's rig tied up outside, and it is too late
once he steps inside. Sherman, a rugged, gruff man unlike his brother in
nearly every way, teases Grant about his dandy dress.

Sherman is unusually cruel to Grant because he himself had been badly
shocked that day, having been turned down for a loan needed to buy a
threshing machine. The man who turned him down, Philo Barkley, and

transplanted Englishman Alfred Courtland, the lone employee of the bank and Myrtle Fargo's husband, sit at the office discussing the schoolteaching job they obtained for Edie Dillon, way up in Misery Creek. Barkley is taking a 20 percent cut of her wages, and Courtland silently disapproves.

On his way home, Sherman is set upon by Bill Simpson, salesman extraordinaire for the World-Wide Harvester Company who tells the stoic farmer he doesn't need a bank loan to get the thresher. Before they reach Sherman's home, he has bought a thresher, mower, and plow on credit.

Pearl Fargo is in her own way just as sick of life as her husband. Entranced by the eloquence of the town preacher, she yearns for a better next world. Lincoln warns that Reverend Whitcomb has "bulldozed a lot of these light-wits into signing over their property to him!"

> Bewildered, Mrs. Fargo proceeded down the walk to the gate. Unlike her husband, she did not deem life to be the slow losing of a gift. It was merely a long trail of hardship which led to a better hereafter. Toward the end, if you had done as you should have, you were permitted to rest in peace and comfort while waiting for the gates to open. But that was all. She was innately a kind and patient woman. She had borne four children to a man who was quick-tempered, harsh-spoken, and away from home as much as he could be. She had reared those children, with reasonably good educations, into healthy maturity. She had supported them over a period of years, seen that they had the little comforts and pleasures that other children had. And not for her own glory, any of this. As wife and mother, she had no individuality; nothing for glory to attach to. She had done it almost mechanically.
>
> Now, she was tired, tired and puzzled. She had entered the last ten years of her three-score and ten, and the pause of peace and quiet was not there. She did not know who was to blame, and, childishly, she did not care. But she knew that she was not; and she was tired.

Pearl's search for peace and meaning has indeed brought her under the spell of Whitcomb. She offers him the piece of paper he covets, but the Reverend notes with dismay that instead of quitclaiming her land in his name she has turned the land over to "God." Before the Reverend can properly convey his disappointment, he and Pearl are set upon by masked men on horseback, who drag Whitcomb away. The chapter ends as she listens to the men tar, feather, and ride the Reverend out of town on a rail.

Winter settles over Verdon. Lincoln and Sherman sit on Lincoln's porch mulling the crucial question of whether to feed cattle or plant wheat; Sherman has come to take Robert back to his house for the night.

Robert does not yet know that his mother has left for her teaching job up-country.

Robert is greeted at Sherman's by his two older cousins, Gus and Ted, who are thirteen and twelve. The boys get into all sorts of trouble with Sherman's wife, Josephine, before settling down in their bedroom for a pipe smoke.

Gus and Ted's mother, Josephine, has lost something irretrievable; "a quaking, bread-pudding of a woman" she is a caricature to the boys, and now, even to herself:

> Some nights—even some days—she dreamed that a gawky rosy-cheeked girl slipped out of the mountain of fat. And with a morose, roughly affectionate young man, she ran laughing across the virgin prairie or lay supple and submissive among the willows of the bayou. She made coffee over a cowchip fire, and sipped from the cup from which the young man drank, and their lips brushed the same things, and their bodies and their souls and their thoughts were one. Together they uprooted the tough sod; together they nursed the cane-bloated yearling. And there was sunlight, sun always upon the snow, the grass crisp or green, the warm or frigid Calamus . . .
>
> It had never happened, though. Time had made it incredible. One cannot believe the unbelievable.

In Chapter Eight Edie Dillon lies in her straw bed at the Jabowskys' house, way up-country near Misery Creek. The students, especially a boy named Mike Czerny, have been torturing her at school. Their parents will do nothing; Edie firmly resolves to stick it out. Meanwhile, Robert lies awake down in the valley at Lincoln's house, wondering what he had done so wrong as to have lost both his parents.

The next chapter opens with Alfred Courtland preparing for a trip up to Misery Creek; Barkley has heard about Edie's mistreatment and wants to take care of the matter before the Fargos, especially Sherman, hear about it. Myrtle, Edie's sister and Courtland's wife, is inordinately proud of her man and his mannerisms; she thinks she married an English baron. Courtland knows this, and puts on an act for her.

After he sets off, Myrtle cannot bear to face another day alone in bed, to which she habitually retires in an effort to save a few pennies worth of coal. She decides to visit her cousin Bella Barkley. When Bella opens the door only after persistent knocking, Myrtle inadvertently looks into the house and spies her brother Grant lying naked on the settee. Bella shakes and threatens Myrtle, who miserably shuffles back home to bed.

Courtland stops for dinner at William Deutsch's farm, where he is heartily greeted and given the best meal he has eaten in months. He also drinks quite a bit, and he notices that it affects him more than usual. By the time he reaches the Jabowsky house, he is seething and aggressive. He threatens Jabowsky with foreclosure on his loans, and does the same to other important men of the area.

At the school Edie identifies Mike Czerny for Courtland, who tells the boy he's already spoken to his father:

> A tiny muscle jiggled in the boy's cheek. "I'm American. This not the old country. My father got nothing to say 'bout having me beat."
>
> "You're a swine. Are you going to get up from there?"
>
> "I'm Amer-"
>
> Courtland struck him in the face with the doubled quirt.
>
> Edie cried out, but her cry was lost in the boy's scream. Blood burst from his face in a dozen places, and a great red welt coiled snake-like across his cheeks. He staggered to his feet, half-blinded, and his great fists doubled and undoubled harmlessly. If Courtland had struck him with his hand he would have fought, but the whip . . . the whip had done something to him. It had broken worse than his skin—something that would always lie festering, unhealed.

Unbeknownst to Courtland, he has spawned a monster. Mike Czerny's wounds not only will never heal on the outside, but he will also be driven mad. Soon Czerny will live only for revenge.

In Chapter Eleven, Sherman and Lincoln consult the only lawyer in town, young Jeff Parker, about a legal matter. Jeff is intelligent and quick-witted, but desperately poor and unsure of himself. The butt of many jokes, he is yet a town favorite.

The Fargos were refused a loan by Barkley because the deed to their land is clouded; Pearl quitclaimed to God. Judge Ritten, Jeff's mentor, later tells him what to do:

> ". . . you go back up to your office and draw up a complaint: Fargo vs. God, with yourself as attorney. . . . When God fails to appear in court, you'll win the action. We won't have wasted any of the county's time or money, and you'll get your laughs—the right kind—and the sort of publicity you want if you handle it right.

Bella schemes to get money out of her father, ostensibly to go back east to find a husband; actually she wants to run away with Grant. She meets Grant at dusk in the fairgrounds yard on the outskirts of town. Before she enters the rundown shack where he awaits, she has a terrible premonition of death. After Grant hears the good news, he takes her brutally, and sets off for town to drink away the money she's given him. Bella staggers outside and vomits.

In Chapter Thirteen Sherman decides he will feed cattle indefinitely, and attempts to return the wheat thresher. He has to enlist the help of Jeff Parker, whose "suit against God" has catapulted him into the spotlight. The sharp young lawyer writes a brilliant letter to the thresher company; the company decides to let Bill Simpson handle Sherman and to look into hiring Jeff Parker as their regional counsel.

So one spring day Simpson arrives, and cons Sherman into once more planting wheat, since if everyone else is feeding cattle, there'll be no money in livestock. Simpson proceeds down the road to Wilhelm Deutsch's farm, where his smooth sales pitch falls on deaf ears. Deutsch has a hundred-and-sixty-year crop rotation plan for his land. Simpson's protest that he'd make more money by planting wheat this year doesn't faze the German farmer; he knows such short-sighted greed will lead to the exhaustion of his land.

The fourteenth chapter continues the genesis of a monstrous killer:

Courtland had hurt the Czerny boy more terribly than he ever knew, and when the boy reached home, he was beaten again by his father and locked in the stable for punishment. This was right, of course, for young Czerny had endangered the living of the whole family by his misconduct. . . . That night he began to howl with pain, and his mother slipped out to him and pushed a saucer of grease beneath the locked door. His fingers stiff with cold, he dropped it to the floor of the stable, and when he anointed his swollen and broken face in the darkness, there was manure on his fingers. . . . By morning he was raving, by that evening his head was puffed to twice its normal size; he was a festering, bleeding, sightless mess. They could not get a doctor up there, and a doctor could have done him no good; and, too, they loved him and did not want him taken away. When his insanity became uncontrollable, they chained him in the cellar, and there he remained for three months. By fall, he seemed completely normal again—except for his looks. His face looked as though it had been branded with a running-iron; his mouth had been chewed and clawed until it was almost twice its original size, and there were only a few stumps of teeth in his rotting gums. He was almost wholly blind, but he could see enough to know what they saw, and he could hear. He was a monster; and a monster could not go back to school, he could not visit a sweetheart, he could never even as much as ride into town. He could only be kept out of sight, be hidden and given work to do. And so he was. And the other hunkys who knew the secret kept it with the Czernys. So the days, the weeks, the months passed for Mike Czerny. Gradually, he gained more freedom for himself. He could not leave the place, but he was not watched so closely. And sometimes he would slip away from his drudgery and lie concealed near the road, peering at the infrequent passers-by out of his almost-blind eyes. Waiting . . .

Mike Czerny is both inwardly and outwardly a monster—a rarity in Thompson's later novels, in which most of the killers have rotted away inside, but show little outward sign to warn of the danger. A different kind of monster, Grant Fargo, will later prove himself to be the first of Thompson's outwardly bland psychotics.

In Chapter Fifteen, Alfred Courtland boards the train to Omaha with $25,000 of Barkley's money in his possession, along with a letter from Barkley stating it all belongs to Courtland. Barkley wants to dabble in the stock market, yet cannot do it in his own name for fear of the word getting back to his depositors. Courtland buys himself a pint of whiskey, and gets unusually drunk and uninhibited, just as he did the day he beat the Czerny boy. He runs into Jeff Parker, recently elected to the state legislature and on his way to Lincoln. Courtland drunkenly insults Parker, and while attempting to apologize, he runs into a cop who takes him in for questioning when he notices the bag of money.

Jeff Parker stops in a small town for lunch between trains, where he soon charms a whole barroom full of people, who parade him back to the train station. Courtland's tirade had shaken him up, but now he feels better.

A wide-eyed innocent in the big city of Lincoln, Parker checks into a swank hotel at three dollars a day, thinking the rate is three dollars a week. He then is puzzled over why they put the bathroom in his room; now everyone on the floor will have to walk through the room to get to it.

The truth of these matters is explained to him by an agent of the railroad, who offers Jeff his first bribe. Jeff realizes he'll never survive in the city on his salary, so he takes the money, not comprehending what he has done.

Courtland is escorted back to the railroad station by the chief of police, who, having spoken to Philo Barkley, is full of apologies. Courtland continues on to Omaha, and immediately sees a doctor who informs him that he has advanced syphilis of the brain.

Courtland returns to Verdon after depositing his new money in two different bank accounts. He stops at Barkley's house after downing a pint of whiskey; he needs it to face Bark. After thoroughly shocking and insulting both Barkley and Bella, he returns home to Myrtle and rages at her, until he collapses sobbing in her arms.

Chapter Eighteen opens with this synopsis of events:

There was much to gossip about in Verdon that year:

Alfred Courtland took over the bank, and Philo Barkley began the operation of a small-loan and commission business from his home.

Jeff Parker sold out to the railroad (there was definite proof, at last).

Link Fargo had a stroke which laid him up for several months.

Edie Dillon assumed proprietorship of the hotel.

And Grant Fargo went to work on the Verdon *Eye*.

Bella forced Grant to get a job after she realized there was no money to be had from her newly destitute father. She is under the impression that Grant is saving money so they can run away, until she realizes that he's been drinking all their savings. Bella then says she's pregnant, threatening to tell the family of her condition if Grant doesn't come up with some money soon.

Edie Dillon has become the proprietor of the town hotel thanks to a loan from Alf Courtland. Robert, who is rapidly growing up, has a mad crush on Paulie Pulasky, who returns his affection by bringing him ice cream and candy from her parents' store; they share their first kiss.

Lincoln is soon feeling much better, having been roused by an attempt by Grant to rob him and flee the town. Lincoln takes his grandson around town with him one day; Robert gets into a lot of trouble, culminating in staging his own hanging from a courthouse window, in view of the whole town.

When he and Lincoln emerge from the courthouse, Robert expects everyone to set upon him; but evidently something else has taken their attention:

> Bob looked around fearfully, then boldly, then with annoyance. For no one paid the slightest attention to him. They seemed actually to avoid looking at him.
>
> He looked up at Lincoln, and saw the old man's accipitrine face suddenly grow more hawklike than ever. Roughly, Lincoln flung their hands apart and shouldered his way into a group.
>
> "What's that you said?" he demanded. "What'd you say about Grant?" . . .
>
> "Honest to Gawd, Link, I didn't say nothing against Grant."
>
> "Just what did you say, anyhow?"
>
> "Nothin'. Honest to—"
>
> "Want me to cane you?"
>
> "But I ain't said nothing, Link! All I done was mention that Grant was with her when she got drowned . . ."

Bella Barkley's body is recovered from slow quicksand at the bottom of a bluff. Doc Jones tells Philo Barkley that Bella was not pregnant, and in fact was a virgin. Sheriff Jake Philips and County Attorney Ned Stufflebean want the real story from Doc. But Jones maintains that she wasn't pregnant, and that she died of a broken neck; he wants no trouble with Barkley or the Fargos.

The two county officials proceed to the Fargo house to "talk to Grant" only to find the whole clan surrounding Grant in the living room. Much to Philips's dismay, Stufflebean presses on, asking Grant what happened in the car:

> Grant shuddered and closed his eyes, and Mrs. Lincoln Fargo looked resentfully at the officers.
>
> "Can't you see he ain't fit to do no talking?" she demanded.
>
> "Oh, I'll tell 'em, Ma," said Grant, his voice peevish. "We were driving along—she was driving—and she was going awfully fast, and I told her she better slow down. She just laughed, and I reached over to push up on the gas, and she kind of jerked the wheel, and the next thing I knew we were—she was—I jumped and she was—"
>
> His voice broke, and he buried his face in the pillow, sobbing . . . .
>
> An uneasy, angry stirring filled the room.

Stufflebean and Philips leave to investigate the crash scene; by the time they reach the wrecked car, still down in the quicksand, they have decided it's an accident. They drive back by the Fargo house on their way back to town, honking and waving to signal their unspoken decision.

> Sherman laughed sourly, and Lincoln stared off across the garden, his veiled eyes bitter with disgust. He wished there had been some way of hanging Grant without disgracing the name of Fargo. He knew, beyond a shadow of a doubt, that his son was guilty of murder.
>
> So that was gone, too—his pride; and there was no pretense that would take the place of it. And there was so little left, now, so very little of the brimming handful with which he had started life.

The realization that his son has become a murderer leads Lincoln to a reevaluation of his life, of all life, which he will offer to his daughter Edie on his deathbed.

In Chapter Twenty-three, Sherman is forced by the bank to plant wheat for the sixth straight year, despite the fact that it will very soon exhaust his land. His boys Ted and Gus, now grown to young manhood, see no future in Verdon. They steal Sherman's prize horse team, sell it, and hop the next train out of town.

They land in Kansas City, where Bill Simpson gets them jobs at the World-Wide Harvester Company. They last about two weeks, and things go downhill from there. They work harvesting crops around the country for a few seasons, and finally decide to go back home. They have heard that Sherman has had to let much of his land revert to the bank, and that things are quite tight back in the valley. Down in Texas, attempting to save enough money to go back to Verdon with their heads high, they get into a fight and are hauled off to jail. They are sentenced to two years in prison.

In Chapter Twenty-five, thirteen-year-old Robert Dillon finally consummates his love for Paulie Pulasky. Alone at the hotel, she is at first hesitant, but then turns the tables on Bobbie:

> There was so much there, so much that was ancient and wise in the great slate-grey pools, that suddenly it was he who felt young and foolish and frightened. And she saw those things, felt them, knew them almost before they occurred; and her eyes closed and her lips parted.

Meanwhile, Edie is out at Lincoln's house, where he lies dying. Lincoln has said good-bye to everyone, and now sits quietly with Edie, waiting for the end. He speaks with regret about Grant, how he had left him apprenticed to a printer back in Kansas City when he was just a little boy; Lincoln thought he was doing the right thing. But now all he can remember are Grant's cries not to leave him behind, and he feels responsible for what Grant later became.

Lincoln tells Edie about marching through the South with Sherman, something he never talked about before. He greatly regrets destroying the land and the people:

> "They'd've done the same thing to you, Pa."
> "I don't know, Edie. Maybe, maybe not. I ain't very smart. It seems to me, though, that there was never a fight or a killin' or a war yet that wasn't started to keep someone from doin' something to someone else. If they got a chance . . . .
> "So we run 'em off their places, their homes, an' then we burnt 'em to the ground after we'd carried off everything that was worth carrying. We done it because we knew they'd've done the same thing to us if they'd had the chance . . . .
> "I guess we don't never learn, Edie. We don't never learn. There ain't none of us can tell whether it'll rain the next day or not. We don't know whether our kids are goin' to be boys or girls. Or why the world turns one way instead of another. Or—or the what or why or when of anything. Hindsight's the only gift we got, except on one thing. On that, we're all prophets.
> "We know what's in the other fellow's mind. It don't make no difference

that we've never seen him before, or whatever. We know that he's out to do us if he gets the chance."

"Pa!"

"You got plenty of time to talk, Edie. I ain't . . . We came to a house one day—not far out of Atlanta it was—and I was bringin' up the rear, an' all I got was a book . . . .

"I don't remember the words no more, but I got the idea . . . There ain't no death, no deed, no o-mission or co-mission that don't leave its mark . . .

"We burn off a forest, an' all we see is the cleared land, an' the profit. We burn the forest because we say it's ours to burn, an' we can do what we want with what's ours. We burn it, an' the birds leave, an' the grubs come, and the grain don't grow so good. And there's hot winds and dust.

"We plow up the prairie because it's ours to plow, and we dam up the cricks because they're ours to dam. We grab everything we can while the grabbin's good, because it's ours an' because some other fellow will do it if we don't . . . And, hell, there's nothin' that's really ours, and we don't know what's in the other fellow's mind . . .

"I had a thousand acres once, said it was mine . . . .

"I had a son, an' he was mine. And what he done was mine, too. Fifty years or more ago we marched through Georgia, and it was ours. And now, Ted and Gus . . . Ted an' Gus . . . ."

Lincoln's eyes grew wider and wider. They stood out in his head like yellow apples. His hands went to his throat, seeming to claw at the rattle there. He gasped and a cable of blood and mucus rolled out of his sunken mouth. He looked around wildly, searching, and one of his hands ceased its clawing and gripped the cane. Twisting, he swung it viciously.

"You sons-of-bitches!" he roared, and then fell back. And with the last twitch of his fingers, he flung the stick from him.

He had no use for canes.

Thus Lincoln's Fargo sums up the theme of *Heed the Thunder,* in which Jim Thompson likens the land and its people; where the short-sighted neglect of the land is reaped in rotting crops and exhausted soil, and the shortsighted abuse of people is reaped in nearly all the characters, but most strikingly in the rotting soul of Grant Fargo, and the rotting flesh of Mike Czerny.

Lincoln Fargo's view of the world will echo through almost all of Thompson's later fiction. His belief that there is no act of omission or commission that does not leave a lasting mark will provide the foundation of Jim Thompson's view of guilt and culpability, upon which the Thompson novels *The Criminal* and *The Kill-Off* are built.

Lincoln's observation of the certainty with which man thinks he knows that which is fundamentally unknowable—the motivations of his fellow man—will become, when extended to include the unknowability of self, the basis of Thompson novels as diverse as *The Killer Inside Me, The Getaway,* and *Child of Rage.*

In Chapter Twenty-seven, set down in Mexico, a man is hit on the head in a barroom fight; when he comes to, he realizes he's Robert Dillon, and can't remember the last seven years of his life.

Next, the story of Grant Fargo reaches a fitting end when he meets his *doppelgänger,* Mike Czerny. Now an alcoholic bum on the streets of Lincoln, Grant is found by Jeff Parker, who fixes him up with food and new clothes, and puts him on the next train to Verdon. As the train nears his hometown, Grant realizes he doesn't want to get off at the town station in his present condition. He decides to leap from the train before Verdon, just as it reaches Fargo crossing.

Grant miscalculates, jumping off too early, away up in Misery Creek. The sun is setting and it is snowing quite heavily. Badly frightened, he spots a cornhusker with great relief. He doesn't know the man is Czerny, and that Grant's current behavior and dress is reminding Czerny of Alfred Courtland:

> He backed away, and the thing merely stood and watched him.
>
> Then it turned and walked over to the fence. The blade of the husking mitt came down on the barbed wire and the wire snapped. The thing walked to the next post and repeated the same process.
>
> It came back to the road, dragging the length of barbed wire. It started toward him.
>
> He could not move for a moment. he could not even cry out. He was like a man in a nightmare.
>
> *Jesus . . . God . . . Jesus . . . I didn't want to kill her . . . she kept after me and I didn't want to, and I'm sorry . . . I've told you how sorry I was . . . Jesus, just let me see Ma again. Don't . . . DON'T . . .*
>
> He screamed. He tried to run at last, and his foot caught in a frozen rut and he sprawled.
>
> And the thing stood over him.
>
> "I . . . know . . . you . . . You know me?"
>
> Grant looked up and screamed again, and the thing bent over him insistently.
>
> "You . . . know . . . me?"
>
> "No!" screamed Grant. "Go 'way. I haven't got any money. I—I——GO AWAY!"
>
> "You . . . stand . . . up."
>
> "I won't stand up! You can't make me! . . . Please, please don't hurt me. I'm sick and I haven't got any money, and *help, help!*"

The husking mitt closed around his neck and the blade bit into his flesh. As if he had been a child, he was lifted into the air.

He struggled, choking, flailing at the hideous face with his hands, and the thing suddenly released him and let him drop to the road.

His terror was so great by now that it was its own antidote. He watched the thing fold the wire, and his voice became almost quiet.

"What are you going to do? Why are you doing this? I haven't any money . . . You—you don't want to tie me up with that. It'll cut me. I'll freeze. Why do you want to tie me up. Why . . ."

"No tie . . . Whip."

"W-whip?" Grant rose to his knees incredulously. "Y-you can't do that. I—"

The thing moved so swiftly that he was still talking when the blow fell. He did not even have time to close his eyes. The barbed wire bit into his face, chopped into his eyes, dragged through skin and flesh and membranes. And when his pain rode through the shock, and he opened his mouth to scream, the wire quirt swung again, slicing his neck, his throat. And his scream died in a choking burbling sound.

A drowning sound . . .

. . . He lay stretched out on his back at last, lay on a scarlet counterpane of blood. And he no longer screamed nor struggled. He no longer breathed.

Mike Czerny let the quirt slide from his fingers. Scornfully he nudged the corpse of Grant Fargo with his foot.

In the last chapter, Thompson offers a final update on all the principal characters. In Verdon, Paulie Pulasky lies weeping in her bed. In Lincoln, Mike Czerny sits in the death cell, and Jeff Parker recommends an investigation of Courtland's bank. In Houston, Gus and Ted lay chained to their bunks, planning some way of killing their guards.

And on the night train out of the valley are Bob and Edie Dillon. Bob can't believe he's finally going home to Papa. Yet he's sad to leave the valley, and will miss not only Paulie, but all the rest:

And so he called them all back, one by one; all, for they were real people, elemental people, understandable people, people of the land, and as good and as bad as the land, their birthright, was good and bad. And in his loneliness he called them all:

Honest, bitter Lincoln; swaggering Sherman; fat Josephine; prissy Myrtle; cool Courtland; mean-eyed Ted and Gus; chipper Jeff Parker; dull Pearl; slow Barkley; proud Bella; dude Grant . . .

He called them and they came into the mirror of the window, seemingly fighting for remembrance even as he fought to remember them. They came brashly and shyly, swaggering and halting and prissing, laughing, smiling, frowning, grimacing. Good, bad, indifferent: the real people, the people of the land. And then they were gone, the last of them; and as he burned them forever into his memory, he pressed his face against the window and fought to hold the land:

The land. The good land, the bad land, the fair-to-middling land, the beautiful land, the ugly land, the homely land, the kind and hateful land; the land with its tall towers, its great barns, its roomy houses, its spring-pole wells, its shabby sheds, its dugouts; the land with its little villages and towns, its cities and great cities, its blacksmith shops and factories, its one-room schools and colleges; the hunky land, the Rooshan land, the German land, the Dutch and Swede land, the Protestant and Catholic and Jewish land; the American land—the land that was slipping so surely, so swiftly, into the black abyss of the night.

So Jim Thompson concluded his second novel, a mainstream historical novel seemingly far removed from the rest of his writing, with an elegy for a lost time, a lost land, a lost people. *Heed the Thunder* is Jim Thompson's declaration of intent, inspiring and foreshadowing what was to come in later years. Within its pages are keys that unlock the more obscure motivations and themes of Thompson's later novels.

Nearly all later Thompson characters seek their fates in the "black abyss of the night," without even the land to rely upon. Rootless denizens with nothing tangible to cling to—least of all their unknowable selves and motivations—they are randomly tossed about by the world and circumstance until the meaninglessness drives them to murder. Patriarch Lincoln Fargo glimpsed what lay ahead for his people as he lay on his deathbed; Jim Thompson later fulfilled that terrible vision in his crime novels.

FIVE

Heed the Thunder garnered mixed reviews: *Weekly Book Review* wrote "the prose is vigorous, and domestic dialogue has barroom bluntness. If sufficient readers are 'interested or amused' says the author, he will do a trilogy. No comment." *The Saturday Review of Literature* found "a number of good stories in this book but the whole effect . . . moderately confusing." Beatrice Sherman of *The New York Times* was more enthusiastic:

> A robust novel of country life in Nebraska—forthright and earthy, boisterous in its humor, cruel in its tragedy. . . . In a minor way the book is a *God's Little Acre* of the West. . . . As [the story] progresses the breaks, good or bad, are handed out in a curiously pat manner by a sardonic and bitter Providence. The odds are definitely long against anybody in Verdon, Nebraska, leading an even moderately satisfactory life.

Heed the Thunder also was "reviewed" in the local *San Diego Tribune:*

> *Heed the Thunder,* the second published novel by Jim Thompson, is off the presses and will be released in local stores tomorrow. . . . [It] is a serious study of the transition from hand to machine industry, illustrated by the life of a small Nebraska town from 1907 to 1914, showing the sacrifice of land and human resources for the "immediate dollar."
>
> A tall, slender, greying man, Thompson, 40, started writing when he was a 15-year-old schoolboy in Anadarko, Oklahoma, and has since written an estimated 7,000,000 words in novels, poetry, articles and other literary production.
>
> He makes long studies of his subjects in his San Diego home, then goes

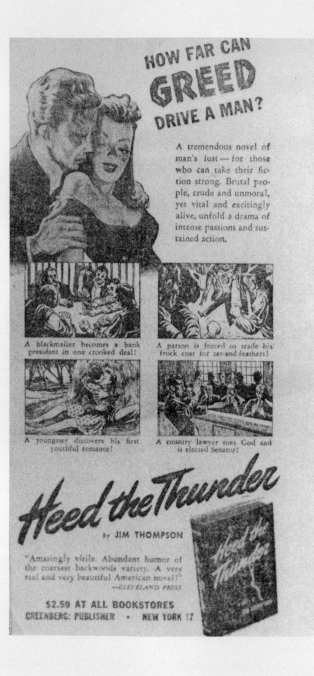

Newspaper advertisement for 1946's Heed the Thunder.

to New York, locks himself in a hotel room, works 16 to 18 hours a day and
turns out a 100,000 word novel in five weeks.

What is his advice to youngsters seeking writing careers? "Take up
plumbing," he grins.

Jim Thompson's wife and children will not speak openly about his
drinking during the late 1940s. But by his own account in "An Alcoholic
Looks at Himself," and Freddie and Maxine's recollections, Thompson
had become all but disabled, and a frequent patient at alcoholic asylums.
Freddie spoke carefully about the subject:

> We had to put him in to dry out a few times—in these places that would
> keep him for two days—in San Diego, when he was a newspaperman.
>
> There were a lot of pressures, not an awful lot of help, or emotional
> support. I always felt that his family didn't understand him—they didn't
> make life easy for him. Because he wasn't that easy to understand. It must
> have been rather difficult for them a lot of the time—it was for all of us.
> Nobody wants to be bothered with somebody who's causing them trouble.
> So if he was causing a disruption of things, naturally it's not popular. That
> caused arguments.
>
> It was hard on Alberta, she didn't have an easy time of it—I don't think
> she ever understood. She came from a totally different background.
>
> We were all *for* Jimmie. Sure, I'd get annoyed if he wouldn't leave a bar,
> but he'd always end up going with me.

From "An Alcoholic Looks at Himself":

> Back home again, my drinking entered a new and terrifying phase.
> Heretofore its tendency had been to make me amiable and gregarious. Now
> I become dopey, antisocial and abusive. I sought a "cure" in one sanitarium
> after another. I got nothing but temporary sobriety and enormous bills.

Evidently drinking steadily through the fall and winter of 1945–46,
Thompson did not complete the second novel for Greenberg. When *Heed
the Thunder* appeared in January 1946, Thompson read the reviews with
despair; once more he felt he'd never write again.

Counterbalancing Thompson's lifelong desire for "success" as a writer
was that innate desire for self-destruction, often symptomatized by his
drinking. Though Thompson thought highly of his own writing, he had
rendered himself incapable of success. All of Thompson's behavior in the
1940s stems from the deeply held belief, instilled by his relationship with
his father, that he was destined to be a failure. In Thompson's conscious
estimation nature and circumstance invariably conspired against him, and
he could do little to change his fate.

This, of course, is exactly the attitude/position of the psychotic killers who narrate the best of Thompson's crime novels. *The Killer Inside Me, A Hell of a Woman,* and *Savage Night* are all stories of men whose desire for a "success" they consider impossible plunges them into a psychic hell from which there is no escape.

Thompson persisted in writing and rewriting the crime novel manuscript and sending it off to publishers; still he found no takers. Finally, when the family's financial affairs demanded it, he obtained a job as a rewrite man on the *San Diego Journal*. From "An Alcoholic Looks at Himself":

> I began to write, forcing out words, hour after hour, from an all-but-exhausted talent for creation. I did one draft, sent it out, got it back. Did another . . . and so on.
>
> Our sole income was my wife's modest earnings, and since I would not stop drinking, our affairs plummeted rapidly from worse to terrible.
>
> When, finally, we actually lacked food and we could beg and borrow no more, I did a high pressure selling job upon a local newspaper and went to work as a rewrite man.

Thompson lasted at the *San Diego Journal* for nearly a year, mostly doing research and rewrite work, although Sharon Reed still recalls one particular story, when her father interviewed Robert Mitchum after the actor had been arrested for possession of marijuana. Thompson would meet up with Mitchum again, on a professional basis, decades later.

Eventually, Thompson was fired for being constantly drunk, according to "An Alcoholic Looks at Himself:

> During my last month, I was absent from the job six of the twenty working days and I was in sanitariums four times. I was regretfully but firmly fired one night when I telephoned the managing editor, rousing him out of bed, and harangued him drunkenly for the many unpardonable sins of which I found him guilty.

The loss of another decent job left Thompson adrift once more, until he received word that the seemingly impossible had occurred. The prestigious publishing house of Harper's, to whom Alberta had insisted he send the manuscript of *Nothing More Than Murder* (Thompson considered it a last resort, as they were about the only publisher he hadn't previously sent the novel to), had unaccountably accepted it. The advance money on the novel got the family through a few more months, but Thompson evidently did not abate his drinking in the least.

Nothing More Than Murder, published in February of 1949, was Thompson's farewell to hardcovers. Max Miller of the *San Diego Tribune-Sun,* who had previously reviewed both *Now and on Earth* and *Heed the Thunder,* wrote up the interesting history of *Nothing More Than Murder,* on February 16, 1949:

> The old truism, "The longer you work on it, the shorter the book becomes," has been proved again. This time by the San Diego writer, Jim Thompson.
> Though his third novel, "Nothing More Than Murder," is being released to the stands today by Harper's, the inside story of the story of the book goes back to 1932—when he began working on it.
> "I've rewritten that book so many times," Thompson said, "that I know each word by heart. I bet I've rewritten it eight or ten times. And I bet it's been to about every publisher between rewrites before Harper's got it."
> Now, after 17 years of fighting that book, brooding about that book, and rewriting that book, it can be picked up and read within an hour. Seems unfair, yet that's how such things go. . . .
> Thompson's case has another peculiar twist. Since starting this book in 1932, and having it turned down, etc., he went to town with two others: "Now and on Earth" (published by the Modern Age Press in 1942) and "Heed the Thunder" (published by Greenberg in 1946). So he does know some of the answers.
> No writer knows them all. That's the catch. Knowing the rather choosy publishing house of Harper and Brothers does not go in for outright murder mysteries, I asked Thompson: "How come on this one?"
> I had not read the book, but had judged only by the title. So he had to do what all authors hate to do: He had to describe his own product to somebody who had not read it. He said it was not a murder mystery as such, but was something else with a murder in it . . ."a novel of suspense" . . . .
> He would have tried to explain it, I presume, but the occasion called for mercy. So we called it off. What he should have done was to turn on his heel and say: "Well, read the book if you want to know."
> If he had done a murder mystery, as I had assumed it was, then in this town right now we would have had quite a few murder mystery writers. There would be Ronal Kyser, who writes under the name "Dale Clark." And we have Raymond Chandler and Jonathan Latimer, who has written both kinds of novels. And then the murder mystery team of Bob Wade and Bill Miller under the joint pen name of "Wade Miller."
> Thompson would have made one more. His home is at 2601 Nye Street, Linda Vista, and the names of his three children are Pat, Mike and Sharon.
> You may recall "Now and on Earth" because it had for its main setting a local aircraft factory, and the whole story was based in San Diego—plus a brief jaunt into Tijuana.

Besides having worked at one time on a local paper, Thompson also has worked on the Fort Worth Press, the Oklahoma City News, the Lincoln State Journal, and the Omaha Bee. During the war he was a private in the Marine Corps.

Previous to that he was director of the Federal Writers' Project of Oklahoma (1938–40) and held a research fellowship in the building industry from the University of North Carolina (1940–41). His yen has always been for writing books—and especially to lick finally that one he started in 1932.

This is not a review of the book, but a review of the writer who rewrote and rewrote the book until he sold it. You may like the book, or you may not. You may find the paragraphs cut too fine and too brisk with all the rewriting. Or you may find the subject material too tough. That's up to you. But, anyway, after 17 years of working on it he sold it.

And that's the story of the story.

Nothing More Than Murder, one of the more intricately plotted of Thompson's crime novels, exhibits many of what would become Thompson's trademark obsessions and techniques: first-person narration by a self-denying psychotic, uncontrollable desire for an objectively unattractive, large-breasted woman, and murder paradoxically viewed as a return to innocence, or the ticket to a happy, decent life.

Joe Wilmot, the first-person narrator, ran the Barclay movie theater for a few years before marrying Elizabeth Barclay, ten years his senior. Though they couldn't have come from more dissimilar backgrounds, he and Elizabeth see the world the same way. Elizabeth recognizes him for the heartless con man that he is, but doesn't mind—she admires him. And Joe will do anything for her. So they get married, and after Joe pulls a series of shady deals, the movie theater is the biggest independent in the state.

Then one day Elizabeth hires a farm girl from up the road to live in the house and help with the chores. Soon Joe notices the drab girl in a new way:

There was a knock on my door, and I said, "Come in, Carol," and she came in.

"I just wanted to show you the new suit Mrs. Wilmot gave me," she said.

I sat up. "It looks very nice, Carol."

I don't know which I wanted to do most, laugh or cry.

She was a little bit cockeyed—maybe I didn't tell you? Well. And she was more than a little pigeon-toed. The suit wasn't new. It was a worn-out rag Elizabeth had given her to make over, and she'd botched it from top to

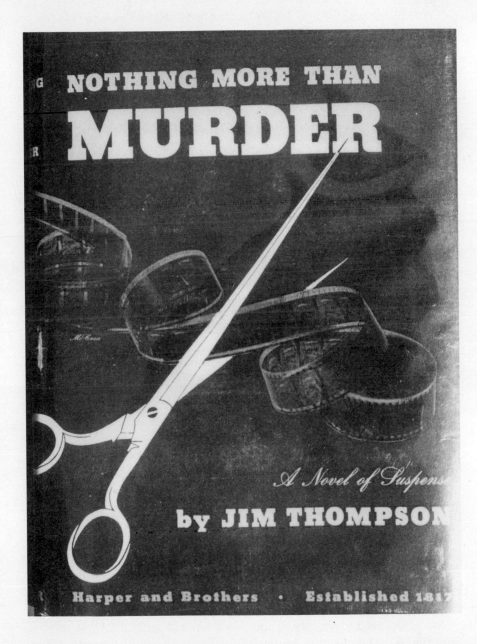

First edition of Nothing More Than Murder, *1949*.

bottom. And she had on a pair of Elizabeth's old shoes that didn't fit her half as well as mine would.

The blouse was too tight for her breasts, or her breasts were too big for the blouse, however you want to put it. They were too big for anything but an outsize. A good deep breath and she'd have had to start dodging.

I felt the tears coming into my eyes, and yet I wanted to laugh, too. She looked like hell. She looked like a sack of bran that couldn't decide which way it was going to fall.

And then the curtain rose or however you want to put it, and everything was changed.

And what I began to think about wasn't laughing or crying.

That tiny bit of cockeyedness gave her a cute, mad look, and the way she toed in sort of spread her buttocks and made a little valley under her skirt, and—and it don't—doesn't—make sense but there was something about it that made me think of the Twenty-third Psalm.

I'd thought she looked awkward and top-heavy, and, hell, I could see now that she didn't at all. Her breasts weren't too big. Jesus, her breasts! She looked cute-mad and funny-sweet. She looked like she'd started somewhere and been mussed up along the way.

She was a honey. She was sugar and pie. She was a bitch.

I said, "Come here, Carol," and she came there.

And then I was kissing her like I'd been waiting all my life to do just that, and she was the same way with me.

I don't know how long it was before I looked up and saw Elizabeth in the doorway.

Carol is the first in a long line of unattractive sirens with an unaccountable pull over Thompson's psychotic killers. Joe Wilmot, like his later brethren, realizes too late that what he sees in, or projects upon, Carol is the small amount of good that is left (or once was) inside him.

Elizabeth is willing to go peacefully enough, and let Carol and Joe be together, but she wants money. The scheme the three eventually decide upon involves staging Elizabeth's death by accidental fire in the film rewind room above the garage. The body will be charred beyond recognition, enabling them to kill some unsuspecting woman instead of Elizabeth. Elizabeth will then leave town, and Joe and Carol will send her the insurance money when they collect it. After a suitable amount of time, Joe and Carol can get married.

Joe places an ad in the city paper for a woman needed for housework, and the respondents are screened by Carol to find someone whose disappearance won't be noted. The rewind room burns to the ground one night when Joe is in the city, as scheduled, but Joe tips his hand to Hap Chance, a sleazy film distributor.

Soon an insurance investigator named Appleton is assigned to the case, and Joe progressively digs himself deeper and deeper, growing to mistrust Carol more and more. Only at the end of the novel does Joe realize that he has given himself away and misunderstood the motivation of nearly every other character. And he discovers that instead of a substitute dying in that fire, Carol actually killed Elizabeth, because Carol knew what Joe couldn't admit even to himself: that he still loved his wife.

The maze of misunderstandings, false intentions, and slip-ups in *Nothing More Than Murder* reveals Joe Wilmot's central problem: he doesn't understand his fellow man, and in his ignorance ultimately attributes to others all the baser motivations which he cannot admit he finds in his own heart. Joe's state of mind is exactly what Lincoln Fargo spoke of to Edie on his deathbed: "We know what's in the other fellow's mind. . . . We know he's out to do us if he gets the chance."

Thompson developed this theme more explicitly in some later novels, but it is the source of much of the evil in every Thompson novel, and the foundation upon which all his psychotic narrators base their reality. Their divided hearts and minds can only attribute the lowest motivations to other humans, just as they rationalize excuses for their own criminal acts.

Lincoln Fargo attributed all the evil in the world, from the North's destruction of the South to his son Grant's murder of Bella Barkley, to this basic human flaw. If we change Lincoln's observation to "We know what's in the other fellow's mind, *but we don't know (or can't see) what's in ours (or that what we see in others is actually in us),*" we come close to locating the secret place from which all Thompson's criminal narrators view their world.

Nothing More Than Murder is an ingeniously structured novel of suspense: Joe Wilmot lies both to himself and to us in his narration of events. As a result, he is both the guilty party and discoverer of his own true guilt (i.e. the inner truth), a dramatic/narrative construct precisely analogous to Joe's own psychotic mind. The importance of this construct cannot be overstated, since Jim Thompson can within its parameters offer a "mystery" as sealed and symmetric in structure as any Ellery Queen short story.

As in the best ratiocinations, the reader doesn't know until the final page of *Nothing More Than Murder* exactly what happened. But the reader doesn't then feel tricked by some clunky plotting device, or disappointed by the arbitrary nature of "the truth" revealed by a seemingly omniscient detective, as is all too often the case in the English parlor mystery.

In *Nothing More Than Murder*, truth of plot is intertwined with truth of character, for at the same time as it is revealing plot points and occurrences, Joe Wilmot's narration can delve into the philosophy of murder and the motivations of the murderous heart even more deeply than can a narrator like Raymond Chandler's Philip Marlowe, who, for all his meditations on a world of crime, remains forever separated from it by his very nature as a good man.

As Wilmot begins to unravel under the pressure of the murder investigation, he begins to probe inside himself, searching for an answer to why he did what he did. He finds nothing. Joe doesn't know why he was so attracted to Carol; he doesn't know that he still loves his wife; he doesn't know why he agreed to the murder scheme. He feels pulled along by some invisible force. Joe Wilmot is not able to find a neat reason for his descent into hell, and that descent is rendered that much more horrible by its seeming randomness and unstoppability.

Of course, Joe's fate is mild compared to those in store for Thompson's ensuing first-person narrators like Lou Ford, Dolly Dillon, Clinton Brown, and Charlie Bigger. But in *Nothing More Than Murder* Thompson had discovered the perfect narrative technique of the crime novel, one that allowed him to leap out of the ghetto of genre fiction in his next book, his masterpiece, *The Killer Inside Me*.

Thompson's first-person psychotic narrative technique achieves full integration of the English "parlor entertainment" (where "the truth" of exactly *what* happened is revealed at the last) with the American detective crime novel (where a meditation on "the truth" of crime and evil is the *raison d'être* for the book). Thompson also combined the "puzzle" that defines the former with the violence that defines the latter, especially in later novels that exhibit much more overt violence than *Nothing More Than Murder*.

Thompson continued to develop his radical construct in his first-person narrations: perfecting it thematically in *The Killer Inside Me*, where Lou Ford's divided nature mines the depths of "guilt" and "evil" and "personality" and "conscience"; perfecting it formally in *A Hell of a Woman*, where Dolly Dillon's divided nature eventually ruptures his very narrative into multiple points of view.

In April 1949, *Master Detective* published another Jim Thompson true-crime story, the undistinguished "Four Murders in Four Minutes." By June, when the second half of the advance for *Nothing More Than Murder* had been used up, Thompson had somehow obtained another newspaper rewrite man job, with the *Los Angeles Mirror*. He lasted on that job for nearly a year, living in a hotel room or a room at the Press Club in downtown Los Angeles and seeing his family infrequently.

According to his own account, he was drunk the whole year, and finally fired as he began the last in a series of binges:

> It may sound hypocritical to say that I am glad I was fired. But that is one of the few absolutely truthful statements I have made during the past fifteen years. That paper was my last chance to earn a comfortable and respectable living and at the same time drink. Nothing else will serve from now on except absolute sobriety. It took the jolt of being fired from that job to bring me finally to my senses.
>
> Sooner or later an alcoholic is faced with the question of not whether to go on or give up drinking but whether to live or die. In three years I was hospitalized twenty-seven times for alcoholism. Obviously, I could not put off answering that question much longer.
>
> Now I have answered it. I have decided to live. The letter of dismissal has helped me reach this decision.

Thompson also decided to travel to New York once again. He left the family behind in San Diego and arrived on the East Coast in July of 1950. He stayed with Maxine and her husband, Joe Kouba, who had recently been transferred to New York. Thompson knocked on the doors of some old acquaintances at McFadden Publications; he was assigned a position on McFadden's *SAGA: Men's True Adventure* magazine.

During Thompson's time at *SAGA* magazine, he authored some rather improbable articles and stories. His first appearance, "Those Amazing Gridiron Indians," in the November 1950 issue, was a tough assignment for a man who knew more about real Indians than football. It was the "true story" of the Carlisle College championship football team of 1912, whose most famous member was native Oklahoman Jim Thorpe. Thompson must have been drinking steadily to churn that one out.

He landed the next issue's cover story, the self-explanatory "A G.I. Returns From Korea," as well as "He Supplies Santa Claus" (credited to Thompson's only known pseudonym, Dillon Roberts) and the anonymous confessional "An Alcoholic Looks at Himself."

The most interesting thing about the G.I piece is not the predictably jingoistic slant on a "regular soldier's" story, but the small piece of autobiography Thompson slips into the narrative. He'd been assigned the story by *SAGA* editor David Dressler, and told to go to Washington, D.C., right away to interview the soldier. Thompson tells Dressler he'll go right down, but it wasn't as easy as just getting on a plane.

Freddie, Jim's sister, vividly recalls Dr. Max Jacobson shooting up Thompson with vitamins and amphetamines to sober him enough to make the trip to Washington in August of 1950. So even as he was writing "An

Alcoholic Looks at Himself," in which he swears future sobriety, Thompson was drinking as much as ever.

Already mined for its autobiographical insights, "Alcoholic" is the story of a man who has been disabled by drink for the better part of a decade. Faced with the loss of yet another good newspaper job, the narrator tells us the story of those past ten years, and grimly promises himself that nothing but total sobriety will do in the future.

"He Supplies Santa Claus" is the story of A.C. Gilbert, founder of the Gilbert Toy company and inventor of toy chemistry and Erector sets.

"Prowlers in the Pear Trees" is an episode from Thompson's childhood that appeared again later in his first "autobiography," *Bad Boy*. It concerns the visit of one of Pop's friends to the Thompson household; at the time Pop was away and Mom was struggling to run a grocery store, in the yard of which was a pear tree. Pop's terminally drunken friend decides that the pears must be protected from thieves, and he rigs them with wires and pebble-filled tin cans. That night the high winds send the pebbles everywhere, pelting the Thompsons and breaking windows. Pop's drunken friend sleeps through it all, but the next day accuses every customer of the store of being the prowler in the pear trees. When Pop returns home he sends his friend for a seven-day cure and sells the store, which he has to admit was a poor purchase in the first place.

The curious "Two Lives of John Stink" has as its central plot device the fact that, once the Osage Indians perform a burial service, the deceased is considered dead forever. This is usually not a problem, but John Stink was mistakenly buried alive. When he escapes from his grave and returns to his home, none of his fellow Indians will recognize him. They are convinced he is a ghost, and the way to handle a ghost is by completely ignoring it. Thus shunned by his own people, John is forced to live a rather unhappy remainder of his life among the whites.

Thompson used the idea of a living death conferred by an Indian tribe once again in 1952's *Cropper's Cabin*.

Thompson returned to current events reportage with "Who Is This Man Eisenhower?" an amusing biographical sketch of the life of the future president. Thompson's final appearance in *SAGA* was April 1951's "Death Missed a Bet," by far the most compelling story he wrote for the magazine. Ostensibly yet another piece of autobiography, it concerns what happens when Jim, exhausted and drunk, picks up a hitchhiker when he is about halfway through a trip from San Diego to San Francisco. The young man mistakes Jim for a "success":

> "H-how do you go about amounting to something, mister?"
> How? I almost laughed out loud. I was a damned poor specimen to

answer a question of that kind. I had a research fellowship from a philanthropic foundation, but it was due to expire in another month, and there was not the slightest chance of getting it renewed. I'd been a reasonably successful short story writer, also, but I hadn't sold a story in more than a year. For months now I'd been a good-time Charlie—I'd played at working. I'd lost much of my one-time skill at writing, and I'd sunk deeper into debt. And, now, my rope was running out. I was pretty well washed up. So . . .

So I bragged to the Kid. I'd always been talkative when I drank, and I probably shot my mouth off more than usual. I told him about the fancy rates I'd drawn as a writer, and this fine travelling fellowship I had. I left no doubt in his mind that he was travelling with a big-time operator.

Unknown to Thompson, "the Kid" plans to rob him and steal the car. Thompson dozes off with the Kid at the wheel; when he wakes up the car is tottering on the edge of a cliff. If he steps carelessly from the passenger side, he will drop hundreds of feet into an abyss. Somehow he finds the right words to use with the Kid, who doesn't really want to kill him. He pretends that he doesn't know what's actually happening, and the Kid goes along:

> Oh, he knew all right! He knew that I knew what he'd had in his mind. But he wasn't a murderer at heart, only an impulsive kid who'd been down on his luck. He had wanted to back down.

Thompson disarms the potential killer by placing faith in the inherent goodness of the killer's heart; it is Thompson's faith that makes it so. This is the flip side to Thompson's belief in the shared nature of guilt: if evil can be spread, so can good. The idea is given its most complete treatment in Thompson's 1955 novel *After Dark, My Sweet.*

Thus Thompson concluded his stint at *SAGA;* his next appearance in print, besides some evidently embarrassing ghostwriting for *Police Gazette*, would be his fourth novel, 1952's *The Killer Inside Me.*

The *SAGA* stories had been written months in advance, and Thompson was able to send for the rest of the family by October of 1950. Sharon Thompson Reed recalls that they moved into a New York City apartment, where the rent was triple what it had been in San Diego. Freddie had also recently moved to New York with a new husband, Irving Townsend; true to form, all the Thompson siblings were now within miles of each other.

Despite the job at *SAGA,* Thompson's drinking problems continued; the family would "lose" him for days at a time while he hopped the hotel bars of Manhattan. Freddie recalls rescuing her brother many times; on one particular drunk, Thompson once more needed the help of his "personal physician," the original "Dr. Feelgood," Max Jacobson:

> There were times when he was drinking (and this appealed to his sense of humor), I'd have to hunt all over town for him, bar to bar, until I'd locate him. He'd leave amiably enough, but usually there'd been a little hassle like he'd in fun poured his beer over someone's head . . . something totally foreign to a man like Jimmie, something if he were sober he'd be horrified. . . .
>
> One time we had lost Jimmie in New York (we were living in Queens). . . . Alberta called and said Jimmie hadn't come home. The idea was nobody ever left him. We'd get up and start searching until we found him. I finally got a call that he was at the Hudson Hotel on the West Side. So I went over there, we were always afraid that he would get hurt, or something would go wrong.
>
> Anyway, I got over there and he was really drunk, he said, "I need help, you have to get a doctor." I was new in New York, I had no idea, it was late at night. "Who will I call?" and he said, "Call Max Jacobson, he's read my books and liked them." Anyway, I called his office, he was in. I got Jimmie in a cab and got him there, and Max injected him with a few things and got him on his feet, sobered him up. Of course that's what got him kicked out later on, his license was taken away. A lot of people went to him—he was a Jewish doctor who had worked in the concentration camps. He won a lot of awards. He gave injections to John Kennedy, people like that.

Thompson dedicated *Nothing More Than Murder* to Max Jacobson.

So Jim Thompson was productive (and evidently sporadically sober) at *SAGA* for nearly a year. He was promoted to managing editor in July 1951, but was gone by the October issue, having written six credited stories (and one anonymous and one pseudonymous) and many pages of rewrites and uncredited filler. Thompson resigned when his editor was fired.

Thompson followed *SAGA* with a short stay at the *Police Gazette*, one of the few jobs he remained forever embarrassed about. He later claimed to have written whole issues of overheated crime stories himself.

Evidently Thompson finally hit bottom in his own mind with his stint at *Police Gazette*. He suspended his drinking and told his agent, Ingrid Hallen, he was sober and ready to write more novels.

Early in 1952, Ingrid Hallen brought Thompson to the offices of Jim Bryans and Arnold Hano of Lion Books, who were looking for writers for a new line of paperback originals. The ensuing association with Hano,

Bryans, and Lion Books yielded the most productive three years and best books of Thompson's career, a time during which, by all accounts, he remained absolutely sober.

Arnold Hano recalled the formation of Lion Books, and how he met Jim Thompson:

> Lion books began as a reprint house, as really all paperback houses were, when I was hired in 1950. It was called Red Circle Books then—I hated that name—we ended up calling it Lion, God knows why.
>
> And then we found we really couldn't bid for the good books to reprint—because we didn't have the money to compete with Bantam and Pocket Books (I had come from Bantam, where I had been managing editor). So we started a line of paperback originals; we weren't the first to do it—Ian Ballantine had started it—but we were among the early ones—Gold Medal also. That way we could get young and new writers to do things for us. And then Jim Bryans, my co-editor, suggested we write synopses of books that had the substance we wanted, and then find writers who could do that sort of book. They were short synopses of about two-thirds of a page.
>
> Fairly early on, Jim Bryans had Jim Thompson and his agent, Ingrid Hallen, come in to meet with us. Jim Thompson was a big sheepdog of a guy, following docilely behind his woman agent, very deferential and polite. He always was the Southern gentleman type. We handed him about five synopses or so, that Bryans and I had worked out—mostly Bryans's. He would take the classics—*Oedipus Rex, Hamlet, Macbeth*—and turn them into modern suspense novels, in synopsis form.
>
> And there was one about a New York City cop who got involved with a prostitute, and ends up killing her. It was a cheapo suspense novel, the first one on the list, and Jim said, "I'll take this one."
>
> And that was how *The Killer Inside Me* was born.
>
> Of course, he took the whole thing and changed it around—made it a Texas deputy sheriff, and did all those other wonderful things to it—but he did begin with that. Also on the list of synopses was *Cropper's Cabin,* the second novel Jim wrote for us.
>
> After he left I remember reading two of his previous novels, the autobiographical one and the mystery, and immediately liking them—not liking them inordinately but liking them.
>
> The arrangement was that you would write three chapters and a synopsis of the remainder, and we would either take it or not on the basis of that. And so not two weeks later he brought in the first 10,000 words or so and a two-page synopsis. I took it home that night and read it—it went through as far as the scene in the jail cell when Lou Ford kills the young Mexican boy. The novel had been okay up until then, but when I got to that scene it exploded on me, and I went, "WOW."
>
> I phoned Jim from work the next morning, and told him how much I

liked it, and we put through the check for the advance, whatever it was (probably $1,000 then and another $1,000 on completion). He finished it within a month of the go-ahead.

Thompson also changed the title of the synopsis to *The Killer Inside Me;* Hano and Bryans's title had been *Sleep With the Devil.*

The unbearably dark view of daily life conveyed in *Now and on Earth,* when combined with themes explored in *Heed the Thunder* and techniques tested in *Nothing More Than Murder,* enabled Jim Thompson to turn a banal, sketchy synopsis about "a New York City cop . . . involved with a prostitute" into a stark novel of ideas written in the voice of the hollowed-out, murderous prophet/savior of a burnt-out, dead-end world.

So Jim Thompson began his association with Lion Books and Arnold Hano, during the first three years of which Thompson would publish thirteen novels, including *The Killer Inside Me, Savage Night,* and *A Hell of a Woman.* For this short time Jim Thompson retreated from his own personal oblivion, sober and committed to writing razor-sharp, pocket-sized trips into the void.

Available at the local newsstand for 25 cents a copy.

SIX

Jim Thompson wrote the bulk of *The Killer Inside Me* while visiting his sister Maxine at the Marine Base in Quantico, Virginia, where she and her husband Joe Kouba were then stationed. Thompson took the train down from New York after getting the assignment from Arnold Hano and Jim Bryans. It's unclear whether he wrote the sample (nearly half) of *The Killer* in New York, and completed it in Quantico, or simply wrote the whole thing down South. Hano does remember first reading the sample, then receiving the finished novel a few weeks later, so it was probably written in two bursts, at least one of which (probably the second) occurred down in Virginia.

Maxine and Joe had an extra room upstairs in their married officer's quarters. Each morning Jim Thompson would be at his typewriter by eight, and Maxine would not see him again until five. Recalls Maxine:

> Jimmie wrote ten pages a day and he'd be so quiet at night, but nice, nice to be around. I guess he was worn out. I don't think it was ever edited. It just came out like he wrote it. Each night I read the next ten pages. I was horrified.
>
> I asked him one night—we'd sit out on the stoop and talk after my husband had gone to bed—I said to him, "What in the world is this, Jimmie, how do you know all this?"
>
> He just said research, a lot of it was research.
>
> And there was a navy doctor who lived next door who loved to sit out with us on the stoop at night and talk to Jimmie. Jimmie would tell stories of the past, the oil fields, and the Writers' Project. He could be so funny when he wanted to be; when he was comfortable with someone, he'd open up a bit.

Sometimes Jimmie would laugh at the strangest things . . . things you'd have to think a minute whether they were funny or not. But they'd really tickle Jimmie.

The process of writing *The Killer* became a habit during the Lion years. He completed most of the books while visiting Maxine, or shut up in a cheap hotel room in New York City if circumstances didn't allow the trip to Virginia. Sharon Thompson Reed recalls that her father believed that any writing he did around the house never sold, so he habitually was away somewhere writing during this time. He was paid about $2,000 per novel by Lion.

Jim Thompson published little besides the nearly bimonthly paperback novel release from September 1952 to June 1955. "Blood From a Turnip" appeared in the December 20, 1952, issue of *Collier's*, as a "short-short," their term for a story that fit onto one of the magazine's oversized pages, illustration included. The "turnip" of the story's title is an old watch, bought by Tulsa Slim, a door-to-door gold buyer. He brings the watch into Duffy's, a gold buyer and wholesaler. Slim is crestfallen, because he bought the watch and a boxful of assorted junk for a few dollars, thinking the watch was quite valuable. But the watch stem won't turn, and now Slim thinks he has a rusted old piece of junk. But Duffy and the narrator, Al, know better; the watch is a valuable collector's item meant to be wound with a jewel-encrusted key.

The sharp Duffy basically steals the watch from Slim, and when the two gold buyers reach the sidewalk outside Al tells Slim how valuable it is. Duffy will get at least fifty bucks for it; and if it had the key, it would fetch five times that. Slim realizes that he *has* the jewel-encrusted key. For once, Duffy won't rook them out of all the profit. He'll have to pay dearly for the key.

In 1988 Lion Books editor Arnold Hano wrote an afterword to the first hardcover edition of *The Killer Inside Me,* published by Craig and Patricia Graham's Blood & Guts Press of Los Angeles. In the afterword, he again recalled meeting Thompson:

I remember his huge size and his gentleness. Soft voice. Diffident manner. Extraordinarily polite with a southern courtesy. Courtliness, perhaps, is better. Deferential to the editor; a shade too deferential. But then I knew nothing about his background. The years he'd spent writing. He was forty-six years old when we met (I was thirty), and he'd spent thirty of those years writing. That's a whole career. With so little to show for it. He'd had bouts of drinking during those years, but he also told us he was dry and had been dry for some time. And that turned out to be true. He would remain dry the first years I knew him.

He smoked lots of cigarettes, letting the butt burn down almost to his fingertips, and he laughed a lot. Quiet chuckles mainly, but occasionally a bigger sound.

I liked him.

He told me early on that he had spent something like nine years in alcoholic institutions. Alberta says that's not so. He may have been on and off away for a while—and she's probably right that he exaggerated.

Anyway, I understood that there was a nine-year period when he was just totally out of it—cause he was trying "to explain" (I don't know when some of his earlier books were published) some gap.

He was forty-six, and was trying to explain where his writing has been—and it hadn't been anyplace for so many years. So he said that he was an alcoholic and institutionalized for nine years.

I tend to go through life taking people at face value until I learn otherwise. And he told me that, so I assumed it to be so. I'm still not sure. Jim would give you the melodramatic side of things and Alberta would gloss them over. Someplace between is the truth.

Anyway he was dry then—he wasn't drinking at all.

And Hano recalled reading *The Killer* for the first time:

He took home the synopsis, and a few weeks later he turned in a chunk of his novel, with a brief outline of the remaining pages.

I read that portion of *The Killer* that night. Immediately I knew it was good, and when he reached the scene of Lou Ford coming to the dark jail cell of young Johnnie Pappas, the Greek kid who'd been arrested with one of the bills that connected him to the first murder, I started to feel the hair on my skin rise. And when Lou Ford reached his hand to the youngster's throat, my brain exploded gently and the top of my head seemed to blow off.

The next day I called Jim. I told him he was writing a terrific book and just to keep it going, and our check for half the advance ($1000 then, $1000 when he finished) would be in the mail within days. It was, and the rest of the novel reached us within a few weeks. He probably wrote the whole thing in less than a month.

According to Hano, *The Killer* and most of Thompson's later Lion novels were printed in a press run of 160,000 to 180,000 books, of which at least 100,000 were sold. Some titles, including *A Hell of a Woman*, later went into a second Lion printing. Lion published nine Thompson novels in 1953–54; as Hano says, "Jim churned them out for us":

He worked fast, yet he worked fastidiously as well. He would write a page on his typewriter and then go over it two or three times or until it pleased him. He had a few theories about writing fiction. He wanted to tell an anecdote—a small story—on every page. Or close to one per page. It made Jim's work much more a series of small stories, linked together. Perhaps this grew out of his pulp days (as has been suggested), but if so he did not have the pulp writer's propensity to throw in purple descriptive paragraphs simply to add wordage; pulp writers often were paid by the word. So he would work on each page as though it were something complete in itself; I never knew another fiction writer to work that way. Most of us would push through as far as we could go, to the end of the novel or the short story if we could. Then we would pretty it up. Jim was different. Each page had to be right. And he set a goal of twenty pages a day. That's a hell of an output, working that way, doing your rewrite as you go along. He didn't always hit his goal; a poor day's volume might have been just ten pages. Phenomenal.

The Thompson family are in agreement with nearly everything Arnold Hano has to say about Jim Thompson except for two long-standing disagreements. The first concerns what Hano wrote about James Sherman Thompson's death and its connection with the writing of *Now and on Earth*, in a brief appreciation of Thompson that appeared in the *Los Angeles Times* at the time of Thompson's death. As previously discussed in the prologue, Hano was told this story by Jim, and that is all he ever claims. Hano is the first to admit he wasn't there, and had no first-hand knowledge of the incident.

The other controversy is somewhat similar in that there really is no dispute. Hano maintains that Jim worked from Lion's synopses for his first two books for the publishers, *The Killer Inside Me* and *Cropper's Cabin*. Alberta Thompson, Patricia Thompson Miller, and Sharon Thompson Reed deny that Jim Thompson ever worked from a synopsis, and are indignant at what they perceive as Hano's attempt to take the credit for Jim Thompson's novels.

Having heard Hano's story a few times, it is clear that he is not trying to take any of the credit for Thompson's books; he's just trying to relate exactly what happened. Arnold Hano marvels at the originality and genius of *The Killer Inside Me;* the synopsis was given to Jim Thompson so that he could produce the *type* of book Hano and Jim Bryans were looking for.

Hano brought up the issue for what he hoped would be the final time in his afterword to the 1988 hardcover edition of *The Killer Inside Me:*

> Now, if you will permit me (or even if you won't; it's my typewriter) I will once again talk about Lion Books and our use of synopses which we gave to some of our interested would-be writers. I have told this story before, and whenever I do, the family, particularly Alberta, Jim's wife,

whom I love dearly and have no desire to tangle with, gets on my back. Jim, they say, never needed anybody to write a synopsis of his novels. Well, I agree. Jim never needed a synopsis. He proved that time and again. But the fact is, he accepted our synopsis of *The Killer Inside Me* and he also accepted a second synopsis and produced from that *Cropper's Cabin.*

That's the truth. I also have said, and I repeat it here, the glory of Jim's writing is what he did with those synopses. He took our banal plot outline and our trite characterizations and he turned them into—well, he turned them into *The Killer Inside Me* and *Cropper's Cabin.*

Take *The Killer,* for a moment. Our synopsis had as its protagonist a big city cop who had a sadistic bent and when he found himself falling in love with a prostitute he'd been ordered to run out of town, he killed her. That was our premise. Look what Jim did to it. He took the sadistic bent, and on page two, he has his protagonist (no longer a big city cop but a Texas deputy sheriff named Lou Ford) indicate the form of the sadism by inflicting cliches upon his cornered listener. And on two thirds of a page he unleashed six lightning cliches, his victim squirming.

That's pure genius. Whoever had thought of triteness as sublimated murder. Jim Thompson, that's who. Just in case you didn't realize the inflicting of those cliches was a sublimated form of murder, Jim concludes that brief page with the chilling thought: "Striking at people that way is almost as good as the other, the real way.". . .

So, yes, he took our synopsis, but no, he wasn't bound by it. He took *The Killer* synopsis and turned it into something very different from what we had in mind. For which I am eternally grateful.

So much for the business of synopses. I hope it is buried forever.

Hano and Bryans's synopsis was little more than the seed of an idea, which in any case Thompson substantially changed. Of course Hano is justifiably proud of his association with Thompson, but his main motivation in telling the story is to illuminate and enhance, not to obscure or diminish, Jim Thompson's accomplishment.

Arnold Hano continued working with Jim Thompson for nearly three years, editing such books as *Savage Night, A Hell of a Woman,* and even *The Nothing Man,* which was published by Dell, not Lion. Hano recalls little editing was required on the Thompson books, or little traditional editing:

> He was never the easiest person to do any rewriting—what he turned in, more or less, is what we went with. I had some questions, he sometimes got more obscure than what I wanted. Of course, some of his power is his obscurity—but sometimes I wanted him to explain to me what he was trying to say, so that he and I could talk it through. And maybe he could

write it so it would be less obscure to the average person who wasn't going to fight his way through it like we were.

Problem was, he didn't always know what it was he was wanted to say—what he said was what he said. To try to explain it was very difficult for him, he had done it, and any explanation of it would have been different.

So impressed was Hano with Thompson's *Savage Night* that he later asked Thompson if he could use it as the basis for a Western he was writing. Flattered, Thompson said sure, and Hano wrote *Flint,* a paperback original with substantially the same plot as *Savage Night.* Written in both first and third person, the Western fails to capture the lyrical lunacy of the Thompson original. Hano, who wrote the novel under the pen name Gil Dodge, intended to thank Jim Thompson on the dedication page, but Gold Medal omitted the dedication.

Arnold Hano summed up the origin and aims of Lion Books, and his rather unconscious support of a set of writers that were developing a new kind of fiction:

> We had two original novelists, Jim and David Karp, who we liked and nurtured, and felt very proud at having. More people at Lion, including Martin Goodman, the publisher, felt that Karp was the better writer, and I knew that Jim was the better writer. Karp was the slicker, more conventional writer, a suspense writer.
>
> We also did a David Goodis novel, more than one I think. Without knowing what we were doing, I gather that we were developing a whole *serie noire,* black, Horace McCoy kind of suspense novel to a greater degree than anyone else had. For that, I guess, I take some credit. All the books that were chosen I chose, whether I found them originally or not I was the last word. Martin Goodman would just okay it. Sometimes Goodman would ball me out for a dirty word—he didn't like to see the word shit in print, but I snuck it by him a few times. So we had a line of books that were quite good.
>
> We did some other things. When I was at Bantam I wanted to reprint *All Quiet on the Western Front.* I had assumed it had been reprinted, so asked one of my bosses "How come no one's ever done that?" He said, "Well, it's a pacifist book, and we don't want to fool with that." This was during the cold war.
>
> So when I got to Lion it was one of the first things I did. We did a Millen Brand novel called *The Outward Room.* We did a bunch of things that were pretty good, or a little left wing that were pretty good. We did eight books a month; it was a lot to do, but I enjoyed it.
>
> Later I did a Western novel for Gold Medal, and the print run was something like 400,000—the print runs were wild in those days, the books

sold for a quarter. So today it sounds like—100,000 of a Jim Thompson novel sold—that's a lot, but that really wasn't a lot of copies for that time.

I guess we didn't realize we were under pricing the books. We knew we could print them up and sell them for a quarter and still make a nickel. It was a sensational buy, but we didn't realize it. Bantam eventually raised the price to fifty cents, but we stayed at twenty-five a long time.

And finally, Arnold Hano offers his opinion of the nature of Jim Thompson and his work:

Jim Thompson was not a pulp writer. I never knew quite what he was, except he was like Horace McCoy but I liked him better. He was like James M. Cain, but I liked him better. There was that inevitability of the Greek tragedy that you see in his things.

I thought Thompson's were good to great books, but I was in the minority, even at the publishing house. I never thought it through much, but I was very glad to have Jim on my list. And since Jim seemed to very much enjoy working with me, it was a very good arrangement.

It occurred to me very early on that what Jim needed was encouragement, more than he needed anything else. You unleash a guy like that, you don't direct him.

In New York he'd rent a hotel room and do his writing there. Often I think he'd finish up his novels renting a hotel room in some terrible hotel. Never a good hotel. Bursts of five or six hours at a time, pounding away at the typewriter.

I suspect he was most alive when he was writing, and other things were just not as important to him.

SEVEN

The Killer Inside Me, published September 1952.
Cropper's Cabin, published November 1952.
Recoil, published February 1953.
The Alcoholics, published January 1953.
Bad Boy, published June 1953.
Savage Night, published July 1953.
The Criminal, published December 1953.
The Golden Gizmo, published February 1954.
Roughneck, published March 1954.
A Swell-Looking Babe, published June 1954.
A Hell of a Woman, published July 1954.
The Nothing Man, published late 1954.
After Dark, My Sweet, published early 1955.

*B*ad *Boy* and *Roughneck,* Jim Thompson's fictionalized, tall-tale "autobiographies," trace his life up until the time of his first published novel in 1942. As we know, a few of the accounts in the two novels are based on real events in Thompson's life and these do provide valuable insights of his attitudes and feelings.

Both *Bad Boy* and *Roughneck* predominantly offer a series of improbable escapades and mythical tales. Very likely many of the adventure yarns Thompson picked up in his wanderings among the oil fields of West Texas and Oklahoma made their way into these books as having happened to him or to his sidekick, the pesky con man Allie Ivers. Narrated with a

Nine Thompson first-edition covers from the 1950s.

sort of jovial hopelessness by a roustabout who dreams of being a writer, the mood and atmosphere of these two books reveal more about Thompson's youth than most of the adventures chronicled in their pages.

One rather startling passage from *Bad Boy* describes a West Texas deputy sheriff with a peculiar, frightening personality. The deputy drives forty miles out of town to pick up Thompson for his failure to appear in court on a disturbing-the-peace violation. Thompson, high up on an oil derrick above the deputy sheriff, thinks for a few moments that he has the upper hand in the situation; he drops down a piece of the block, nearly hitting the implacable deputy on the head. Finally, with a laugh, Thompson climbs down.

> He was a good-looking guy. His hair was coal-black beneath his pushed-back Stetson, and his black intelligent eyes were set wide apart in a tanned, fine-featured face. He grinned at me as I dropped down in front of him on the derrick floor.
>
> "Now, that wasn't very smart," he said. "And that's—"
>
> "And that's a fact," I snapped. "All right, let's get going."
>
> He went on grinning at me. In fact, his grin broadened a little, but it was fixed, humorless, and a veil seemed to drop over his eyes.
>
> "What makes you so sure," he said, softly, "you're going anywhere?"
>
> "Well, I—" I gulped. "I—I—"
>
> "Awful lonesome out here, ain't it? Ain't another soul for miles around but you and me."
>
> "L-look," I said. "I'm—I wasn't trying to—"
>
> "Lived here all my life," he went on, softly. "Everyone knows me. No one knows you. And we're all alone. What do you make o' that, a smart fella like you? You've been around. You're all full of piss and high spirits. What do you think an ol' stupid country boy might do in a case like this?"
>
> He stared at me, steadily, the grin baring his teeth. I stood paralyzed and wordless, a great cold lump forming in my stomach. The wind whined and moaned through the derrick. He spoke again, as though in answer to a point I had raised.
>
> "Don't need one," he said. "Ain't nothin' you can do with a gun that you can't do a better way. Don't see nothin' around here I'd need a gun for."
>
> He shifted his feet slightly. The muscles in his shoulders bunched. He took a pair of black kid gloves from his pocket, and drew them on, slowly. He smacked his fist into the palm of his other hand.
>
> "I'll tell you something," he said. "Tell you a couple of things. There ain't no way of telling what a man is by looking at him. There ain't no way of knowing what he'll do if he has the chance. You think maybe you can remember that?"
>
> I couldn't speak, but I managed a nod. His grin and his eyes went back to normal.

As he goes on to write, the deputy posed a great riddle to Thompson—
had he been bluffing, or had he meant to kill him? The man haunted
Thompson for years, and many times he tried to capture the character on
paper:

> The riddle, of course, lay not so much in him as me. I tended to see
> things in black and white, with no intermediate shadings. I was too prone
> to categorize—naturally, using myself as the norm. The deputy had
> behaved first one way, then another, then the first again. And in my
> ignorance I saw this as complexity instead of simplicity.
>
> He had gone as far as his background and breeding would allow to be
> amiable. I hadn't responded to it, so he had taken another tack. It was
> simple once I saw things through his eyes instead of my own.
>
> I didn't know whether he would have killed me, because he didn't know
> himself.
>
> Finally, as I matured, I was able to re-create him on paper—the sardonic,
> likeable murderer of my fourth novel, *The Killer Inside Me*. But I was a
> long time in doing it—almost thirty years.
>
> And I still haven't got him out of my mind.

A chance meeting out in the far West Texas oil fields, and the
long-term effect it had on Jim Thompson's thinking and writing, is in no
small way responsible for Thompson's brilliant first-person novels of the
criminal mind. Thompson's ability to crawl inside a character's head and
view the world from a new perspective opened up a wide range of
narrative and thematic possibilities.

Because Thompson himself was leading a kind of double life, a lonely
intellectual submerged beneath a rather banal family man, his split-
narration first-person narratives closely resemble the state of his own
mind and life. Thompson himself was quite used to saying one thing, and
meaning another; used to watching the world from a secret place, never
giving voice to his true thoughts. Thompson's first-person narratives
allowed him to be himself, in a way that is both poignant and frightening.

Conversely, Thompson's third-person crime novels generally lack the
impact and cohesiveness of the first-person books; oddly schizophrenic in
their own right, they are never as analytical or objective as Thompson
probably intended. In the first-person narrations, the occasional lapses
into philosophy, social observation, and commentary on the human
condition work on two levels: what the narrators are actually saying, and
what their statements say about them. Thus the random attacks and flights
of ranting that seem out of place in the third person, in the first person
reveal the twisted mind of the narrator even as they map the twisted
terrain of his world. These crime novel passages often prove to be

Thompson's most autobiographical writing, offering more truth than any anecdote from *Bad Boy* or *Roughneck.*

Only when he slipped into the voice of a deputy sheriff, or a collection agent, or a hit man—shallow personas which the world took at face value but veiled razor-sharp, disturbed depths—could Jim Thompson give full vent to the rage inside *him.*

The Golden Gizmo, the eighth Thompson novel published by Lion Books, was actually written years before any of the other Lion novels, when Thompson and family were living in San Diego. Thompson came up with the idea in the mid-1940s, evidently inspired by his brief stint as a door-to-door gold buyer. Recalls Arnold Hano:

> *The Golden Gizmo* Jim had written before he came to us, and he brought it into me one day, and I took it home and read it, and I liked it pretty well, but not as much as the stuff he had been doing for us. We made a few changes. We suggested that we not pay him as much for that as for something he did fresh for us. I think he was a little hurt by that. But it wasn't as good, and it was already finished. I don't know, we did skinflint people, that wasn't very nice. Instead of $2,000 he got $1,500 for that one.

The Golden Gizmo is the well-plotted, somewhat awkwardly written story of Todd Kent; the gizmo of the title is his talent and his curse. A sort of inner radar for the big money, the gizmo has led Kent through the usual marginal con man occupations, from bellboy to crap shooter. Now, he seems to have a perfect setup, buying gold for honest Milt Vonderheim, whose store lends Toddy a much-needed air of legitimacy.

We come upon Toddy the day his world falls apart, when he inadvertently steals a solid gold watch from a man who also numbers among his possessions a face with no chin and a fearsome talking dog. Toddy then returns to his hotel room to find his wife "murdered." He promptly flees, but can find no escape; soon he is neck-deep in a Nazi scheme to smuggle large quantities of gold out of the United States. By the end, Toddy has learned the truth about Elaine, his psychotic wife; Milt, his evil boss; and Dolores, his new love. As usual, the "truth" of each character's essence is pondered throughout, and that truth, when finally ascertained, seems arbitrary and indeterminable.

Narrated in the third person, *The Golden Gizmo* has none of the obsessional themes or structural symmetry that marks Thompson's better third-person novels. It's basically a good piece of genre writing; despite some Freudian underpinning the novel has little psychological resonance.

The same can be said of *The Alcoholics,* a "twenty-four-hour" novel about an alcoholic asylum, its staff, and patients. Probably Thompson's worst novel, it is obtuse, sermonizing, and nearly plotless; it doesn't even offer the expected insights into Thompson's own battle with alcohol. Upon reflection this is no surprise, since Thompson never did conquer fully his alcoholism.

Recalls Arnold Hano:

> Only *Killer* and *Cropper's Cabin* were commissioned. Later Jim would say, "Well, I want to do a book about alcoholics." His marketing theory was "There are forty million alcoholics, I'll sell forty million books." And I said okay, sure, but it's gotta be a novel. We talked about it, and we decided it would be one of those twenty-four-hour novels. So I said okay, Jim, do it. And mostly that was what I did, I just gave him the green light.

The Alcoholics takes place entirely during what is likely the last day of El Healtho sanatorium, an alcoholic asylum run by Dr. Pasteur Semelweiss Murphy. Murphy must come up with $15,000 to pay off his creditors and keep the place open; he thinks himself a failure, having let down both himself and his patients. In fact, he has not cured one man of alcoholism yet.

His only chance to raise the money is to accept the job of "burying" the latest arrival to the sanatorium, an embarrassment to a rich family who has just been given a prefrontal lobotomy. If Dr. Murphy agrees to "take care of" the patient (which he isn't qualified to do) while keeping the whole matter quiet, the family will give him the money to keep his asylum running.

What to do about the lobotomy case weighs on the doctor's mind as he goes through the rounds of this extraordinary (and decidedly improbable) day. Murphy rapes his sadistic head nurse, thus curing her of her illness and making her fall in love with him; he delivers a baby to a patient he didn't realize was pregnant; and, of course, he cures all the patients of their alcoholism. To top it all off, Murphy tricks the rich family's doctor into signing complete control of the lobotomy case over to him, enabling Murphy to then blackmail the family. Murphy thus gets both the needed money and proper care for the patient.

The Alcoholics is most memorable for the check-in to El Healtho by Thompson himself, which closes the novel. Murphy recognizes him as just the man to do a certain job:

> "Better rig up a saline drip . . . What's his name, anyway, his job? His job?"
>
> "Couldn't quite get his name, Doctor. But he was babbling something about being a writer."

"Well, we'll wash out his bloodstream, get him back to work as soon as possible. That's what all these birds need. Something to keep—grab him!"

They grabbed him together, the puke-smeared, wild-eyed wreck who staggered suddenly into the corridor. He struggled for a moment, then went limp in their arms sobbing helplessly.

"T-tomcats," he wept. "S-sonsbitches t-thirty-four f-feet tall an' . . . n' got eighteen tails, n' . . . n' . . ."

"Yeah?" said Doctor Murphy."

". . . n' oysters for eyeballs."

Doctor Murphy chuckled grimly. "Yes, sir," he said, "we'll knock him out, wash him out, and get him back to work. I've got a job all picked out for this character."

"A job? I don't—"

"C-cats," sobbed the writer. "N' every damn one a lyric soprano . . ."

Doctor Murphy regarded him fondly. "A grade-A nut," he said. "A double-distilled screwball. Just the man to write a book about this place."

Recoil is about as close to a straight suspense thriller as Jim Thompson ever wrote. Because the narrator, an ex-convict named Pat Cosgrove, is not a psychopathic killer, *Recoil* does not feature the free-floating rationalizations, bursts of violence, or unknowable motivations of Thompson's more characteristic first-person novels. Here, the first-person narration works almost entirely on another plane: it supplies the pieces of a puzzle which Cosgrove must solve before a trap is sprung that will end his life or send him back to prison. Since Pat Cosgrove is not chiefly investigating his own motivations and guilt, *Recoil* is one of Thompson's lighter books, although the intricate plot makes it a swift and satisfying one.

Pat "Airplane Red" Cosgrove was a bright teenager trapped in a seemingly dead-end life when he foolishly tried to escape it by robbing a bank. He was caught, tried, convicted, and sentenced to ten years to life by a judge whom he kidnapped in his getaway attempt. Fifteen years later, he is still in Sandstone Prison, since he has no family to take an interest in getting him paroled. One of his letters asking for help falls into the hands of Doc Luther, a corrupt political lobbyist for whom Cosgrove represents the final element needed in an unexplained plot.

Luther cashes in a lot of political favors to obtain Cosgrove's parole, including help from his lawyer, Hardesty, and several state senators. The one honest political official in the state is Myrtle Briscoe, head of the parole board, who had to be tricked into letting Cosgrove out. Briscoe is certain that Luther is up to no good, and intends to keep an eye on him.

Cosgrove soon is of the same mind, when he gets to know his benefactor and realizes Luther does no one such a great favor as he has done him without getting something out of it. Luther obtains for

Cosgrove a sinecure on the State Highway Commission, and puts him up at his own house. The only problem for Cosgrove seems to be the behavior of the beautiful Mrs. Luther, who is less than discreet in her advances toward Red. Cosgrove fears that if Doc finds out about him and Mrs. Luther, Doc will have him sent back to Sandstone.

The other major character is Madeline, a mysterious figure who works for Luther in some unknown capacity. Cosgrove and she fall for each other right away, and he visits her almost daily, confiding in her his worries and concerns.

Soon Cosgrove's head is spinning, since everything he knows about Doc Luther, Hardesty, Madeline, and Lila Luther could point two ways. Any of them could be on his side, and any of them could be out to murder him:

> But what about Hardesty? Why, when he so obviously distrusted and detested Doc, had he told him of my visit? He wanted me to share his distrust and hatred. He meant to work me up to the point where I would. That was my answer: I was not yet, in his opinion, sufficiently worked up. I was not ready to be used. Until I was, he was chiefly interested in seeing that I did nothing which might cause me to be returned to Sandstone.
>
> Myrtle Briscoe—I stopped in my pacing and sat down again. Myrtle. She was using me to get Doc. I was a rope she was giving him to hang himself.
>
> And Doc . . . Doc had foreseen that she would know, and guessed that she would react as she had. He was tolling out rope of his own. He was certain he could tighten it before she could tighten hers.
>
> And Mrs. Luther? Was she working with one of the three or did she, too, have a plan?
>
> And Madeline . . . ?
>
> No, not Madeline. I'd never had the slightest doubt about her. My instinct told me just one thing about her: that she was good and that she loved me. If I was wrong about that, then I was wrong about everything. And maybe I was.
>
> I didn't know anything. All I had was guesses. Guesses which, when you probed them and tried to follow them out, became ridiculous.

This impossibility of ascertaining anyone's true innocence or guilt is axiomatic in Thompson's crime novels, having evolved from Lincoln Fargo's observation in *Heed the Thunder* that we can't be sure of anything, except that the other fellow's out to get us if he gets the chance. Only by living by "Fargo's creed" do the inhabitants of the Thompson world defend themselves against that which they are unable to fathom. Think the worst of other people, the best of yourself, be always on the lookout. This tenet is the foundation upon which Thompson built novels as diverse as *The Criminal, Recoil,* and *The Killer Inside Me.*

Sensing the trap is closing fast around him, Cosgrove hires a private detective to investigate his suspicions. The detective is quickly murdered, and Cosgrove unwittingly frames himself for the crime.

The denouement involves an insurance scheme, the identity of Luther's real wife, the betrayal of Luther by Hardesty, and a full pardon for Cosgrove. Myrtle Briscoe comes to the rescue at the last moment and hauls the bad guys away. Madeline, whom Cosgrove believed was playing a role, actually does love him, and they start a life together.

Cropper's Cabin concerns eighteen-year-old Tom Carver, another bright young man trapped in a dead-end life. At the beginning of the novel Tom offers the "facts" of his life: he has labored out on the cotton fields for as long as he can remember, having been raised by his adopted father and Mary, a woman thirteen years his elder whom Pa supposedly took from a large family glad to be rid of her.

Tom is in love with Donna, the beautiful daughter of Matthew Ontime, the largest landowner and wealthiest Indian in the county. While many other white families sharecrop Ontime's land, the Carvers consider themselves a little above the rest. They own ten acres, smack in the middle of Ontime's land, as well as cropping forty more for him.

That ten acres is the cause of great trouble between Pa Carver and Ontime. Carver has had countless lucrative offers for the mineral rights to his ten acres—offers which are invariably withdrawn when the oil company finds that Ontime won't allow his surrounding land to be drilled. Carver can't understand why Ontime won't approve the drilling, and is tortured by the fortune the Indian is preventing him from acquiring. He's certain that if he sells his land to Ontime, the Indian would then drill all the land.

When Ontime is stabbed and dumped into the hog trough at his estate, Tom is accused of the murder. This triggers Tom's discovery of the truth of many things, most important the fact that Pa is his real father, and his mother died while giving birth to him, alone. Pa stayed in the city sleeping with a whore for three straight days, only to return to find his dead wife and infant son. The whore, of course, was Mary, whom Pa has kept trapped and frustrated on the farm all these years.

Kossmeyer, the great lawyer (and one of the few continuing characters of the Thompson world), is brought in to defend Tom on the murder charge by Tom's teacher and the school principal. Kossmeyer's defense entails smearing Donna Ontime's good name, and Tom does get off lightly with twenty years in jail. But he is inconsolable for another reason:

he knows that things will never be the same between Donna and him again. The hate and mistrust caused by the trial will never fully go away.

After a hellish few months in prison, Tom is cleared when Abe Toolate, a no-good Indian whom his people have mysteriously condemned to a living death, confesses to the murder. All the months in prison Tom has dreamed of his return to the sharecropper's farm, of chopping up his father and Mary, who betrayed and framed him.

But what he finds upon his return to the farm is not what he had dreamed. Mary has abandoned the old man, resuming her previous profession out on the oil fields; his father has let everything waste away. Tom begins to help his father, despite knowing he will be trapped in the same life once again; there seems nothing he can do about it. Then his wheedling, evil father tries to put him back to work, and Tom is freed from his sense of duty and pity toward the old man.

He walks down the road, and finds Donna at their old rendezvous, where they dream of the life they will have together.

Cropper's Cabin is a mediocre performance by Jim Thompson, showing signs of being rushed out with little inspiration; not surprising, considering that Thompson had just finished writing *The Killer Inside Me*. Still, Tom Carver's first-person narration has that distinctive put-upon, had-enough attitude, defining him as a true descendant of *Now and on Earth*'s James Dillon. His trip into psychic and physical hell charts the course from boyhood to manhood, but he averts having circumstance make him a true criminal. The happy ending, in which Carver reconciles with Donna Ontime, is not what Thompson originally intended. According to Arnold Hano:

> His endings would sometimes puzzle me, or not be clear enough, or not satisfy me. When we did *Cropper's Cabin* we asked him if he could come up with a more upbeat ending, and he said, oh, like ———, and he mentioned another novel, and I said yeah, like that. And he said sure. In that instance he was able to do that—upbeat—that removed him from his own life, and his own feelings about things, and he could be the craftsman.
>
> But since he tended to think only in the downbeat, dark side of things in his writing and in his internal life—he didn't always seem able to step back from that.

The revised ending of *Cropper's Cabin* contradicts Thompson's belief that the hate that grows from suspicion and misunderstanding leaves a residue that never goes away. At the last moment, as Tom Carver sees Donna, another voice inside his head tells him what really lies in store for the two of them:

She kept on coming, and I began to tremble; in another second I knew I'd be running . . . Save something? Hell, how could a man save something when he couldn't save himself? There was a great silence, and out of it came only one voice, yelling at me to run and keep on running forever. Yelling at me not to do anything, not to try to rebuild. *You'll be disappointed, Tom. It just isn't worth the disappointment, and heartbreak. They'll never forget that trial, kid. They'll never let you or her forget it. They'll laugh at you; or worse, they'll pity you. And you're ignorant, uneducated, and your health isn't good and— What can you do anyway? What can you rebuild with? Think it over, Tommy. Think of everything you've got to fight. Keep thinking—that you'll lose even if you win. Then go and hide. Bury yourself. And stay buried. Run away from—*

Her hands went around mine, steadying them on the nest. And it was odd that they should steady them, for hers were trembling, too, but that's the way it was. Like in algebra, sort of; the two minuses together had made a plus.

Tom Carver seems determined to face the rest of his life, fully aware of the difficulties ahead of him. Despite Thompson's uncharacteristically upbeat ending, the grimmer passages of *Cropper's Cabin* leave a lasting impression on the reader. A few months later Thompson wrote *The Criminal,* again in which a teenage boy is accused of murder, and Thompson more explicitly indicts society for its role in *murder,* a society in which murder seems far from the worst crime.

The Criminal is a masterful, underrated Jim Thompson novel, directly addressing one of the underlying themes of his body of work. Narrated in the first person by ten different characters over fourteen chapters, the novel is a structural tour de force. Ostensibly a murder mystery, *The Criminal* is a study of collective guilt.

The story is straightforward enough: a young teenage boy, Robert Talbert, is suspected of raping and murdering the girl next door, who by all accounts has grown to be a flirtatious tramp. Having no real evidence against Talbert, the D.A. is leaning toward dismissing the case when the godlike local newspaper owner, the Captain, decides to make the case a front-page sensation. The boy is then badgered into a confession, and Kossmeyer, the famous lawyer, is hired to get him off. Eventually Kossmeyer pays some Negro squatters to give the boy an alibi (it's unclear whether they're lying); still the case is not dismissed. Finally the Captain, whose paper is now suffering because of the excessive hammering it gave to Talbert, orders the story slant swung the other way, and the boy is set free.

The Criminal is a subtle, satirical novel, which indicts and implicates nearly every character within its pages, up to and including the Captain, the God substitute. Substitute, for in this world there is no God, only those who play the part—and almost all the characters take a crack at it. With various degrees of self-awareness, each rationalizes his own role in the murder, and his own accountability for what is happening and has happened, due to their own actions or inactions. The resultant portrait of a hateful world is bleaker, subtler, and harder to dismiss than those painted by the more violent and idiosyncratic psychotic narrators of other Thompson novels. There's no denying the resemblance *The Criminal's* world bears to our own, or the familiarity of each seemingly innocent narrator.

William Willis, the *Star* reporter assigned to do the hatchet job on the teenage boy (a dirty job given to him because of his union activities), is one of the clearest-eyed narrators. He decides to give his superiors more than they asked for in a nasty story, but can only hope that the boy is guilty:

> I was rationalizing, hoping subconsciously that the kid was guilty. I couldn't be impartial. I was using him, swinging him as the club in my grudge play against the *Star;* I was going to knock his brains out in the course of trepanning Dudley and Skysmith, and I needed justification. If he was guilty, good. If he was innocent, bad. Very bad. That would make me a supersonic jet-propelled heel instead of the slow-flying, propeller-driven model which I had become reasonably well adjusted to.

Clinton, the supposedly ethical district attorney, has a sudden change of opinion concerning the boy's guilt when Willis tells him what he's going to write in the paper; Clinton then gives the boy the third degree until he signs a confession.

Kossmeyer, later arguing with the D.A. to drop the charges, explains how bad it'll be for the boy, even if he is let go. It's an echo of the voice telling Tom Carver what lies ahead for him, at the end of *Cropper's Cabin:*

> "And Clint, that still leaves it plenty bad for the boy. It leaves it lousy for him and his parents. If he walked out of the place this minute, he'd still be getting the rawest deal a kid could get. He'll suffer for it the rest of his life. Think of it, Clint! Think of what it's going to mean to him at school, and after he leaves school, starts looking for a job, or when he meets some nice gal and wants to get married . . . Would you want a child of yours to run around with a kid who was the prime suspect in a rape-murder case? . . .
> Don't tell me people will forget. They'll forget all right—that he wasn't

convicted. It's like the old song: the words are ended but the melody lingers on. And it'll get louder and uglier wherever he goes, whatever he does, as long as he lives."

The D.A's tormenting wife gleefully strikes to the heart of the matter, when she asks him why he's not dismissing the case, despite the testimony exonerating the boy. Clinton responds to her, and to himself:

> "I thought it [the new evidence] was reasonably conclusive, and I believed that the public would think it was. Since the public apparently wasn't and isn't completely convinced, I may have been wrong. At any rate, I can't dismiss the case."
>
> She nodded slowly. Her forehead puckered in a frown, creasing the face cream into white, greasy little worms.
>
> "I see," she said. "Then, it doesn't really matter whether he's guilty or not, does it? Whether he could actually prove that he was innocent. It isn't what he is, but what other people are. If they say he's guilty—"

When the D.A. tries to cite the newspaper as a reflection of public opinion, and then denies that he's influenced by it, his wife laughs him down. He protests even more vehemently:

> "I'm not influenced by the newspapers, but I am by public opinion as reflected in the newspapers. They don't mold it or make that opinion, to any great extent, but they do reflect it. They're a barometer of what the public wants, or is about to want. They may get a little ahead of the public, but they're never behind it. They're never greatly in disagreement with it. When they are, they get in agreement quickly or they go out of business . . . Do you understand what I'm saying, Arlene?"
>
> "Of course. Certainly, dear." She nodded earnestly. "Not influenced by newspapers . . . only what's in newspapers. Is that right, darling?"
>
> "You know it isn't!" I said. "You're deliberately twisting my words. What I said was that—that—oh, to hell with it."
>
> "Poor darling." She patted my arm. "I just hate myself for being so silly and stupid when you have so many troubles."

A world where appearance is more important than reality, and opinion more important than fact, begs the very question of guilt and innocence. Subconsciously knowing, but never consciously admitting, the evil they are capable of, each character in the novel is more than willing to let Robert Talbert be "guilty." His role as scapegoat allows them to believe that "evil" is "out there" and to go on ignoring the unacknowledged, truer guilt within themselves.

Donald Skysmith, chief editor of the *Star* and answerable only to The Captain himself, has a different motivation for his actions: his wife is dying of cancer, and he must go on doing The Captain's bidding in order to care for her. Fully aware of the evil consequences of the schemes that The Captain orders carried out, Skysmith dreams of one day incinerating the old man: "I'd kill him! By God, I would kill him! I'd sneak into that castle at night, and he'd be ass deep in teletype flimsies and whores, and I'd have that good old gasoline and those good old matches—big kitchen matches—and I'd burn him alive! BURN HIM—."

The Criminal concludes when Skysmith finally disobeys an order from The Captain:

> ". . . I suggest you go downstairs and get yourself a cup of coffee."
> "N-No! No," I said, "Who the hell do you think you are, anyway? Who the hell do you think you are? Do you think you're God?"
> "Yes. Don't you think that you are? Get the coffee, Don."

Skysmith goes to a bar and gets a shot of whiskey rather than a cup of coffee, and the omniscient Captain calls him at the bar and fires him. But before he hangs up, The Captain seems to have one more thing to say:

> "Spit it out!" I said. "What have you got to say?"
> He coughed apologetically. He didn't sound at all like The Captain.
> "I'm afraid I can't say it, Don. I don't seem to be able to find the words to express what I feel. All I can say is that I'm sorry. I was very sorry to learn of Teddy's death."

Without the burden of his wife's illness, Skysmith is freed of The Captain's control, and the novel ends. The question of whether the boy actually murdered the girl is never answered.

In *The Criminal,* Thompson offers a full-length meditation on one of his favorite sayings: "Better the blind man that pisseth out the window than the knowing servant who leads him thereto." Thompson always saved his highest contempt for those who *have* a choice, those who were *not* born with "the crooked cue," yet still propagate evil. The people who, actively or passively, are responsible for the fact that the lives of millions of their fellow men are nearly unbearable: politicians, bureaucrats, management men—anyone with the power to change things for the better but who doesn't do it, because of a lack of courage or caring.

These people may have excuses, but so do those they've driven to violence and murder. Thompson's interest lies with the plight of the killers, who can act only in the way that nature and circumstance compel them.

* * *

Jim Thompson's best crime novels are meditations on the nature of guilt and culpability in a deterministic society; depictions of the desperate need to recover a lost innocence or discover a new one, in an upside-down world; chronicles of the crimes of compulsive killers, as they search for answers to fill the yawning emptiness inside themselves. The free-floating "personality" of *The Killer Inside Me*'s Lou Ford is the unknowable essence of others internalized: the unknowable becomes self. Lincoln Fargo's creed that one can't know anybody else's motivations, what's in their heart, is extended in *The Killer Inside Me, A Hell of a Woman,* and *Savage Night* to the unknowable, unexplainable capacity for evil within a single human heart.

Lou Ford has his capacity for evil underlined by his father's reaction to his sadomasochistic affair with Helene, the housekeeper, when Lou is fourteen. Lou did not realize what he was doing was wrong—in fact, Helene approached Lou because his father was no longer servicing her in that way—in an Oedipal twist, Lou was only doing what his father had done. The ensuing condemnation of his actions as weird, twisted, and evil leaves Ford uncertain of any of his actions, or from where they spring. Seeking revenge against Helene, he sexually assaults a little girl, and his adopted brother, Mike, takes the blame.

Lou frantically searches for the source of his compulsions, probing his own motivations, only to find no answer. Eventually he is rendered hollow inside by the festering of this unresolved adolescent crisis, and can only fill the emptiness with a semblance of personality. How he's *supposed* to act, since his "true nature" has been condemned as dangerous and evil.

The resultant mask which Ford dons to live the daily life of a dumb deputy sheriff in the small town that is his prison becomes in itself a more stifling prison. His very real personality crisis assumes epic proportions when the mask ensures the further rotting of whatever true personality lies beneath it. Ford tries to resolve the "two sides" of him, despite knowing it's impossible: "All I can do is wait until I split. Right down the middle."

In fact, by the end of his story Lou Ford is as uncertain of the reality of what is "inside him" as he is certain of the emptiness of the bland, kidding persona that is "outside him." These two versions of Lou Ford may fight each other for control, but neither can fully cover or begin to fill the utter emptiness of his soul. In the end, when Ford is feverishly searching for a reason *why,* he finally recognizes that even the "condition," *the sickness,* is not answer enough.

Dolly Dillon—the narrator of *A Hell of a Woman*—lacks Ford's self-awareness, but offers a sharply delineated schematic of a similar war waged inside himself when his very narrative splits, representing the two sides of his rent psyche. Charlie Bigger of *Savage Night* searches for an answer to the riddle of his hollow self right up to the end, hoping the answer might reveal itself in death.

In *The Killer Inside Me, A Hell of a Woman,* and *Savage Night* Jim Thompson extended his vision of the culpability and guilt of a lost society to the interior of the marginal products of that society—where a horrible internal battle is waged. More than the irreparable split, the emptiness and uncertainty of the dualities that fight for control of personality—good and evil, innocence and guilt, love and hate, success and failure—are the ultimate horror awaiting Lou Ford, Dolly Dillon, and Charlie Bigger. Their internal struggles to understand what is in fact a meaningless void echo the moral vacuum at the center of a whole society, as best conveyed in Thompson's *The Criminal.*

The inverted society that relies on conscious or unconscious manipulation of appearance and reality, rather than acknowledge the capacity for "evil" inherent in both it and its members, becomes the true *Criminal;* its naturally bred killers both toxic by-products and victims.

Lou Ford opens *The Killer Inside Me* with a depiction of the incessant needling that has become his only safe method of lashing out at people. An intelligent man forced to live the life of a corny, boring deputy sheriff in a small West Texas town, Ford believes he can never live a normal life. He has spent the years since an unresolved psychosexual adolescent crisis burying the truth of the event deep inside himself. He explains that a fresh sadomasochistic relationship with Joyce Lakeland, a prostitute that he was supposed to run out of town, has reopened the psychic floodgates and started him toward the revenge scheme that will bring about his downfall:

> She began fumbling at my tie, my shirt, starting to undress me after I'd almost skinned her alive.
> I went back the next day and the day after that. I kept going back. And it was like a wind had been turned on a dying fire. I began needling people in that dead-pan way—needling 'em as a substitute for something else. I began thinking about settling scores with Chester Conway, of the Conway Construction Company.
> I won't say that I hadn't thought of it before. Maybe I'd stayed on in Central City all these years, just in hopes of getting even. But except for her I don't think I'd ever have done anything. She'd made the old fire burn again.

Joyce has even shown Lou the way to get even with Conway, the object of his revenge—Conway's no-good son Elmer is in love with Joyce and wants to run away with her. Lou, who has been relating all this in flashback, steps out of the Greek's diner and is hit up by a bum. He doesn't know it then, but he makes the biggest mistake of his life:

> "Something to warm you up, eh?" I said.
> "Yeah, anything at all you can help me with, I'll . . ."
> I took the cigar out of my mouth with one hand and made like I was reaching into my pocket with the other. Then I grabbed his wrist and ground the cigar butt into his palm.

After flashing his badge and telling the astonished bum to scram, Ford meets with Joe Rothman, the head of the local building trades union. They discuss the mysterious circumstances of the death of Lou's adopted brother, Mike—a death Ford knows was engineered by Conway, because Mike, in his capacity as building inspector, was going to cost Conway a lot of money rebuilding a below-code project. Mike took the blame for Lou's assault on a three-year-old girl when Lou was sixteen:

> "Dad and I knew Mike hadn't done it. I mean"—I hesitated—"knowing Mike, we were sure he couldn't be guilty." *Because I was. Mike had taken the blame for me.* "I wanted Mike to come back. So did Dad." *He wanted him here to watch over me.*

Rothman's information is not new to Lou Ford. He has known for a long time that Conway killed his brother—but he lets Rothman think he's satisfied that Mike's death was an accident. Rothman sees through Ford's dumb act, and tells Lou to "save the bullshit for the birds."

Lou returns home, where he relaxes by reading a few articles in foreign languages and working out a few calculus problems. He ponders his fate, why he lives a charade:

> Dad had wanted me to be a doctor, but he was afraid to have me go away to school so he'd done what he could for me at home. It used to irritate him, knowing what I had in my head, to hear me talking and acting like any other rube around town. But, in time, when he realized how bad I had *the sickness,* he even encouraged me to do it. That's what I was going to be; I was going to have to live and get along with rubes.

Lou is surprised by Amy Stanton, the town schoolteacher and his steady love, who is in the house waiting for him. He is more able to be himself around Joyce Lakeland than Amy, to whom his act seems genuine. When she again brings up the topic of marriage, Lou is hesitant; he offers a reason why, and Amy shows how little she knows about Lou:

"Well, I don't want to go on being a deputy sheriff all of my life. I want to—well—be somebody."

"Like what, for example?"

"Oh, I don't know. There's no use in talking about it."

"A doctor, perhaps? I think that would be awfully nice. Is that what you had in mind, Lou?"

"I know it's crazy, Amy. But—"

She laughed. She rolled her head on the pillow, laughing. "Oh, Lou! I never heard of such a thing! You're twenty-nine years old, and y-you don't even speak good English, and—and—oh, ha, ha, ha . . ."

She laughed until she was gasping, and my cigarette burned down between my fingers and I never knew it until I smelled the scorching flesh.

"I'm s-sorry, darling. I didn't mean to hurt your feelings, but— Were you teasing me? Were you joking with your little Amy?"

"You know me," I said. "Lou the laughing boy."

Amy is so intent upon getting married that she uses the ploy Lou's been expecting: she tells him she's pregnant. Before he can think it through, Lou tells her that since he is sterile, she can't be pregnant. He goes on to explain that, yes, it had been done to him by his father around the time Mike was involved with the little girl . . .

Too late, Lou realizes he's placed too many of the pieces of the truth in Amy's hands: "The answer was trying to crash through and it couldn't make it—quite. I was standing in the way. It couldn't get around the image she had of gentle, friendly, easy-going Lou Ford."

Chester Conway drops by Ford's house the next day. Lou is supposed to make sure everything goes right with the payoff to Joyce Lakeland. Joyce has insisted that Elmer personally make the payoff to her, so she can see him one more time before she leaves town. Later Elmer Conway arrives to visit Lou. Elmer thinks Ford is helping him and Joyce run away from town on his father's money. Suspicious of exactly why Ford wants to "help him" so much, Elmer reluctantly offers Lou some money, which Lou takes to stop his wondering.

Lou's real plan is to kill both Elmer, to exact revenge upon Chester Conway, and Joyce, who has awakened *the sickness* inside him—and make it look like they killed each other.

That night, after sleeping with Joyce one last time, he explains to her that he's going to beat her to death, as he calmly draws on his gloves:

"They won't catch me," I said. "They won't even suspect me. They'll think he was half-stiff, like he usually is, and you got to fighting and both got killed."

She still didn't get it. She laughed, frowning a little at the same time. "But, Lou—that doesn't make sense. How could I be dead when—"

"Easy," I said, and I gave her a slap. And still she didn't get it.

She put a hand to her face and rubbed it slowly. "Y-you'd better not do that, now, Lou. I've got to travel, and—"

"You're not going anywhere, baby," I said, and I hit her again.

And at last she got it.

She jumped up and I jumped up with her. I whirled her around and gave her a quick one-two, and she shot backwards across the room and bounced and slumped against the wall. She staggered to her feet, weaving, mumbling, and half-fell toward me. I let her have it again.

I backed her against the wall, slugging, and it was like pounding a pumpkin. Hard, then everything giving away at once.

When Elmer arrives at Joyce's cottage, Lou smilingly sends him back to her room:

"I'd bet money though that she's all stretched out waiting for you."
I wanted to laugh out loud. I wanted to yell. I wanted to leap on him and tear him to pieces.

Lou gives Elmer some time to discover the body, and then walks in on him.

He looked up at me, his mouth hanging open.

I laughed—I had to laugh or do something worse—and his eyes squeezed shut and he bawled. I yelled with laughter, bending over and slapping my legs. I doubled up, laughing and farting and laughing some more. Until there wasn't a laugh in me or anyone. I'd used up all the laughter in the world.

Lou shoots Elmer six times in the mouth.

As Lou calmly is making his getaway, pulling out onto the road without his headlights, he is nearly plowed into by Chester Conway's oncoming Cadillac.

Conway orders Ford to follow him back up to the cottage, seemingly accepting Ford's feeble excuses for being there in the first place. Lou overhears Conway on the phone—evidently Joyce is not yet dead, and Conway wants to keep her alive so he can make her pay for what she did to his only son.

Things get complicated for Ford pretty quickly. On the way home after close questioning by Howard Hendricks, the county attorney, he stops in at the gas station where young Johnnie Pappas is now working. A

harmless juvenile delinquent, Johnnie looks up to Lou and Lou has in turn
tried to keep the boy from going bad. Lou returns home to find Amy in
his bed, and tells her what's supposed to have happened. She then
discovers that he's been sleeping with another woman, probably Joyce:
"You're dirty. I can tell. I can smell it on you. Smell her."

Lou thinks fast—Amy's injured pride is so far preventing her from
seeing the greater import of her discovery. Lou does the only thing he
can, the only thing that will shut her up. He asks Amy to marry him.

Next morning Howard Hendricks tries to disprove Lou's alibi about
having a flat tire, but Lou is too smart for him. Then Lou and Bob Maples,
the sheriff, ride along with Conway in a plane to Fort Worth—Conway is
flying Joyce there to make sure she has every chance to live. Conway orders
Lou to wait at the hotel, and takes Maples along with him to the hospital.

Lou sits in the hotel, regretting that he can't see more of "Cowtown"—
he'd never been out of Central City before, and he'd fallen asleep on the
plane, and was now shut up in this hotel room on account of Conway:

> . . . I had to stay here by myself, doing nothing, seeing nothing,
> thinking the same old thoughts.
> It was like there was a plot against me almost. I'd done something
> wrong, way back when I was a kid, and I'd never been able to get away
> from it. I'd had my nose rubbed in it day after day until, like an overtrained
> dog, I'd started crapping out of pure fright.

Bob Maples returns from the hospital quite upset about something; Lou
thinks it a reaction to being pushed around by Conway. Maples gets
passed-out drunk, just after telling Lou that Joyce died after all. Lou carts
him off to the train back to Central City. Bob wakes up during their ride,
and hints at what actually is wrong:

> "Stop man with grin, smile worthwhile—s-stop all a' stuff spilt milk n'
> so on. Wha' you do that for, anyway."
> "Aw," I said. "I was only kidding, Bob."
> "T-tell you somethin'," he said. "T-tell you somethin' I bet you never
> thought of."
> "Yeah?"
> "It's—it's always lightest just before the dark."
> Tired as I was, I laughed. "You got it wrong, Bob," I said. "You
> mean—"
> "Huh-uh," he said. "You got it wrong."

Next, Lou has to calm the fears of Joe Rothman, who realizes he's in
a hell of a spot if it's shown that Lou actually killed Elmer. It could be

proven that Joe was an accessory before the fact. But Lou's personality disarms Joe; even he can't figure Lou for the job: "Putting together everything I know about you . . . I couldn't make it tally with the picture I've got of *that* guy. Screwy as things are, that would be even screwier. You don't fit the part, to coin a phrase."

Lou goes down to the courthouse to make sure he's in the clear there. He takes up the needle again, giving a real hard time to the phony Howard Hendricks, who was elected county attorney by virtue of some shrapnel wounds inflicted in the last war. Ford slyly points out that the two victims almost had to kill each other after they were dead, something that Joe Rothman had been concerned about. Lou figures that'll give ol' Howard something to ponder.

That night Lou discovers an old photograph of Helene, his father's housekeeper who seduced him into a sadistic sexual relationship after his father stopped sleeping with her. In fact, the photograph shows the scars on Helene's backside, marks of many nights of violent lovemaking.

Lou burns the photograph, but it is too late—all the blocked memories flood back to him. *"But you'll like it, darling. All the big boys do it . . ."* Lou remembers overhearing Helene and his father, after Dr. Ford has found out about them. Helene warns the doctor this need not be a big deal:

> *"Has it hurt you any? Have you harmed anyone? Haven't you, in fact—I should ask!—gradually lost all interest in it?"*
>
> *"But a child! My child. My only son. If anything should happen—"*
>
> *"Uh-huh. That's what bothers you, isn't it? Not him, but you. How it would reflect on you."*
>
> . . .
>
> *"Get out or I'll kill you!"*
>
> *"Tsk-tsk! But think of the disgrace, Doctor . . . Now, I'm going to tell you something . . ."*
>
> *"Get—"*
>
> *"Something that you above all people should know. This didn't need to mean a thing. Absolutely nothing. But now it will. You've handled it in the worst possible way.*
>
> . . .
>
> I'd forgotten about it, and now I forgot it again. There are things that have to be forgotten if you want to go on living. And somehow I did want to; I wanted to more than ever. If the Good Lord made a mistake in us people it was in making us want to live when we've got the least excuse for it.

As Lou finishes burning the photograph, he notices how much Helene looked like Joyce. And Amy too.

Howard Hendricks calls Lou with some news—they've captured the real killer. Evidently the Conway payoff money was marked, and Johnnie Pappas broke one of the marked twenties in a drugstore that morning. The boy refused to talk, and is locked up in isolation. Hendricks wants Lou to persuade him to confess.

Johnnie Pappas, who considers Lou about his only friend in town, has not told the cops that Lou gave him the marked twenty on the night of the murders. Johnnie tells Lou that he was actually stealing some tires off a parked car at the time of the murders, but he wanted to give Lou a chance to figure out a story. Lou tells him he shouldn't have done that:

> "You mean they'll be sore?" He grunted. "To hell with 'em. They don't mean anything to me, but you're a square joe."
> "Am I?" I said. "How do you know I am, Johnnie? How can a man ever really know anything? We're really living in a funny world, kid, a peculiar civilization. The police are playing crooks in it, and the crooks are doing police duty. The politicians are preachers, and the preachers politicians. The tax collectors collect for themselves. The Bad People want us to have more dough, and the Good People are fighting to keep it from us. . . .
> "Yeah, Johnnie, it's a screwed up, bitched up world, and I'm afraid it's going to stay that way. And I'll tell you why. Because no one, almost no one, sees anything wrong with it. They can't see that things are screwed up, so they're not worried about it. What they're worried about is guys like you.
> "They're worried about guys liking a drink and taking it. Guys getting a piece of tail without paying a preacher for it. Guys who know what makes 'em feel good, and aren't going to be talked out of the notion . . . They don't like you guys, and they crack down on you. And the way it looks to me they're going to be cracking down harder and harder as time goes on. You ask me why I stick around, knowing the score, and it's hard to explain. I guess I kind of got a foot on both fences, Johnnie. I planted 'em there early and now they've taken root, and I can't move either way and I can't jump. All I can do is wait until I split. Right down the middle. . . .
> "I killed her, Johnnie. I killed both of them. And don't say I couldn't have, that I'm not that kind of a guy, because you don't know."

Johnnie's trust of Lou Ford, his inability to discern what is really beneath the deputy's bland exterior, costs him his life. Lou quickly knifes his hand against Johnnie's throat, knocking him out. Lou then hangs Johnnie with his own belt, and leaves him strung up in the cell, an apparent suicide.

Ford tells Hendricks he's "broken the case," and to give Johnnie some time to think about things. He adds that Howard should call him at home, because "I'm kind of curious to know if he talks."

Ford thought he had gotten rid of *the sickness* with the murder of Joyce, but it has only made him worse. Soon Amy takes the place of Joyce in a sadomasochistic sexual relationship. Lou prefaces the next chapter—his summary of his last, peaceful weeks with Amy Stanton— with a stunning meditation on the fleeting nature of love:

> I've loafed around the streets sometimes, leaned against a store front with my hat pushed back and one boot hooked back around the other—hell, you've probably seen me if you've ever been out this way—I've stood like that, looking nice and friendly and stupid, like I wouldn't piss if my pants were on fire. And all the time I'm laughing myself sick inside. Just watching the people.
>
> You know what I mean—the couples, the men and wives you see walking along together. The tall fat women, and the short scrawny men. The teensy little women, and the big fat guys. The dames with lantern jaws, and the men with no chins. The bowlegged wonders, and the knock-kneed miracles. The . . . I've laughed—inside, that is—until my guts ached. It's almost as good as dropping in on a Chamber of Commerce luncheon where some guy gets up and clears his throat a few times and says, "Gentlemen, we can't expect to get any more out of life than what we put into it . . ." (Where's the percentage in that?) And I guess it—they—the people—those mismatched people—aren't something to laugh about. They're really tragical.
>
> They're not stupid, no more than average anyway. They've not tied up together just to give jokers like me a bang. The truth is, I reckon, that life has played a hell of a trick on 'em. There was a time, just for a few minutes maybe, when all their differences seemed to vanish and they were just what each other wanted; when they looked at each other at exactly the right time in the right place and under the right circumstances. And everything was perfect. They had that time—those few minutes—and they never had any other. But while it lasted . . .

When Lou gets home from his visit to Johnnie's cell, Amy can't quite bring herself to ask him to beat her—she's heard some women like it—embarrassed, all she can do is hint. Lou knows what she wants, and gives it to her.

Soon Hendricks calls with the expected news about Johnnie. Lou hangs up the phone and turns once again to Amy, who's ready for more of the same:

> Sure, I know. Tell me something else. Tell a hophead he shouldn't take dope. Tell him it'll kill him, and see if he stops.
>
> She got her money's worth.

It was going to cost her plenty, and I gave her value received. Honest Lou, that was me. Let Lou Titillate Your Tail.

Lou takes to his sickbed for a week after Johnnie Pappas's "suicide." He has an uneasy feeling that "they" are closing in on him, but he can't quite pin it down. Amy notes that Conway hasn't called to thank Lou for helping solve the case.

When Lou is finally back up and around, he notices that "something was sure enough eating on" Howard Hendricks. Ford even visits Johnnie's father, who's renovating his diner in memory of his dead son. Joe Rothman tells Lou that Johnnie was buried in sacred ground—the church didn't call it suicide—and that Conway Construction is handling the renovation of the diner.

Lou Ford can't believe he's not in the clear, so he rationalizes away all the ominous portents. Rothman offers Ford the final bit of evidence. Rothman knows Johnnie stole the tires off that car, so he couldn't have killed Elmer and Joyce.

Rothman has alerted the legendary lawyer Billy Boy Walker, just in case things get that bad for Ford. Lou is shaken by that news most of all: "It sort of worried me that Rothman thought I needed that kind of help." Rothman tells Lou he better get out of town in a couple of weeks, and Lou begins to mourn for Amy, since that's about all the time she has left to live.

Lou often has to remind himself of *why,* as he attempts to justify his need to murder:

> I knew I had to kill Amy; I could put the reason into words. But every time I thought about it, I had to stop and think *why* again. I'd be doing something, reading a book or something, or maybe I'd be with her. And all of a sudden it would come over me that I was going to kill her, and the idea seemed so crazy that I'd almost laughed out loud. Then, I'd start thinking and I'd see it, see that it had to be done, and . . .
>
> It was like being asleep when you were awake and awake when you were asleep. I'd pinch myself, figuratively speaking—I had to keep pinching myself. Then I'd wake up in reverse; I'd go back into the nightmare I had to live in. And everything would be clear and reasonable.

Lou has no clear plan to rid himself of Amy until one night when the bum whose hand he burned with the cigar butt shows up at his door. The bum followed Ford and heard him talking to Rothman that first night, and saw Lou outside Joyce's cottage on the murder night. Lou finally "gives in" to the bum's blackmail, telling him to come back in two weeks to collect his blackmail money.

After the bum leaves, Lou wonders at how circumstance always seems to point the way for him, and the cowardice of his victims:

> I grinned, feeling a little sorry for him. It was funny the way these people kept asking for it. Just latching onto you, no matter how you tried to brush them off, and almost telling you how they wanted it done. Why'd they all have to come to me to get killed? Why couldn't they kill themselves?

Ford is paid a visit by a man he eventually recognizes as an infamous quack psychiatrist. He toys with the man, frightening him and kicking him out of the house.

The days pass too quickly for Ford; before he knows it it's the night when the bum will return, and Amy Stanton will die. The chapter in which Ford relates the murder of Amy is masterfully structured, opening with the news of her murder and running back over the days to the night when it happened. When finally he can bring himself to do it, Lou promises to tell us everything, so we'll understand exactly how it was. And he does tell everything:

> And I hit her in the guts as hard as I could.
> My fist went back against her spine, and the flesh closed around it to the wrist. I jerked back on it, I had to jerk, and she flopped forward from the waist, like she was hinged.
> Her hat fell off, and her head went clear down and touched the floor. And then she toppled over, like a kid turning a somersault. She lay on her back, eyes bulging, rolling her head from side to side.

Lou has to wait for the bum, while Amy writhes in agony on the floor. He tries to read the paper, but Amy gets a grip on his crotch; he drags her around the kitchen before she'll let go. Later she reaches for her purse, but Lou thinks nothing of it. He sits there working up his anger, knowing Amy hasn't taken a real breath in thirty minutes. He's been "suffering" right along with her—and he's going to make that bum pay. When Lou finally hears the bum coming up on the porch, he kicks Amy a few times in the head to finish her off.

Lou quickly hands the bum the rest of the marked money, and the bum follows him back into the house, nearly stepping on Amy. The bum begins to scream and wiggle his arms like a "two-bit jazz singer":

> That's the way he looked, and he kept making that damned funny noise, his lips quivering ninety to the minute and his eyes rolling all-white.
> I laughed and laughed, he looked and sounded so funny I couldn't help

it. Then I remembered what he'd done and I stopped laughing, and got mad—sore all over.

"You son-of-a-bitch," I said. "I was going to marry that poor little girl. We were going to elope and she caught you going through the house and you tried to . . ."

I stopped, because he hadn't done it at all. But he *could* have done it. He could've done it just as easy as not. The son-of-a-bitch could have, but he was just like everyone else. He was too nicey-nice and pretendsy to do anything really hard.

So in Lou's inverted world, the fact that the bum didn't kill Amy becomes a worse crime than killing her—since the bum won't admit to his part in making Lou kill her. The bum represents all the people and circumstances that made Lou as he is, but won't share part of the blame. Thus Jim Thompson twists his theme of shared responsibility into justification for murder:

> But he'd stand back and crack the whip over me, keep moving around me every way I turned so that I couldn't get away no matter what I did, and it was always now-don't-you-do-nothin'-bud; but they kept cracking that old whip all the time they were sayin' it. And they—he'd done it all right; and I wasn't going to take the blame. I could be just as tricky and pretendsy as they were. . . .
>
> . . . I went blind ma— angry seeing him so pretendsy shocked, "Yeeing!" and shivering and doing that screwy dance with his hands—hell, he hadn't had to watch *her* hands!—and white-rolling his eyes. What right did he have to act like that? I was the one that should have been acting that way, but, oh, no, I couldn't. That was their—his right to act that way, and I had to hold in and do all the dirty work.

The bum tries to run, and Lou grabs up his knife and takes off after him. Lou slips in the puddle Amy made on the floor, and goes sprawling. He hopes for a fleeting moment that the bum will take the knife and finish him off, but then he realizes he won't ever get off that easy.

Lou chases the bum through the streets of town, screaming that he murdered Amy. Deputy Jeff Plummer, one of Lou's few remaining supporters down at the courthouse (along with Bob Maples) shoots the bum dead.

The next morning, when Lou wakes from the sedative given him when he beat the bum's corpse, he realizes that things aren't right. There's no one there to comfort him, like there should be.

The truth is undeniable now. They may know . . . but they can't prove anything.

Howard Hendricks and Deputy Plummer arrive to question Lou, to no avail. Hendricks has no real evidence, since Conway can't admit Lou's reason for killing Elmer. Hendricks's political future—what Lou calls the shrapnel—is tied up with Conway.

Howard Hendricks does have one piece of surprise "evidence"—a note to Lou found in Amy's purse, which hints at the truth. Amy intended to give it to Lou the night before, when they stopped for a bite to eat on the road. She was going to give him plenty of time to get away, if that's what he needed to do. The heart-wrenching note destroys the little bit of humanity left inside Lou Ford:

> . . . But I'm afraid—are you in trouble? Is something weighing on your mind? I don't want to ask you more than that, but I want you to believe that whatever it is, even if it's what I—whatever it is, Lou, I'm on your side. I love you (are you tired of me saying that?) and I know you. I know you'd never knowingly do anything wrong, you just couldn't, and I love you so much and . . . Let me help you, darling. Whatever it is, whatever help you need.

Ford has no choice once again—Amy's already dead—and he won't reveal himself to Howard Hendricks, king of the phonies. He fights to emerge from the hell the letter dropped him into:

> What are you going to say when you're drowning in your own dung and they keep booting you back into it, when all the screams in hell wouldn't be as loud as you want to scream, when you're at the bottom of the pit and the whole world's at the top, when it has but one face, a face without eyes or ears, and yet it watches and listens . . .
>
> What are you going to do and say? Why, pardner, that's simple. It's easy as nailing your balls to a stump and falling off backwards. Snow again, pardner, and drift me hard, because that's an easy one.
>
> You're gonna say, they can't keep a good man down. You're gonna say, a winner never quits and a quitter never wins. You're gonna smile, boy, you're gonna show 'em the ol' fightin' smile. And then you're gonna get out there an' hit 'em hard and fast and low an'—an' Fight!
>
> Rah.
>
> I folded the letter, and tossed it back to Howard.
>
> "She was sure a talky little girl," I said.

Hendricks is stunned; Jeff Plummer has to threaten to shoot Lou before he will get dressed and let himself be taken away. They lock Lou up in a jail cell, and try to shake him by playing a recording of Johnnie Pappas's voice over and over again. Lou just laughs.

Lou Ford has plenty of time to muse on what has happened. Plummer told him that Bob Maples shot himself when he heard the news about

Amy Stanton, and that leads Lou to the truth of what Bob was trying to tell him that night. They *do* have evidence against Lou: "I let it go by me because I had to. I couldn't let myself face the facts. But I reckon you've known the truth all along."

Lou can now admit that he had no reason for all his crimes—rather, that the reasons he'd thought up at the time weren't the real reasons at all. He offers a new "truth," likely just another set of rationalizations:

> Once I'd admitted the truth about that piece of evidence, it was easy to admit other things. I could stop inventing reasons for what I'd done, stop believing in the reasons I'd invented, and see the truth. And it sure wasn't hard to see. . . .
>
> [It] had started back with the housekeeper; with dad finding out about us. All kids pull some pretty sorry stunts, particularly if an older person edges 'em along, so it hadn't needed to mean a thing. But Dad made it mean something. I'd been made to feel that I'd done something that couldn't ever be forgiven—that would always lie between him and me, the only kin I had. And there wasn't anything I could do or say that would change things. I had a burden of fear and shame put on me that I could never get shed of.
>
> She was gone, and I couldn't strike back at her, yes, kill her, for what I'd been made to feel she'd done to me. But that was all right. She was the first woman I'd ever known; she *was* woman to me; and all womankind bore her face. So I could strike back at any of them, any female, the ones it would be safest to strike at, and it would be the same as striking at her. And I did that, I started striking out . . . and Mike Dean took the blame.

Lou says he kept Amy at a distance all those years not because he didn't love her but because he did. He was afraid she might ask him to do what Helene had made him do . . . and when she finally did, when Amy responded to being beaten, she became Helene, and had to die. It worked the same way with Joyce. Amy and Joyce wouldn't have caused him trouble, that's not why they had to die. They had to die because they had become *her*.

And his other victims, Elmer, the bum, Johnnie, Bob Maples? Settling the score with Conway over Mike's death partially explains Elmer:

> That was my main reason for killing Elmer, but it wasn't the only one. The Conways were part of the circle, the town, that ringed me in; the smug ones, the hypocrites, the holier-than-thou guys—all the stinkers I had to face day in and day out. I had to grin and smile and be pleasant to them; and maybe there are people like that everywhere, but when you can't get away from them, when they keep pushing themselves at you, and you can't get away, never, never, get away . . .
>
> Well.

Knowing it is a shaky house of cards that he has built from his new reasons, Lou resorts to a textbook definition of dementia praecox, schizophrenia, paranoid type. Even that's just an easy answer, as he finally admits:

> Plenty of pretty smart psychiatrists have been fooled by guys like me, and you can't really fault 'em for it. There's just not much they can put their hands on, know what I mean?
> We might have the disease, the condition; or we might just be cold-blooded and smart as hell; or we might be innocent of what we're supposed to have done. We might be any one of those three things, because the symptoms we show would fit any one of the three.

The central mystery of Lou's actual nature is unsolvable—there's not even enough left inside him to render him guilty or innocent, sane or insane. The facts, the symptoms, are supposed to reveal a reality—but all that's left to be revealed is a vacuum where personality, motivation, or a soul should be. In the end Lou will let his pursuers think they've solved the mystery—that he's just a mad killer. Lou Ford alone assumes the burden of the eternally unknowable.

Lou is moved to the insane asylum run by the psychiatrist who visited his home. One night he genuinely enjoys a slide show they give him of pictures of Amy Stanton—but he makes the mistake of asking them to show the pictures a little more slowly the next time. They don't show them again.

Lou is in the asylum a few weeks when Rothman's lawyer, Billy Boy Walker, arrives and rescues him. Lou figures they probably let the lawyer get him out; they should be just about ready to use that piece of "evidence."

On the drive back to Central City, Lou opens up to Walker, after the lawyer reveals his own thinking. Billy Boy's slant on Lou's plight is Jim Thompson's own, thinly disguised: note the nature of Billy's analogy, and his formal education:

> "I never had any legal schooling, Mr. Ford; picked up my law by reading in an attorney's office. All I ever had in the way of higher education was a couple of years in agricultural college, and that was pretty much a plain waste of time. Crop rotation? Well, how're you going to do it when the banks only make crop loans on cotton? Soil conservation? How're you going to do terracing and draining and contour plowing when you're cropping on shares? Purebred stock? Sure. Maybe you can trade your razorbacks for Poland Chinas . . . I just learned two things there at that college, Mr. Ford, that was ever of any use to me. One was that I couldn't do any worse than the people that were in the saddle, so maybe I'd better

try pulling 'em down and riding myself. The other was a definition I got out of the agronomy books, and I reckon it was even more important than the first. It did more to revise my thinking, if I'd really done any thinking up until that time. Before that I'd seen everything in black and white, good and bad. But after I was set straight I saw that the name you put to a thing depended on where you stood and where it stood. And . . . and here's the definition, right out of the agronomy books: 'A weed is a plant out of place.' Let me repeat that. 'A weed is a plant out of place.' I find a hollyhock in my cornfield, and it's a weed. I find it in my yard and it's a flower.

"You're in my yard, Mr. Ford."

Jim Thompson here offers a version of the central analogy of *Heed the Thunder,* in which the corruption of the people and the destruction of the land are both criminal wastes of natural resources. Circumstance, time, and place—that which forms all of us—have conspired to make Lou Ford considered a weed by society.

Billy Boy listens quietly to Lou Ford's story, and Lou marvels that Billy "understood me better'n I understood myself." More than anything, Lou now needs another reason for his actions—something to fill the emptiness. Billy Boy offers a reason why:

> ". . . and, of course, you knew you'd never leave Central City. Overprotection had made you terrified of the outside world. More important, it was part of the burden you had to carry to stay here and suffer."
> He sure understood. . . .
> "I couldn't have gone, no matter how things were. It's like you say, I'm tied here. I'll never be free as long as I live . . ."

Lou Ford knows there's not much time left. After Billy Boy drops him off, he goes through his house soaking everything with grain alcohol and setting up some slow-burning candles. He slides a butcher knife up the sleeve of his shirt, and practices dropping it into his palm a few times. Then he sits in the kitchen smoking and drinking coffee, awaiting the arrival of Joyce Lakeland.

Lou is sure the house is surrounded by men with guns, but he peeks out the door to confirm his suspicions. Then he hears the car, just as he's finishing his last cigarette.

They walk into Ford's kitchen—Conway, Hendricks, Hank Butterby, and Jeff Plummer—and ahead of them comes Joyce Lakeland, a living mummy:

> Her neck was in a cast that came clear up to her chin like a collar, and she walked stiff-backed and jerky. Her face was a white mask of gauze and tape, and nothing much showed of it but her eyes and lips.

Joyce mumbles to Lou that she didn't tell them anything, and Lou nods: "I didn't figure you had, baby." Unafraid, Joyce shuffles to him, and Lou springs at her with the knife, to finish the job he had botched:

> And it was like I'd signaled, the way the smoke suddenly poured up through the floor. And the room exploded with shots and yells, and I seemed to explode with it, yelling and laughing and . . . and . . . Because they hadn't got the point. She'd gotten that between the ribs and the blade along with it. And they all lived happily ever after, I guess, and I guess—that's—all.

But that's not all—Lou Ford has found one more—or perhaps two—reasons *why:* "We might have the disease, the condition; or we might just be cold-blooded and smart as hell; or we might be innocent of what we're supposed to have done." Lou's final actions offer Hendricks and the rest the simple "answer" to that conundrum—he was a mad killer after all. That is enough for them, but that doesn't solve anything for Lou Ford. His final "answer" lies in Billy Boy Walker's mention of the "burden" he always had to carry. All of Ford's victims were people just like him—trapped, hopeless victims of life.

It became Ford's mission to take care of them, to send them to the next world where they might get a better roll of the dice. Ford has come to believe he's a high priest of murder—a conviction Nick Corey would act out more thoroughly in *Pop. 1280.* Ford is both the savior and the scapegoat of his world, a world in which there's no difference between the two.

So Lou Ford closes his story with a prayer for himself and his victims—a prayer that is also a blessing upon those for whom he has performed the sacrament of murder:

> Yeah, I reckon that's all unless our kind gets another chance in the Next Place. Our Kind. Us people.
> All of us that started the game with a crooked cue, that wanted so much and got so little, that meant so good and did so bad. All us folks. Me and Joyce Lakeland, and Johnnie Pappas and Bob Maples and big ol' Elmer Conway and little ol' Amy Stanton. All of us.
> All of us.

On this twisted note of hope Jim Thompson closes the tale of a lost man, of a lost world. A world where belief is the only separation between salvation and damnation, and good and evil a matter of perspective—"a weed is a plant out of place."

The Thompson world.

* * *

When Jim Thompson slipped into the voice of Lou Ford, a trapped intellectual forced to play a dumb, sardonic clown, he came as close to the realities of his own life as he ever did in a first-person narration. It's easy to believe that Thompson, the quiet family man who became broken up at bad news on the radio, was as stifled and deceptive as Lou Ford. He didn't just understand the deputy sheriff's dual nature, Thompson lived his own version every day, and poured the truth of his own daily deception into the writing.

Was Jim Thompson really like the killers he so convincingly wrote about—secretly lashing out, sublimating an urge to kill through his writing? Although it's not that simple, the validity of the question does give one pause—Thompson *was like* Lou Ford, but in a more subtle, sadder way than one might initially expect. Thompson felt that he had to put on an act, just like Ford, in the following passage from one of Thompson's uncompleted novels, *A Penny in the Dust*. The narrator is Thompson surrogate Robert Hightower, a high school student/bellboy in Fort Worth. He's decrying the loss of a favorite teacher, one man who recognized his intelligence and with whom he could be himself:

> You see, you see, he was all I had. My only friend. The only person in the world I had to talk to. As I liked to talk, and be talked to. A way that apparently seemed natural and unaffected only to the two of us. As much as I loved and respected them, I could not talk to my parents. . . .
>
> I could not talk to my peers (and it had been a very long time since I had tried) without being accused of swallowing a dictionary or showing off. As for conversing with an adult, well, that too could be done only with the utmost wariness. And even then, according to the adult's station in society, I was apt to be dismissed with a patronizing word or the suggestion that I stop flogging my dummy.
>
> I could only talk by being what I was not.

"I could only talk by being what I was not" seems Lou Ford's central plight in a nutshell. Other factors notwithstanding, in everyday life in Central City, Ford must act like a "corny bore" or never fit in among the people. Thompson felt forced to hide his true nature as a young man, and later he easily assumed the role of a banal family man. One can only guess at the secret thoughts buried deep within himself—only guess, except for the answers submerged in his writing.

Two of Jim Thompson's later novels, 1957's *Wild Town* and 1961's *The Transgressors,* feature versions of Lou Ford, the dual-natured deputy sheriff, in appearances more geared to outright sympathy and understand-

ing of a man who must live life being untrue to his inner self. There seems
no good reason for Thompson to return to the "Lou Ford" character in
later, weaker books, in which circumstance hands Ford a better fate; no
good reason, except perhaps Jim Thompson was writing and rewriting his
own story all along.

A Hell of a Woman is the story of Frank "Dolly" Dillon's final chance
to fulfill his dreams of success. He's been on the road since he was kicked
out of high school for making a pass at his teacher—Dolly lets us know
she was really asking for it. Since then he's been selling magazines, pots
and pans, burial plots, buying old gold. You name it, he's done it. But
now he's thirty, and he's been on the same treadmill for years, running
himself ragged and getting nowhere:

> And then you take a good look at yourself, and you stop wondering
> about the other guy . . .   You've got all your hands and feet. Your health
> is okay, and ambition—man! you've got it. You're young, I guess you'd
> call thirty young, and you're strong. You don't have much education, but
> you've got more than plenty of other people who go to the top. And yet
> with all that—with all you've had to do with—this is as far as you've got.
> And something tells you, you're not going much farther if any.

Soon a young blonde named Mona Farrell is offered to him as payment
for some silverware he's hawking to her "aunt"; Dolly falls hard for the
girl. He tells us that's easy, considering what he's married to: Joyce, the
latest in a seemingly endless series of tramps. Joyce leaves him after
he slugs her and knocks her into a bathtub full of dirty water. And just
when things can't get any worse, Dolly's boss, Staples, catches him
stealing from his receipts and Dolly's thrown in jail.

Inexplicably (and fatefully), Mona bails Dolly out, and soon arrives at
his doorstep with some money she's stolen from her aunt's cache in the
cellar. Dolly shakes his head at the fistful of bills, telling her they'd need
a lot bigger stake if they were going to run away and keep running.
Puzzled, Mona tells him there's more to get, a lot more . . .

The resultant murder scheme, involving one of Dolly's deadbeat
customers, Pete, goes off without a hitch. Pete and the aunt both end up
dead, supposedly a mutual double murder. And Dolly ends up with
$100,000, the American Dream come true. As he sits in his squalid
shack, staring at the treasure for which he committed a double murder,
Dolly's narrative abruptly changes tone and style. He whitewashes his
murderous actions in a breezily psychotic imitation of a Horatio Alger
story:

I dropped the rest of the pack back into the satchel, and started to fasten the catch. And I was a happy man, dear reader. I had won out in the unequal struggle with every son-of-a-bitch in the country, even my own father, giving me a bad time. I had forged onward and upward against unequal odds, my lips bloody but unbowed. And from now on it would be me and all this dough, living a dream life in some sunny clime—Mexico or Canada or somewhere—the rest of the goddamned world could go to hell.

But though I seldom complain, you have doubtless read between the lines and you know that I am one hard-luck bastard. So now, right as I stood on the doorstep of Dreams Come True, my whole world crumpled beneath me. I had all this dough and I had Mona—or I soon would have her—and then I looked up and (TO BE CONTINUED)

Joyce has returned and snapped him out of his reverie. Dolly must now decide which woman he wants to run away with. And his boss, Staples, seems to know more than he's letting on about what Dolly's up to. Things get very complicated very fast.

The stress continues to manifest itself in Dolly's narrative. He increasingly relates his tale in the second person, and in the Horatio Alger–style chapters, the first titled "Through Thick and Thin: The True Story of a Man's Fight Against High Odds and Low Women."

What has become most important to Dolly is the "truth" about the women in his life. Is Mona the tramp evidence hints she is? And what about Joyce? Has she really changed her ways?

Dolly's mind is made up for him when Joyce accuses him of killing Pete and the aunt. In one of the most gruesome murders in Jim Thompson's novels, Dolly kills his pregnant wife in the bathtub and buries her in a railroad coal car.

A little detective work of his own helps Staples discern the truth of the aunt's identity, and Dolly's murderous actions. Staples gets all the money, and sends Dolly out of town with the girl. Dolly soon kills Mona after deciding she is a useless tramp after all.

Months later, broke, disguised, and desperate, Dolly meets up with Helene, a female version of himself. In her hotel room one day, he reads a newspaper article that reveals the improbable truth about Mona and the money. It is a "truth" he himself hit upon in his earlier, desperate search for Mona's "goodness":

The 20-year-old Stirling kidnap case appeared to be solved today with the arrest of an ex-store manager and admitted associate of the notorious Farraday gang.

The suspect is H. J. Staples, 55. . . .

Ramona Stirling was the only child of multi-millionaire oil-man, Arthur

Stirling, and his semi-invalid wife. Three years old at the time, Ramona was snatched from the grounds of the family's luxurious Tulsa estate. . . .

Dolly had speculated that Mona had probably been born "with a silver spoon in her mouth," and he had been right. A Stirling silver spoon.

In another of Thompson's sly literalizations, the news drives Dolly "over the edge." In a hallucinatory final few pages, with lines alternating in roman and italic type, Dillon is castrated/throws himself out a window. Here's the roman type version of the ending:

> I laughed and laughed when I read that story. I felt good all day. And then evening came on, and I didn't laugh any more and I didn't feel good any more. Because it was quite a tragedy, when you got to thinking about it; and I guess you know dear reader I'm a pretty soft-hearted son-of-a-bitch. Yes, it was a terrible tragedy and whoever was responsible for it ought to be jailed. Making a guy want what he couldn't get. Making him so he couldn't get much, but he'd want a lot. Laying it all out for him every place he turned—the swell cars and clothes and places to live. Never letting him have anything, but always making him want. Making him feel like a bastard because he didn't have what he couldn't get. Making him hate himself, and if a guy hates himself how can he love anyone else? Helene came home, my fairy princess, and she saw I was feeling low so she fixed me a big drink. And right after that I began to get drowsy. I was sleepy; I went and stretched out on the bed, and she came in and sat down beside me. She had a big pair of shears in her hand, and she sat snipping the ends of her hair, staring down at me. And I looked at her, my eyes dropping shut. And she made herself look like Joyce and then like Mona, and then . . . all the others. She said I'd disappointed her; I'd turned out like all her other men. You deceived me, she said. You're no different from the rest, Fred. And you'll have to pay like the rest. Don't you want me to, darling. I nodded and she began unfastening and fumbling and then, then she lowered the shears and then she was smiling again and letting me see. There, she said, that's much better, isn't it? And, then, nice as I'd been, she started laughing. Screaming at me.

Boasting Thompson's most frightening ending, *A Hell of a Woman* is one of his best-crafted books—ingeniously plotted and structured, full of puns and ironies. Like the best Thompson crime novels, the first-person narration once again conveys and disguises an ingenious "mystery" plot, in which the truth is concealed/revealed as a direct result of the narrator's delusions and observations. An explicit portrayal of the foul, twisted interior of a debased American dreamer, *A Hell of a Woman* is also an implicit indictment of the societal values that spawned him.

* * *

Arnold Hano:

On *Savage Night* Jim came in and said, "I want to do a syndicate-type novel and I want to use just 500 words, 500 basic words, cause I think that will reduce it to what I want to reduce it to." A minimalist kind of thing, but nobody used those words. I said go ahead, do it. So he did, but someplace along the line that 500 word thing got lost. Still, it's a wonderfully spare book, and my own favorite of all the Jim Thompson books. I have three favorites, by the way, *Savage Night, A Hell of a Woman,* and *The Killer Inside Me. Savage Night* still gets me.

Savage Night is the story of Charlie "Little" Bigger, a five-foot-tall, consumptive hit man rousted out of hiding and retirement by syndicate chief The Man, who needs the legendary killer for a special job. A former payoff man, Jake Winroy, is going to testify against the mob to save his own neck. Charlie's job is to kill him and make it look like an accident.

As Charlie admits early on, he doesn't know if he's up to the job anymore. He had been living out in Arizona, with a kindly old couple who treated him like a son, and he'd eventually stopped coughing up blood. But there's never been very much to him, weighing in at around a hundred pounds, with false teeth and contact lenses. Somehow he knows that this job may be too tough for him to handle. Sure, he would kill Jake, no problem, but The Man needs the job done just right. If it isn't, then that's the end of Charlie "Little" Bigger.

This seemingly commonplace mafia novel setup soon evolves into a meditation on death and dying, as Charlie searches for answers to the whys of his life and his world. *Savage Night* is Jim Thompson's most inspired, lyrical novel.

The setting of *Savage Night* echoes its theme, as Charlie Bigger notes on arrival in the college town of Peardale: "The whole place had a kind of decayed, dying-on-the-vine appearance. . . . There was something sad about it, something that reminded me of bald-headed men who comb their side hair across the top." Charlie is supposedly going to be a special student at the teacher's college, and he's taken a room at the Winroys' house.

Fay Winroy, Jake's wife, is a type familiar to Bigger (and to most Thompson readers). He knows just how to play her. Charlie comes on to her quickly, revealing his identity and his mission; a little too fast, according to The Man, who reminds Charlie that there's a lot of reward money available for a person who can identify the infamous little killer.

The other woman in the Winroy household is Ruthie Dorne, a crippled young college student from a white trash family; she does the cooking and household chores. Like the sirens of *Nothing More Than Murder* and *A Hell of a Woman* before her, Ruthie exerts an unexplainable pull on Charlie:

> But what I saw interested me. Maybe it wouldn't interest you, but it did me.
>
> She had on an old mucklededung-colored coat—the way it was screaming Sears-Roebuck they should have paid her to wear it—and a kind of rough wool skirt. Her glasses were the kind your grandpa maybe wore, little tiny lenses, steel rims, pinchy across the nose. They made her eyes look like walnuts in a plate of cream fudge. Her hair was black and thick and shiny. But the way it was fixed—murder!
>
> She only had one leg, the right one. The fingers of her left hand, gripping the crosspiece of her crutch, looked a little splayed.

Charlie sees in her a reflection of himself, and his own inadequacies. But as he will discover, the real attraction of Ruthie is due to Thanatos, not Eros.

Charlie realizes he has something of more immediate concern than Ruthie: he thinks The Man might have another agent right there in the house, to watch him and report back if he seems to be slipping up badly. The obvious suspect is the other boarder, Mr. Kendall, a retired academic who now runs the local bakery and immediately strikes up a friendship with Charlie, who's using the name Carl Bigelow:

> All at once I had a crazy idea about him, one that kind of gave me the whimwhams. Because maybe everyone doesn't have a price, but if this dull, dignified old guy *did* have one . . . Well, he'd be worth almost anything he asked as an ace in the hole. He could throw in with me, in case of a showdown: back me up in a story, or actually give me a hand if there was no other way out. Otherwise, he'd just keep tabs on me, see that I didn't try a runout . . .
>
> But that was crazy. I've already said so. The Man knew I couldn't run. He knew I wouldn't fluff the job. I shoved the notion out of my mind, shoved it damned good and hard. You just can't play around with notions like that.

Jake Winroy arrives home, drunk as usual, and is spooked out of his shoes by "Carl Bigelow." He runs to the sheriff, claiming that Charlie Bigger has been sent to kill him. The sheriff investigates "Carl's" past—he was well known and liked by the county judge and sheriff in Arizona. The sheriff curses Winroy for being a drunken fool.

One night Ruthie visits Charlie's room, and he finds out more than he wants to know about what's under her skirt:

> I looked down, my head against hers so she couldn't see that I was looking. I looked, and I closed my eyes quickly. But I couldn't keep them closed.
>
> It was a baby's foot. A tiny little foot and ankle. It started just above the knee joint—where the knee would have been if she had one—a tiny little ankle, not much bigger around than a thumb; a baby ankle and a baby foot.
>
> The toes were curling and uncurling, moving with the rhythm of her body . . .
>
> "C-Carl . . . Oh, *Carl!*" she gasped.
>
> After a long time, what seemed like a long time, I heard her saying, "Don't. Please don't Carl. It's a-all right, so—so, please, Carl . . . Please don't cry anymore—"

Thus three dualities are established: Bigger feels a bond with Ruthie, because they are both malformed; with Kendall, because they are introverted intellectuals; and with Winroy, because in killing him he will likely be killing himself. Before the novel reaches its conclusion, each of these characters will inform Bigger about some aspect of death.

Bigger takes a trip to New York City, where he meets with Fay Winroy for a fling that solidifies her assistance, if needed. But before their assignation, he meets up with The Man, who warns him about the small missteps he's already made. The Man orders Bigger to kill Fruit Jar, whom The Man claims holds a grudge against Bigger because he rubbed out his brother long ago.

Bigger, all too eager to kill Fruit Jar, does so before he realizes the real reason The Man wants him dead:

> Fruit Jar . . . He could have told me. I could have made him tell me—the thing that might mean the difference between my living and dying. And now he couldn't tell me.
>
> His brother . . . HIS BROTHER HELL!

Fruit Jar had known who The Man's insurance was in Peardale, if indeed The Man did have another operative on the Winroy case. But now Bigger can't find out until too late.

While unable to sleep because of Fay's incessant snoring, Bigger recalls a crazed character who once gave him a lift:

> He was a writer, only he didn't call himself that. He called himself a hockey peddler. "You notice that smell?" he said, "I just got through

dumping a load of crap in New York, and I ain't had time to get fumigated." All I could smell was the whiz he'd been drinking. He went on talking, not at all grammatical like you might expect a writer to be, and he was funny as hell.

He said he had a farm up in Vermont, and all he grew on it was the more interesting portions of the female anatomy. And he never laughed or cracked a smile, and the way he told about it he almost made you believe it. "I fertilize them with wild goat manure," he said. "The goats are tame to begin with, but they soon go wild. The stench, you know. I feed them on the finest grade grain alcohol, and they have their own private cesspool to bathe in. But nothing does any good. You should see them at night when they stand on their heads, howling. . . .

"Oh, I used to grow other things," he said. "Bodies. Faces. Eyes. Expressions. Brains. I grew them in a three-dollar-a-week room down on Fourteenth Street and I ate aspirin when I couldn't raise the dough for hamburger. And every now and then some lordly book publisher would come down and reap my crop and package it at two-fifty a copy, and, lo and behold, if I praised him mightily and never suggested that he was a member of the Jukes family in disguise, he would spend three or four dollars on advertising and sales of the book would swell to a total of nine hundred copies and he would give me ten percent of the proceeds . . . when he got around to it."

This detour in Bigger's narrative is a cameo appearance by Jim Thompson himself, offering a savage satirical attack on the state of his career and publishers, and a peculiar vision of hell that is what lies ahead for Charlie Bigger. The story of a Vermont vagina farm with howling, fertilizing goats leaves a great impression on Charlie Bigger, as does:

> "Sure there's a hell . . ." I could hear him saying it now, now, as I lay here in bed with her breath in my face, and her body squashed against me . . . "It is the drab desert where the sun sheds neither warmth nor light and Habit force-feeds senile Desire. It is the place where mortal Want dwells with immortal Necessity, and the night becomes hideous with the groans of one and the ecstatic shrieks of the other. Yes, there is a hell, my boy, and you do not have to dig for it . . .

Charlie Bigger doesn't doubt the veracity of those words; words that are an echo of those used by *Heed the Thunder*'s Edie Dillon to her father as he lies dying, wondering if there's a hell:

> Edie nodded her head firmly. "I know doggoned well there is. And you don't have to dig for it."
> Lincoln laughed. Comforted, he took another drink.

Birdie Myers Thompson
and James Sherman Thompson
on their wedding day.

James S. Thompson (far right) with deputies,
Andarko, Oklahoma, circa 1906.

Jim Thompson,
ten years old in 1916.

Jim Thompson in Oklahoma City,
twelve years old in 1918.

Jim Thompson and Alberta Hesse Thompson
in Lincoln, Nebraska, 1931.

(From left) Michael, Sharon, Jim and Patricia Thompson in Tijuana, Mexico, 1940s.

(From left) Joe Pascovar, Louis L'Amour and Jim Thompson in Oklahoma City, 1937.

On the beach in San Diego, late 1940s.

Alberta and Jim in San Diego, late 1940s.

Thompson with cat named Deadline on the back cover of
Nothing More Than Murder.

(From left) Joe Kouba, Maxine,
Alberta and Jim in San Diego, 1946.

Joe Kouba and an overweight Thompson
dressed for the Writers' Guild awards
ceremony in Hollywood, 1958.

(From left) Jim Thompson, Maxine Thompson Kouba and Freddie Thompson Townsend in the early 1960s.

Sharon Thompson and Jim Reed's wedding. Alberta and Jim are on the far left, 1963.

(From left) Alberta, Michael, Sharon and Jim Thompson, early 1960s.

Alberta and Jim, late 1960s.

*(From left) Thompson, Robert Redford and Tony Bill
at Redford's Utah ranch, 1970.*

*Thompson as Judge Grayle
in production still
from* Farewell, My Lovely.

*Robert Mitchum as Philip Marlowe
and Thompson as Grayle
in* Farewell, My Lovely.

Hollywood Hills, 1975.

1975

Hollywood Hills, 1975.

Death doesn't seem so bad to Lincoln Fargo, a man with a clear vision of hell on earth.

Charlie Bigger slogs ahead, surviving an attempt kill him when Winroy locks him in the freezer at the bakery. But the episode takes a great toll, and Bigger begins to emphasize the shrinking, the rotting, the steady loss of his being: "I didn't have much pain. Like I said, I was just weak and tired. And I had a funny feeling that a lot of me had been taken away." And: "I had to go on waiting and hoping, losing more of the little that was left of me."

Bigger's plans fall apart about as quickly as he does, and soon he no longer holds out hope of surviving. He realizes, too late, that Kendall is just what he appears to be, a kindly old man who has taken a liking to Bigger:

> ". . . Do you believe in immortality, Mr. Bigelow? In the broadest sense of the word, that is? Well, let me simply say then that I seem to have done almost none of the many things which I had planned on doing in this tearful vale. They are still there in me, waiting to be done, yet the span of time for their doing has been exhausted. I . . . but listen to me, will you?" He chuckled embarrassedly, his eyes blinking behind their glasses. "I didn't think myself capable of such absurd poeticism!"
>
> "That's all right," I said, slowly, and a kind of chill crept over me. "What do you mean your span—"
>
> I was looking straight into him, through him and out the other side, and all I could see was a prim, fussy old guy. That was all I could see, because that was all there was to see. *He wasn't working for The Man. He never had been.*

In a typical bit of Thompson irony, Bigger sees the truth, but too late for it to do any good. He truly understands Kendall now, since there is nothing left at stake.

In fact, Kendall has made "Mr. Bigelow" his heir. Bigger barely has time to weep over Mr. Kendall's actions when he realizes that leaves only one person who could be The Man's inside operative: Ruthie.

Ruthie, taking care of the job Bigger has botched, knifes Winroy— nearly cutting his neck off. With Winroy dead, and Kendall dying, Ruthie and Bigger flee Peardale. Bigger knows his destination is Jim Thompson's personal vision of hell—the hell you don't have to dig for. This hell on earth is Thompson's literalization of the empty burden that Charlie "Little" Bigger has had to carry with him his whole life.

Ruthie and he take up residence at the Vermont farm, where eventually the howling goats drive Bigger mad, and Ruthie begins walking around on her knee and little foot. In a series of increasingly brief chapters, Bigger chronicles the end.

Bigger locks himself in the cellar, but one day Ruthie chops at him with an axe, until all that's left of him is a bloody torso. He crashes over some bottles into an open closet, certain that the answer awaits him there. He finds no answer, and dies.

In the last few pages of *Savage Night* Bigger hurtles toward death—any excerpt or summary here could not convey the fierce momentum. As with many of Thompson's endings, it's impossible to say what's "real" and what's imagined by Bigger, but it is clear that he's found "the hell that you don't have to dig for."

Just like Lou Ford and Dolly Dillon, Bigger's hell has been inside him all along: an emptiness, a void that even death, the savage night, cannot fill.

Jim Thompson worked and reworked the themes of *Savage Night, A Hell of a Woman,* and *The Killer Inside Me* in the rest of the novels written before 1956.

A Swell-Looking Babe, published in 1954, is the story of young, ambitious Bill "Dusty" Rhodes, who has been forced to work the bellboy night shift at the Manton Hotel for more than a year, since his father was dismissed from his teaching job for signing a controversial petition. Dusty resents having to take care of the old man, who seems increasingly senile; his mother died some time before.

The only real danger to a bellboy's job is getting involved with a female guest, about which Dusty has been quite careful until the arrival of Marcia Hillis:

> Sure, he'd seen some good-looking women before, at the Manton and away from it. He'd seen them, and they'd made it pretty obvious that they saw him. But he'd never come up against anything like this, a woman who was not just one but *all* women. That was the way he thought of her, right from the first moment. All women—the personification, the refined best of them all. She was twenty. She was thirty. She was sixty.

Marcia Hillis brings to a boil the psychic hell that's been simmering inside Dusty since preadolescence. He was adopted when he was five, and his mother was quite a bit younger than his father. She smothered him with affection, and when the boy was eleven he coolly plotted to receive and give that affection in a new way. As he lay in bed with his mother, he convinced her to uncover her breasts for him, just like she used to:

> "B-baby. Turn around, baby . . ." And he turned around.
> Then, right on the doorstep of the ultimate heaven, the gates clanged shut.

She lay perfectly still, breathing evenly. She did not need to push him away, not physically. Her eyes did that. Delicately flushed a moment before, the lovely planes of her face were now an icy white.

"You're a very smart boy, Bill."

"Am I, Mother?"

"Very. Far ahead of your years. How long have you been planning this?"

"P-planning what, Mother?"

"You had it all figured out, didn't you? Your— poor old Dad, sick and worn out so much of the time. And me, still young and foolish and giddy, and loving you so much I'd do anything to save you hurt."

"I— you mad at me about somethin', Mother?"

"Stop it! Stop pretending! Don't deceive yourself, Bill. At least be honest with yourself."

"M-Mother, I'm sorry if I—"

"Not nearly as sorry as I am, Bill. Nor as shocked, or frightened . . ."

Now Marcia Hillis has walked into Dusty's life, a reincarnation of *her*. His descent is swift and irreversible.

When Dusty makes his inevitable play for Marcia, it is the trap he somehow knew it would be. He runs to Tug Trowbridge, a mobster who lives at the hotel, to get him out of the jam. Dusty is soon involved with Tug in a scheme to rob the hotel's safety deposit boxes. Dusty tries to convince himself that he's both been dragged into the scheme and that nobody will get hurt. Knowing, but never admitting to himself, that Bascom, the night clerk, will be killed in the robbery, Dusty proceeds.

Three people recognize Dusty's true evil: Trowbridge, the mobster who uses him but underestimates him; Kossmeyer, his father's lawyer, who knows Dusty actually signed the petition that cost his father his job; and his father, whose final realization of what his son has become makes him drink a bottle of whiskey that kills him.

Dusty's one goal throughout is final attainment of Marcia Hillis, the woman he's desired so long without consummation. At the end of the novel she is nearly his; he's foiled the police, who know he was involved in the robbery but can prove nothing. But Kossmeyer has sworn "to get" Dusty, and the little lawyer doesn't care how he does it; he'll play by Dusty's rules:

[Dusty] paused helplessly. He couldn't express the thought, present it as the pure truth in was. But Kossmeyer must see it. Kossmeyer was an expert at separating truth from lies, and he must know that— that— Dusty gasped, his eyes widening in sudden and terrified understanding. He had chosen to play the game on the strict ground of proof: to disregard the rules of right and wrong, truth and falsehood. Now Kossmeyer was playing the same way. Kossmeyer knew that he was guilty, of the old man's death and more. He *knew,* and as long as there were no rules to the game . . .

Kossmeyer lays out the evidence, and Dusty knows that Marcia, listening from the bedroom, will believe the lawyer. Dusty's dreams are dashed, and Kossmeyer, a wonderful imitator, pantomimes what lies ahead for the boy: swinging from a hangman's noose . . .

A Swell-Looking Babe is a frustrating Jim Thompson novel; the plot and its psychological underpinning are as compelling as those in his better books, but the third-person narration is awkward, only distancing the reader from Dusty's inner machinations and rationalizations.

Dusty Rhodes's technical innocence of the murder of his father will do him no good; he will hang, as he deserves to, but for the wrong reasons. *The Nothing Man,* published later in 1954 by Dell, is in many ways the flip side of *A Swell-Looking Babe,* for Clinton Brown, first-person narrator and alcoholic psychotic, ostensibly kills three times in the novel only to find himself technically innocent (and thus ostensibly incapable) of murder.

Clinton Brown comes across as a basically good man, driven into a self-hating, bitter hell by the loss of his penis in an explosion while in the army. Brown is the prize rewrite man for the *Pacific City Courier,* where his boss is Dave Randall, the man responsible for sending him into the mine field which emasculated him. Brown drinks constantly, and constantly tortures those around him, especially Randall, the one man who knows his secret.

Brown has even kept that secret from his wife, having immediately divorced her upon his discharge from the army. Evidently Elaine has descended into a life of prostitution, yet she dreams of reuniting with Brown. Fearing discovery of his secret, Brown "kills" his wife one night by knocking her out with a bottle and setting her on fire. This "murder" leads to two more; and only at the last does the impotent Brown, in one of Thompson's sly psychic/physical dualities, discover that he's not even capable of consummating murder.

The Nothing Man is Thompson's most radical take on the nature and reality of guilt; throughout the novel we believe, along with Brown, that he is a murderer. Clinton Brown is as likable and smart as Lou Ford, and his narration every bit as self-aware and bitter. What Ford calls "the sickness" Brown recognizes as "the two-way pull":

> He looked at me, trying to appear concerned and worried while he sized me up. But there wasn't anything for him to see. The two-way pull had

taken hold and he wasn't looking at the real me—the me-in-charge-of-me. I'd moved off to one side, and I was moving faster every second. I was miles away and ahead of him.

Like Ford, Brown struggles to know himself, discover his motivations, especially those concerning his ongoing torture of Dave Randall:

> In a way, I liked him; I felt sorry for him. Yet there was another side of me that hated him, that was determined to make him go on suffering for what he had done to me. I wanted to steer clear of trouble for two reasons. Because I liked him—because I hated him. He was a nice guy—and I wanted him to stay right where he was. Where I could get at him. Dig at him day after day until . . .
>
> I don't know. It's hard to be specific about one's emotions. It is difficult to stop a story at a certain point and give a clear-cut analysis of your feelings, explain just why they are such and such and why they are not something else. Personally I am a strong believer in the exposition technique as opposed to the declarative. It is not particularly useful, of course, when employed on an of-the-moment basis, but given enough time it invariably works. Study a man's actions, at length, and his motivations become clear.

Of course, *The Nothing Man* is a "lengthy study" of the "actions" of Clinton Brown. And for most of the novel we believe, along with Brown, that his actions include murder. That actions can reveal motivations seemingly contradicts Thompson's theme of the unknowability of human nature. In fact, Thompson is proclaiming that if motivation/intent is purely good—even though unknown—then the resultant action cannot be anything but pure good.

A true analysis of action would yield the truth of intent—but man is ordinarily incapable of such analysis, due to subjective perspective. Clinton Brown could easily be Lou Ford, and a weed be "a plant out of place."

In the end, Lem Stukey, the city sheriff, shows Brown the truth of his actions and the murders. Stukey knows Brown's secret, and also knows he is basically a good man, embittered by bad fate and circumstance. Stukey sets Brown on the road to recovery at the end of the novel.

In the rather improbable plot of *The Nothing Man*, Thompson goes to great lengths to explore the possible guilt and the ultimate (active and passive) innocence of Clinton Brown. That a man could be as close to murder as Brown and yet be "innocent" points out not only the slippery, undefinable nature of guilt but the possibilities of redemption and innocence within even the most twisted murderers.

When Brown does actually see himself as he is (or as he could be), he believes himself incapable of the Sneering Slayer murders. The belief makes it so.

Circumstance and its instrument, Lem Stukey, conspire to ensure Brown's previous and future innocence, while in *A Swell-Looking Babe* circumstance and its instrument, Kossmeyer, conspire to ensure Rhodes's guilt and punishment.

After Dark, My Sweet, another important Thompson psychotic narrator novel, is the last of the thirteen books he published in three years. Prone to unthinking acts of violence, "Kid" Collins has been kicked in and out of uncaring mental institutions since he killed a man in a boxing match. Ostensibly stupid, he can't stand to be made fun of or teased, and has a much greater awareness of possible motivations of other people than they give him credit for. His main problem is one common in the Thompson world—like Cosgrove in *Recoil,* he can envision the many permutations of the truth of any given person, plan, or situation, but is unable to choose between these possible versions of the truth. Each fact, each action points in as many directions as there are possibilities.

Predictably, Kid Collins cares most about the innocence or guilt of a woman, Fay. Just in time he comes to the realization that innocence and guilt are ever changing, ever evolving, affected by other people (just as Lem Stukey was able to set Clinton Brown back on the road to innocence). He sacrifices himself for Fay, not only to save her life, but to give her a new life in which she can fulfill all the good that is in her.

The narrator of *After Dark, My Sweet* is William "Kid Collie" Collins, who gets mixed up in a kidnap scheme with Uncle Bud, a crooked ex-cop, and Fay Randall, a crazed, alcoholic young widow. Uncle Bud recognizes Collie as the man he's long needed to pull off the actual kidnapping. Bud's lame attempt to double-cross Collie and collect a reward fails when Collie shows he is miles ahead of Bud in his thinking.

Collie then relishes watching Fay and Bud squirm, now tied up in a kidnapping with an addled lunatic and able to do nothing about it. Then Collie realizes he's gotten himself into a hell of a spot by kidnapping the boy, and spends the rest of the novel trying to figure a way out for himself, the boy, and Fay—if Fay is all that he hopes she is.

Once again, personality, what is going on inside another's head, is an unknowable thing, yet something that must be known.

Only after everything has gone sour—Uncle Bud is dead, the ransom is lost, and Collie, Fay, and the sick boy are fleeing the police—can Collie see the truth about Fay, or the potential truth of Fay:

When a man stops caring what happens, all the strain is lifted from him. Suspicion and worry and fear—all the things that twist his thinking out of focus—are brushed aside. And he can see people as they are, at last. Exactly as they—as I saw Fay then.

Weak and frightened. Self-pitying, maybe. But good, too. Basically as good as a woman could be, and hating herself for not being better . . .

Suddenly it made sense for Fay to live; it was the only way my having lived would make any sense. It was why I had lived, it seemed. It was why I had been made like I was. To show her something, to prove something—to do something for her that she could not do for herself. And then, to protect her so that she could go on. So that she would have the reason for living that I'd never had.

Collie tells Fay they have to kill the boy so that there are no witnesses left to involve them in the crime. She doesn't believe him, so he seals the deal:

I laughed, cutting her off. "I guess I had you fooled, didn't I? Well, I guess I should have, all the practice I've had. I started in almost fifteen years ago—I was up for a murder rap, see, and it was the only thing I could think of. So I went into the act, and it got me out from under. And then I went into the Army, and it got me out of that. It looked like such a sweet deal that I started working the act full time."

"*What* act?" she said. "W-what are you saying?"

"The crazy stuff," I laughed again. "Hell, it's better than a pension. I could just roam about doing what I pleased—acting stupid, and cracking down when people fell for it . . . .

"I don't know why people never get wise," I said. "You do all sorts of things to give yourself away—to prove, you know, that you're plenty good at looking out for yourself. But somehow they never seem to catch on."

Fay finally believes him, believes he will kill the boy. Collie "accidentally" loses his gun, and Fay does what he expects her to do. She shoots Collie in the back and scoops up the boy to make a run for it.

Collie lies dying, happy in the knowledge that the cops will believe Fay's story, and she will have a fair chance at a good life.

Thus Jim Thompson portrays a violent psychotic as a true savior—rather than a deluded savior like Lou Ford of *The Killer Inside Me* or Nick Corey of *Pop. 1280*—of his inverted world. Kid Collins finds a reason for his actions, his unknowable nature, his seemingly meaningless existence. For a brief instant, in the upside-down world of Jim Thompson, truth has come from deception, love has come from hate, and good has come from evil.

* * *

Jim Thompson and Arnold Hano, and their wives, Alberta and Bonnie, became good friends during the Lion years. They invited each other to dinner, played cards, went to the movies, talked about the kids. The Thompson family continued to live out in Astoria, Queens, in the apartment about a block from the East River to which they had moved in October of 1950. Arnold and Bonnie Hano lived at Broadway and 105th Street in Manhattan.

Happily buried in work, these were good times for Jim Thompson and his family. Not since the Writers' Project had Thompson felt this happy and secure in a job. And his work was finally getting noticed; many of his novels had been favorably reviewed by Anthony Boucher in his weekly column on crime and mystery novels for *The New York Times Book Review*. This was no small feat; Thompson's were the first paperback originals of any kind of be reviewed in *The Times*. Boucher remained a loyal fan, reviewing each new release from the prolific Thompson.

Eventually, due to Jim Thompson's lifelong proclivity for failure, the bubble had to burst. Lion was not doing as well as the owners had hoped, and they were considering ceasing the publication of original novels. Larger competitors pushed the Lion books out of or to the back of the newsstand racks, and the whole paperback market's reader base was steadily decreasing due to the growing popularity of television. Fewer people were spending their evening reading a book.

In the meantime, Thompson had come to depend on the current situation, and had grown greatly attached to Hano. Arnold Hano:

> I think (it's hard for me to talk about this) I became some kind of surrogate father, or uncle, or big brother, God knows what. He was a few years older, but it didn't seem to matter. He was always needy in terms of having other people, he had to have other people, because he didn't really take care of himself.
>
> And to the best of my knowledge during the time I was working with him—he was totally sober. I emphasize this because it became so much a part of his life later on, that he wasn't. And when I told him that I was leaving Lion to freelance and I wasn't sure that Lion was going to continue, Jim panicked at my no longer being his editor, and maybe the whole venture dying on him. And immediately after that he started to drink.
>
> He got a job very briefly at the *New York Daily News* on the copy desk. Well, he came to the apartment that Bonnie and I had on 105th and Broadway one evening after work, and he was slightly sloggered. He said he had been laid off—he didn't know why, he thought he'd been doing very well, and thought that they had complimented his work. He then spent most of the evening with us. He ate a little bit, he drank a lot and then it was time

for him to go home. He lived in Queens with Alberta and I had to take him home.

We walked through the driving rain to my car, which was parked on Riverside Drive; I turned the key and nothing happened, literally nothing. I opened the hood and the battery was gone. They had left the four screws neatly in the corners—nice of them.

It didn't matter to him, it mattered to me—he was so out of it. We walked to the subway in the driving rain.

And we got there and he said to Alberta, who was frantic by this time—I think we had called her, but she was still frantic—he said, "Alberta, they laid me off today." And there was one instant where her face showed what he had said, and then she said, "Oh, Jim, you should have seen what the wind did before I got the window closed—it knocked down a lamp." She just shifted the thing to some little domestic problem—like it wasn't important as—that was the way she handled things.

I've never forgotten that moment.

Hano moved out to Laguna Beach, a suburb south of Los Angeles, soon after, and Thompson evidently felt abandoned.

Thompson had published thirteen books in the past three years, yet again believed that all the work had gotten him nowhere. Despite good notices from Anthony Boucher and the few other critics who bothered to review his books, he knew that as a writer of lowly paperback originals, "potboilers" as he himself called them, he would never garner any real literary acclaim. His vision would go unnoticed.

As the market for his writing continued to soften, Thompson's money-making ability remained only as good as his next book. He could have sold as many books as he could write if he could continue the pace and quality of the Lion years. But the fate of his father, his own dreams and failures, and the deeply held belief that, like the characters in his novels, he was born "with a crooked cue" piled up to paralyze him once again.

Thompson was drinking more and more, and the atmosphere at home was chilly. As Sharon Thompson Reed recalls, 1955 (her senior year in high school) was a very bad time.

Nearing the end of his fifth decade and having experienced his greatest acclaim as a novelist, circumstance would soon change the course of Jim Thompson's lifelong pursuit of "success." A young filmmaker named Stanley Kubrick and his producer partner James B. Harris had read Thompson's *The Killer Inside Me*. They wanted to speak to him about a film project they were trying to get off the ground.

Thompson, despite his bleak worldview and ingrained allegiance to failure, never completely gave up hope; he eagerly grabbed the chance to work in the movies. The rest of his life and career developed into a maddening flirtation with the ultimate success offered by Hollywood; a flirtation that eventually would destroy him.

Excited by the chance to succeed in a new field, Jim Thompson would have done well to recall Sheriff Bob Maples's advice to Lou Ford in *The Killer Inside Me:* "It's always lightest just before the dark."

THE HELL YOU DO NOT HAVE TO DIG FOR

■

The darkness and myself. Everything else was gone. And the little that was left of me was going, faster and faster.

I began to crawl. I crawled and rolled and inched my way along; and I missed it the first time—the place I was looking for.

I circled the room twice before I found it, and there was hardly any of me then but it was enough. I crawled up over the pile of bottles, and went crashing down the other side.

And he was there, of course.

Death was there.

Savage Night, **1953**

EIGHT

Jim Thompson moved his family from the apartment in Astoria to a house in Flushing, Queens, in June of 1954; they moved out about a year later, back to another apartment, at 48-02 43rd Street in Woodside, also in Queens.

While living in these neighborhoods Thompson wrote *After Dark, My Sweet,* which Popular Library published in 1955. After that success, three more Thompson efforts—*The Expensive Sky, King Blood,* and a short novel, *This World, Then the Fireworks*—all failed to find publishers. *King Blood* finally was published in England in 1973, *Fireworks* in a posthumous collection of Thompson's fiction published in 1988; *The Expensive Sky* remains unpublished at this time. Though it's impossible to say whether it was cause or effect, Thompson was drinking steadily once again by the time he wrote the three futile efforts.

Each of the three novels was so oddly skewed that it is no surprise Thompson found no takers for them. *King Blood* begins as a familiar Thompson con man tale and mutates into *King Lear* set in the Old West; the poorly written *The Expensive Sky* is a melodramatic chronicle of the last days of a Manhattan Hotel. *This World, Then the Fireworks*'s theme of childhood trauma as predestination gives it an important place in Thompson's canon, but the Greek tragedy storyline of matricide and incest, along with the condensation of the narrative to the bare essentials, made it unpublishable in the 1950s.

King Blood and *Fireworks* are discussed further in Chapter Nine and the epilogue, respectively; an excerpt from *The Expensive Sky* appears in Appendix III.

Unwilling to labor out yet another novel only to see it turned down, Thompson once more turned to short stories, publishing seven efforts in

1956. The first two, "Bellboy" in February's *Mercury Mystery Magazine* and "Prowlers in the Pear Trees" in March's, were not really new. "Bellboy" was actually Chapter Twenty of 1953's *Bad Boy;* and "Prowlers," evidently one of Thompson's favorite tall tales, had been published in *SAGA* in 1951, as well as appearing in a condensed version in Chapter Three of *Bad Boy.*

A new Thompson short story, "The Flaw in the System," appeared in the July 1956 issue of *Ellery Queen's Mystery Magazine.* A sociopolitical parable of sorts, it concerns the ability of a mysterious, kindly old beggar to swindle tough department store employees out of hundreds of dollars worth of merchandise.

Joe, the narrator, works in the credit department in an "installment house," a store which offers "easy" credit at murderous prices and interest rates. Usually the down payment covers the cost of an item. There is a set of iron-clad rules as to whom to approve for credit and under what circumstances. Even the inept con artists know of this "unbeatable" system, so few ever try to swindle the store.

One day, a kindly old man is sent up from the sales floor to be approved for a large amount of merchandise, despite having no job, no address, and no down payment. He's clearly a turn-down, but Joe just can't do it. He gives the case to Dan, his superior, who can't turn the old man away either.

Joe and Dan eventually approve the account, and wait for the inevitable ramifications. They have done the unallowable, the unexplainable. Soon Dorrance, the company's credit manager, arrives for an audit of the books.

Dorrance finds nothing amiss, besides the approval of the old dead-beat's account. He tells Joe and Dan that he has audited ten other stores in the past few weeks, and that four of them didn't check. The employees had figured a way to beat the unbeatable system. Dorrance continues:

> "I've been wondering why I didn't foresee that it would happen. We've discouraged individuality, anything in the way of original thinking. All decisions were made at the top and passed down. Honesty, loyalty—we didn't feel that we had to worry about those things. The system would take care of them. The way the system worked—supposedly—a man simply had to be loyal and honest.
>
> "Well, obviously we were all wet; we found those four stores I mentioned, and God knows how many others there are like them. And about all I can say is we were asking for it. If you won't let a man think for you, he'll think against you. If you don't have any feeling for *him,* you can't expect him to have any for *you.*"

The old con man's campaign triggered the store investigations; in a way, Dorrance is in debt to the old man. Still, Dorrance asserts he is a dangerous guy: "Why, a man like that—he could wreck us if he took a notion to. He could wreck the entire economy!"

The nature of the "old man" is left a mystery, but it's broadly hinted that he's a Christlike or savior figure, holding up a mirror to each man he meets; a mirror that demands they reassert their own humanity—and act like a human being rather than part of the "system."

Thompson's indictment of the system is here more pointed and spare than in any writing he did after the WPA, but the single theme of this short story underlies each of his more characteristic crime novels. The subversive idea that a modern-day savior would be opposed to the rote workings of capitalism is at the heart of "The Flaw in the System."

The title of "Murder Came on the Mayflower" (*Mercury Mystery Magazine,* November 1956) does more to evoke the Thompson world, and the inseparable intertwining of murder and the New World, than do the "facts" of the story itself. Based on the story of John Billington, the first man to be hanged for murder in America, this true-crime effort reads more like a synopsis by a historical journalist than a story by Jim Thompson. Still, Billington's story itself offered fascinating possibilities; Thompson evidently thought so, for he published another version of the story, "America's First Murderer," in September's *For Men Only,* and left behind an unfinished novel about the ill-fated pilgrim, entitled *Billington.* (See Appendix III).

Later in 1956 Thompson succeeded in selling two novellas to *Alfred Hitchcock's Mystery Magazine,* which published them in December 1956 and February 1957. Entitled "The Cellini Chalice" and "The Frightening Frammis" they entail the exploits of Mitch Allison, an engaging, somewhat inept con man. The first centers around a complicated revenge sting executed against Mitch by his jealous wife and associates. The second, taking up the narrative where the first left off, concerns Mitch's attempt to steal $50,000 from some fellow con men, including a character named The Pig.

Thompson probably intended the adventures of Mitch Allison to be lighthearted, action-filled con man stories; neither explore Thompson's trademark themes or obsessions to any great degree. The only interesting passages within these novellas are the instances of grotesque violence, which seem inappropriate for the tone Thompson has set. In "The Cellini Chalice," Allison seals a man inside a cesspool, up to his neck in filth; in "The Frightening Frammis," Allison entombs The Pig in a bathtub full of plaster.

Like "Murder Came on the Mayflower," Thompson must have thought the Mitch Allison stories held some unfulfilled promise; an unfinished novel entitled *Mitch Allison* was left among his papers when he died. (See Appendix III.)

Besides the Mitch Allison episodes, Thompson published another story, under the pseudonym Dillon Roberts, in the December 1956 issue of *Alfred Hitchcock's Mystery Magazine*. Entitled "The Threesome in Four-C," it concerns the efforts of the narrator to quiet the noisy neighbors upstairs. Only at the end do we find that the apartment upstairs is empty, and the noises he has been hearing are only in his mind. The narrator murdered his wife and two children, but their voices ceaselessly haunt him. His delusions give him away to the police.

Thompson wrote at least one more story, for a less distinguished magazine, during this time. The September 1957 issue of *Man's World*, a typical 1950s men's magazine, featured Thompson's "Bert Casey, Wild Gun of the Panhandle"—a fanciful retelling of the adventures of a legendary Oklahoma Territory outlaw.

In late 1955 a young agent named Robert Goldfarb at the Jaffe Company in Los Angeles was contacted by Stanley Kubrick and James Harris about *Clean Break,* a caper novel by Lionel White, whom Goldfarb represented. Goldfarb knew Harris as the son of a big film distributor, Joe Harris, and knew Kubrick from his work as a still photographer for *Life*. The twenty-five-year-old Kubrick previously had made two small features, *Fear and Desire* and *Killer's Kiss*, and the two new collaborators were interested in the Lionel White novel as a basis for their first film as a production team. They acquired the option rights from Goldfarb, who figured that would be the last he'd hear of it.

James Harris recalls:

> After we acquired the rights, Stanley brought to my attention that there was this terrific writer. He'd read some of Jim Thompson's books—*The Killer Inside Me*, among others—and Stanley thought he should be brought in to work on the screenplay.

Alberta Thompson and daughter Sharon recall Stanley Kubrick's frequent visits to their apartment in Woodside, where Thompson and Kubrick soon pounded out a working relationship. They would discuss what each scene was about and how long it should run, and then Thompson would write them up. Later Kubrick would look the work over, and changes would be made. Evidently Thompson and Kubrick had no awareness of conventional screenplay format: the resultant script was on legal-sized paper, and about three times too long.

Some time later, Bob Goldfarb received the first draft of the screenplay at his Hollywood office:

> I'll never forget the script's arrival—in a cardboard carton big enough to house a family—and the script was something like 300 pages, legal sized, clipped at the top. The whole thing looked like amateur night. It was written by Stanley Kubrick and Jim Thompson.
>
> I don't claim to have read that script and announced that a star had risen in the east. In fact, I was terribly skeptical of the suspense device that proved in the picture to be absolutely stunning. . . . The stroke of genius was to keep going back to a point in the story and running all the threads simultaneously up to a point, and then going back and running them back to a further point. I must say that the name Jim Thompson meant nothing to me. And, of course, Kubrick's didn't mean much either.

Eventually Goldfarb traveled back to New York to advise the young filmmakers and their screenwriter:

> I told them you just can't show something like this, it's not professional. No one can handle a script that's written on legal sized paper. I [gave] them a sample script to show them how to put it in conventional studio screenplay form. . . .

Adds James Harris:

> Jim had never written a script before and Stanley had only written his own things. I always remember that it opened up the way you would read a yellow legal pad. We recruited Bob Goldfarb's help to go after our list of actors to get a lead.
>
> I'm pretty sure that when Thompson wrote *The Killing,* he didn't write it as a screenplay. He probably wrote scenes like he would in a book chapter. And Stanley would put it into screenplay form. I know Thompson wasn't aware then of things like "fade in" and "fade out."

Goldfarb represented the property for Kubrick and Harris, and when Sterling Hayden agreed to play the lead role of Johnny Clay, United Artists offered to finance the remaining shooting amount in return for a distribution deal. From a *New York Times* newspaper clipping in the Thompson family collection:

> Mr. Harris, who was seeking more rewarding film fields, found a kindred soul in Mr. Kubrick and the pair, under the corporate tag of Harris-Kubrick Film Corporation, now are launching another independent feature, "The Clean Break" for United Artists. Last week, the Messrs.

Kubrick and Harris signed Sterling Hayden to play the lead. They described "Clean Break" as a story by Lionel White (the script has been written by Kubrick and James Thompson) dealing with "an ingenious attempt to rob a local racetrack of $2,000,000."

It will go before the camera in Manhattan, at the Biograph studio in the Bronx and at a racetrack here, starting next month. "Clean Break," Kubrick said, will be filmed on an eight week schedule.

About this time Bob Goldfarb took an interest in Thompson's previous work, and agreed to represent his interests out on the West Coast. He remembers his first impression of Jim Thompson:

> I was impressed by Jim Thompson's size, he was a big man, very tall. And I sensed immediately something that I always felt characterized him: in common with many people who are physically imposing, he had a very gentle manner and way of speaking—terribly insecure, very diffident. Stanley was always calling on him and Thompson claimed that although he did the work, it was Stanley's name on the page. And I didn't doubt it.
>
> But when I got to know Stanley better, I realized what a bloody genius he was, and I realized that no one else would have given Jim the opportunity that he did, or put up with the things—I don't know—I hesitate to say that Jim was an alcoholic—but he was what I call a whiskey fighter. He fought booze every hour of his life and sometimes the booze won. He was a guy always trying not to take a drink.

Thompson's drinking evidently did not cause the filmmakers undue worry; recalls Harris:

> His drinking didn't get in the way of the work. He always had money problems. There were calls at odd hours of the night—when he was "under the weather" and needed help. Money was tight all over in those days for us, but we'd always help him out when we could.
>
> [Thompson's drinking] may have held up delivery of some pages at one point or another. Thompson would call Stanley for bail-outs and help. Stanley cared, he liked the material. If we had to wait a couple of extra days, what difference did it make?
>
> We never socialized much. He was a loner as far as we were concerned. He was substantially older than we were. It was more of a business relationship than anything else.

While the young filmmakers had some trouble with Thompson's drinking, Thompson in turn found Kubrick's personal style hard to deal with. Sharon Reed vividly recalls Kubrick's "beatnik" clothes and mannerisms: "Stanley was strange and eccentric when it wasn't 'cool' to be that way. Sometimes he'd embarrass Daddy at restaurants—he wouldn't wear a tie, things like that. Daddy would be mortified."

The whole Thompson family turned out for the New York premiere of *The Killing*. According to Alberta, Sharon, Pat, and Michael, Thompson "nearly fell off his chair" when the writing credits flashed on the screen: Screenplay by Stanley Kurbrick; additional dialogue by Jim Thompson. Says Sharon: "There were fireworks when my father saw Stanley after the screening."

The Thompson family maintains that Jim Thompson sued for proper screenwriting credit with the Writers Guild and won, and as part of the settlement Kubrick was forced to hire Thompson to write his next picture, *Paths of Glory*.

That is not what happened. There is no record of an arbitration at the Writers Guild, and Harris has no recollection of there ever being one. When Thompson, more than a decade later, did sue for a screen credit over *The Getaway,* he stated in his letter to the Writers Guild that it was the *first time* he ever instigated a credit arbitration.

Very likely, when Thompson approached Kubrick and Harris about the credit matter (if he ever did so directly), and they told him how much they valued his work and offered $7,500 to write their next picture, Thompson accepted the desperately needed praise, work, and money as fair settlement.

James Harris says he doesn't recall any great dispute over the writing credit, and bristles at the idea that he and Kubrick cheated Jim Thompson of his rightful credit:

> We weren't the kind of people to do that sort of thing—to have a ghost writer come in and not give him any credit.
> Kubrick must have believed that he had done enough work overall. Stanley not only did revisions, he put it into screenplay form—and therein may lie the evaluation of how the credits were decided.
> Maybe it was a bit unfair in the sense that we were adjudicating those kinds of things ourselves. I guess we felt Stanley had written the majority of what went into the final screenplay.

The Killing is a classic caper film, a harder-edged, cooler descendent of films like John Huston's version of W. R. Burnett's *The Asphalt Jungle*. Like the Huston film, it involves an intricate scheme to steal millions of dollars. Johnny Clay, played by Sterling Hayden, recruits the men he needs and efficiently lays out his plan to rob the local racetrack of about $2 million. The five principals will split the take, while two men hired to create diversions will be paid straight fees for their tasks. The

Insert poster and three lobby cards for The Killing.

main "diversion" is the shooting of the favorite in the big race of the day as the horses reach the backstretch.

As usual in such films, something goes terribly wrong. Sherry, the tramp wife of George Peatty, the meekest of the criminals, is sleeping with a small-time hood. They conspire to steal the loot from Johnny and his men. In a final shootout everyone dies except Johnny and his girl. They are arrested at the airport when a cheap suitcase containing the $2 million bursts open on the runway.

Jim Thompson's mark on the film is most apparent in the crisp dialogue, and the dark comedy found in the most unexpected situations. The "gimmick" of cutting to different characters and plotlines at different times of the caper is lifted straight from the novel; Lionel White's own stroke of brilliance, not Kubrick's or Thompson's. In fact, the swift, lean novel reads like a screenplay; all it really needed was the tightening and streamlining that Kubrick and Thompson gave it.

Nonetheless, Jim Thompson's hand is evident; his best lines are given to Johnny Clay and Sherry Peatty, who is a pure distillation of a familiar Thompson icon. An exchange between Johnny and Sherry, after Johnny discovers her spying on the gang is undoubtedly Thompson's work:

SHERRY

You don't know me very well.

JOHNNY

I know you like a book. You're a no good, nosy little tramp. You'd sell out your own mother for a piece of fudge. But you're smart along with it. Smart enough to know when to sell and when to sit tight. And you know you better sit tight in this case.

SHERRY

I do.

JOHNNY

You heard me. You like money. You got a great big dollar bill sign there, where most women have a heart. So play it smart. Stay in character and you'll have money. Plenty of it. George'll have it. And he'll blow it on you. Probably buy himself a five cent cigar.

SHERRY

You don't know me very well, Johnny. I wouldn't think of letting George throw his money away on cigars.

Another bit of trademark Jim Thompson writing is hidden in an exchange between Johnny Clay and Maurice Oboukhoff, the chess-playing, philosophical side-of-beef Johnny hires to create a diversion at the racetrack. A deep thinker, Maurice knows that in this world where mediocrity is the accepted norm, Johnny will be punished for his ambition. It's a twist on the plight of Lou Ford and his hidden brilliance, this time applied to a different all-American stereotype—the gangster:

> MAURICE
>
> You have my sympathies, Johnny. You have not yet learned that in this life you have to be like everyone else. The perfect majority. No better, no worse. Individuality's a monster, and it must be strangled in its cradle to make our friends feel competent. You know I've often thought that the gangster and the artist are the same in the eyes of the masses. They are admired and hero-worshipped, but there is always present an underlying wish to see them destroyed at the peak of their glory.
>
> JOHNNY
>
> Yeah, like the man said, "Life is a glass of tea," huh?
>
> MAURICE
>
> Oh, Johnny, my boy. You never were very bright, but I love you anyway.

Still, the sharpest move Thompson and Kubrick made in adapting *Clean Break* was staying as faithful to the novel and its structure as possible. In the rush to praise Kubrick's breakthrough film, not only was Jim Thompson's contribution overlooked, so was Lionel White's.

On July 6, 1956, Jim Thompson signed a contract with the Harris-Kubrick Pictures Corporation to write a screenplay of *Paths of Glory,* from the novel by Humphrey Cobb. From the contract:

> 8. In the event a motion picture based upon the work shall be produced, screen credits shall be given to Jim Thompson on the positive release prints of the Photoplay in the manner following: "SCREENPLAY BY STANLEY KUBRICK AND JIM THOMPSON."
>
> 9. In consideration of the sale, transfer and assignment herein made, and in full payment thereof, you shall pay to Jim Thompson (hereinafter referred to as "Thompson") a sum of Seventy-five Hundred Dollars, payment to be made as follows:
>
> a) Five Hundred Dollars per week for ten consecutive weeks commencing the week of July 9, 1956, totaling Five Thousand Dollars.
>
> b) Twelve Hundred Fifty Dollars on January 1, 1957.
>
> c) Twelve Hundred Fifty Dollars upon the first day of commencing of principal photography of the picture, "PATHS OF GLORY."

Kubrick and Harris had decided to make Hollywood the base of operations for this picture, so Jim and Alberta Thompson rented an apartment in the Hollywood Hills for the ten weeks it took Jim to write the first draft. They then returned to New York to prepare a more permanent move to the West Coast. Later that year they moved the family to 907 Buena Vista in San Clemente, where they remained for several years.

The writing of *Paths of Glory* was essentially a very well-paid part-time job for Thompson; with renewed spirit and a burst of creativity he wrote and sold two new novels later in 1956: his last Lion Book, *The Kill-Off*, and *Wild Town*, for Signet. Both were published in 1957.

The Kill-Off, composed of twelve first-person chapters in the voices of twelve different characters, is another of Thompson's structural tours de force. Like its formal predecessor, *The Criminal*, it centers around a murder and the likely suspects.

Luane Devore is the leading gossip of the dying seaside town of Manduwoc—a bitter, twisted old woman who has sealed herself up in her bedroom and uses the telephone to exact revenge against any and all perceived enemies. Many people have more than enough reason to kill her, including her husband, Ralph. Twenty years Luane's junior and now in love with beautiful jazz singer Danny Lee, Ralph Devore has a small fortune in cash saved up from his handyman jobs over the past twenty years. But Luane keeps the money stored in the mattress of the bed she never leaves, and Ralph can't figure a way to get his money, short of killing her.

Her vicious speculation into others' lives has led Luane to guess the true lineage of Bobbie Ashton, whose mother supposedly died giving him birth; actually he is the son of the town doctor and his Negro housemaid. Bobbie had suspected the truth for years, intending to use it in his own way. Now Luane has ruined his plans.

Luane also has guessed the truth of County Attorney Henry Clay Williams's sister's "stomach tumor": she is pregnant with her brother's baby. And long ago Luane's father swindled honest Pete Pavlov out of a large sum of money on a construction job Pavlov was doing. Now Pavlov needs the money, since his fortune has slipped away from him. Even Kossmeyer, her lawyer, has been stung by Luane's anti-Semitic remarks . . .

Like *The Criminal, The Kill-Off* is a study of a small society and collective guilt; the mapping of the route of infectious evil as it travels from one person to the next. The one undoubtedly "good man," Pete Pavlov, is also the one who divulges that he kills Luane Devore and two other people.

Kossmeyer, the diminutive lawyer, narrates Chapter One, in which Luane Devore confesses her basic fear: she thinks Ralph is trying to kill her. Kossmeyer reminds her that a lot of people have good reasons to want her dead. In Chapter Two, Ralph takes over the narration.

Ralph Devore explains that Luane, ostensibly the fount of all this poison, was herself the victim of gossip when she married him, a man young enough to be her son (some whispered that he *was* her son . . .):

> I felt awful sorry for Luane. She'd sure given up a lot on my account. She was a lady, and she came from a proud old family. She'd been a churchgoer and a charity worker, and everything like that. And then just because she wanted someone to love before she got too old for it, why there was all that dirtiness. Stuff that took the starch right out of you, and filled you up with something else. . . .
> . . . it did something pretty terrible to Luane. She didn't show it for a long time. . . . But the hurt was there inside, festering and spreading, and finally breaking out.

Rags Maguire, narrator of Chapter Three, is another of the wounded of this world. A jazz musician, he says he hired Danny Lee as the singer in his band because "she has the music in her." Although her talent is rough and undeveloped, Rags is determined to make Danny a star.

Danny reminds him of his wife, Janie, whom Rags claims is not touring with him this summer because she's taking care of their two sons. Actually, their sons were killed in the car crash that has left Janie without a face.

Rags sets up Ralph and Danny as a practical joke on the girl, telling her Ralph is one of the richest men in town. Rags doesn't realize he's telling her the truth.

Bobbie Ashton, the doctor's super-intelligent but twisted son, takes over in Chapter Four. He has figured out that Ralph must have a lot of money saved up, and intends to steal it as part of his master plan to gain revenge on his parents and Luane. Bobbie's rage has rendered him impotent, and he in turn has made Myra Pavlov, Pete's daughter, a junkie. The absence of love is the source of his impotence, and one night while spying on Ralph and Danny, basking in the glow of their love for one another, he discovers he has an erection. After deciding not to kill them on the spot—during what he considers the happiest moments of their lives—Bobbie rushes to Myra. He demands her love, pleading with her in the only way he can:

> I kissed her. I crushed her body against mine. And her lips were stiff and lifeless, and her body was like ice. And the glow was leaving me. The life and the resurrection were leaving me.
> "D-don't," I said. "I mean, please. I only want to love you, only to love

you and have you love me. That's all. Only sweetness and tenderness and—"

Suddenly I dug my fingers into her arms. I shook her until her silly head almost flopped off.

I told her she'd better do what I said or I'd kill her.

"I'll do it, by God!" I slapped her in the face. "I'll beat your goddamned head off! You be nice to me, you moronic bitch! Be sweet, you slut! Y-you be gentle and tender and loving—you love me, DAMN YOU, YOU LOVE ME! Or I'll . . . I'll . . ."

The character of Bobbie Ashton was resurrected and further developed as Allen Smith, the half-black, impotent high school student/savior of Thompson's last novel, *Child of Rage*.

In Chapter Five, Dr. Ashton offers excuses for his actions over the years; yet by the end of his chapter he sees the string of rationalizations for what they are, and admits he's always been a man without the courage of his convictions.

Chapter Six offers the ruminations of the town idiot, Marmaduke "Goofy" Gannder. Waking on his grandmother's grave in the "City of Wonderful People," Goofy has a "conversation" with his dead Grandma, a conversation during which he offers his own story of the state of the world:

"Certainly, Grandma," I said. "Certainly . . . 'Once upon a time, there were two billion and a half bastards who lived in a jungle, which weighed approximately six sextillion, four hundred and fifty quintillion short tons. Though they all were brothers, these bastards, their sole occupation was fratricide. Though the jungle abounded in wondrous fruits, their sole food was dirt. Though their potential for knowledge was unlimited, they knew but one thing. And what they knew was only what they did not know. And what they did not know was what was enough.' "

I stopped speaking.

Grandma stirred impatiently. "Well, go on."

"That's all there is," I said.

"But I thought you said you'd finished. That's no more than you had before."

"It's all there is," I repeated. "As I see it, there is nothing more to say."

Goofy's sly parable is a twist on Lincoln Fargo's story, changed by the additional element of man's insatiable need and greed: "what they did not know was what was enough." Thus is man's central plight implicitly linked to the desire for money and power—the desire upon which the capitalist system is based.

Later in his chapter, Goofy offers another crucial musing, after Pete Pavlov hints at Goofy's helping him stage a fake holdup so he can collect on the insurance. When Goofy puts the matter too explicitly, Pete angrily denies that that's what he was talking about:

> "Yes, sir," I said. "And I don't know what you said. I didn't hear you. I wasn't listening."
>
> I turned and left. I went out onto the boardwalk, wondering if this after all was not the original sin, the one we all suffer for: the failure to attribute to others the motives which we claim for ourselves. The inexcusable failure to do so.
>
> True, I was not very prepossessing, either in appearance or actions. I was not, but neither was he. He was every bit as unreassuring in his way as I was in mine. And as you are in yours. We were both disguised. The materials were different, but they had all come from the same loom. My eccentricity and drunkenness. His roughness, rudeness, and outright brutality.
>
> We had to be disguised. Both of us, all of us. Yet obvious as the fact was, he would not see it. He would not look through my guise, as I had looked through his, to the man beneath. He would not look through his own, which would have done practically as well.
>
> It was too bad, and he would be punished for it—as who is not?

Goofy Gannder's view of original sin is the most explicit statement of a theme central not only in *The Kill-Off,* but in all of Thompson's novels; the best diagnosis of the condition of the entire Thompson world since Lincoln Fargo's observations in *Heed the Thunder.* Man walks through life acknowledging only his own disguise, his own truth behind the mask. Others he takes at face value, refusing to consider even the existence of something else underneath.

Goofy's parable and his exchange with Pete reveal his deep understanding of the plight of his world and people; but in a typical Thompson irony, this visionary's glimpses of the truth have only driven him insane—or insane as judged by his society.

The remaining chapters of *The Kill-Off* are narrated by Hattie, Bobbie Ashton's mother, in which Bobbie hints at helping out a friend; by Luane Devore, in which she glimpses her murderer; by Danny Lee, in which she and Doctor Ashton provide each other with alibis for the time of Luane's murder; by Henry Clay Williams, in which he makes the mistake of crossing Kossmeyer; by Myra Pavlov, in which she explains why she's so afraid of her father; and by Pete Pavlov, in which he kills Bobbie and Myra as they make love in the woods, and then frightens Luane into falling down the stairs and killing herself. At least, Pete thinks he killed her. He has a funny feeling someone else may have finished the job.

Like *The Criminal, The Kill-Off* offers no final solution to its central crime. In fact, Pete Pavlov claims that all the other principal suspects really should not be suspected at all, because of the kind of people they are:

> The very fact that they had good reasons for wanting Luane dead—and that everyone knew it—would be the thing that would keep them from killing her. They'd be too afraid, you know, that the job might be pinned on them.
>
> Aside from that, and maybe excepting Danny Lee, all the prime suspects were too fond of living to commit murder. They'd proved it over and over, through the years; proved it by the way they lived. They'd give up their principles, their good name—everything they had; just as long as they could go on living. Living any damned old way. And people like that, they ain't going to take the risk of killing.

Pete speculates that Henry Clay Williams's secretary, who has long been secretly in love with her boss, probably killed Luane because of her gossip about his sister's "stomach tumor." That is, if Pavlov himself didn't kill her. And we know that Bobbie Ashton really committed suicide there in the woods—he planned that Pete would discover and kill him and Myra.

Once again, in *The Kill-Off* guilt is a slippery and an arbitrary concept, if only because everyone must share in guilt, not just the man who pulled the trigger. Like *The Criminal, The Kill-Off* offers a more panoramic vision of the inverted Thompson world than do Thompson's single narrator novels.

In *Wild Town*, ex-convict Bugs McKenna is hired on as a hotel detective by millionaire Mike Hanlon. Bugs is a basically honest man who's had more than his share of bad luck and bad scrapes; although life has made him extremely suspicious and watchful, he doesn't seem a killer. But he's afraid that's exactly why he's been hired—he thinks Hanlon's wife, Joyce, wants him to knock off the old invalid so she can inherit all his money. Bugs is sure that Deputy Sheriff Lou Ford is mixed up in Joyce Hanlon's schemes.

Further complicating matters, Bugs falls in love with Amy Standish, the town schoolteacher and Lou Ford's assumed betrothed. None of these peculiar West Texans will come out and speak plainly about anything, and before long Bugs's poor head is spinning from his search for the truth.

The rest of *Wild Town* is a passable Jim Thompson "mystery," emphasizing the unknowable nature of personality and motivation. As usual, we don't know until the end exactly who is doing what and why. Lou Ford here acts as the brilliant detective who figures everything out; Lou Ford as Hercule Poirot. Bugs McKenna eventually discovers the innate goodness inside himself, and ends up getting the girl. Lou Ford is portrayed as a tragic, sacrificial character, who gives up his own slim chance at contentment so that Amy and Bugs can be together.

In this, Thompson's second chronicle of the life of a "Lou Ford," Ford does play a heroic role, unable to find any true happiness. But through most of the novel, it is very easy to believe that Ford is the evil, grinning clown that Bugs McKenna takes him to be:

> Bugs got up and paced nervously around the room. As attractive as this set-up seemed, in some ways, he was worried about it. Suspicious of Ford. Ford's clownish mannerisms were too exaggerated, no more than a mask for a coldly calculating and super-sharp mind. He wouldn't go to these lengths simply to place an efficient house detective in the Hanlon Hotel.
>
> Still—Bugs thought—how could he be so sure? He didn't think like an ordinary man any more; he'd reached the point where he was suspicious of everyone.

Only Amy Standish understands this Lou Ford, as she explains to an incredulous Bugs:

> "You see," she went on, "Lou feels his own life is wasted. He hates what he's doing. He's not suited to it, and it's twisted him. Actually, he's very scholarly. He was a brilliant student, and—"
>
> "*Him?* Ford?"
>
> "It's hard to believe, isn't it?" Amy nodded. "But, yes, Lou's very brilliant. He graduated from high school when he was fifteen. He went through pre-med in three years. Then, in his first year of medical college, his father took very ill and Lou came home. Doctor Ford—his father, that is—didn't get any worse, but he didn't get any better, either. He just lingered on, year after year. And Lou . . ."
>
> Ford had felt that he had to stay with the old man. But there was nothing in the small town for him to do. No suitable work, no real challenge for his mind. Still, he had to do something, and because he was "old family" he had been given a deputy sheriff's appointment. It was no job for a book-learned dude, obviously. For a man with ambitions which would be interpreted as pretensions. You had to blend with those around you, with the public's perception of a cowtown deputy. So Ford had blended. He had fitted himself into the role with a vengeance, exaggerating it until it bordered on caricature. And with this outward twisting of the man, there

had been an inward one. In the brain—the intelligence—which could not be used as it had been intended to be.

In the end, Bugs discovers the truth of Amy's statements about Ford, as Ford teaches Bugs a few things about himself. Thompson gives his final attention to Lou Ford, a solitary, tragic figure in the West Texas landscape:

> The loneliness swept over Ford again, the loneliness and the bitterness. But only briefly; it was gone almost as soon as it came. He grinned and stood up quietly. He tiptoed out of the room.
> He went down the hall, Stetson shoved back on his head, cigar gripped between his teeth, rocking in his high-heeled boots. Laughing at himself, jeering at himself. Laughing away the unbearable. He reached the entrance, and he stood there for a moment. He breathed in the cold air of darkness and stared up into the heartbreaking beauty of the Far West Texas sky.
> It sure was a fine night, he decided. Yes, sir, it sure was, and that was a fact . . .

The difference between this Ford and his predecessor of *The Killer Inside Me* is not as great as one might like to think; Thompson here emphasizes that only random circumstance and its resultant effect on personality makes the difference between anyone being a "good man" or a hollow, twisted killer. Although its sometimes awkward third-person narration renders *Wild Town* a minor Thompson novel, its new take on Lou Ford makes it essential for understanding the Thompson worldview.

Thompson still was not through with the character of Lou Ford; he returned to the deputy's story one more time, giving him a new name in 1961's *The Transgressors*.

Stanley Kubrick and James Harris eventually hired Calder Willingham to rewrite Jim Thompson's screenplay drafts of *Paths of Glory;* Harris says Thompson "understood that sometimes you write yourself out on a particular project. We wanted to bring a new mind in." Willingham had worked on the screenplay for *The Burning Secret,* which MGM had proposed to Harris-Kubrick as their next film after *The Killing*. After the main promoter of *The Burning Secret,* Dore Schary, was fired from MGM, that development deal went down the drain.

Recalls Arnold Hano:

> I knew Jim was working with Kubrick, he complained about Kubrick and how difficult it was to work for him, and he told me Kubrick allegedly tried to steal the credit again. I gather he took it to the Directors Guild. Jim

Half-sheet posters for The Killing *and* Paths of Glory.

had all the manuscripts, and he did assure me that the finished Calder
Willingham version was so close to his that it was practically impossible to
tell the difference.

There is no record of an arbitration over the credit for *Paths of Glory*
at the Directors or Writers Guild. Once again, if Thompson felt his credit
was not all that it should have been, he did nothing official about it.

The final screen credit for *Paths of Glory* is screenplay by Stanley
Kubrick, Calder Willingham, and Jim Thompson. The film opened on
Christmas Day, 1957, and immediately won great critical acclaim and
eventual worldwide success, despite being banned in France.

Paths of Glory is set in the French Army of 1915, when the Germans
and French were waging many bloody and pointless battles. General
Broulard calls on General Mireau one day, announcing a promotion will
ensue if Mireau's men take the anthill, a nearly impossible-to-capture
German stronghold. After mild protestation, the ambitious General
Mireau agrees to take the hill.

Mireau in turn visits Colonel Dax, who informs Mireau of what he
already knows: ravaged from previous battles, his exhausted men
couldn't possibly capture the hill. Mireau threatens to relieve Dax of his
command; faced with little choice, Dax tells the general that he and the
men will do their best on what amounts to a suicide mission.

When the assault turns out as all knew it would, some of the soldiers
refuse to leave their trenches to face instant death. Mireau orders the
artillery officer to bomb the French trenches. Further enraged at the
debacle, Mireau orders Dax to have three of the surviving men chosen for
court-martial for cowardice in the face of the enemy.

The court-martial is a farce; the men are convicted despite being defended
by Dax, who formerly was a renowned civilian lawyer. As a last resort, Dax
goes to General Broulard with information about Mireau ordering his own
men bombed. Yet Broulard lets the executions take place as scheduled.

When they meet the next day, Broulard makes Mireau the scapegoat
for the anthill incident after all. Broulard offers Dax the disgraced
general's rank, mistakenly assuming that was what Dax was after all
along—rather than trying to save the court-martialed men. Dax insults
General Broulard and refuses the promotion. Dax rejoins the rest of his
men, who are listening to a German cabaret singer. Little has changed—
soon they must return to battle.

Paths of Glory shows subtle signs of Jim Thompson's hand, especially
in the maze of misunderstood motives, the conundrum of ultimate guilt or
innocence, and the punchy dialogue. James Harris still recalls Thompson's coming up with one of the best lines in the film, when a soldier

accuses a cowardly superior of "having a streak of spit where his spine oughta be." It's also unmistakably Thompson when Mireau claims that Dax's men have "skim milk in their veins instead of blood."

A third-draft screenplay of *Paths of Glory,* dated March 24, 1957, and credited to Kubrick, Willingham, and Thompson, was left among Thompson's papers; some of the changes made and scenes later excised are of particular interest. This exchange, left out of the film, seems prime Jim Thompson:

DAX
Don't you think the men should deserve shooting?

BROULARD
Well, Colonel, all men deserve shooting, if you come right down to it.

DAX
In other words, it doesn't matter if the execution is an injustice.

BROULARD
My dear Colonel Dax, injustice is as much a part of life as the weather. Besides don't you think it would be incredibly arrogant for us to decide what's just and what isn't?

DAX
(sarcastically)
I'm afraid, sir, that your reasoning is a little beyond me.

BROULARD
Those three men aren't being shot for a crime. They're being shot as examples. It's their contribution to winning the war. And a heroic one, too, if you like.

DAX
In other words, these men are dying for their country.

BROULARD
There is no doubt about it. They're dying gloriously for France.

DAX
What you're saying, sir, is that executing these men serves a higher purpose, by protecting the General Staff, and by simultaneously welding the army into a more efficient fighting force.

BROULARD
Precisely. And since you understand it so clearly, I'm sure you'll agree with me that their death is necessary.

DAX
Sir, even if killing these men would achieve that higher purpose, it would be brutal and inhuman. The truth however is that it won't achieve a thing.

BROULARD

Perhaps you're right.

(rises)

Well, Colonel, although it's been a great pleasure discussing this with you, I'd better get back to my guests.

DAX

At the risk of being tedious, sir, I'll ask you one final question. Do you sincerely believe that good can come from evil?

BROULARD

Why, certainly, Colonel—where else can it come from?

Upon the release of *Paths of Glory* Stanley Kubrick's reputation was secured. Both Kubrick and Harris felt they owed a great debt to Jim Thompson, and wanted to continue to work with him. Having by this time recognized that Thompson's strength lay in novel writing, not screenplay adaptation, they commissioned Thompson to write them a new novel, which they could then turn into a film.

Jim produced *Lunatic at Large,* which, unfortunately, we can now judge only by its title. Thompson gave Kubrick and Harris the only copy of it (he apparently made no carbon). After glancing at it, they put it in their "next project" file. Kubrick was then preparing the actual shooting of *Paths of Glory,* and according to Harris, they lost the original Thompson novel in the confusion:

I'm embarrassed to say that not only did I lose the book, but now I can't even remember what it was about, except for a long scene in the subways of New York. *Lunatic at Large,* it was called. We were all guilty of not having the brains to think we might lose it.

Nearly twenty years later, just before Thompson died, he contacted Harris and Kubrick and asked them if he could have the rights to *Lunatic at Large* if he rewrote the novel. According to Harris, they said sure: "At that point, Kubrick and I both felt, why not? Give it back to him, if he wants to take the time to re-create it." Thompson evidently never got very far with it; there is no sign of *Lunatic at Large* among the manuscripts he left behind.

Throughout his career as a director, Kubrick continued to have a keen eye for source material. His brilliance lies not only in his technical abilities as a director, but also in his determination to stay true to the vision of the bleak novels to which he is attracted. This is not to be underrated in the film world, where every decision is made by committee, and the final choice made always the safest, blandest, and least likely to offend. Kubrick remains one of the few film directors whose plots and themes have their own inner logic and obsessions, and who do not change a character or tack on a happy ending for the sake of conventional wisdom or box office receipts. Luckily free of financial dependence on Hollywood by the early 1960s, Kubrick has produced an as fiercely individualistic body of work as, well, Jim Thompson. Despite any personal differences they may have had, they each must have recognized how much they were alike.

Ironically, today Stanley Kubrick remains one of the few directors who would be able to bring one of Jim Thompson's books to the screen with its full impact intact, undiluted and uncompromised.

The *Lunatic at Large* fiasco ended Thompson's association with Kubrick and Harris. Kubrick moved on to direct *Spartacus,* and Harris eventually directed some films of his own. Jim Thompson should have benefited from his association with Kubrick and Harris, and was undoubtedly expecting offers to write more films.

The offers never came.

In the meantime, Thompson began work on another novel, a caper type possibly inspired by his experience with Lionel White's *Clean Break;* it was called *The Getaway.* Bob Goldfarb recalls: "I loved Thompson's work—especially *The Getaway.* I read it in manuscript and I remember that he couldn't get it published—it was very different from his usual thing."

Back on the East Coast, Thompson's agent was Ad Schulberg, the mother of author Bud Schulberg. She wrote to Thompson on March 24, 1958:

> Dear Jim:
>
> ### THE GETAWAY
>
> It was nice talking to you. NAL's check arrived this morning and I am rushing mine for $1,125 to you. . . .
>
> Please keep me posted on Studio interest. Kubrick should see it and certainly the majors and some of the independents.
>
> As you know, I have only one copy which I need for the magazines.
>
> My fondest regards to you, Alberta and the family.

Added in handwriting to the typed note was: "It does look like a splendid start for 1958—Ad."

Things did indeed look bright for the winter. *Paths of Glory* had been nominated for a Writers Guild award as best screenplay adaptation of

1957. Thompson, basking in the acknowledgment of his work by his peers, attended the black-tie ceremonies at the Moulin Rouge in Hollywood with Alberta and Maxine and Joe Kouba. Unfortunately, *Paths* did not win the award.

Thompson's *The Getaway* stirred no great interest among Hollywood's film producers. It would not be made into a film until thirteen years had passed; thirteen years in which Thompson, who had seemingly established himself as a screenwriter through his work with Kubrick, would see only one mainstream film assignment, and would have to resort to writing for second-rate television shows.

Thompson wrote at least three teleplays for Ziv Production's *Mackenzie's Raiders* later in 1958. Thompson's own synopses of the episode, from the title pages of the screenplays:

Episode 10b: "Indian Agent." Story by David Victor and Herb Little. Screenplay by Jim Thompson. 22 August 1958.

SYNOPSIS: Protected by a crooked Indian Agent who shares in their loot, a gang of young Indian braves goes on a rampage of murder and robbery. Col. Mackenzie sets a trap for the gang, and manages to catch them alive. Then, allowing their leader to escape, he trails him to the Indian Agent's office, where there is a three-man showdown with Mackenzie emerging the victor.

Episode 19b: "Death Patrol." Written by Jim Thompson. 6 October, 1958.

SYNOPSIS: After mopping up on an outlaw gang, Mackenzie must get his patrol back to Fort Clark—a 150-mile journey through drought-stricken wasteland. He has three prisoners. Two of his own men are unable to walk, and he is critically short of food, water and ammunition. Pete Lemond, the gang's leader, snipes at the patrol. Two of Mackenzie's men are killed. He and the one remaining able-bodied man are wounded. Mackenzie ultimately enlists the aid of one of the prisoners, Chief Redwing, and is thus able to kill Lemond and reach the fort.

Episode 28b: "Joe Ironhat." Written by Jim Thompson. 19 December, 1958.

SYNOPSIS: Despite the sympathetic help of Mackenzie, Joseph Topanga, the first educated Indian in the Fort Clark area, is thwarted and insulted at every turn as he attempts to find suitable employment. Criminal Indians—taking advantage of his discouragement—dupe him into taking part in a robbery. Believing that he has killed the victim, he flees into Mexico with the criminals. Mackenzie's task: To bring the true culprits to justice without harm to the innocent man, Topanga.

Thompson's *Mackenzie's Raiders* scripts were mostly rote work, employing many conventional plot elements and situations. Showing none of his trademark themes and obsessions, at best these "true-cavalry" efforts have a folkloric quality resembling some of his anonymous true-crime stories of years previous.

Thompson was stymied by the low-budget production values, as he expressed in this holiday letter to his sister Freddie and husband, Irving Townsend, who were living in Westport, Connecticut. Despite the imminent publication of *The Getaway,* the nomination of *Paths of Glory* for a Writers Guild award, and the steady teleplay work, Thompson seemed no happier or financially secure at the tail end of 1958, though his hopes remained high and his sense of humor intact:

San Clemente, California
December 27, 1958

Dear Freddie and Irving,

A few lines to thank you for the very fine Christmas gifts—not, I'm afraid, adequately reciprocated by us. Perhaps we can do better when I start drawing my old age pension. And Alberta and I both feel qualified for them after these past two weeks. I was particularly glad to get the Atlantic Monthly for another year. It's one of the very few magazines I enjoy reading, yet somehow I seldom get around to buying it.

At long last, I've got my foot firmly in the door of television—I'd like to put it up the industry's collective butt—and hope to have a really good year in 1959. Everything I've done so far has been for Ziv Productions, which is polluting the air waves with a dozen-odd idiots' delights, and is a very low-pay, slave-driving outfit, but by no means the worst. (Give me time, give me time.) I dropped in to see them just before Christmas, and was informed that they were counting on me for five or six programs during the coming year. Meanwhile, I've received encouragement from Warner Brother TV and Revue, who pay quite a bit better and do not bracket writers so severely as to production costs. (My spies tell me that all Ziv productions are shot in the producer's garage with a Brownie camera.) Believe me, it's a hell of a job to stage an Indian war with only one Indian. At the moment, I'm finishing a novel—I still have most of it to do—which must be delivered before January 15th.

Pat is feeling much better, and is due to pick up the baby tomorrow. She and Max, her husband, were not able to join us at Maxine's and Joe's for Christmas dinner, due to her illness. But the rest of us enjoyed it very much. Joe and Maxine went to Barstow today to visit with the Stairs; and will drop in again tomorrow to see us.

My latest book [The Getaway] will be out soon, and will send you a copy.

I'm enclosing a recent snapshot of Alberta and me. I appear on the left, wearing pleased smile and new permanent. Fat and frowning party on right is Alberta. As you can see, she is really putting on the blubber. Suspect this is due to secret guzzling, a vice she has long been addicted to.

Very best regards to you all—Suzy, Nicole, Jeremy and Randi. And hope you had a magnificently happy Christmas.

Love, Jimmie

Despite Thompson's hopes for the new year, 1959 was not a good year for him and his family. He did not complete the book that was due on January 15; in fact, he did not publish a follow-up to *The Getaway* until 1961's *The Transgressors*. He concentrated on his screenwriting, but found little or no success.

The Getaway is the best third-person crime novel Jim Thompson ever wrote. Written just after his screenwriting experiences with Kubrick and Harris, it's clearly a novel written with an eye toward the big screen. *The Getaway* contains more external "action" than most of Thompson's earlier efforts, and the bank robbery that opens the book is told with a scene-shifting/time-changing technique similar to that used by Lionel White in *Clean Break* (and Thompson-Kubrick's screenplay for *The Killing*).

Ostensibly a straightforward crime novel tracing a husband-wife team's getaway from their final big caper, it leaps the genre to chronicle the loss of trust between them, the resultant disintegration of their marriage, and their arrival in a hell specially designed for people like them.

The first four chapters introduce the main characters while they are pulling off the bank robbery. Carter "Doc" McCoy, recently paroled from his second long stretch in the pen, is the mastermind and coolest of the crooks. Stationed across from a small-town bank in a room in the only hotel in town, he calmly shoots the bank guard with an air gun, and creates a diversion with a couple of sticks of dynamite.

Rudy Torrento and a punk named Jackson pull the actual robbery, after which Rudy gleefully disembowels Jackson. Ugly, abused from birth, with almost no intelligence, Rudy is Thompson's version of a born criminal. Rudy is aware that Doc will try to kill him after the job is pulled, as he killed Jackson, but he can't quite believe it. Envious of all that Doc has that he does not—all that Doc is that he is not—Rudy is determined to kill Doc first.

Carol Ainslee McCoy is Doc's wife and disciple. McCoy rescued her from a drab life as a small-town librarian and introduced her to crime. Now:

Reform? Change? Why, and to what? The terms were meaningless. Doc had opened a door for her, and she had entered into, adopted and been adopted by, a new world. And it was difficult to believe now that any other had ever existed. Doc's amoral outlook had become hers. In a sense, she had become more like Doc than Doc himself. More engagingly persuasive when she chose to be. Harder when hardness seems necessary.

Rudy meets up with Doc after the job is pulled, and takes away the shotgun Doc has tried to hide in his raincoat. Rudy then drives down a deserted road, where he intends to kill Doc. Doc confuses Rudy with quick talk of investments and global inflation, trying to show Rudy that killing him would be a big mistake—the money will run out before Rudy knows it. When Rudy agrees to let him live, Doc takes off his hat as if to wipe his sweaty brow. He removes a pistol from the hat and shoots Rudy right in the heart.

Doc and Carol have no time for a reunion—they haven't seen each other since Doc went to jail—for they now must pay off Beynon, the corrupt official who obtained Doc's release. Doc heads straight for Beynon's house, as planned; Carol seems unexpectedly nervous about it.

When Doc speaks to Beynon, he finds out why—Beynon hints that Carol slept with him to obtain Doc's release, and that they schemed to let Doc pull the bank job and then kill him and run away together with the money. Too late, Doc hears Carol enter the house, and he cannot totally dismiss Beynon's words. Doc doesn't know whether Carol will shoot him or Beynon. Even when Carol kills Beynon, Doc cannot be sure the man wasn't telling the truth, or some of the truth.

Carol, furiously sobbing over Beynon's body, denies that she planned to betray Doc. Doc instantly recognizes the truth when he hears it, and is slightly comforted. But he also realizes that Carol must have slept with Beynon—she didn't deny that part of the story.

Doc's doubt makes him uneasy, for he knows what it inevitably leads to:

He was ready to admit that his shaky faith was a personal thing. As a professional criminal, he had schooled himself against placing complete trust in anyone. And as a criminal, he had learned to link infidelity with treachery. It revealed either a dangerous flaw in character, or an equally dangerous shift in loyalties. In any case, the woman was a bad risk in a game where no risk could be tolerated.

Against his better judgment, Doc shakes off these thoughts. He loves Carol.

Carol, in many ways Doc's twin, knows what Doc is thinking. They both realize talking about it will do no good—the kind of people they are leaves no easy answer to this new problem. Doc tells her:

"It leaves me without a corner to go to. If I'm agreeable, it's pretense. If I'm not, that also is cause for alarm. You see, my dear? You just can't think that way. It's foolish and it's dangerous, and—you do see that, don't you?"

"I see it," she nodded; and then desperately, with what was almost a cry, "Then it's all right, Doc? Honestly? You're not sore or suspicious about—anything? Everything's just like it always was?"

"I said so. I've done everything I could to show you."

"But you might do that anyway! You might act just as sweet as pie, and all the time you'd be planning t-to—to . . ."

"Carol," said Doc soothingly. "My poor darling little girl."

And she sobbed harshly, sighed, and fell asleep against his shoulder.

The lost trust can never be recovered; suspicion and resentment now grow between them.

Soon their getaway becomes as complicated as their relationship. A report Carol hears on the radio leads her to believe that Rudy is still alive, but Doc dismisses it: he knows he plugged Rudy right in the ticker.

But Rudy *is* still alive; the mass of knotted bones, cartilage, and muscle that is his rib cage deflected the bullet and saved his life. Burning for revenge, he's determined to meet up with Doc and Carol again at their scheduled hideout in San Diego, and this time he'll kill them both.

Rudy kidnaps Clinton, the veterinarian who took care of him, and his tramp wife, Fran. The three head for San Diego. Clinton soon kills himself after lying awake listening to Rudy and Fran make love in the same hotel room with him: "feeling no shame or anger but only an increasing sickness of soul."

The McCoys next drive up to Kansas City, altering their plans due to Beynon's death. Carol is short-conned out of the bag of money by a thief working the switched-key routine at the train station baggage locker. Doc catches and kills the man, unaware that he has already taken some of the money out of the bag and placed it in his suitcoat pocket. When the man's body is discovered on a train, and the money discovered on him, the police identify Carol and Doc as the bank robbers. Now every lawman in the country is looking for them.

Her foul-up at the train station has further widened the gap between Doc and Carol:

She couldn't quite locate the cause of her anger; explain, in absolute terms, why she had viewed him and almost everything he had done with distrust and distaste practically from the moment of their post-robbery meeting. It wasn't so much what he'd done, she supposed, as what he had not. Not so much what he was, as what he was not. And in her mind she

wailed bridelike for what she had lost—or thought she had; for something
that had never existed outside of her mind.

After jumping off the train, Carol and Doc hitch a ride from a man
whom Doc promptly kills, and they steal the car. They learn from a radio
broadcast that they have been identified. Thompson summarizes their
next moves:

> Flight is many things. Something clean and swift, like a bird skimming
> across the sky. Or something filthy and crawling, a series of crablike
> movements through figurative and literal slime, a process of creeping
> ahead, jumping sideways, running backward.
>
> It is sleeping in fields and river bottoms. It is bellying for miles along an
> irrigation ditch. It is back roads, spur railroad lines, the tailgate off a
> wildcat truck, a stolen car and a dead couple in lovers' lane. It is food
> pilfered from freight cars, garments taken from clotheslines; robbery and
> murder, sweat and blood. The complex made simple by the alchemy of
> necessity.

They finally creep cross-country to Los Angeles, hidden among the
children in a migratory sharecropper's beaten-up old truck. They disguise
themselves as best they can and take a train south to San Diego, where
Rudy awaits them.

Doc shoots Rudy and Fran dead, yet is shaken by Rudy's very
existence. Doc and Carol pile into a cab, ordering the cabbie at gunpoint
to drive them to Tijuana. The cabbie leaves his squawk box open, and the
police soon close in on Doc and Carol from all sides.

Doc decides to drive straight for one of the roadblocks, hoping for a
miracle. One appears by the side of the road in the form of the legendary
Ma Santis, a woman whom Doc had credited with such exploits that
Carol doubted she truly existed. Doc swerves the car up and over the
embankment, following Ma into the darkness and the promise of safety.

Now Doc and Carol's descent into a literal and figurative hell is
inexorable and irreversible. First Ma hides them out in two coffin-like
underwater caves, where Carol's doubts about Doc soon lead to feeble
rationalizations that in turn give way to an uncontrollable, claustrophobic
terror:

> Doc would get her out. After all, she was his wife and they had been
> through a lot together, and she'd done a lot for him. And—and—if he'd
> really wanted to get rid of her, he'd had plenty of chances before this.
>
> He'd get her out all right, as soon as it was safe.
>
> Ma would make him.

Next they hide out for nearly three days in a hollowed-out manure pile, literally a shit oven during daylight hours: "The heat brought out hordes of flies. It brought out swarms of corpse-colored grub worms . . . and it brought a choking, eye-watering stench, which seemed to seep through every pore of their skins."

Finally Ma Santis obtains Doc and Carol a boat ride to Mexico, during which Doc cuts the whole crew of a Coast Guard cutter in two with a few shotgun blasts. But it doesn't seem to matter—the happy couple have reached the kingdom of El Rey, where finally they can live the good life they have done all that killing and stealing and hiding out to obtain.

Jim Thompson has reserved the worst fate for Doc and Carol, nearly the only criminals he allows to "get away" with it. What awaits them in the kingdom of El Rey? Only the high life they've always dreamed of and, of course, themselves—the one thing that they can never get away from. Gangster heaven rapidly mutates into gangster hell—a literally cannibalistic existence for those who have always been society's cannibals.

Everything at El Rey's is first-class—from the three-bedroom villas to the exotic cuisine—and quite expensive. Of course, the criminals who have reached this paradise have only a finite amount of funds. To make things worse, the bank charges, rather than pays, interest on all accounts:

> Most immigrants to the kingdom come in pairs, married couples or simply couples. For the journey is an arduous one, and it can seldom be made without the devoted assistance of another. In the beginning, each will handle his own money, carefully contributing an exact half of the common expenses. But this is awkward, it leads to arguments, and no matter how much the individual has he is never quite free of the specter of want. So very soon there is a casual discussion of the advantages of a joint account, and it is casually agreed that they should open one. And from then on—well, the outcome depends on which of the two is the shrewder, the more cold-blooded or requires the least sleep.

So the "immigrants" fall back on their natural instinct to kill in order to survive. And when the money does finally run out on a survivor, he is eligible to live in a separate section of the kingdom, where the only food available is the roasted flesh of fellow criminals. The sickening truth slowly dawns upon Doc one day:

> "B-but—" Doc brushed a shaky hand across his mouth. "B-but . . ."
> *That smell that filled the air. The odor of peppery, roasting flesh. Peppers could be had anywhere, for the picking, the asking, but the meat . . .*

"Quite fitting, eh señor? And such an easy transition. One need only live literally as he has always done figuratively."

Carol and Doc now race to see who can kill the other first. Both of them try to enlist the help of Dr. Max Vonderscheid, who, unknown to them, was Rudy Torrento's mentor and only friend. Vonderscheid takes great pleasure in letting Doc know that his wife has already asked for much the same assistance as did he.

So Carol and Doc share a final exchange, in which they both muse on their natures, and the nature of their predicament. They actually do love each other, but it makes no difference. Because they are so alike all trust is gone, if ever it existed:

> . . . Doc turned to her with thoughtful wonderment. "Do you know," he said, "I believe you really love me."
> "Love you?" she frowned. "Why, of course I do. Don't you love me?"
> "Yes," Doc said slowly. "Yes, Carol, strangely enough I love you very much. I always have and I always will and I could never love anyone else."
> "And I couldn't either. I—oh, Doc. *Doc!*"
> "And it doesn't make any difference, does it, Carol? Or does it?"
> "Does it?" she dabbed her eyes with her handkerchief. "T-tell me it does, Doc, and I'll tell you it does. And what the hell difference will it make?"

The hell that patiently awaited Carol and Doc McCoy has finally caught up with them in the kingdom of El Rey, but like Charlie Bigger and other inhabitants of the Thompson world, it has been inside them all along. And they are forced to see themselves all too clearly, since each is a mirror for the other.

As Thompson mentioned in his Christmas letter to his sister Freddie, Warner Television was interested in hearing a few ideas from him for their Westerns, namely *Maverick* and *The Lawman*. Thompson pitched his story idea "Satan's Quarter-Section" to Warner on January 30, 1959, according to studio records. The one-page pitch, dated January 26, 1959, turns on an idea first used by Thompson in *Heed the Thunder:*

"SATAN'S QUARTER-SECTION"

The Ames homestead is so worthless that its cantankerous owner calls it "The Devil's Quarter-Section" and he and his daughter are barely able to scratch a living from it. Yet two men ("heavies") meet him on the way home from town and attempt to buy it from him. Suspicious, he refuses to sell. They kill him, confident that they can buy the place from his daughter, who won't be able to run the place on her own. By way of covering up their motive, they'll buy up other cheap farms in the area for the nominal purpose of turning them into pasture.

Meanwhile, the girl sees our hero approaching the place, shoots at him, then apologizes when she recognizes him. She's glimpsed two men skulking in the badlands behind the house. And with her father away, she's been frightened.

The hero investigates the area where she saw the men (they didn't come close enough to be recognized). He finds evidence—carefully concealed—that the land has been prospected, and that the prospectors have discovered gold.

He tells the girl. They start for town to look for her father, and find his lifeless body. Hero is certain that the prospectors are the murderers. To force them to show their hand, he and the girl keep discovery of the gold secret.

Ames' will is read. As a sardonic joke, he's willed his farm to the Devil, "who probably owned it in the first place." It was his intention, of course, for his daughter to have the farm. But the will is entirely legal and binding, and under its terms the Devil is now the lawful heir.

The two heavies show up at the farm. After all, they have as much right to be there as the girl has. Hero agrees that this is true, but points out that they have *no more* right than does anyone else and that if they try to take advantage of a legal technicality, a great many others are certain to do the same. Now, he, the hero, has a plan for clearing the title to the farm. And if they, the heavies, will hold off, the girl will sign an agreement to sell to them as soon as she becomes the owner. The heavies don't see how they can lose; they go along with the plan.

Hero files suit against the Devil to recover property for the girl, duly giving notice in the local newspaper, etc., as required by law. When the Devil fails to appear in court to defend his claim, the girl automatically becomes owner of the farm.

Heavies are exultant. They're all ready to buy the property "at the going market price for such land." The hero stalls them; he'll have to check the place over very carefully before the sale can be made. Heavies get nervous, make larger and larger offers for the farm. At last, hero tells them coldly that the girl isn't selling to them at all. Nor, despite the agreement, can they force her to. For it's a legal axiom that criminals may not profit from their crimes . . . and by their wild bidding for nominally worthless land they've proved themselves Ames' killers . . . Heavies are punished—either by law or shootout. Hero and girl return happily to farm.

Though Warner expressed no interest, Ziv's *Man Without a Gun* eventually did use Thompson's "Satan's Quarter-Section" story idea in an episode entitled "Devil's Acres." Thompson's ideas met with little more success over the next few years. He repeatedly pitched things to any story editor who would listen (or pretend to listen). At Warner alone, he pitched a *Maverick* episode and his own *Wild Town* novel in 1957, "The Cellini Chalice" in 1958, and "Satan" in 1959.

In 1960 Thompson briefly returned to magazines, with an appearance in the May issue of the short-lived magazine *Shock*. "Forever After" is one of Thompson's better and more characteristic short efforts, depicting the special hell awaiting Ardis Clinton, who breaks her neck while helping her boyfriend chop her cliché-spouting husband into little pieces.

Back in Hollywood, Thompson raised his sights to ideas for new series: in September 1960 he suggested to Warner, without success, "Mike Flanagan's Fleet" and "Manzi's Millions." In 1961 he received a co-teleplay credit for an episode of MGM's *Cain's Hundred* entitled "Five for One." In 1962 he submitted four novels, *A Hell of a Woman, The Nothing Man, The Transgressors,* and *The Golden Gizmo* to the readers at Warner, in addition to another try with "The Cellini Chalice" and something called "Jeanie."

By 1963 Thompson apparently gave up on Warner. In 1964 he received full story and co-teleplay credit for an episode of *Dr. Kildare* entitled "Pardon Me for Living," which by family accounts is about how Hollywood had made Thompson feel by this time.

According to Thompson's sisters Freddie and Maxine:

Freddie: "Hollywood basically killed him—he just didn't understand the workings of it—he'd go into the studio and some creep would sit there picking his nose while Jimmie was trying to lay out a story for him."

Maxine: "He stood it, though, he'd take it. He fell apart later a little bit."

Freddie: "But these things did damage, they hurt him."

As usual, Thompson's daughters and wife recall the scripts he sold and the credit he received, and acknowledge that it all was a struggle, but offer no illuminating comments upon this time in Thompson's life.

For a glimpse of how Thompson may have felt, we can turn to his unfinished novel *Sunset and Cienega,* which concerns the plight of Sanderson Blake, a once-successful novel writer, now an alcoholic writer of bad television shows when he can find work at all. Blake's Hollywood story is similar to Thompson's own, being brought out by some independent producers to adapt a novel for the screen, and later feeling lucky to write low-budget television. Thompson's own painful experiences leak through scenes such as this, when Blake is humiliated by a story editor with a grudge against him:

If you were lucky, you have to do your selling to only one or two people—the producer and/or the story editor—and that could be tough enough with guys who yawned in your face, talked over the telephone while you were talking and assured visitors that they would be through with you "in just a minute." Sometimes, however, you might have an audience of as many as four—producer, executive producer, story editor and story analyst. All of them poisonously critical, pitching curveball questions at you, doing everything they could to rip your story apart.

Blake opened the doors to two deserted offices before he located the story editor's. He went in briskly, and appeared amazed at the sight of Crossland.

"Why, Matt! Are you on this show? I thought you were still over at Cal-Tel."

"Isn't that receptionist out there?" said Crossland.

"I just saw the screening," said Blake. "Mind if I throw a few ideas at you?"

"You're goddamned right, I mind," said Crossland; and then, catching himself, he nodded curtly. "All right. As long as you're here."

Blake began to talk. Crossland fixed him with a cold, deliberately disconcerting stare, grinning inwardly as it began to have its effect on the writer. He hated Blake's guts. A minuscule portion of his mind whispered that he had no right to, but he did, by God, and he would never stop.

. . .

It was all Blake's fault. *Yes, by God, it was!* He had tried to help Blake, to make him look better than he was, and Blake had repaid him with a double-cross. It had to be that way. Matt Crossland could not be to blame, so Sanderson Blake had to be. And now the rotten double-crosser had the nerve to try to sell him a story!

". . . so there's this newspaperman," Blake was saying. "A columnist. He's going to tag along on the case, and see just how Dirk operates. Well, Dirk catches on to the tag fast, but he's good-natured about it. He lets the guy tail him, keeping an eye on him to see that he doesn't get into trouble. And when the natives capture him, Dirk risks his life to save him. Now, here's the gimmick, Matt. The guy ain't really a newspaperman. He's working with the heavies—"

"Oh, shit!" said Crossland in a loud voice. "What are you trying to hand me, Blake?"

"Well . . ." The writer put a trembling hand to his mouth. "Let me throw you another one. There's this millionaire; he has a big hunting lodge bordering on the Rio Grande River. One of Dirk's insurance company clients has issued a policy on the place. Well, this millionaire is rotten spoiled, a poor sportsman. So he and his playboy buddies start dynamiting the river for fish—you can cover that with stock shots, of course—and they use too much of the Dyna and change the course of the river. The lodge winds up on the Mexican side instead of—"

"Jesus Christ!" Crossland groaned loudly. "This is getting worse and worse!"

Blake mopped his face. He said desperately, "Well, listen to this, Matt. This one will really kill you. I—"

"Sandy . . ." said Crossland gently. "Sandy, boy."

"—Dirk meets this dame in a bar, and she— Yes, Matt?" said Blake.

"Don't keep torturing yourself, Sandy. Don't make me keep turning you down. It's too hard on both of us."

"But, Matt"—Blake gulped. "I—"

"You're washed up, kid. Don't you understand that? You've lost your touch. I know you've been hit pretty hard, losing your boy and your wife and everything, and God knows I sympathize with you. It's a wonder you aren't on Skid Row already. But I can't buy stuff from you out of pity. If you had even the germ of a decent story—anything but this terrible shit you've been handing me this morning—"

"I guess I'd better go," said Blake shakily. "T-thanks a lot, Matt."

1961's *The Transgressors* marked the third time Jim Thompson used the Lou Ford character in a novel; this time he's named Tom Lord but his personality and situation are nearly identical to Lou Ford's. Lord is the son of a small-town doctor, in fact a long line of doctors; he was traumatized not by a sexual relationship with his nanny, but by the loss of his mother when she runs away with another man when Lord is quite young. Lord later enters medical school, but his father is taken ill and Lord must suspend his studies to care for the old man. His father lingers and dies a slow death over several years, and by this time Lord thinks it's too late to resume his medical studies.

His father's medical bills have absorbed the entire family fortune, so Lord needs a job. Since he is "old family" only certain jobs are appropriate, one of these is deputy sheriff. Sheriff Bradley initially believes that Lord won't be liked by his fellow deputies, but Lord astonishes him by easily donning the mask of a local yokel:

"I see. You're thinking I wouldn't fit in with your other men. I'd act in a way they'd resent."

"Well"—Bradley squirmed—"you wouldn't mean to, of course. Know it ain't like you to be uppity. But—"

"Now, looky, Sheriff Dave," Tom drawled, "gimme a chance, huh? You just gimme a chance, an' there won't be no kicks. Those men o' your'n'll cotton to me like burrs to a dog fox."

"Like I was sayin'," the sheriff continued. "You wouldn't"— He broke off, his eyes popping in a wide double take. "What'd you say, boy?"

"I mean it," Tom grinned. "I'll fit in, an' that's a fact. Won't stand out no more than a fly turd in a box of pepper."

He got the job, and he kept it. It was easy, frighteningly easy. Descent always is . . .

Actually the transformation never took place. For behind—inside—the drawling, doltish Tom Lord, there was another, the real man. The Lord of the conquistadors, the Lord who could not live the role he was cast in and was unmercifully denied the right to die.

He, then, the real man, became smaller and smaller as the years went by, and the outer shell became thicker. But he was there, all right. A little of him was constantly poking through to the surface, showing up in exaggerated Westernisms and savagely sly gibes—blindly, bitterly striking back at the world he could not change.

Thompson's third-person narrative explanation of Tom Lord seems also to be an "explanation" of the plight of Lou Ford of *The Killer Inside Me,* a character so emblematic of Thompson's fictional and personal world that he returned to him time and again as a model of what circumstance and environment might do to a man.

Lord takes up with the town prostitute, Joyce Lakewood, and is soon involved in the accidental shooting of an oil field executive who swindled him out of millions of dollars. The setup of *The Transgressors* is thus far essentially convergent with *The Killer Inside Me,* but the rest of the plot and the happy ending is so divergent, it seems as if Thompson has returned to the character determined to give him a final chance at happiness.

To all outside observers, Tom Lord and Lou Ford are twins, but Lord does not have the deep-seated sickness inside him. As much as circumstance has conspired against him, the rotting of his soul has not yet advanced to the murderous stage. Thompson even allows Lord a happy ending with the widow of the man who swindled him, in which the desolate West Texas locale is evoked as starkly beautiful—a modern Eden.

Why Thompson wrote a book such as this, beyond the customary financial need, does seem a mystery. Was he backing off of the bleak world view of *The Killer Inside Me?* Joyce Lakewood, of course, is essentially similar to Joyce Lakeland of *The Killer Inside Me.* It is important to realize that she and Lord do not live in a different Thompson world, but a different part of it; their "re-use" emphasizes how many of "us people" are out there—on the edge of psychosis and murder. Only random circumstance and environment keep Tom and Joyce from replaying Lou and Joyce's story. And the flip side to that, of course, is that only the same factors kept *The Killer*'s Lou Ford from being an "innocent" man.

Here, as always, his upbeat approach is less convincing than his more usual downbeat take on things; possibly Thompson considered the theme and tone of *The Transgressors* more commercially viable than his more characteristic books.

Nevertheless, Thompson did write on personal themes and obsessions in *The Transgressors,* sometimes more explicitly than in his better books. The very title evokes the Thompson world, where everyone is either actively or passively guilty of something grave. Here's Tom Lord musing on the subject of the unknowable motivations of the human heart:

> Absently, he lighted a cigar, stood outside of himself as he puffed it; curiously considering the man at the desk.
>
> Looked about like anyone else out here. Talked like them, acted like them. *Was* like them except for what went on inside of him. And yet that, the last, was the most important thing of all, the only important thing when you got right down to cases. It was him, not what showed up on the surface. It was what made him love or hate, die or give death. Yet no one was aware of it; no one could diagram its workings or predict their results. Certainly not he, the man it inclined and impelled, could not. The machinery had become too complex; too many moments had been added to its sum.
>
> It was easy to believe, of course, that the irking contradictions of his own life justified almost anything he did. He'd had it tough all the way down the line. Obviously—obviously, to his own way of thinking—he was a classic case of the square peg in the round hole, and he should be excused where others should not. And, hell. How stupid and blind did you have to be to think that way? Everyone was unique particularly, but no one generally. Every man's life was a different road, but all paralleled one another. Everyone was a son of a bitch, everyone an angel, everyone both.

Again, Thompson emphasizes the basic similarities between seeming polar opposites—devil and angel, guilty and innocent—not so much to depict the duality of man but the slipperiness of the concepts by which he defines himself. The stories of Tom Lord and Lou Ford, Joyce Lakewood and Joyce Lakeland, are more similar than we might like to think.

In early 1963 Jim Thompson was stricken with bleeding ulcers, and was incapacitated for a few months. The illness may have brought about a short-term change in priorities and a return of his lost muse, for he briefly turned away from Hollywood to turn out two of his best books, *The Grifters* and *Pop. 1280,* published in 1963 and 1964. Despite uniformly good reviews, the two books did little to enhance his bank balance or his Hollywood reputation.

Only in his novels did Thompson unleash his true voice and his true view of things. He knew television and film were not prepared for his bleak vision. When he tried to alter or soften his themes, he was working against his strengths, and did not produce quality work. And as always, his personality further stifled him.

Stakes were much lower for Thompson and his paperback publishers than for Thompson and Hollywood producers; after all, the cost of a failed paperback edition was only the author's $2,000 advance and the printing costs. Thompson could go comfortably wherever his strange muse led him; he sporadically produced great novels until the end of his career.

Nearly sixty years old, Thompson was an eccentric, forgotten writer whose unique worldview was both his genius and his curse. The fact that—like his fiction's murderous psychotics—he brought it on himself only made the burden of failure heavier. Now only his drinking and his writing could ease the pain of the hell that he carried with him every day.

The Grifters, one of Thompson's better third-person-narrative novels, is the story of the last days of short-con artist Roy Dillon, whose fate has been predestined by unresolved psychosexual obsessions involving his mother. Thirteen years his senior, Lilly Dillon arrives back in her son's life in time to save him from a mortal wound—only to kill him herself a few months later.

For most of the length of *The Grifters*, it seems a relatively lighthearted (for Thompson), well-balanced look at the lives of a group of small-time con artists, centered around Roy Dillon. Only in the final four chapters does Dillon's fate close in on him via a burst of unnarrated action involving the reported death of his mother, and the actual death of his girlfriend, Moira, who was a Lilly Dillon look-alike.

Lilly Dillon has washed herself up with her syndicate boss, and after killing Moira (whom the police think was Lilly) she tries to steal the money Roy has accumulated from years of operating in Los Angeles. Roy walks in on her as she's removing the money from its hiding places in his hotel room. Soon they are discussing each other and their future, and Roy tries to explain to Lilly why the money won't help her—at the same time realizing a truth about himself:

> "Okay," Lilly said. "So you're on the level. So you don't need the money, do you? You don't need or want it. So why the hell won't you give it to me?"
> Roy sighed; tried to explain why: to explain acceptably the most difficult of propositions; i.e., that the painful thing you are doing for a person is really for his or her own good. And yet, talking to her, watching her distress, there was in his mind, unadmitted, an almost sadistic exulting. *Harking back to childhood, perhaps, rooted back there, back in the time*

when he had known need or desire, and been denied because denial was good for him. Now it was his turn. Now he could do the right thing—and yes, it was right—simply by doing nothing. *Now now now the pimp disciplining his whore listening to her pleas and striking yet another blow. Now now now he was the wise and strong husband taking his frivolous wife in hand. Now now now his subconscious was taking note of the bond between them, the lewd, forbidden and until now unadmitted bond. And so he must protect her. Keep her from the danger which the money would inevitably lead her to. Keep her available . . .*

Lilly knows what her son is thinking; she has had the same thoughts about him. Unashamed, she knows how to use their unspeakable attraction for each other to her own advantage:

> There was a peculiar glow in her eyes, a strange tightness to her face, a subdued huskiness to her voice. Watching him, studying him, she slowly crossed one leg over the other. . . .
> *The leg was swinging gently; hinting, speaking to him. Holding him hypnotized.*

Lilly asks her son what he wants, what she needs to do to get that money. Just as Roy begins to tell her she swings the bag of money against the glass of water in his hand, shattering it and sending a shard of glass deep into his throat. As Roy lies dying, Lilly collects the blood-spattered money, and coolly looks around the hotel room, knowing she's in the clear. Then:

> Bracing herself, she let her eyes stray down to her son. Abruptly a great sob tore through her body, and she wept uncontrollably.
> That passed.
> She laughed, gave the thing on the floor an almost jeering glance.

The Grifters shows flashes of brilliance, and the lead women are more fleshed out than usual, but this odd blend of Sophocles and Freud is kept from being one of Thompson's top books by uneven tone and awkward structure that leave the reader nearly baffled at the abrupt ending. Although Thompson probably deliberately saved his most characteristic writing and obsessions for the last few pages of the novel, by then they seem to come out of nowhere.

Moreover, the subplot concerning the concentration camp experiences of Dillon's nurse, Carol, is ineffective, and decidedly more offensive than illuminating—right out of the sleazy paperback original handbook, and not what we expect from Thompson.

* * *

Jim Thompson's final "crime novel" masterpiece is *Pop. 1280,* in which he returns once again to the first-person story of a psychotic sheriff, this time in the service of a savage satire of small-town life and corruption featuring a familiar but powerful blend of guilt, evil, identity loss, and human nature.

Nick Corey, High Sheriff of Potts County, shares many characteristics and circumstances with Lou Ford. He seems a little more easygoing, and Corey doesn't let the reader in on as many of his inner thoughts as does the narrator of *The Killer Inside Me.* Corey keeps up the dumb act with the reader and himself, never quite acknowledging his inherent sharpness and self-awareness.

In fact, he has lived the dumb ol' sheriff routine so long that he has become his role. Corey doesn't meditate on the psychic prison his life has become—he just lashes out at the world that has made him so, while searching to rediscover an identity, and a reason why. In the end he'll discover "why"—the only *possible* reason why he's been sent to Potts County, in one of Jim Thompson's most daring and brilliant conceits.

Nick Corey lays out his big problems for us right away. It's a tough job to be sheriff, especially when the people of the town don't really want a sheriff to do what he's supposed to do. Nick struggles to keep up the pretense of efficiency that is his best insurance of continued reelection. Corey can safely enforce the law only against blacks and other people who can't vote.

Nick Corey is a ladies' man, unfortunate enough to have been roped into marriage by the horrific Myra, who delights in torturing him. To make things worse, Myra's idiot "brother" Lenny lives with them, slobbering all over himself when he's not out at night peeping in windows. Myra had ruined Nick's plans to marry Amy Mason, "one of the quality." Still, Nick is getting along tolerably well, since he quite often sleeps with Rose Hauck, Myra's best friend.

What's really bothering Corey as he begins his tale is the disrespect shown to him by the town's two black pimps. He "innocently" consults a "wiser" man, Sheriff Ken Lacey of a neighboring county, about his problem. While Corey plays the buffoon and Lacey plays right into his hands, Corey tips himself to Buck, Lacey's deputy and chief whipping boy:

> "Hurt your arm?" Ken said. "Whereabouts?"
> "I'm not positive," I said. "It could be either the radius or the ulna."
> Buck gave me a sudden sharp look out from under his hatbrim. Sort of like I'd just walked in the room and he was seeing me for the first time. But

of course Ken didn't notice anything. Ken had so much on his mind, I reckon, helping poor stupid fellas like me, that he maybe didn't notice a lot of things.

Buck assists Corey in getting exactly what he wants out of Ken Lacey:

> "You're actually lettin' 'em off pretty easy, Nick," Buck said. "I know I'd sure hate to be in the same room if any pimp sassed old Ken here. Ken wouldn't stop with just kickin' 'em. Why, a-fore they knew what was happening, he'd just yank out his pissoliver and shoot 'em right in their sassy mouths."
>
> "Pre-zackly!" Ken said. "I'd send them sassy skunks to hell without no foolin' around about it."

Buck and Nick discuss a few things as Buck walks Nick back to the train station: "we were getting along real fine, just like I thought we might." Nick then relates a dream he's always having, a nightmare about his childhood. His mother died giving birth to him, and his father always blamed him. Nick knows he was never loved, and maybe that's why he gets along so well with women—he's looking for something he's never had.

Nick returns to Pottsville, treks out to the whorehouse by the river, and promptly shoots the two pimps dead. He seems quite surprised when Ken Lacey pounds his door in the middle of the night; evidently Buck has convinced Ken that Nick took his advice about shooting the pimps *literally*. Nick calms Ken's fears, and sends him out to the whorehouse, which Nick says is the only place in town where Ken can get a bed to sleep in at this hour of the night. Nick adds that the pimps probably won't be there, and Ken can have a lot of fun with the girls, especially if he tells them that he took care of the pimps and they have nothing to worry about anymore . . .

Before he leaves town next morning, Ken practically frames himself for the murders of the pimps, telling everyone he meets he "took care of 'em." Nick then points out to a paling Ken what a spot he would be in if the pimps *did* turn up dead, along with the advice that Ken should be real nice to Buck in the future: "I got kind of a funny idea that he don't like you very much as it is, so I sure wouldn't do no more talkin' about making him peck horse turds with the sparrers."

Next on Nick's hit list is Tom Hauck, Rose's big, ornery husband who beats her when she's not doing all the farm chores. Tom Hauck puts Nick in a ticklish spot by beating up an old black man, Uncle John, in view of the whole town. Nick ingeniously wriggles off the hook; since he can't arrest Tom for beating a "nigger," he warns Tom about beating Uncle John with a plank paid for with taxpayers' money.

Nick later follows Hauck out in the woods, and after telling him he's been sleeping with Rose for a long time, and intends to keep on sleeping with her, Nick shoots him in the guts with a double-barrel shotgun.

> It didn't quite kill him, although he was dying fast. I wanted him to stay alive for a few seconds, so that he could appreciate the three or four good swift kicks I gave him. You might think it wasn't real nice to kick a dying man, and maybe it wasn't. But I'd been wanting to kick him for a long time, and it just never seemed safe until now.

Nick proceeds to Rose's farm, where he tells her the good news and she rewards him in the usual way.

Soon Nick reunites with Amy Mason, who finally forgives him for marrying Myra. This launches Nick's final plan—to get rid of Myra, Lennie, and Rose, and run away with Amy.

But first poor Nick has to service Rose not long after sleeping with Amy. By some miracle of God he's able to satisfy her, when they hear noises out on the porch. Rose thinks Tom must have survived, but it is only Uncle John leaving Tom's body on the porch. Unfortunately for Uncle John, he sees Rose and Nick together, and Nick now must kill him.

Nick and Uncle John drive Tom's body back out into the woods, and along the way Nick tells the terrified Uncle John the hard facts of the world:

> "I'll tell you somethin' Uncle John," I said. "I'll tell you something, and I hope it's a comfort to you. Each man kills the thing he loves."
>
> "Y-You don't love me, Mistah Nick . . ."
>
> I told him he was god-danged right about that, a thousand per cent right. What I loved was myself, and I was willing to do anything. I god-dang had to go on lying and cheating and drinking whiskey and screwing women and going to church on Sunday with all the other respectable people.

Nick follows this startling explanation of his plight, his masquerade, with the reason he feels no pity for Uncle John—a psychotic twist on a familiar Thompson theme:

> "I'll tell you something else," I said, "and it makes a shit-pot-ful more sense than most of the goddam scripture I've read. Better the blind man, Uncle John; better the blind man who pisses through a window than the prankster who leads him thereto. You know who the prankster is, Uncle John? Why, it's goddam near everybody, every son-of-a-bitch who turns his

head when the crap flies, every bastard who sits on his dong with one thumb in his ass and the other in his mouth and hopes nothing will happen to him, every whoremonger who thinks that piss will turn to lemonade, every mother-lover supposedly made in God's image, which makes me think I'd hate like hell to meet him on a dark night. Even you, particularly you, Uncle John; people who go around sniffing crap with their mouths open, and acting surprised as hell when someone kicks a turd in it. Yeah, you can't help bein' what you are, jus' a pore ol' black man. That's what you say, Uncle John, and do you know what I say? I say screw you. I say you can't help being what you are, and I can't help being what I am, and you goddam well know what I am and have to be. You goddam well know you've got no friends among the whites. You goddam well ought to know that you're not going to have any because you stink, Uncle John, and you go around begging to get screwed and how the hell can anyone have a friend like that?"

I gave him both barrels of the shotgun.

It danged near cut him in two.

In this remarkable burst of rationalization Nick not only indicts those guilty of sins of omission and commission, but saves his greatest contempt for those who have a choice in how to act and still actively or passively promote evil. Nick is willing to do what he was made to do, what he has to do—and to carry his burden of his acts with him. Everyone is guilty in Nick's world, and those who won't admit it—won't admit that the world is a cesspool populated by living excrement that makes things filthier—are liars who deserve something worse than death.

Nick does admit that Uncle John can no more change himself than he can, but it doesn't matter—they both have their roles to play.

Nick makes it look like Tom and Uncle John shot and killed each other (apparently a psychotic's favorite, since Dolly Dillon and Lou Ford did the same thing). He gets away with it, and seems in the clear until he learns that Amy saw him kill the pimps on that dark night by the river. Amy agrees not to say anything about the pimps, but she won't stand for the frame-up of Ken Lacey: it would make her an accessory to murder, and that's where she draws the line. Nick starts hoping the pimps' bodies don't surface from their watery graves.

Eventually George Barnes of the Talkington Detective Agency arrives in town to investigate the death of Curly, one of the pimps, who apparently had some family who cared about him. Nick gives Barnes some of the savage needling he reserves for phonies:

"Let's see now, you broke up that big railroad strike, didn't you?"
"That's right." He showed me the tooth again. "The railroad strike was one of our jobs."

"Now, by golly, that really took nerve," I said. "Them railroad workers throwin' chunks of coal at you and splashin' you with water, and you fellas without nothin' to defend yourself with except shotguns and automatic rifles! Yes, sir, god-dang it, I really got to hand it to you!"

"Now, just a moment, Sheriff!" His mouth came together like a buttonhole. "We have never—"

"And them low-down garment workers," I said. "God-dang, you really took care of them, didn't you? People that threw away them big three-dollar-a-week wages on wild livin' and then fussed because they had to eat garbage to stay alive! I mean, what the heck, they was all foreigners, wasn't they, and if they didn't like good ol' American garbage why didn't they go back to where they came from?"

Eventually Nick allows Barnes to explain his mission in Pottsville. Nick teases the detective along, letting him think he will cooperate in pinning the murders on Ken Lacey. Now relatively comfortable, Barnes makes the mistake of discussing some philosophical questions with Nick, who seizes the chance once again to debate the topics he first brought up with Uncle John, in a page of Thompson prose unequaled in satirical brilliance and importance:

"Now here's what I was going to ask, Nick, and it's something I've worried about a great deal. Does the fact that we can't do anything else— does that excuse us?"

"Well," I said, "do you excuse a post for fittin' a hole? Maybe there's a nest of rabbits down in that hole, and the post will crush 'em. But is that the post's fault, for fillin' a gap it was made to fit?"

"But that's not a fair analogy, Nick. You're talking about inanimate objects."

"Yeah?" I said. "So ain't we all relatively inanimate, George?"

Here we have the reason that many of Thompson's other narrators, from Joe Wilmot to Dolly Dillon, are so uncertain about their vital signs. They're really not alive, not in the sense that one thinks a human should be alive. Their lack of vital signs is a literalization of their lack of free choice. As Nick continues:

Just how much free will does any of us exercise? We got controls all along the line, our physical make-up, our mental make-up, our backgrounds; they're all shapin' us in a certain way, fixin' us up for a certain role in life, and George, we better play that role or fill that hole or any goddang way you want to put it or all hell is going to tumble out of the heavens and fall right down on top of us. We better do what we're made to do, or we'll find it being done to us."

As Lincoln Fargo's creed makes a brief appearance, George protests: " 'You mean it's a case of kill or be killed?' Barnes shook his head. 'I hate to think that.' " Nick replies first with the Thompson theme of shared culpability, and then, evidently grasping at straws like Lou Ford, Nick lights upon the idea that he's the Savior himself:

> "Maybe that's not what I mean," I said. "Maybe I'm not sure what I mean. I guess mostly what I mean is that there can't be no personal hell because there ain't no personal sins. They're all public, George, we all share in the other fellas' and the other fellas all share in ours. Or maybe I mean this, George, that I'm the Savior himself, Christ on the Cross right here in Potts County, because God knows I was needed here, an' I'm goin' around doing kindly deeds—so that people will know they got nothing to fear, and if they're worried about hell they don't have to dig for it. And, by God, that makes sense, don't it, George? I mean obligation ain't all on the side of the fella that accepts it, nor responsibility neither. I mean, well, which is worse, George, the fella that craps on a doorknob or the one that rings the doorbell?

And Nick returns to the blind man pissing out the window. By this time, George is sure that Nick is putting him on, and can barely control his laughter. But Nick turns the screw a few more times in a final indictment of God:

> "Like the poem says, you can't fault a jug for bein' twisted because the hand of the potter slipped. So you tell me which is worse, the one that messes up the doorknob or the one that rings the bell, and I'll tell you which got twisted and who done the twisting."

Nick walks George back to the station, waiting until the last moment to drop the bomb on him: Nick tells George that he saw the pimps alive the day *after* Ken Lacey was supposed to have killed them. Nick then has to explain to Amy exactly what happened, since she got the wrong idea after seeing Nick and the detective together.

Soon Nick decides that circumstance has made it time to do what he has to do: ". . . it had to be done, I reckoned. It had to be, and I didn't have no choice in the matter."

He lures Lennie all the way out to Rose Hauck's house, giving Rose a chance to use her colorful vocabulary on him. She tells him the truth as part of Nick's unexplained plan:

> "You just wait! I'm gonna tell Myra on you! I seen him! I seen ol' smarty Nick! He come sneaking all the way out here so's you 'n' him could do somethin' nasty!"

"You mean screwing?" Rose said. "What's nasty about screwing?"

"Ooh!" Lennie pointed a shaky finger at her, his eyes popped as big as saucers . . .

. . . "What's the matter?" Rose said. "You screw Myra all the time, and don't tell me you don't, you stupid-looking jackass! That's what makes you goofy, banging her so much. You've tossed it to her so often you've thrown your ass out of line with your eyeballs! . . .

. . . "The hell you didn't! You're not her brother, you're her boy friend! That's what she keeps you around for, to diddle her fiddle. Because you're low-hung and she's high-strung!"

"It a-ain't n-neither! I *de-ed* not! You—you're just a m-mean ol' story teller, an—"

"Don't lie to me, you liver-lipped bastard!" Rose shook her fist in his face. "I've seen you pouring it on her! I peeked in the window, and goddamn, you were pounding it like a drum. The way you were banging the bunghole, you damned near fell in!"

Lennie flees back to town to tell Myra, as Nick knew he would. Nick pretends to leave for town, but actually waits near Rose's house for Lennie and Myra's arrival. Since Rose's words about Lennie and Myra were actually the truth, Myra has to shut her up. She shows up at Rose's with Lennie and a camera in hand.

Nick emerges from his hiding place and peeps in the window to watch the fun. Myra intends to photograph Rose with Lennie, as a way of ensuring her silence. But before Nick can take note of the action, a strange alienation overtakes him, and he sees the house as if for the first time:

I'd maybe been in that house a hundred times, that one and a hundred others like it. But this was the first time I'd seen them for what they really were. Not homes, not places for people to live in, not nothin'. Just pine-board walls locking in the emptiness. No pictures, no books—nothing to look at or think about. Just the emptiness that was soakin' in on me here.

And then suddenly it wasn't here, it was everywhere, every place like this one. And suddenly the emptiness was filled with sound and sight, with all the sad terrible things that the emptiness had brought the people to.

There were helpless little girls, cryin' when their own daddies crawled into bed with 'em. There were the men beating their wives, the women screamin' for mercy. There were kids wettin' in the beds from fear and nervousness, and their mothers dosin' 'em with red pepper for punishment. There were the haggard faces, drained white from hookworm and blotched with scurvy. There was the near-starvation, the never-bein'-full, the debts that always outrun the credits. There was the how-we-gonna-eat, how-we-gonna-sleep, how-we-gonna-cover-our-poor-bare-asses thinkin'. The kind of thinkin' that when you ain't doin' nothin' else but that, why you're better off dead. Because that's the emptiness thinkin' and you're already dead inside, and all you'll do is spread the stink and the terror, the weepin' and wailin', the torture, the starvation, the shame of your deadness. Your emptiness.

Paradoxically, Nick Corey has reached deep inside himself and found the existential vision of his world that is the ultimate excuse for his murdering. These people are already dead, and he'll be doing them and the world a favor by getting rid of them. Thus the act of murder becomes not only a way to a better life for Nick, but a better world—he's an instrument of God, performing the sacred act of murder:

> I shuddered, thinking how wonderful was our Creator to create such down right hideous things in the world, so that something like murder didn't seem at all bad by comparison. Yea, verily, it was indeed merciful and wonderful of Him. And it was up to me to stop brooding, and to pay attention to what was going on right here and now.

Nick wakes up just in time to hear Myra accusing Rose of knowing the truth, and so Nick is confirmed in his suspicions about Myra and Lennie—they *were* sleeping together. Myra orders Lennie to rip Rose's clothes off, as she prepares the camera. But Rose gets away, and runs for the gun that Myra (at Nick's suggestion) insisted she have to protect herself from Tom. Rose shoots them both dead.

Nick returns to town, calmly awaiting Rose's hysterical arrival. Rose saw him leave the farm, and knows that he set everything up. As she frantically tries on some of Myra's clothes that she will need to make her getaway out of town, she accuses Nick of doing it all so he can marry Amy Mason without any problems. But strangely enough, this doesn't seem to be his reason anymore, if ever it was:

> ". . . I'm afraid marryin' her might interfere with my work. Y'see, I got my job to do, Rose; I got to go on bein' High Sheriff, the highest legal authority in Potts County, this place that's the world to most people here, because they never see nothin' else. I just got to be High Sheriff, because I've been pec-cul-yarly an' singularly fitted for it, and I ain't allowed to give it up. Every now an' then, I think I'm going to get out of it, but always the thoughts are put in my head and the words in my mouth to hold me in my place. I got to be it, Rose, I got to be High Sheriff of Potts County forever an' ever. I got to go on an' on, doin' the Lord's work; and all He does is the pointin', Rose, all He does is pick out the people an' I got to exercise His wrath on 'em. And I'll tell you a secret, Rose, they's plenty

of times when I don't agree with Him at all. But I got nothing to say about it. I'm the High Sheriff of Potts County, an' I ain't supposed to do nothing that really needs doing, nothin' that might jeopardize my job. All I can do is follow the pointin' of the Lord's finger, striking down the pore sinners that no one gives a good god-dang about. Like I say, I've tried to get out of it; I've figured on runnin' away and stayin' away. But I can't, and I know I'll never be able to. I got to keep on like I'm doin' now, and I'm afraid Amy would never understand that or put up with it. So I misdoubt I'll be marryin' her."

The novel ends with Nick's final problem: Buck, Ken Lacey's put-upon deputy, is upset about Nick's failure to complete the framing of Ken for the murder of the pimps. Nick reveals his divine nature to Buck, who is not impressed. Then, in an effort to make Buck realize everyone has their own problems, Nick tells Buck a little parable about why dogs go around sniffing each other's asses. The story has little effect.

Finally Nick has to give Buck an answer:

> "Well, Nick? I ain't waiting much longer."
> "And you don't have to, Buck," I said. "You don't have to because I finally come to a decision. I've been a long time comin' to it; it's been the product of thinkin' and thinkin' and thinkin', and then some more thinkin'. And depending how you look at it, it's the god-dangest whingdingest decision ever made, or it's the skitty-assed worst. Because it explains everything that goes on in the world—it answers everything and it answers nothing.
> "So here it is, Buck, here's my decision. I thought and I thought and then I thought some more, and finally I came to a decision. I decided I don't no more know what to do than if I was just another lousy human bein'!"

The realization that "God" can be just as dumbfounded and confused as any "lousy human bein'" explains the fouled-up nature of things, but it leaves no one ultimately responsible for this world. So Nick Corey's world has become truly godless—a meaningless cosmic joke.

In *Pop. 1280* Thompson utilized his most effective narrative technique and characterization, that of a first-person psychotic killer, to write a bitterly funny satire that incorporates nearly all of his thematic obsessions. Since Thompson was not as concerned here as in *The Killer Inside Me* with imparting the inner sickness of his psychotic narrator, Nick Corey is better able to launch savage attacks on his deterministic world in general and the phonies of his society in particular.

Thompson thus offers his clearest, hardest-hitting takes on the themes that unite all of his novels. As always, Nick's observations are made in the service of excusing himself for his crimes but, frighteningly enough, his rationalizations still have a horrible validity—Nick Corey's world resembles our own too closely for them not to.

More than any other novel, *Pop. 1280* proves that when Thompson was writing in top form about what he wanted to, he didn't write crime novels at all—he wrote subversive, sociopolitical novels anchored by philosophy.

In *Pop. 1280* a Thompson hero completes the search for a reason for his existence, a reason for the state of the world, which so haunted Lou Ford, Charlie Bigger, Dolly Dillon, and other Thompson psychotics. And what does Nick Corey find? Only that in his upside-down world he can be a true savior, and still it can mean absolutely nothing. In *Pop. 1280* the concept of God is as empty and twisted as Nick Corey's psychotic mind.

Thompson would return once more to the idea of a hollowed-out psychotic as savior in his final novel, *Child of Rage,* which sounds a note of regeneration and hope and puts a sly end to the godless Thompson world.

Jim Thompson is renowned as the blackest, fiercest of the *noir* writers not because his novels are full of violence and sex, or hookers, grifters, and pimps—pick up any 1950s pulp novel and you'll find those commonplace elements—but because his criminals and their actions are only the most extreme examples of a whole world gone wrong. Thompson's world is not a stylization like that of most other *noir* or pulp novels—it is an organic whole, and the tough streets, tough people, tough actions are manifestations of a diseased environment. Robbed of free choice and all hope, many of Thompson's victims are "dead" long before a killer finishes them off.

Thompson's unique view, sharpened by the events of his own life, made him very well suited to chronicling the adventures of psychotics on the edge. Thompson's need for answers for the bleakness of his own life imbued the searches of Lou Ford, Charlie Bigger, and Nick Corey with a desperation and poignancy that lend *The Killer Inside Me, Savage Night,* and *Pop. 1280* an awesome power.

Jim Thompson found crime novel conventions particularly useful in conveying his vision of the world; his vision thus disguised has a subversive power lacking in more mainstream novels of similar, but more obvious, ambition.

I hesitated, thinkin' I should be able to come up with somethin'.
Because it was all so clear to me, Christ knew it was clear; love one
another and don't screw no one unless they're bendin' over, and forgive
us our trespasses because we may be a minority of one. For God's sake,
for God's sake -- why else had I been put here in Potts County, and why
else did I ~~break my back~~ to stay here? Why else, who else, what else but
Christ Almighty would put up with it?

But I couldn't make him see that. He was as blind as the rest
of 'em.

"Well, Nick? I ain't waiting much longer."

"And you don't have to, Buck," I said. "You don't have to,
because I finally come to a decision. I've been a long time comin' to
it; it's been the product of thinkin' and thinkin' and thinkin', and
then some more thinkin'. And dependin' on how you look at it, it's the
god-dangest whingdingest decision ever made, or it's the skitty assed
worst. Because it explains everything that goes on in the world -- it
answers everything and it answers nothing.

"So here it is, Buck, here's my decision. I thought and I
thought and then I thought some more, and finally I came to a decision.
I decided I don't no more : know what to do than if I was just another
lousy human bein'!"

                        ### End ###
                        POP. 1280
                        a novel by
                        Jim Thompson

The final page of Pop. 1280 *from Thompson's original manuscript. He crossed
out the last two lines, which read: "I whirled around, drawing my gun. We both
fired at the same time."*

NINE

In August of 1964, Jim Thompson's Hollywood agent, Jerry Bick, had obtained for him one of his last television assignments, writing an episode of the popular *Dr. Kildare*. The final draft of the teleplay, dated October 20, 1964, is co-credited to James F. Griffith, from a story by Jim Thompson.

Dr. Kildare production 6968, "Pardon Me for Living," is the story of a mousy young nurse who gains some self-respect (with the help of Dr. Kildare, of course) after being accused of beating up a woman patient. An insurance investigator proves the woman is a fraud who beat herself black and blue with a few oranges tied in a sheet; Lisa, the nurse, moves away from the controlling aunt who has kept her down over the years.

The story actually exhibits some of Thompson's trademarks—the con game with the oranges and the overbearing aunt who has kept the nurse stifled and repressed. Still, Bick recalls that Thompson just was not suited to television or film writing: "He could write a novel in ten days. He couldn't write a screenplay in ten years." A few months later Thompson received story credit for "Adventure in the North Atlantic," a special two-hour episode of *Convoy*.

Jim Thompson earned no additional original screen credits the rest of his career.

It had long been clear to Thompson and those around him that his drinking was an addiction that he'd never shake. His home life had deteriorated, and he did not have to step far out of line to get into trouble with his wife. He came to depend more and more on drink to anesthetize his pain; when that didn't work, he would turn to his sister Maxine when he needed someone to talk to.

Nine later Thompson first editions.

Thompson would see Arnold Hano on occasion, but the get-togethers were becoming less frequent because of the difficulties Jim was experiencing.

Arnold Hano:

> After Bonnie and I moved to Laguna Beach, Jim and Alberta followed shortly after; they moved to San Clemente. I think it was all still part of his need to be close. We were still friends, but were three thousand miles apart, so he closed that gap. He always got these attachments. Later when he lived in Hollywood he banked in San Clemente or he would get his hair cut there. Found it very hard to tear up roots, whatever they might be.
>
> We would see them every so often, not so frequently, and it became difficult when he was drinking, and he was drinking nearly all the time once he started to become "successful" in Hollywood.
>
> An evening with the Thompsons was no longer fun. He never passed out, he just became less coherent and rambling. I never knew how he did it; the amount he drank in the beginning was phenomenal and then after a while he didn't need a lot to get drunk, he'd get drunk very quickly.
>
> But he drank all the time. And then he'd be sober enough to write a book. I never knew how he did that.

Thompson's son, Michael, who had joined the army in 1960, left the service in March of 1962 after a twenty-six-month hitch. Michael had experienced more than his share of the usual teenage problems before joining the service at the age of twenty-two, but his time with the army only exacerbated some more deeply seated problems.

Michael Thompson had a nervous breakdown in 1963, and remained a constant worry to Jim and Alberta throughout the decade. He attempted suicide more than once, and Jim often stayed up all night talking to his son, trying to keep him from hurting himself. Jim and Alberta were now living in an apartment in Hollywood, having moved up from San Clemente in 1962. Michael lived with them after he got out of the army, and for most of the rest of the 1960s. Recalls Michael Thompson, who is now a professional gambler:

> We used to talk quite a bit. He tried his best to talk, see what was bothering me. Try to keep me away from going to bed all the time, things like that. Try to keep me alive. Which at that particular time was quite a job.
>
> We used to talk whether he was drinking or not. He did his best to try to talk to me out of a lot of problems. We didn't always agree—my lifestyle, whatever. But I do give him credit for being very loyal, and standing by me in a crisis. I've found out since, some of the people around

me I really have my doubts about. But with him—pardon the expression—he was the most loyal son of a bitch I ever met in my life. He stuck by me when other people deserted me. He was down to the core. You don't really appreciate it till you get around other people for years—there aren't that many people like him. Completely loyal down the line.

Thompson's problems with his son haunted him throughout the decade, adding to the already overwhelming burden he put on himself in his quest for greater success in the movies and in his novels.

On November 28, 1964, Thompson received the first half of an advance for a new paperback original novel commissioned by Fawcett Books. It was due on January 18, 1965, and he spent most of the holiday season pounding out the book relating the Texas adventures of a slick con man and his beautiful assistant. Fawcett Gold Medal published *Texas by the Tail* late in 1965.

Texas by the Tail is another of Thompson's con man stories—which evidently had become a favorite topic—though not his most successful. The hero of this third-person adventure novel is Mitch Corley, a practitioner of various short-con swindles, ably assisted by the curvaceous Harriet, better known, for obvious reasons, as Red.

Red and Mitch have been making a lot of money on their way around Texas, and Red is looking forward to the day they retire, buy a house with a white picket fence, and live off their ill-gotten gains. Unknown to Red, almost all of their savings have gone directly to Mitch's wife, Teddy, whom Red thinks is dead.

Mitch runs afoul of both the infamous Gidge Lord, matriarch of one of Texas' oldest and richest families, and Jake Zearsdale, presently the state's most powerful and richest man. Unable to take advantage of a generous investment offer made to him by Zearsdale, Mitch makes Red suspicious that they don't have any savings after all, which of course, is the truth.

Mitch knows that if Red finds out about the money, or worse, finds out about Teddy, she'll probably kill him. By the end of the novel, Red finds out both things . . .

Texas by the Tail is a decent, workmanlike job by Thompson, but it shows little inspiration or enthusiasm, and few of the usual themes or obsessions. Perhaps he was drained by the effort of writing the brilliant *Pop. 1280* months before. The tone of *Texas by the Tail* is seriocomic throughout, which doesn't lend itself to the familiar psychological underpinning Thompson gives the novel. One passage, about the origin of oil drilling in Big Spring, seems at least semiautobiographical, and was excerpted earlier in this book.

There is one stunningly successful passage which does address, in a new way, one of Thompson's familiar themes. Red likes to go on shopping sprees in dime stores, limiting her daily expenditure to five dollars. It fulfills a childhood fantasy of hers, and makes her happy like nothing else can:

> She would be very touchy about the armload of "bargains" she brought home (they would disappear in a day or so, just where he never knew). Once he had teased her, asking if she had left anything in the store, and the color had risen in her cheeks and she had called him a mean stupid darned old fool. And then heartbrokenly she had begun to cry. He had held her, cuddled her small body in his arms, rocked gently to and fro with her as the great sobs tore through her breast. And there were tears in his own eyes, as at last he understood the cause of her sorrow; for it was his also, and perhaps everyone's. The loss of innocence before it had ever endured. The cruel shearing away of all but the utterly practical, as pastoral man was caught up in an industrial society.
>
> She was an extreme case, yes, as was he. But the tenant farmer's shack and the hotel room were merely the outer limits of a world which inevitably shaped everyone. He did not need to wonder about her thoughts when her schoolbooks had related the adventures of Mary Jane and her Magic Pony. He suspected that in a different way they had been akin to his as he read of the joyous conspiracy between Bunny Rabbit and Mrs. Stork (while the couple overhead were damned near pounding the bed apart).
>
> So she wept, and he wept a little with her. Not for the idealized dream of things past but for the immutable realities of the present. Not for what had been lost but for what had never been. Not for what might have been but for what could never be.

Here is the post *Heed the Thunder* "black abyss of the night" in which all Thompson's later characters live. The ramifications of a loss of innocence in a world in which innocence may be the most precious of possessions is pretext or subtext in nearly all of Thompson's first-person narrator novels. *Lack* of innocence may be more correct, since this seems a world where there is no innocence, even in childhood. After all, the true damage done to Lou Ford by his involvement with Helene was done by the *knowledge,* later gained, that he had done evil, not the act itself. And of course, knowledge represents the first and ultimate fall from innocence.

The impact of a childhood loss of/lack of innocence is cause and effect in Thompson's short novel *This World, Then the Fireworks,* which, though written in 1955, was published posthumously. It is discussed in the epilogue.

Fawcett now took an interest in resurrecting Jim Thompson's career; having done well with 1964's *Pop. 1280* and happy with the manuscript of *Texas by the Tail,* they decided to reissue *The Killer Inside Me* later in 1965. In fact, to celebrate the reissue of *The Killer* they placed a full-page, back cover advertisement in the June 8, 1965, edition of *Daily Variety,* replete with quotes from favorable reviews and mention of "censorship":

ANNOUNCING STILL ANOTHER HUGE PRINTING OF THE
BOOK THAT CENSORSHIP COULDN'T KILL.
JIM THOMPSON'S
great crime classic
THE KILLER INSIDE ME
A GOLD MEDAL BOOK   AT ALL NEWSSTANDS

Favorable quotes included Stanley Kubrick's *"The Killer Inside Me* is probably the most chilling and believable first-person story of a criminally warped mind I have ever encountered"; Anthony Boucher's *"The Killer Inside Me* is one of the most remarkable psychological studies conceived within the crime novel form"; and R.V. Cassill's *"The Killer Inside Me* is exactly what French enthusiasts for existential American violence were looking for in the work of Dashiell Hammett, Horace McCoy and Raymond Chandler. None of those men wrote a book within miles of Jim Thompson's."

The Cassill quote is from the first serious study of the novel published in the *New York Herald-Tribune,* and later reprinted in a collection of essays entitled *Tough Guy Writers of the Thirties,* edited by David Madden. Jerry Bick asked Thompson what he thought of Cassill's essay, which identified *The Killer Inside Me* as a novel of ideas that transcends its paperback origins. Thompson replied with a shrug and a grin that he didn't know what Cassill was talking about.

Arnold Hano recalls a similar incident with Thompson. Hano was discussing *The Getaway* with Jim, and raving about the literal hell on earth that is the Kingdom of El Rey. Hano says that Thompson seemed genuinely puzzled by this idea; in fact, Thompson insisted to Hano that Doc and Carol did get away with it. Thompson seemed to have known that for his writing to be truly subversive he couldn't go around explaining how subversive it was.

In any case, the ad in *Daily Variety* did nothing more than temporarily bolster Thompson's flagging spirits. It had so little effect that Jerry Bick, who was listed as Thompson's agent at the bottom of the ad, never knew about the ad until it was mentioned to him years later.

Thompson's work on the *Dr. Kildare* script at MGM had resulted in a chance meeting with Sam Peckinpah, who was then affiliated with the studio. Peckinpah had greatly admired both *The Killing* and *Paths of Glory,* and was familiar with Thompson's novels. The director soon struck a deal to have Thompson write a first-draft screenplay based on Sam Ross's 1964 novel *Ready for the Tiger.*

The project lingered in development at MGM for well over two years, during which Peckinpah himself wrote several screenplay drafts; a complete draft authored by Peckinpah, dated March 15, 1965, was among Jim Thompson's private papers. Oddly enough, there are no pages written by Thompson to be found among his own papers; instead, a half-finished draft written solely by Thompson was among Peckinpah's private papers.

Ready for the Tiger is the story of an American mercenary/outlaw named Mike who has come to a small Central American town to kill a man who betrayed him years before. He knifes and kills the man in an alley, and is protected from arrest by Eddie, a young boy who lives with his teenage sister Emelita. Emelita and Eddie's parents both are dead.

The two youngsters provide an alibi for Mike, but there's a catch to it; the local police captain, Wallens, killed their brother, and they want revenge. Soon Mike and Emelita fall in love. Eddie also cares about Mike, but revenge burns in him, and he'll do anything to see Wallens dead. When Mike sleeps with Emelita any qualms the jealous Eddie had about using him vanish.

Eddie turns Mike in for the first killing, and Emelita and Mike flee to another city. Eventually she has to start prostituting herself again so that they can survive.

In the final confrontation Mike kills Wallens and is himself killed by the police. Finally Eddie is distraught by what has happened; he got exactly what he wanted, but lost what little he had. Emelita, long the wiser of the two, shakes her head and takes him home.

Thompson's screenplay is similar in structure to Peckinpah's, but Thompson's violent scenes are even more violent. The first knifing scene, as written by Thompson, is an excruciatingly slow exercise in sadistic revenge; an interrogation scene with a sap is quite a bit more graphic. Peckinpah was probably saving his more ingenious bits of violence for the actual shooting, but it is startling to see Thompson's takes on violence outdo the master of screen violence himself.

Thematically, we can guess that Thompson was drawn to the subject matter of the novel, especially the characters of Eddie and Emelita, who have suffered a childhood trauma that could be right out of any Thompson book. Unfortunately, Thompson evidently had no great involvement in the project beyond his first draft, and the film was never made by Peckinpah.

Peckinpah had recognized a kindred spirit in Thompson and was enthusiastic a few years later when the novelist's *The Getaway* was offered to him as a star vehicle for Steve McQueen and Ali McGraw.

Meanwhile, Robert Mills, Thompson's agent in New York, was informed by the French publishing house of Gallimard that they wished to publish Thompson's *Pop. 1280* as the thousandth book in their *Série Noire* line of paperbacks. The *Série Noire* had been established decades before, and was dedicated to publishing great hard-boiled American novels. The offer of being the thousandth book in the series was a gesture of how highly they thought of *Pop. 1280* and the rest of Thompson's work.

Three Thompson books, all retitled, had been previously published in the *Série Noire:* in 1950 *Nothing More Than Murder* as *Cent Mètres de Silence;* in 1959 *The Getaway* as *Le Lien Conjugal;* in 1965 *Wild Town,* as *Éliminatoires.* Thompson was invited to a party in France celebrating the publication of *Pop. 1280* (French title: *1275 Âmes*), but he could not afford to fly over.

The French title, which means 1275 souls, seems a mystery in itself. The loss of five souls may have been intended to take into account Nick Corey's victims, but he kills six people, not five—the two pimps, Tom Hauck, Uncle John, Myra, and Lennie. Perhaps some of the inhabitants of Pottsville are soulless? Nick Corey seems obvious, but who else— Myra, Lennie, Rose, and Amy? The only other possible answer lies in Ken Lacey's assessment of blacks as less than human; the pimps and Uncle John are black, but where then are the other two soulless humans?

After the January 1966 publication of *Pop. 1280* as the thousandth in the series came editions of *The Nothing Man, A Hell of a Woman, The Killer Inside Me, A Swell-Looking Babe,* and *Cropper's Cabin,* in 1966 through 1970.

By now, in fact, quite a bit of Thompson's earlier work had been translated into foreign languages. Robert Mills, working with British agent John Farquharson, sold Thompson books to France, Spain, Germany, Japan, Portugal, and elsewhere. Though most of the advances were small, they were steady, and Thompson came to depend on them.

Thompson's 1965 Fawcett Gold Medal novel, *Texas by the Tail,* had been initially commissioned as an untitled "pipeline novel"; sometime

Foreign editions, including Spanish, French, German and Czechoslovakian.

later the title "South of Heaven" was scribbled onto the contract. But when the novel appeared in 1965, it was the con man adventure *Texas by the Tail*. It's unclear whether Thompson went ahead and wrote a different book, or it was just retitled. In any event, Thompson approached Gold Medal about doing the pipeline novel *South of Heaven* as the next book after *Texas,* and he wrote a novel based on his own youthful adventures in the far West Texas oil fields. For the by now customary advance of $2,000, Thompson delivered the novel and Fawcett Gold Metal published it in 1967.

South of Heaven is the story of the coming of age of Tommy Burwell, a hobo out on the West Texas oil fields in the mid-1920s. Based on Thompson's own adventures years before, *South of Heaven* is a wistful novel of a time gone by, built around Tommy Burwell's determination to foil a plan to rob the payroll of a big pipeline job, and to rescue a girl with whom he's fallen in love.

Tommy Burwell's been alone out on the oil fields since his grandparents blew themselves up with some sticks of dynamite while trying to blast a new latrine. He meets up with Four Trey Whitey, a strange, distant character who gruffly takes Tommy under his wing. Four Trey is aware of Tommy's inherent intelligence, especially after Tommy recites some clever, if dirty, poetry. In his own way, Four Trey tells Tommy the oil fields are no place for a guy with a brain:

> I broke off, for Four Trey had rolled over on his side, back to me. I waited a moment, and when he didn't say anything, I asked him what was the matter.
>
> "You," he said, his voice coming to me a little muffled because he was speaking into the wind. "You're the matter. You know, if I was really a friend of yours, I'd kick the crap out of you."
>
> "What?" I said. "What are you talking like that for?"
>
> "Prometheus," he said. "Oedipus Rex. Cosmic reciprocity. Goddammit . . ." He rolled over and faced me, scowling, "What kind of a life is this for a kid as bright as you are? Why do you go on wasting your time, year after year? Do you think you're going to stay young forever? If you do, take a look at me."

Tommy's already aware of what Four Trey is talking about, since he took a personal inventory earlier that morning and found himself wanting:

> I took a long look at myself, trudging along in the dust, with my hat brim turned up front and back and my belly burning with before-breakfast booze. And the picture wasn't a nice one at all. There was nothing romantic or dashing about it. I was a drifter, a day laborer, a tinhorn gambler—a man

wasting his life in a wasteland. That's what I was now. That's what I'd be in another twenty-one years if I lived that long, unless I started changing my ways fast.

I told myself I would. The telling made me feel better, sort of removing the need, you know, to actually do anything.

Tommy meets a girl named Carol, and he's instantly smitten by her. Four Trey tells Tommy to forget about her, that he should know what she is, what she has to be, a woman all alone out on the fields—a prostitute, to be had by any man with enough pay in his pocket.

Tommy gets angry, so Four Trey drops the subject. He tells Tommy that he needs an assistant on the pipeline job he just got. What Four Trey neglects to tell Tommy is that the pipeline job involves shooting dynamite.

The rest of *South of Heaven* takes place out on the oil pipeline job. Tommy sleeps with Carol in the strange, truck-like automobile in which she lives. He has a running feud with Bud Lassen, a "hired lawman" who killed Tommy's friend Fruit Jar. When Lassen ends up dead, Tommy is hauled off to jail for the murder.

Tommy is set free after three witnesses come forward and swear Lassen's death was an accident. Tommy is suspicious that the "witnesses" are up to no good, and had a selfish reason for getting him out of jail.

Eventually, with the help of Four Trey Whitey, Tommy is able to figure out exactly what the crooks' scheme is, and he turns himself into a living bomb in order to bring down the payroll robbers. Carol, though involved with the robber gang, turns out to be the innocent he "knew" she was.

South of Heaven is an interesting, colorful reminiscence of the life of pipeliners and hoboes in West Texas, but it lacks the power of Thompson's best novels. Although the novel imparts a good sense of a unique time and place, only the passages which seem to be autobiographical have any real impact.

By this time, Jim Thompson had evidently built a new, mostly fantasy image of himself, and for himself. He was living in an apartment on Whitley Avenue, just up the street from the Musso and Frank Grill, Hollywood's oldest restaurant and a former haunt of such literati as Faulkner, Chandler, and Hammett. Thompson became a fixture in the bar at Musso's, and he regaled anybody who would listen with tales of his life, and how he personally knew all the great writers who hung out there.

Arnold Hano recalls Thompson asked him a favor during this time:

There was bitterness that he was not famous. He once wanted me to write a magazine article about him. He thought it would help if he was presented to Hollywood in *California* or *Los Angeles* magazine, or some other magazine. I was doing a lot of magazine writing then, I was in *TV Guide* all the time. So he thought I'd be able to do that. So I said let me think about that, it would be really hard.

So what arrived in the mail a few days later but such an article, written by Jim, about Jim. About this courtly gentleman who would show up at Musso and Frank's and he always had the same table, and people knew him and respected him, and he was this writer. It was so totally unlike my version of Jim, I said to him I can't sign off on this and I don't know what I could write that would be of use to him.

When the internal pressure and pain got too great, Thompson would frequently end up at Maxine and Joe Kouba's house in West Los Angeles. He would arrive some time in the early evening, and Maxine, familiar with the routine, knew what invariably would take place. She first would call Alberta and tell her that Jimmie was okay. Then she'd sit up most of the night with her brother, as he drank and talked about what was bothering him.

Maxine Kouba:

He spent many nights with me, we'd be up talking until five in the morning. He would come out—I just knew what was going to happen. He could consume an awful lot—but he never got bad, always gentler.

You might think they were wild stories, tales of the past and so on, but they never varied. If he repeated a story it was always the same. It was always the same few things. Not drunken talk or anything.

The drinking just opened him up to where he did talk, otherwise he wouldn't. His stories never varied. People say it was just drunken talk; well it wasn't.

He always came here. I never told Alberta if it was a long night or a bad night, because I didn't want him to go home and be reproached. Which would be normal, from her standpoint. So nothing was ever told. I'd say, oh, he was all right, he just went to bed. But he would always leave and come out here. Always.

He did not stay at home and carry on, and I guess he had a reason for it. He was never violent or argumentative. He just wanted to talk. And he wouldn't stop.

They were just stories of the past, how he felt—I hope it did him some good. Then he'd be fine for a while.

Next morning, he'd straighten himself up, but he'd be afraid to go home. He'd hang around, and I'd call Alberta. I'd say, do you want me to call her, I'll see how things are.

So then usually nobody'd want to come and get him. So we took him back when he got ready.

When Maxine was asked what she thought caused this behavior, she responded:

Jimmie'd open up a lot in later years, but he was introverted all his life. Always wanted to be successful, always wanted to do the best for his family. He tried.

Maxine Kouba refused to be specific about "the stories" that Thompson would rehash on his periodic visits. She just reiterated that they never varied, and so she thought them true, despite "other people's" saying they were just drunken talk.

We know that Thompson was obsessed by the myriad missed opportunties of his career, and his endless string of bad luck. But with his sister Maxine, one person who truly knew how close he had been with Lucille Boomer decades previous, he probably speculated on how his life might have been different if it had been spent with Lucille.

And without doubt Jim Thompson relived that fateful time in New York City when he failed to rescue their despondent father before he gave up hope and died. Reliving it, retelling it, searching for a relief from the burden of guilt and pain that he had carried around with him for three decades.

In April of 1967 *Ellery Queen's Mystery Magazine* published Thompson's "Exactly What Happened." Neil Keller's plan to steal an old man's fortune and pin it on Jake Goss, his one-eyed, toothless co-worker, goes horribly wrong when Jake turns out to have an ingenious plan of his own.

In the end, like many Thompson heroes, Keller is doomed by himself—or, more correctly, by Jake Goss disguised as Neil Keller—a literal twist on a familiar Thompson theme:

In his last brief moments all he saw was himself. The one man he had not guarded against. The one man every man faces sooner or later. All he saw was that he was about to be murdered by himself—which, in a sense, was exactly what happened.

Thompson soon learned from Arnold Hano that an old friend, Jim Bryans of Lion Books, had become a vice-president and editor-in-chief at Popular Library. Bryans commissioned Thompson for three "novelizations" beginning with 1967's *Ironside,* based on the hit television series.

Thompson was paid $2,000 for the book, which he evidently pounded out in about six weeks: the contract was signed June 16, 1967, and the manuscript due August 1. Two novelizations from films followed in 1969: *The Undefeated* and *Nothing but a Man*. Jim Thompson seemingly had reached the nadir of his career with these efforts, but *Ironside* does contain flashes that are distinctly his work. And as Thompson knew, things were never so bad that they couldn't get worse.

Of the three novelizations to which the steady descent of Thompson's writing career had now brought him, only *Ironside* features a plot conceived by Jim Thompson. Rather than have Thompson use a plot from one of the television episodes, the publishers of *Ironside* wanted Thompson to use the television characters in an original story of his creation.

This renders *Ironside* an interesting hybrid, containing more of Thompson's characteristic writing than one might expect. In fact, the whole first chapter, in which a murderer meets his victim in a bar, is a stunning set piece. It's not until the second chapter that we meet Robert Ironside and his crew, and the more pedestrian investigation of the murderer's crimes begins.

After quickly setting the scene in a hellish bar, Thompson zeroes in on the Killer, and his position as a deity of his world—in his mind and in his actions:

> Tolerantly, which is not to say approvingly, the Killer effortlessly absorbed the sights and sounds of the saloon. The unforgivable stench. The unmusical music. The irredeemable people. He understood such places—the reason for their being. He understood the habitues—the myriad dark byways which had brought them here. He understood so he did not condemn, just as he would not have condemned a hole or the poisonous snakes which populated it. Just as God would not have condemned his own creations.
>
> The Killer's condemnation was reserved for creatures of free will. For those who might have done very well and had, perversely, done very badly. As with God (reputedly), the Killer had tolerance and understanding for the hapless evil of predestination. But for the wickedness which need not have been, for the willful doer of evil, the Killer had nothing but death.

The Killer's opinion of "willful doers of evil" is quite familiar, being about Thompson's own opinion of outright criminals like *The Getaway*'s Doc and Carol McCoy, and the passive evildoers of novels like *The Criminal*. And the Killer's role in his world is an obvious variation on Nick Corey's and Lou Ford's roles as deities. In *Ironside,* the Killer traces the evil careers of such wasteful people of privilege—seeming to blackmail them, but really just setting them up for extermination.

The Killer is expecting his latest victim to meet him in the bar, and she has just walked in:

> She was twenty-four years old. As a human being, she wasn't worth a plugged nickel. But the bank and tax authorities assayed her at approximately 16 million dollars. Her maiden name, reacquired after each of her five divorces, was a very distinguished one—Eleanor McNesmith Chisholm. But it was not the name which the habitues of the bar would have applied to her. They had never seen her before, but they had met all her sisters and cousins and other kindred. So they knew her name well.
>
> They spelled it t-r-a-m-p.

In her constant search for new kicks, Eleanor Chisholm had starred in a stag film, and the blackmailer has recognized her. When she tries to make the payoff, the Killer pretends not to be the blackmailer that she thinks he is. Finally the Killer suggests that she dropped a key on the floor, along with a small bag containing a bikini. She understands immediately, actually looking forward to her meeting with the Killer in a room behind the bar—instead of being afraid for her life, as she should. "She glanced inside [the bag] briefly, and a sudden flush flooded her patrician features. *But, wow! This promised to be something else again!"*

The Killer follows her back to the room, after giving her time to change into the bikini. He accepts the payment of $10,000, now satisfied she is not wired for sound. He then turns down her expected offer: "Certainly not! Do you think I'm as filthy as you are?" The chapter ends with the Killer and Chisholm still in the room.

The rest of the novel deals with the investigation by Ironside and crew of two seemingly unrelated murders. The first is a hit-and-run fatality; the driver was the rich spoiled son of Coleman Duke, against whom Ironside refuses to drop charges—making the powerful Coleman Duke his enemy. The hit-and-run victim was Eleanor Chisholm.

The second murder is charged to Ironside's young black protégé, Mark Sanger. Sanger was set upon on his way to night school by a rich white couple out for a laugh. Mark gets into a fistfight with the man, and is knocked out. When Mark comes to, the police are hauling the white man to the hospital, where he later dies.

Eventually Ironside proves the two murders did not occur the way they seemed to—both victims were poisoned (by the Killer, of course), and the sloppy work of the coroner did not catch it.

Meanwhile, Eve Kendall, a beautiful young cop whom Ironside loves, is doing a favor for a friend who's being blackmailed. Eve's taking the friend's place in meeting the would-be blackmailer at a sleazy bar in downtown San Francisco . . .

Everything turns out happily, as it must, but not before Thompson offers a few more scenes with the Killer in the bar. As the Killer once again listens to the preposterous piano player, Thompson finally extends his dim view of the world and its inhabitants to its only logical end: nuclear holocaust.

> There was beauty in the music, or more accurately, the memory of beauty, now as lost as a lost love; something that lay buried in an unknown dimension like the final decimal of pi. Now, as though avenging itself upon an evil and uncaring world, it had sprouted into hideousness—a seed gone mad. And its terrible blossoms of sound hinted at a greater terror to come. Here, said the music, was a taste of Armageddon. Here, the Ultima Thule. Here the inevitable destination of a planet whose mass of six sextillion, four hundred and fifty quintillion short tons was turned into a slaughterhouse instead of a garden. Here, the fruit of neglect, that socially approved form of murder. Here, the basic lie in its final extension.
>
> A whole *was* greater than its parts . . . or was there no Bomb, no minute amalgam of neutrons and protons? Add three billion to the planet's mass, and subtract kindness and caring, and you were left not with an unkindly, uncaring three billion, but death. So said the seed, the music, now sunk in the morass of a wilderness from which it had vainly cried out. There would be no refuge from the coming terror. No place to hide. No familiar thing to cling to. Something would become nothing, robbed of its intrinsic beauty and safety, and all else. There would be only a smoking, steaming blown-apart, crushed-together mishmash where brother was himself eaten by brother while eating brother, ad nauseam, ad infinitum.

With the Thompson world now finally blown to bits by the ultimate cataclysm, Jim Thompson would return once more to familiar terrain and themes in *Child of Rage,* in an effort to determine the nature of an actual, not a deluded, savior of a godless world.

The Undefeated and *Nothing but a Man* do not have any important Thompson passages buried within their pages. Thompson basically wrote them up directly from the films, frequently going so far as to open chapters with a few words setting the scene, like "Dawn . . . ," "Southwest Texas . . ." and "Night . . . ."

The Undefeated, set just after the Civil War, chronicles how a band of Northern adventurers and displaced Southerners come to need each other and eventually work together against a common enemy: Mexican revolutionaries. The leader of the Northern group falls in love with a young Southern widow, with predictable results.

Nothing but a Man is the story of Duff Anderson, a resentful young black day laborer in Alabama. He falls in love with and marries Josie, a schoolteacher and small-town preacher's daughter. Duff always seems to be asking for trouble, although he doesn't need to ask for it since he's black and in the South. Through the death of his father he learns to face life in a different manner, and stop expecting the worst. He returns to Josie, whom he had abandoned, and brings his three-year-old son with him. He's going to try his best, and with the help of his family, hopes to make it.

In late 1967, Thompson's new Hollywood agent Dick Brand had sealed an option contract with an independent producer intent on filming *The Killer Inside Me*. The deal was for $20,000 upon the commencement of principal photography, but the project never got off the ground, and all Thompson saw was the $1,000 option fee, less commissions. Many other Thompson novels were optioned during the late 1960s and early 1970s, including *Pop. 1280* and *A Hell of a Woman*, though none made it to the screen except *The Getaway*.

It would be eight years and several options later that *The Killer Inside Me* would be turned into a film, with disastrous results.

By the late 1960s, Jim Thompson had gained quite a following overseas—especially in France, where he was increasingly considered the peer or better of such worshiped American writers as James M. Cain and Horace McCoy.

One Thompson fan was *cinéaste* Pierre Rissient, who wrote to Thompson from Paris in hope of meeting with the writer when he visited Los Angeles a few weeks later. Thompson was receptive, and the two met for drinks at the Beverly Wilshire Hotel. Rissient was a great admirer of both *The Killing* and *Paths of Glory,* though *Paths* had been banned in France and Rissient had seen it only once in New York in 1964.

According to Rissient:

> [Thompson] was bitter and sour about Kubrick. He felt his credit was not as it should have been on *The Killing*. Also the fact that he did not finish *Paths of Glory*. He was very much hurt and defeated by life. And you wouldn't think it from reading his books, but he was always very naive, even gullible with people. When he was working with Kubrick he was thinking it could be a long-term relationship. He felt let down that Kubrick turned to other writers. Jim anticipated it as a natural thing that they would keep working together.

He would write what he called "samples"—the first thirty or forty pages of a novel to try to get a publisher. One of them was *Child of Rage*, which

I liked very much. At the time it was called *White Mother, Black Son*. I thought it could be turned into a terrific film. I got a French producer to pay for his writing it in exchange for the movie rights. To be honest, the final book was not as good as what I felt it promised to be. By that time, Jim was quite diminished—in terms of creative powers—even his eyesight was starting to fail. His hands bothered him. And I remember him telling me that typing was very important to him.

Circumstances were difficult for him; his problems with his son were acute. An artist should have calm around him to create. For Jim Thompson there was no calm.

He would say that all books, not just his own, had only one plot—somebody finds out that things are not the way they had been told they would be.

Thompson included this credo in his unfinished novel *A Horse in the Baby's Bathtub*. If he thought that all stories had that as their central plot, he must have felt that his own life story had not turned out the way he had been told or expected it would. This particular cameo appearance of himself is similar to that in *Savage Night;* Thompson once again portrays himself as a washed-up alcoholic writer who now deals in "asses and tits."

From *A Horse in the Baby's Bathtub:*

His name was Tomlinson or Thomas or something of the kind, and I gathered from certain things he said that he was a writer. But he insisted, spattering me with an alcoholic spray, that this was not the case.

"Got my own brokerage business," he said. "Biggest dealer north of Staten Island in asses and tits. Ain't allowed to advertise 'em," he added, with a lascivious wink, "but I handle some mighty nice uteri, too." . . .

He gulped down a sob, and took another long drink of the free booze. Then, he vouchsafed moodily that he had used to deal in other things.

"Brains, faces, smiles, thoughts. Beauty and profundity, if there is a difference. Out of the little I had, I created the much that I had not, bringing into the world the only wealth which does not deprive another. . . ."

And I seemed to hear a . . . . voice, to see a bloated red-eyed face, and to smell the sour sachet of whiskey.

"*Plot? There ain't but one plot in the world, m'boy. Give 'em somethin' else they'd clobber you with it.*"

"*Polti says there are thirty-two plots.*"

"*They all got the same daddy, one basic plot. Things're not as they seem, that's the papa of the whole thirty-two. Things're not as they seem.*"

"*Nothing? Nothing is ever as it seems?*"

"*Only—hic!—only if it stinks. If it stinks then that's the way it is. Livin' proof of it . . .*"

"Things are not as they seem." Yes, it could be applied to all of Thompson's novels, where every motivation is hidden and every personality masked by a persona. But it's more importantly a clue to Thompson's own life; the version of his life that is now offered up by many of his friends and acquaintances, and strictly adhered to by his widow and daughters. Jim Thompson knew no one understood him or shared his inner thoughts. He didn't let them know, but even worse, it seems that no one really wanted to know.

Pierre Rissient continues:

> We took him to Paris for *Child of Rage*, but it was an abortive trip, because he received a telegram from his wife that his son was going to commit suicide if he didn't come back. He had never been to Europe or Paris but he drank so much that he had no reaction to his surroundings, and he had to leave three days after arriving.

So thirty years later, history must have seemed to repeat itself to Jim Thompson. He had produced his first novel under the pressure of getting his father out of the rest home in Oklahoma City before his father gave up hope and died. Thompson failed, and for the rest of his life considered his father's death a suicide for which he held himself responsible. If James Sherman Thompson intended to give his son guilt and inferiority complexes, he succeeded only too well.

Thirty years later in a bizarre, symmetrical echo of the past worthy of one of his novels, Thompson was threatened by the suicide of his son, Michael, while writing what would turn out to be his last novel. Character and circumstance had again conspired to confirm Thompson in the darkest of his tenets about life.

And one can't help but note that Thompson's abortive trip to the bright lights of Paris, the one time he escaped from the American continent, resembles quite strongly Lou Ford's short, dismal trip to the big city of Fort Worth, which the deputy spends shut up in a hotel room.

On November 22, 1971, Thompson signed a contract with Lancer Books for paperback publication of *Child of Rage*. The book made it to the stands in early 1972. Thompson would publish no more books in America; in 1973 Sphere Books of London published *King Blood*, a completed novel which Thompson had written years before while living in Queens. Sphere also reprinted *The Killer Inside Me* and *The Getaway* in 1973.

The original title of *Child of Rage—White Mother, Black Son*—gives all one really needs to know about the plot of this strangest of Thompson novels. Narrated in the first person by "black son" Allen Smith, a super-intelligent, psychosexually tortured high school senior, *Child of Rage* often succeeds as biting social satire. However, Thompson's handling of both the racial and Freudian elements in the tale are sometimes so outrageous that, while they often hit the mark, they leave one wondering how Thompson ever got this book published.

Still, the novel is critically important in Thompson's canon, written with a no-holds-barred urgency that suggests Thompson knew it might be his last book; it is easily his most ambitious effort since *Pop. 1280*. Ancillary to the tale of Allen Smith, Thompson launches angry attacks on many of America's sacred cows, including marriage, motherhood, education, and work—topped off by a sly parody of Norman Mailer's *Why Are We in Vietnam?* at the end of Chapter Six. Thompson had obviously read and been inspired by Mailer's 1967 novel.

Eccentric as the novel is, the main story of Allen Smith contains essential takes on Thompson's trademark themes and obsessions, including child abuse, incest, and identity crisis; and a final exploration of the nature of a savior in a twisted world. In fact, Allen Smith is perhaps the ultimate Thompson split narrator—both black and white, good and evil, sane and insane, guilty and innocent, loving and hateful, right and wrong—God and the devil.

Allen Smith begins his story on the day he and his mother, Mary, having recently moved into a deluxe apartment building in New York, go to the nearby public school to get Allen enrolled. On the way there, Allen torments his mother, whom he's clearly ten times brighter than, with clever wordplay and bitter jokes. But as he closes the first chapter, he admits the biggest joke's on him:

> I didn't blame her, of course.
> If I'd been in her place, a swell-looking white broad who had the bad luck to be stuck with a kinky-haired nigger kid, I'd have hated it too.
> Hated him.

At the school, Mary Smith tells the principal, Mr. Velie, that Allen is likely to cause trouble. The promise of some of Mary's ample charms eventually convinces Mr. Velie to allow Allen to enroll at school.

Allen had a chock-full first day at school. He tortures a pretty young black student, Josie Blair, who works part-time in the principal's office, by slamming a gate on her and cracking lascivious jokes. Josie sees through most of Allen's act:

"Don't you feel sorry for me, you silly-looking coon! Take your goddam pity and shove it up your—"

A bell began ringing loudly, drowning out my voice. The bell for the changing of classes. The room doors opened, and kids swarmed out into the halls, and Josie Blair disappeared among them. Going back to work, or wherever she went at that time of day.

So I didn't get a chance to tell her how sorry I was.

I didn't get a chance to leap on her and smash that gently understanding look from her face, and tear out her hatefully sympathetic eyes.

In geometry class, Allen first acts like a "dum ol' nigger," then dazzles the class with a theorem he's memorized from a doctoral thesis. He then meets the Hadley siblings, Steve and Lizbeth, two stuck-up, phony blacks—doctor's children—against whom Allen instantly plots revenge: *"Why, you put on little suck ups, I thought! Boy, am I going to get you!"*

Allen is called to the principal's office, where Velie beats him for stealing a fountain pen. When Josie produces the pen in question, supposedly left on her desk, Velie apologizes to Allen, who seems to accept the apology. But we know he's just added Velie to his revenge list, if he wasn't there already.

Next Allen meets "Doozy" Rafer, a black radical with a shaved head who's trying to form a Black Students Club. Allen enlists him in the plan against Velie, which, unknown to Rafer, is actually a plot against him as well.

Finally Allen lets Lizbeth Hadley know exactly what he expects of her, if she wants to be "friends":

> "W-Well, I just thought we could talk, and—and maybe have a little snack together. S-Some potato chips and coke, an'—"
>
> I interrupted her to say that she and I would have a Coke. A warm one. Foam up a warm Coke and it made a first-class douche.
>
> "And instead of a little snack, we'll have a little snatch. Only a slight change in plans, see? Practically the same thing you'd counted on."

As Allen waits for Josie, whom he'd arranged to meet after school, he ponders his actions of his first day at school:

> Yes, being human, or a reasonable facsimile thereof, there were doubts in my mind on my conduct of the day; the many, many days preceding it. Momentary doubts and recriminations. And, of course, very-very, crappy-crappy rationalizations.
>
> Judging people? Being absolutely fair in my judgements? *Owl offal! Dingo dung!*

Of course, I judge them. And being absolutely fair about it, I find them all guilty, and sentence them to hang by the balls until they turn red (or some other cheerful color). They're all guilty, we're all guilty. We come into life filled with sinful shit, and we have to get it kicked out of us before we can be raised to glory. (H'it say so, right in de good Book. De Lawd is a tired old man wit' de miseries in his back, an' he sho' can't be histin' shit an' sinners *bofe* up to hebbin.)
    Sympathy? Pity? *Horse Hockey! Snake stools!*
    No one ever actually feels such emotions because they are non-existent.

Allen explains that he considers himself the only true son of a bitch in the world, because he does all these terrible things, yet cannot find a reason why:

The fact is and was that I was and am as I am and was because I was and am an unadulterated, .999 fine, 24-karat, 180-proof, 100-percent pure son-of-a-bitch. The *only* one in the fiction-history from which life is copied.
    All the other so-called sons-of-bitches of other races and mine are merely semis. Their son-of-a-bitchery is motivated, which is another way of saying that there is a reason, and excuse, for it.

That is what Allen really must know—why he acts the way he does. If he knew why, it might solve all his problems. He is searching for an answer to the emptiness he feels inside himself, just like Lou Ford, Dolly Dillon, and Charlie Bigger.
    Allen meets up with Josie, and he feels some real emotions for her, which he cannot admit to himself. He walks her home, where he discovers her father is a cop. A white cop, who gets the wrong idea about Allen. As Allen flees home to his apartment building, he knocks over a baby buggy, which eventually results in the death of the young contents inside. Fortunately for Allen, Mr. Blair saw the whole thing, and swears it was an accident.
    That night we finally discover part of the reason Allen acts the way he does, when his mother lets him crawl in bed with her, in what is evidently a nightly ritual. She gains satisfaction, but he never does:

Her legs were crossed. Firmly crossed. And when a women's legs are that way, that is that. That's all there is, there isn't any more.
    So there we were. A naked man and a naked woman, holding each other tightly in the darkness. And we might as well have been a thousand miles apart. For it was as meaningless as that.
    As meaningless, at least, for me.

After a long time—minutes for her, centuries for me—I felt her body go limp and I heard a soft, ecstatic sigh. I knew she had achieved what I had been denied.

Mary Smith now tortures her son, pretending not to know exactly what just occurred, and feigning shock at what Allen seems to be asking for. She makes Allen probe his motivations once again—maybe he is the sick one, and his nightly visits with his mother as innocent as she pretends.

In any case, Allen desires only his mother—he is impotent with any other woman. The rest of *Child of Rage* chronicles the execution of his revenge schemes against the other characters, as he tries to free himself from the sexual grip of his mother.

First he explains his problem to Josie, who, try as she does, elicits (literally) no reaction from him. Then he watches as Steve and Lizbeth Hadley commit incestuous sodomy. Still no reaction. He weans Doozy's sister from a heroin habit, but she does nothing to stir him.

One night Allen sits with Josie, and explains his theory of the life of an intelligent man in this society—the Lou Ford rule book, and perhaps Jim Thompson's own:

> "Well, it's this way," I said. "The intelligent man can only function behind a mask of stupidity, or conformity, if you will excuse the redundancy. His attitude must always be colored by that of the company he is in. If he is suspected of irreligiosity, he should pray publicly every hour on the hour, falling out of his chair and rolling on the floor, and speaking in unknown tongues. On the other hand— Why for is you-all laughin', gal?"
>
> " 'Scuse me, sah. Ah jest swallered me a feather an' h'it tickles me."
>
> I gave her a fiercely reproving scowl, and resumed. "On the other hand, if our subject is believed to be straightlaced, he should pinch girls on the butt and pee in alleys instead of going to the john. Always, whatever the circumstances, he must reveal his intelligence in an aw-shucks, turd-kicking manner; as much as to say, Well, gosh-durn! Look what I went down . . . Is I learnin' you anything, gal?"

Eventually Allen sends Josie away from him, after having sexually initiated her with his thumb. She soon starts sleeping with Mr. Velie, as Allen intended.

Allen sends pictures of Lizbeth and Steve in the act to Dr. Hadley, who discovers them once more engaged in incest at a sleazy motel on the Connecticut Turnpike. And Allen verifies one more thing, something that he already suspects—Dr. Hadley is one of his mother's clients. In a chapter narrated by Dr. Hadley, he relates something Mary Smith once told him:

> Once, when we had both had far too much to drink, she told me that she was the Virgin Mary and that her son was Jesus Christ, born of an immaculate conception.
>
> "That's why I must keep him pure and untouched," she declared owlishly. "That's why he must be made to suffer, for only through suffering can he redeem humanity."

Only Doozy's junkie sister is able to see the good Allen's actions effect. After she has survived the critical period without her heroin shot, she kisses him, her supposed torturer:

> "What the hell?" I jerked away from her. "What the hell is this?"
>
> "Man . . ." Her voice came to me in a faint whisper. "How come you love me so much when you don' even know me?"
>
> "Love *you?*" I said. "Holy God, what a riot!"
>
> "Reckon you loves most everybody, don't you? 'Bout have to, if you could love me."
>
> I shook my head, wearily. Sick and tired, and sick and tired of being sick and tired. There was a time when I would never tire, and I could make a banquet out of a chunk of bread and fish. But that was long, long ago. Now, everything is tasteless to me, and I am so goddamned tired that I wish the world's entire population had but one asshole so that I could screw it and be done with my work, instead of dealing one by one with individuals.

By the end of the novel Allen will come to understand that most of his actions have resulted paradoxically in good—that he is a sort of savior for his world.

Allen has befriended Mr. Blair, and one night when the time is right he leads Blair to the high school, where they discover Velie and Josie in the act. Blair nearly kills the principal, who of course loses his job.

Allen now is ready to learn the truth, and exact his final act of revenge against his mother. Allen has always suspected his mother is a whore, and via a simple telephone call, he confirms it. He makes an appointment to meet her in a hotel, under the name of Dr. Hadley. When Mary Smith arrives, Allen is in the shower, and she begins to talk to him, thinking he's Dr. Hadley:

> "You know something, Steven? I've been putting two and two together, and I've just about decided that he could be *your* son. The time certainly fits. It was just about nine months after our first date—when I got sore at

you, remember?—that he was born. Of course, I was pretty scatter-brained in those days; still just a kid. But . . ."

I turned up the water because I didn't want to hear any more; thinking Jesus, that would be *too* damned much to bear. But when I turned it back down, two or three minutes later, she was still chattering away on the same subject.

"So I'm probably wrong, since I never was much good at figures. Anyway, don't get your back up about it. I don't have any idea of filing a paternity suit, or doing anything else silly. Besides that, well, you've probably forgotten what I told you about the time we both got high, or else you thought I was joking. But it could be that way. You told me yourself that there had been cases where a woman conceived without being impregnated by a man, and, well, why not me? My name's Mary, and—"

Jesus Christ, I thought again. *Double Jesus Christ!* And I started to turn the water back up.

Allen finishes his shower, and begins to dry himself, trying to decide what to do to his mother. Then she reveals the answer that he's been searching for all his life:

". . . hell, Steven who am I kidding? That Virgin Mary crap sounds good when I'm high, but I buy about as much of it as you do. I know I can level with you, because you understand white people's problems. You can understand what a lousy thing it would be for a white woman to have a black child. Me, getting stuck with a wooly-headed little nigger! (Sorry, Steven, no offense.) I hated that black bastard from the first time I laid eyes on him. And believe me, I made him pay for what he'd done! Of course, I fed him; saw that he had his bottle whenever he wanted it. But I made him nurse between my legs. Peeled it back where he could get at the clitoris. And why the hell not, anyway? It felt good and it didn't hurt him any. The little black brat was too young to even remember . . ."

Too young? TOO YOUNG!

The subconscious never forgets. I would be bound to her, forsaking all others, impotent with any other, without ever knowing why.

Allen emerges from the shower, intent on revenge.

Although Mary is startled to see that it is he, she is even more startled by his erection. She opens her mouth and crawls toward him, begging him to give it to her. Allen refuses. He tells her they must leave the hotel, and he will give her what she wants at home. When they arrive home, he gags her and ties her to her bed.

Allen is off the hook; he knows the source of his actions:

"You did the kiss and make-up bit the night before I started to school here. And just in case that wasn't enough to throw me hard, you set me up for a bouncing around by Velie. That was bound to do the trick. It would send me ricocheting into more trouble, as you knew it would and as it did. With a nice girl and her father. But that wasn't the end of it. I was so punch-drunk by then that I didn't know which end I was standing on, and I stumbled over a perambulator with the tragic consequences you are aware of."

"Now, Allen, that perambulator should never have been parked there. You're no more to blame for—"

"You killed that baby," I said. "Killed it with hatred. And you're going to pay for it."

Allen lets Mary know he is free of her power over him:

I'd always *thought* I'd wanted her, but that was due to the sick seed planted in my subconscious so long ago and gradually brought to evil flower by her sexual teasing of me. But now I was cleansed of her. Completely.

"You arouse me about as much as a syphilitic rattlesnake."

Allen goes shopping for the objects he needs to exact a proper revenge upon Mary. He intends to give Mary to the parents of the dead baby, and he wants to deliver her appropriately wrapped. He ties her up and dresses her in pink:

The perambulator I had bought was extremely large, being intended for triplets, so I had no great trouble in loading her into it and tucking the pretty pink blankets around her. Then, I got the two salamis I had purchased out of the refrigerator.

I put one of them under the blankets, sliding it up into the opening which I had once slid from. I popped the other into her mouth, after removing the washrag.

Allen picks the lock of the apartment of the bereaved parents, and leaves Mary to await their arrival home.

Allen takes a walk along the river, musing upon what has happened, and why:

I had tried to do right, when ever and wherever I could. But right and wrong were so intertwined in my mind as to be unidentifiable, and I had had to create my own concepts of them.

Then all of Allen's "enemies" descend upon him. First Velie, whom Allen carves up a little with a razor blade he keeps hidden in his lapel.

Mary Smith then drives up in a taxi and takes Velie away, screaming and swearing at Allen.

Steve and Lizbeth arrive next, but Doozy unexpectedly wards them off and sends them away. Doozy alone understands that Allen's stunts taught them all a lesson, and that any trouble they got into was their own fault.

Doozy tells Allen that all his tricks were fair, except the one he pulled on Josie. Josie loves him, and she's waiting for him back at her apartment. Allen goes to her, and he discovers something after being with her a few moments:

> "I have remembered that bit of news, Josie."
> "So give," said Josie.
> "It concerns what's-his-name—you know—God," I said. "A major miracle has happened. God has just recovered his sanity."

So the novel, effectively Thompson's last, ends.

Allen Smith is a true Thompson psychotic narrator, having been abused as a child and lashing out blindly at the world in return. His life and world seem to be meaningless, as he searches for the source of his anger and its resultant actions. But Thompson lets Allen discover, in time, the root of his psychosis, and the discovery is also the cure. Fittingly, in *Child of Rage,* Jim Thompson's last novel, the godless, meaningless Thompson world is no more, for "God has recovered his sanity." Allen's life has some meaning, and the whole world is brighter for it.

Child of Rage lacks the finesse and tightness of Thompson's earlier novels; the skewed vision of racism and the sexual explicitness only diminish the themes which Thompson wants to address. As Arnold Hano noted, "Some of Jim's power is his obscurity," but Thompson leaves little to the imagination in *Child of Rage*. Allen's sexual abuse as an infant seems too easy an answer, but Thompson evidently means it be *the answer*.

Thompson's novel-writing career was over. His New York agent, Robert Mills, continued to circulate Thompson's samples without success. By this time Thompson had about twenty unfinished novel samples in his drawer. And though some were near completion, Thompson refused to finish any of them. When a publisher offered a book deal, he would complete the novel. He had always worked that way, and he would continue to work that way. Adds Arnold Hano:

> I remember those half-finished manuscripts; I read quite a few of them, and Alberta read them as well. She was to some degree a critic, but mainly

a friendly critic. She would say, I like it but this one maybe is a little too strong, meaning the language. And they were, they were getting to be too explicit, without much of the other stuff.

Thompson also had three completed works, *King Blood, The Expensive Sky,* and the novella *This World, Then the Fireworks,* which had been around since the mid-1950s. Thompson did eventually agree to write synopses of some of the novel samples, including *The Concrete Pasture* and *The Jesus Machine,* and he completed *The Rip-Off.*

Thompson wrote a letter to Robert Mills, explaining what *The Jesus Machine* was about and where the rest of it was going. It is the one extant letter in which Thompson describes his creative process, acknowledges the various levels of his work, and describes what he was attempting to achieve. An excerpt from the letter:

Dear Bob,

Here are my ideas about *The Jesus Machine;* its characters, its general direction, its conclusion. I hope they will be useful in clearing up any questions about the book.

The Jesus Machine is, of course, told on two levels: one with its outright action story, which needs no comment, and the underlying level, with its story of meaning and character, which, hopefully, particularizes a general situation and makes some useful comment on it. Similarly, the book's several protagonists exist on upper and underlying levels, so that we not only know what they do but why they are impelled to do it. Needless to say, however, since I am not creating another *Strange Interlude* nor a detailed blueprint of a duplex, there is no stratification of the book, *per se.* Without a program, we always know who the player is; without footnotes, we know why he won't say mush when he has a mouthful. . . .

Of the three leading characters, Mister Jack is the least complex. He is an unbending advocate of prejudice, simply because it works for him. Divide and rule, play one group against another—thus, Mister Jack. A shrewd man, and a student of history, he knows he has the time-tested formula for successful bossism. Regardless of friendship or personal sympathies, he is—as in the case of the head housekeeper—absolutely merciless with anyone who deviates one iota from that formula. Mister Jack has a good thing going for himself, as Boss Crump did and as several less well-known figures still do, and he means to let no one louse it up.

Bunk Hascom is, I believe, reasonably representative of a class: the South's poor-white, bigots by environment and circumstance, who generally regard themselves as being quite fair-minded and high-minded. As a Southerner by birth and a long-time resident of the area, I know that most of them *do* so regard themselves. They are in the right, in their own opinion, and they are ready to die to preserve that right.

Bunk has done many bad things in his life, but he has never thought of them as being so. Honesty and a firm conviction of self-righteousness are all that life has given him. Just as Mister Jack must behave in a certain way to exist, so must Bunk Hascom—and that way is threatened by his unintended rape of the Negro girl, Mona. He has done her wrong. Whatever the cost to him, he has to correct that wrong. He has to, despite the fact that it puts him on a collision course with an equally determined and far more powerful Mister Jack.

As for the girl, Mona, I think she is, fortunately, a much more common type than we normally hear about. Personable, self-respecting and well-spoken, she has the patience to accept what she can't change and the determination to change what she can, and the wisdom to distinguish between the two. Since she rightly sees the root problem of all oppression as an economic one, she is determined to make herself more valuable through education. If, in obtaining it, there must be a temporary and surface sacrifice of dignity, so be it. Confident of her own worth, she can and will endure what she must. . . .

Thompson explains the rest of the plot of *The Jesus Machine,* in which Bunk takes on Mister Jack and ends up marrying Mona. Unfortunately, it evidently didn't help Mills sell the novel. *The Jesus Machine* was never completed.

In another, shorter note Thompson told Mills that he wanted *This World, Then the Fireworks* in print so badly that he would give the publication rights away for nothing. Mills canvassed the men's magazines, which he felt were the only possible market for this story of incest and matricide, but *Playboy* found the story "inappropriate." One can imagine Hugh Hefner and cohorts blanching at Thompson's vision of sexuality.

John Farquharson had a little more luck with Thompson's 1954–55 novel *King Blood,* which Sphere of England agreed to publish in 1973. It was effectively Thompson's last appearance in print before he died.

Set in the Oklahoma Territory around the turn of the century, *King Blood* concerns the adventures of Critchfield King, third and youngest son of Ike King, the largest landowner in the territory. "Kidnapped" when a child by his mother and her con man lover, Critch has grown to be something of a con man himself. He returns to King's Crossing having just stolen $72,000 from a pair of sisters, who made the money murdering and robbing men who believed them prostitutes. The money is in turn stolen from Critch by his sharp brother Arlie, who has already killed the other King brother, Boz.

Critch's attempts to get the money back, to win his way into the heart of his tough old father, and to avoid getting killed by the vengeful sisters and Arlie take up the rest of the novel.

King Blood is a strange hybrid—Critch seems molded after Roy Dillon, Mitch Corley, Mitch Allison, and other Thompson slick con men, and for the first quarter of the novel it seems we are to be treated to another story of the grift. But once Critch arrives home to King's Crossing, the novel evolves into a sort of historical/mythical fantasy, clearly inspired by *King Lear*.

James Sherman Thompson makes an interesting cameo appearance in the novel, as a deputy to his Uncle Harry, the United States marshal who's about the only person in the novel whom the Kings fear, besides each other.

In 1970, a young Hollywood producer named Tony Bill became interested in making a film about the American hobo. Someone familiar with Jim Thompson's work mentioned his name to Bill, who went in search of Thompson's novels. He tried the Cherokee Bookshop, a used bookstore on Hollywood Boulevard close to where Thompson was living at the time. Tony Bill recalls the response to his inquiry:

> I remember very well the guy said, "Oh, if I did I wouldn't have it here very long. Anytime we get a novel by Jim Thompson in here, we call him and he comes down and gets it because he doesn't have any of his own books. We always save it for him. He lives just up the street."
>
> I decided to track him down. I went to pick him up for lunch one day and took him to Musso and Frank and talked about his life. At that time, at least according to him, he was absolutely destitute and forgotten by everyone. He was clearly a ninth-stage alcoholic and I remember he told me he lived in this little squalid apartment in the Whitley Arms with his wife and demented son. Once he told me that his son was so prone to these fits of psychotic outbursts that he had to sit on him at night. It's my image of Jim Thompson—this man sitting on his adult son in order to keep him in his bed at night—just a horrible thought.
>
> I got to know him pretty well. And through getting to know him and wanting to do a movie about the American hobo, I started to work with him on this script, which I was developing in the hopes that Robert Redford might do it.

Redford was a friend of Bill's, and soon Thompson was meeting with Bill, Redford, and Vern Zimmerman, who as "Biplane Cinemetograph" were trying to get the hobo film off the ground at Columbia Pictures. On May 15, 1970, Thompson optioned the rights to *South of Heaven* to Tony Bill, for an amount unspecified in the copy of the contract that still exists.

Soon, however, it was decided that Thompson should write an original script about a hobo's adventures, with a lead more suitable to being played by Robert Redford than *South of Heaven*'s Tommy Burwell.

Thompson was paid at least $5,000 in 1970 for his screenplay drafts, entitled "Hard Times" and " 'Bo." Only about half of the "Hard Times" script was still extant among Thompson's papers, and not all of the scenes are sequential.

"Hard Times" is set out on the familiar West Texas/Oklahoma oil fields during the 1920s. The hero is Joe "Big Rocky" Rock, a character clearly based on legendary union activist Joe Hill. A guy just looking for a fair deal for everyone, Rocky has a wide reputation as a Communist and violent troublemaker. He runs afoul of the law in a corrupt small town and lands in the prison farm. Nancy, the rebellious young daughter of a local rich man, gets Rocky out of jail. That's where the first draft of the script breaks off.

The second draft, now entitled " 'Bo," follows Rocky out onto a pipeline job, after he falls in love with and then abandons the rich man's daughter, Nancy. The pipeline scenes are probably why the producers wanted the rights to *South of Heaven,* since much of the action is similar to that of the novel. Joe tries to organize the pipeline workers, with little success. Nancy catches up with him, and tells him she's going to buy him a pardon. But Joe knows they can never be together; he's fighting for something, and she can't help.

NANCY

All right. If that's what you have to do, do it. But—

JOE

Maybe someday, what's simply fair and decent will become law. Safe working conditions and a decent wage. A five or six day week instead of seven. Maybe even a forty-hour week. Disability pay when you're hurt, and unemployment when you're out of work. I know it all sounds pretty far-fetched, but—

Nancy continues to argue with him, saying she wants to get married. Joe seems to acquiesce. In the meantime, the law is closing in on Joe Rock. Nancy and Joe see them approaching, and Joe makes his getaway as Nancy distracts them with her nudity. The script ends as Joe is rattling along on another train, heading for the copper mines of Utah. A character called the Singer has the last words:

> *'Bo was always for the poor,*
> *But not against the rich.*

A sort of fair-is-fair an'
play-it-square son-of-a-bitch.
Tes-ti-tickles like watermelons,
An' a yingyang like a whale
An' you could hear him clean to Kansas
When a hobo scratched his tail.

Recalls Bill:

Thompson worked on the script and it turned out okay, but not really okay enough. I think he gave us short shrift. He told me he was used to writing his novels in bursts of days or weeks at the most.

Despite a few more meetings with Redford, the project went no further. Bill recalls visiting Robert Redford in Utah with Thompson:

That was fun. You had to keep an eye on Jim to make sure he was still sitting upright at the table. But he was well behaved.

I remember Jim was very anxious to please—not in a kowtowing sort of way—but very malleable, very open-minded about what might be appealing, what might work. He had a bag of ideas—if you didn't like this one, roll out another one. We were only there for an afternoon, drove up to Redford's place in Provo. He wasn't drinking a lot. He had acquired the sort of ravaged demeanor of a guy who has a hundred miles of roadbed under him. He was craggy and stooped and shaky and mumbly, but not at all incoherent or off-putting.

Although no film was ever made, the project did leave a lasting controversy. The Thompson family is furious at Tony Bill and all others associated with the project. The Thompsons feel that Bill and company basically stole the film rights to *South of Heaven*, rights that if sold now would be quite lucrative. Thompson evidently signed a contract assigning the rights to *South of Heaven* over to Tony Bill and company for ten dollars. Says Sharon Thompson Reed and Alberta Thompson:

Sharon: "It was totally stolen. They used him. They paid ten dollars for *South of Heaven*. And only $10,000 for my daddy's original screenplay, which was low at the time."

Alberta: "They probably gave him a few drinks, and he signed whatever they put in front of him."

Sharon: "He would never have knowingly done such a thing! And Tony Bill says that Daddy offered to give him all his books for five hundred dollars! Come on!"

Tony Bill does remember Jim Thompson offering him the film rights to all his novels, but Bill had to turn him down, because he didn't have the money and he didn't think it would be the right thing to do. Tony Bill:

> I believe the reason we have the rights to *South of Heaven* is that Columbia, which financed the hobo script, insisted on it. Jim wanted to be able to use some of his original characters and incidents from his hobo novel. So Columbia, to protect themselves, said, okay, it's an original screenplay, but throw in the right to use stuff from the book. I'm positive that's how it came about. So for a dollar or whatever, the rights to the book were conveyed. He was paid a lot of money for the original screenplay.

Alberta Thompson: "[Tony Bill's] story sounds plausible, but that's not the way it happened."

In any case, the rights to *South of Heaven* currently belong to Columbia Pictures, through that original ten-dollar contract signed by Thompson. As this is written there is a film of *South of Heaven* in preproduction, although no settlement has been made with the Thompson estate.

Ironically, Thompson's association with Bill eventually led to Thompson's last "success," the film version of *The Getaway* in 1972. According to Bill, at the time Thompson offered to sell his body of work for $500, he also gave Bill a copy of *The Getaway* to read:

> I loved it and thought it would make a fabulous movie. However at the time I was a struggling producer. I had no access to money or money of my own.
>
> I was so struck by the quality of the book that I made what perhaps one might call the mistake of mentioning it to several people—one of whom was my agent at the time, Mike Medavoy, at Ashley Famous, as it was called then. So I gave Mike my Xerox copy and as luck would have it, he gave it to a producer [David Foster]. And the producer gave it to Steve McQueen and the movie got made.
>
> Mike represented Jim in making the deal for *The Getaway*. I never felt any real upset over the fact that I didn't make it clearer that I wanted to be a part of this and produce *The Getaway* as one of my first films.

Mike Medavoy did pass the novel on to David Foster, a producer who worked closely with Steve McQueen. Steve McQueen was in Paris at the time, but immediately loved the novel and sent word back to "lock it up."

Medavoy represented Thompson's interest, obtaining for him $25,000 for the screen rights to the novel and a crack at writing the first draft of the screenplay. The screenwriting deal was evidently a step-deal, with Thompson being paid more money the more drafts he was involved with, and still more money if he received on-screen screenwriting credit. The film was produced by Warner Brothers, and Peter Bogdanovich was tentatively attached as director. The more appropriate Sam Peckinpah later came on board when Bogdanovich left to do a Barbra Streisand movie.

Unfortunately, Jim Thompson's writing powers had undeniably diminished by then. His screen treatment of *The Getaway,* dated February 2 through 9, 1971, shows little understanding of the novel's strong points. Absurd, but true. The treatment is full of talky, obvious dialogue and awkward action scenes. Even when Thompson remained relatively faithful to the book, he made changes that weakened, rather than strengthened, the original scenes. Witness the last scene, which in the novel is a wonder of irony, understatement and economy:

> As the tinny band swings into an off-key version of *Home, Sweet Home,* and the macabre, last dance begins, Doc fills his and Carol's champagne glasses.
> "May as well drink up, baby. After all, we paid for it."
> "Yeah, didn't we?" Carol laughs harshly. "Tell me, Doc. I'm trying to figure it out. How the hell did we get here, anyway?"
> Doc shrugs. "By boat. Don't you remember?"
> "You know what I mean. How did we get to—to this?"
> "That's an easy one," Doc says. "Somewhere along the road, we took the wrong turn."
> "Well"—Carol touches her glass to his. "Here's to you, and your wonderful getaway."
> "Oh, well," Doc says modestly. "It isn't over yet. Not for me, at least."
> "Not for me either, Doc. Not by a long, long way."
> "Oh"—casually. "Got some ideas have you?"
> "You'll see."
> "So will you, honey. So will you."
> They smiled at each other, their eyes hate-filled.
> And we fade out to End.

The only possible explanation for Thompson's wretched performance on the treatment and screenplay, beyond his having lost most of his faculties, is that in an attempt to please the producers of the film he was giving them what he thought they wanted rather than following his own instincts.

Thompson surely knew the stakes were high, and once again he managed to stumble right on the doorstep of great success. Like all his fictional creations, he was incapable of success because of something planted deep inside him: the seeds of lifelong failure sown long ago by James Sherman Thompson.

The final option contracts for *The Getaway* were signed on April 13, 1971, and Thompson worked on a first-draft screenplay throughout the summer of 1971. David Foster would go over the scenes Thompson wrote, offering suggestions, changes, and deletions. Though Foster's notes back to Jim were couched kindly, Thompson surely found them humiliating. For every page of Thompson's script or treatment, there were two pages of comments from Foster. Some examples:

> PAGE 30: You can cut considerably their whole arrival in San Diego. Just have them in a cab approaching Goalie's and we know everything else before has transpired. When they get to Goalie's Doc gives the cab driver some money, asks him to fetch some food for them. . . .
>
> Regarding the scene with the cab driver, let's be much more subtle with Doc's use of the gun. I would much prefer him having the gun in his pocket and pushing it into the cab driver's side than having him stick it in his ear. . . .
>
> Incidentally, Ma's line to Carol is much better in the book, where she simply says, "Just tryin' to help." Also in the book Ma makes it clear that she wants to know where things stand before she gets further involved with the two of them because of Carol's panic and distrust. As you will recall, in the book, she not only fears the depths of the water and the enclosure, but Carol also thinks Doc is trying to eliminate her once he gets her down there. . . .

Foster was surprised and dismayed at Thompson's evident inability to recognize and play off the strengths of his own novel. Eventually a young writer named Walter Hill was brought in, and Hill's script was used as the shooting script. At that point Thompson became obsessed with the movie actually being shot and released, so that a paperback movie edition of *The Getaway* would be published. Recalls Foster:

> I can't tell you the number of calls I would get from him as the film got closer to going into production about how excited he was the book would be reissued—and there would be a chance for him to make money. He looked at the movie primarily as a means of being able to make some extra money from the book.

Thompson's step deal led to a lot of problems when he was taken off the script and it was given to Walter Hill, who started from scratch without seeing Thompson's drafts. The producers eventually decided that Hill should receive sole screenwriting credit, though the book was based on Thompson's novel and Thompson had completed a first draft.

Walter Hill:

> I was quite surprised that I got the sole screen credit. I never read Thompson's script, but he had written a draft from his novel and that will usually guarantee a credit.

Thompson took the matter to the Writers Guild for arbitration, without success. According to his contract, he would have been paid $25,000 if he had received a screen credit; Thompson believed that was the answer to the whole thing. From his July 11, 1972, five-page letter to the Guild explaining his contribution to the film:

> In conclusion:
>
> I have now been a member of the guild for some fourteen years. During that time, naturally, I have been subject to many credit arbitrations (though none was ever instigated by me; and this is the first time I have protested a producer's designation of credits).
>
> In so doing now, I am not denying that Mr. Hill's work is substantial and excellent—even, perhaps, to a far greater degree than mine.
>
> However, I worked sixteen weeks on this script, and I have provably made very substantial contributions to the work. Also, despite the introduction of new material—characters and scenes—the basic story and numerous scenes are my own creations.
>
> In my other arbitrations, some of which dealt with far less work than I did on *The Getaway,* I have always received some credit; the very least was screenstory credit. To be excluded from any credit at all is, to me, an unprecedented experience. And I find it very hard to account for.
>
> Under the terms of my contract with the producers, I was to be paid a bonus of $25,000 if I got screen credit. Or, to put it another way, the producers would save themselves $25,000 if I could be excluded from credit. I would not say this is the reason for their otherwise baffling attitude. I am merely stating a fact.

The Getaway, starring Steve McQueen and Ali McGraw, directed by Sam Peckinpah from a screenplay by Walter Hill based on the novel by Jim Thompson, opened on Tuesday, December 18, 1972, in Los Angeles. The whole Thompson family had turned out for the premiere the night before. Alberta Thompson recalls: "At the screening David Foster came down and joking told me to keep ahold of Jim, he might make a fuss. But he didn't."

By now the producer was well aware that the film was quite unlike the novel. Gone was the ending in the Kingdom of El Rey, and without that, the whole film seems pointless—or, rather, innocuous. Walter Hill also

French poster for The Getaway, *with Thompson's name displayed more prominently than in the American posters.*

understood the film wasn't true to Thompson's vision—it even compromised Hill's screenplay:

> We made changes for budget, for Steve, for Ali. I thought they were all for the worse. . . .
>
> I felt that the scenes where McQueen and McGraw were jumping in the water and making omelettes together were crap. I'm not sure Sam was fond of that stuff either. And God only knows what Thompson must have thought. . . .
>
> In my opinion, *The Getaway* is a good film. But although there are many elements of Jim Thompson in the movie, it is not particularly a movie that represents the vision of Jim Thompson. It's much more a Sam Peckinpah film than it is anything else. [Thompson's] unyielding, endlessly repeated vision is representing the criminal-pathological-paranoid mind. That is not an attitude that has ever, or probably will ever, become a mainstream of the American commercial cinema.
>
> Had somebody done a script that was absolutely representative of the Jim Thompson spirit, Steve McQueen wouldn't have done the movie nor would anyone have financed it.

Those are the facts of life in Hollywood, but it is unfortunate that the filmmakers did not stay true to the Thompson vision. The resultant film was a huge financial success, though it garnered mixed reviews. Kevin Thomas summed up the popular view of the film in his review in the *Los Angeles Times:* "If 'Bonnie and Clyde' was brought up to date and enlivened with the spectacular action sequences from 'Bullit,' the result would roughly approximate 'The Getaway.' "

The film should have triggered interest in Thompson's other books, but it did not. Thompson was still upset over the loss of the screen credit, and the $25,000. Jerry Bick chalked it up to Thompson's lack of business sense, and his odd propensity for failure.

> *The Getaway* was his one chance to really score. I wasn't around. He was represented by ICM [Medavoy] and I don't think he had a real connection or relationship there. After all, their client was Steve McQueen. I think that Jim didn't get the long end of the stick. . . . People are in business and do the best they can. But Jim was like a storm-tossed waif. He didn't know how to handle himself at all—and I mean at all.
>
> I think he somehow psychologically wanted to be in the position of begging, as much as he hated it on one level. He ended up in that spot all the time. I treated him as though he were a baby. I would always call him back within minutes, because I could visualize him on the other end just shaking.
>
> He was in such pain, that I shied away. It was difficult to spend much

time with him, he was in such emotional pain—he really had a lot of pins stuck in him. I think that he was a tortured guy. Not that he couldn't laugh or have a sense of humor, but the imprint for me was of a man who was tortured. I didn't know how to help him.

Thompson couldn't be helped. If most of Thompson's narrators are self-tortured murderous "saviors," perhaps it's natural that Thompson became a more conventional scapegoat, a self-sacrifice at the altar of unachievable success.

In June of 1973, Thompson wrote Medavoy a letter, firing him as his agent. Bick once again took over Thompson's Hollywood affairs, with little or no success. A few months later, Bick was involved in the production of a remake of Raymond Chandler's *Farewell, My Lovely*. Thompson was interested in playing the part of Charlotte Rampling's husband, the cuckolded judge.

The Thompson family maintain that Jim tried out for the part and got it, without any assistance. But Jerry Bick says he gave Thompson the part because Thompson was in desperate need of medical insurance and the acting role enable him to join the Screen Actors Guild and qualify under their coverage.

Thompson is only on screen briefly in *Farewell, My Lovely*, but he makes a memorable impact. First, in a rather bizarre moment for aficionados of crime fiction, Jim Thompson, great *noir* writer, is introduced to arguably the most famous American fictional detective: Chandler's Philip Marlowe, played by Robert Mitchum.

Later Thompson opens the door to a room to discover his wife in the arms of Philip Marlowe. Arnold Hano gave the best description of Thompson's performance in the scene: "There is a look on his face that is part bewilderment, part despair, and all forgiveness."

The film was released early in 1975.

Later in 1975 the film industry delivered the final blow to the staggering Jim Thompson. Having bounced around through various option deals for nearly a decade, MGM and director Burt Kennedy finally made a film version of *The Killer Inside Me*. Translating the internalized action and tension of Lou Ford's story to the screen is admittedly not an easy task, but this ambitiousless B-movie adaptation is nearly impossible to view. Dripping faucets evidently drive the otherwise mild-mannered deputy sheriff, woodenly played by Stacy Keach, to his murderous acts. Laughable if it weren't so sad, *The Killer Inside Me* gets everything wrong except the perfect casting of Susan Tyrrell as Joyce.

MGM knew it had a bomb on its hands, and gave the film only a limited release in America. So limited, that a deal Robert Mills had struck to have the novel reissued in a movie edition fell through when the publishing company refused to acknowledge that the film had been released at all.

Sharon Thompson Reed recalls that her father's disappointment in the film was so deep that he was left speechless after seeing it. His terrifying novel of the black vacuum at the center of the American psyche had been absorbed by the American dream machine and turned into a laughable schlock film.

In some ways, Jim Thompson was probably glad he didn't have much time left.

Jim Thompson had been in declining health for years; in Arnold Hano's opinion, he had been suffering periodic minor strokes for some time. A look at his performance in *Farewell, My Lovely* lends credence to this idea. Early in 1976, however, Thompson suffered the first in a series of major strokes. According to Michael Thompson:

> It was a Saturday, I remember, and they always used to do the food shopping on Saturday. Dad was in the kitchen reading the food ads, and when my mother walked in she found him slumped over the newspaper, at the table.
> From then on he just got sicker and sicker.

Thompson spent the rest of his life in and out of hospitals. He lost most of his speech and the use of his left arm in the first major stroke. Writing was now out of the question, although, as Sharon Reed recalls, "You could tell Daddy was still in there, in his eyes. He'd be trying to tell us something, but just couldn't always get it out."

Adds Freddie Townsend:

> When he first got sick, but he could still talk, he said, "You know, I'm a man of words, this is the worst thing in the world for me."
> Toward the end what was so tragic—he was trying to tell us something. There were things he wanted to talk about and he just couldn't. We couldn't understand him. He couldn't get it out.

Sharon Reed:

> The last Christmas [1976] he spent down with me [in Huntington Beach]. He asked for ice cream, we couldn't understand him. And he wanted to see the ocean.

We took him, he got to see the ocean. He sat there a long time looking out to sea.

Sharon recalls that her father was still upset by the film of *The Killer Inside Me*, and even more disturbed by the *South of Heaven* contract:

> When my dad was really sick he sat there with tears rolling down his face and said, "How could anybody do this to me?" I sat there and held his hand. This is a man who was dying.
>
> All those people—they never showed up when my dad was dying. [Only] Jerry Bick, Arnold Hano, and Bob Goldfarb. That was all.

But Thompson was most haunted by something else. Sharon Reed:

> My father worked his butt off to go get his father out of that place, and he didn't do it. Daddy had the biggest guilt complex ever—I know, because I'm the same way. He felt he wasn't able to do it fast enough. His biggest dream was to get Pop, to bring him out to San Diego. And when it all fell apart, because Pop died—it was like Daddy's fault.
>
> When my daddy was dying he would say to me, "I'm sorry," over and over again. Just "I'm sorry." And I'd say, "You don't have anything to be sorry about, Daddy."
>
> I mean, why would he keep saying I'm sorry?

Michael Thompson remembers that his family eventually put Jim Thompson in a nursing home for a short while. Thompson had a lifelong fear that he'd end up like Pop, and finally his fear was realized: he had been placed alone in a home. Michael recalls visiting the nursing home:

> I went there one night, and it was dirty and there was no help. I remember he said to me, "Mike, for God's sake, get me out of here." We took him home that night, and it wasn't long after he died.
>
> I remember that he would signal to me like he was smoking a cigarette, and then I'd light one up, and smoke for both of us.
>
> I would go over regularly. I knew he was dying, he was starving himself to death. But it really got me sick to look at him, the way he was dying made it even worse, so prolonged.
>
> At first he fought like mad, but then he gave up because it was so futile. He knew he couldn't write anymore, he was better off dead.
>
> So he proceeded to do what he had to do.

Jim Thompson died on April 7, 1977, in Los Angeles. It was Holy Thursday, so his Catholic family did not hold a memorial service until after the Easter weekend, on Monday, April 11. Twenty-five people attended the ceremonies in Westwood; the only people other than family members were Arnold Hano, Jerry Bick, Bob Goldfarb, and Ned DeWitt.

Jim Thompson was cremated and his ashes scattered over the Pacific Ocean.

Arnold Hano:

I don't remember much about the funeral. I was feeling bad, and I was feeling bad there were so few people in the room.

It struck me that it was just another Jim Thompson story.

EPILOGUE:
THE CITY OF
WONDERFUL PEOPLE

■

It was a crowded city; neighbor elbowed against neighbor. Yet no one felt the need for more room. They dwelt peacefully side by side, content with what they had. No one needing more than what he had, nor wanting more than he needed. Because they were so wonderful, you see. They were all so wonderful.

This World, Then the Fireworks, 1955/1988

Jim Thompson was gone, but his proclivity for outright failure—or success tempered by failure—haunted the slow but steady comeback of his popularity and reputation.

Although he died with none of his books in print in the United States, the Robert Mills Agency of New York continued to represent his estate. Most of the interest in Thompson's writing remained overseas, particularly in Paris, where a handful of self-proclaimed "Thompsonists," including *cinéastes* Pierre Rissient and Jean-Jacques Schleret, film directors Alain Courneau and Bertrand Tavernier, book editor François Guerif, and bookseller Stephane Bourgoin stirred up most of the activity.

La Nouvelle Agence of Paris and John Farquharson of London sold many of Thompson's titles to various publishers, including Ediciónes Jucar of Madrid and Ullstein Krimi of Berlin. In May 1979, Gallimard paid 4,000 francs per novel to reprint *Pop. 1280* and *The Killer Inside Me;* in February 1981, Fayard published translations of *The Kill-Off, The Criminal, Bad Boy,* and *Roughneck* under the editorship of François Guerif. Fayard paid the Thompson estate 7,000 francs per title.

Back out on the West Coast, Alberta Thompson had moved in with her daughter Sharon's family, in Huntington Beach, after Thompson's death. Alberta traveled frequently with her other daughter Patricia to such destinations as Las Vegas and Boston. Former Thompson agent and friend Jerry Bick offered Alberta Thompson any assistance she might need in handling Jim's affairs.

In early 1978 French film producer Maurice Bernart reached an agreement with Alberta Thompson, as executrix of Jim Thompson's estate, obtaining the rights to make a film of *A Hell of a Woman.* Though the resultant film, Alain Corneau's *Série Noire,* did much to revive interest in Thompson's work both in France and America, the contract's terms were most unfavorable for the Thompson estate, assigning the film rights to the novel to the French producers "exclusively and forever."

Alberta Thompson maintains she is still owed money by the makers of *Série Noire;* even more frustrating to the Thompsons is the loss of the American film rights to *A Hell of a Woman,* which could now easily be sold for a large amount of money.

Série Noire, starring Patrick Dewaere as the desperate door-to-door salesman Frank "Puppy" Poupart (Dolly Dillon), opened in Paris on April 25, 1979. Set in France, the film follows the plot line of the book closely, but omits the ending in which Dillon/Poupart meets his end at the hands of his distaff double. The film closes as Staples takes all the money, leaving Dillon/Poupart only with Mona.

The success of *Série Noire* triggered additional interest in Thompson's writing in France; in July 1980, Vanessa Holt of the John Farquharson Agency notified Robert Mills that famed French film director Jean-Luc Godard was interested in bringing *Pop. 1280* to the screen. But Holt also had heard that French producer/director Bertrand Tavernier already had a script from the same novel.

Mills hastily checked that all previous options on the novel had expired, and met with Godard in Paris in early August. Negotiating over the next month, Godard and Mills eventually agreed on an option of $3,500 against a pickup of $35,000, plus various percentages of the film's worldwide receipts.

What happened next is summarized in a letter Mills sent Vanessa Holt on September 2:

> Dear Vanessa:
>
> I come to you with bad news about Jean-Luc Godard.
>
> He came to see me last Wednesday late afternoon, and we had a pleasant meeting, and worked out a deal, as I think I reported to you, and I called Alberta Thompson, who was pleased. I sent the modified contracts to her on Thursday, called her on Saturday to see if she had received the papers, and she said that she had but that she wasn't going to sign them. It seems that somebody in Hollywood offered her $30,000 on signing, plus $20,000 on completion of shooting, and her lawyer told her to take the money in hand. I pointed out that she had authorized me to give her word in my negotiations with Godard, and she said she realized that, felt very badly about it all, but she must do what her lawyer tells her.
>
> Godard called me this morning, and I told him the sorry news and apologized profusely. He seems a most civilized and philosophical man, and appeared to understand Alberta's decision and my embarrassment.

MAURICE BERNART et GAUMONT présentent

PATRICK DEWAERE

MYRIAM BOYER · MARIE TRINTIGNANT
BERNARD BLIER

SÉRIE NOIRE

un film de ALAIN CORNEAU

avec JEANNE HERVIALE · ANDREAS KATSULAS
d'après le roman "A HELL OF A WOMAN"
de JIM THOMPSON
paru dans la Série Noire - Editions Gallimard
sous le titre "DES CLIQUES ET DES CLOAQUES"
Adaptation de ALAIN CORNEAU
et GEORGES PEREC
Dialogues de GEORGES PEREC
UNE CO-PRODUCTION PROSPECTACLE - GAUMONT Ⓖ

The empty psychotic glare of Patrick Dewaere as Puppy Poupart dominates the poster for Série Noire.

French poster for Coup de Torchon, *featuring mention of the source novel as the thousandth* Série Noire.

I'm sorry about all of this, for your sake and also for the sake of Mme. Germain.

Best,
Bob Mills.

Mills wrote back to Alberta Thompson on October 15, 1980:

Dear Alberta:

Herewith another piece on Jean-Luc Godard which just appeared in the New York Times.

And I do feel sorry, I must confess, that you didn't wish to go ahead with M. Godard—he is an imaginative director whose basic attitudes towards life are, it seems to me, somewhat like Jim's were, and I think he would have made a very interesting movie out of POP. 1280, one that might have helped the sale of that book here and abroad, and might have led to interest in other books of Jim's.

Of course, whoever it is that's buying the property may have similar qualifications, and I do look forward to hearing from you who it is and what sort of plans if any there are for production.

I've not made much of this point before, but I'm afraid your revoking your authorization to me to negotiate on your behalf without telling me you were doing so has put me in a very bad light with M. Godard—I doubt that he will trust me enough to deal with me again. Which does sadden me some.

However, your lawyer may well be right, and maybe you've indeed done the best thing for yourself—I do hope so for your sake.

Best wishes,
Bob Mills

Bertrand Tavernier's *Coup de Torchon,* based on Thompson's *Pop. 1280,* was the film that resulted from the contract that Alberta Thompson signed in October of 1980. The film was a huge success in France, and opened to critical acclaim in America in December of 1982. It was nominated for an Academy Award as best foreign film of 1982.

A slightly compromised version of the Thompson novel, *Coup de Torchon* is set in French colonial Africa, rather than the American South. Clearly made with great care and admiration for Thompson's source material, the film offers a more objective view of the Thompson world than does the first-person novel. Nick's actions seem more clownish and coldly psychotic than they do in the novel—the overall effect is closer to Thompson's better third-person books, like *The Getaway,* or the multiple-narrator *The Kill-Off.* The cast is brilliant, especially Philippe Noiret as Nick Corey.

The Thompson family was quite pleased with all the acclaim for the film, but dismayed to find that they once more had signed away the rights to an American remake of the film. Though not as clearly unfavorable as the contract for *Série Noire*, the terms of the *Coup de Torchon* contract are muddy enough to tie up the worldwide rights to *Pop. 1280* for the foreseeable future.

In December of 1982, Zomba Books of London paid 2,500 pounds to the Thompson estate for the rights to a four-novel Thompson omnibus edition, featuring *The Grifters, The Getaway, Pop. 1280,* and *The Killer Inside Me*. In August of 1983, Barry Gifford of Black Lizard Books of Berkeley, California, obtained the publishing rights to *A Hell of A Woman, Pop. 1280,* and *The Getaway*. And in November of 1983, Morrow/Quill obtained the publishing rights to *The Killer Inside Me*. Robert Mills died shortly after he worked out these first few reprint deals; Richard Curtis Associates took over representation of Jim Thompson's estate.

The four American titles, plus the availability of the British collection, triggered an avalanche of Thompson reprints in America in the rest of the 1980s. Black Lizard led the way, with editions of *The Grifters, Recoil, Nothing More Than Murder, Savage Night, After Dark, My Sweet, Wild Town, A Swell-Looking Babe, Cropper's Cabin,* and *The Alcoholics*. Harcourt Brace Jovanovich's *The Black Mask Quarterly* serialized Thompson's previously unpublished *The Rip-Off* in 1986. Donald I. Fine returned Thompson to hardcovers with two omnibus editions of three novels: 1986's *Hardcore* contained *The Kill-Off, The Nothing Man,* and *Bad Boy;* 1987's *More Hardcore* contained *The Golden Gizmo, The Rip-Off,* and *Roughneck*. Finally in 1988, Fine published *Fireworks,* a collection of Thompson's uncollected short fiction, including true-crime stories, selections from his unfinished novels, and the novella *This World, Then the Fireworks*.

The Rip-Off, available first in *The Black Mask Quarterly,* then *More Hardcore,* and finally a paperback edition, offers little to warrant such a frenzied publishing history. *The Rip-Off* is the story of Britton Rainstar, the last member of a once-proud family, whose life has more than fallen apart. Rainstar's life is full of familiar Thompson plot elements, including a burdensome ex-wife who may be trying to kill him, an unknowable, unpredictable girlfriend who may be trying to kill him, and an ominous corporation, which may be out to kill him. After a close shave with death, Rainstar is nursed back to health by the beautiful Kay Randall—who may be out to kill him!

Like most Thompson narrators, Rainstar is as uncertain of himself as he is of anyone else. In the end, with the assistance of local policeman Jeff Claggett, Rainstar straightens out his confused life and sheds his paranoid delusions. Someone *was* out to kill him, but it wasn't any of the people he thought it was.

The Rip-Off, likely one of the last manuscripts he worked on, is a weak effort by Thompson.

Although written in the mid-1950s, a more fitting cap to Thompson's career is the novella *This World, Then the Fireworks*. Stripped down to the barest essential of narrative, the novella is narrated by a murderous psychotic and contains almost all of Thompson's trademark elements.

This World, Then the Fireworks could serve as the textbook for a course entitled "How to Write a Jim Thompson Novel." It's all there in the symmetrical tale of the Lakewood twins: innocence lost before it can be experienced; a traumatic childhood incident as predestination; psychotic rationalization as mournful philosophy; murder as redemption of a lost world; confusion of good and evil, right and wrong, guilt and innocence in an inverted world; child abuse, incest, matricide, homicide, suicide.

By stripping down the narrative and including important takes on his central themes and obsessions, Thompson likely hoped to make his readers recognize what he was up to. Unfortunately, the novella wasn't published until six years after his death, initially in an edited version published by Fedora Press; the unedited manuscript version of *This World, Then the Fireworks* finally appeared in America in 1988 in *Fireworks: The Lost Writings*, published by Donald I. Fine.

This World, Then the Fireworks opens with a prologue, entitled "1-Minus," on the night of the fourth birthday of twins, Martin and Carol Lakewood. They follow their mother across the street at the sound of a second shotgun blast:

> Mom had caught part of the second blast as she burst into the house. She wasn't seriously injured, merely branded for life. We didn't know she'd been injured at all, despite the spurting pinpricks on her face. So meager was our knowledge of life, of good and bad; and Mom was laughing so loudly.

The twins' father had been discovered in bed with the neighbor's wife; Mr. Lakewood had shot the husband's head off with the first shotgun blast. Now Lakewood and the woman were standing there naked, staring at the headless corpse on the floor. The children find this all very "funny":

We laughed and laughed, Carol and I. We were still laughing occasionally—shrieking and screaming—weeks later. It was so funny. It seemed so funny, I remember.

And I remember the night well.

Martin Lakewood tells us his father went to the electric chair, and the woman committed suicide.

Chapter One takes up the narrative years later, as Martin returns to a coastal California town where his mother and Carol now live. After briefly greeting his mother, who is clearly afraid and ashamed of him, he bounds up the stairs to awaken his beloved sister. After they embrace and kiss for quite a while, Carol asks what happened in the "Chicago matter"; it turns out an already convicted murderer took the rap for a murder of which Marty had been accused.

Marty just lost his newspaper job in another city because he was blackmailing some crooked politicians. Carol then asks Marty the one question he doesn't want to ponder: how did he get caught?

How? Why? I wasn't sure of that question. Or, perhaps, rather, I was more sure than I cared to be . . . I'd wanted to be caught? I'd subconsciously brought about my own downfall. I was tired, fed up, sick of the whole mess and life in general?

Martin cannot fully face the likelihood that something inside him wanted to be caught, but he knows how grave the implications are if that is in fact the case. He warns Carol about it, until he realizes that his warning might itself be a rationalization:

"At some point, you know—at *some* point—you'd better look squarely at the truth or look squarely away from it. You can't risk rationalizations. There is the danger that the rationalization may become truth to you, and when you have arrived at this certain point—"

I broke off abruptly. It had struck me with startling suddenness that this might be that certain point and this, the words I was speaking, a rationalization.

I sat stunned, unseeing, my eyes turned inward. For a terrifying moment. I raced myself about a swiftly narrowing circle. Faster and faster and—and never fast enough.

Carol tries to comfort her brother, offering to kill their mother for him, whom she thinks is the cause of his being upset. Martin snaps out of his reverie, and they go down to breakfast.

At breakfast we learn that Carol was raped by her cousins when she was quite young, and that since her divorce, she has been working this seaside town as an independent prostitute. Carol gives Marty some money she had saved; he's puzzled she has so much.

Marty has tried to put their childhood out of his mind, or, rather, to dismiss it as normal. He tells us why:

> You may be wrong, and exist comfortably in a world of righteousness. But you may not be right and live in a world of error, the kind of world we had once *seemed* to live in. It is impossible. Believe me, it is. The growing weight of injustice becomes impossible to bear.

In the next chapter, Marty relates his meteoric rise at the local newspaper; he makes the rest of the writers look so bad that most of them are fired or resign. When finally he is promoted to managing editor, he resigns, leaving the paper in shambles.

Marty then "accidentally" bumps into Lois Archer, whom he propositions on the spot. Marty tries to tell us (and himself) that he doesn't care if Lois takes up his offer; but there seems something else going on that he can't quite pin down:

> I really didn't care, you know. At least, I cared very little. She was a cop, of course, and it was a cop that Dad had killed. But I wasn't sure that I cared to do anything about that or her, to take care of that by taking care of her. I just didn't know.

Lois is both embarrassed and burning with desire; finally she takes Marty to her house, where they make love. Marty tells her about his wife, who suffers from elephantiasis, and his three mongoloid children. Lois doesn't know whether or not to believe him.

Lois in turn tells him that she has been a policewoman for two years, and that she has a brother overseas in the army, with whom she jointly owns the house. There's a rule on the force that policewomen cannot be married; this supposedly explains her enthusiasm for Marty's proposition.

Marty is planning to persuade Lois to sell the house, ostensibly so they can run away together; actually he plans to kill Lois and run away with Carol.

Two obstacles soon appear in Marty and Carol's path. Carol's ex-husband (and ex-pimp) has hired a local private detective to watch her activities. Marty corners Krutz, the private eye, up in his shabby office:

> "I see you know all the facts, Mr. Krutz," I said. "You're thoroughly grounded in the case."

"Sure. That's my business, know what I mean? . . . What's the matter with the guy, Mr. Allen? I'm tickled to have the job naturally, but why does he want it done? How can he do a thing like this just to save himself a few bucks?"

"I wonder," I said. "How can you do it to make yourself a few bucks?"

"Me? Well, uh"—he laughed uncertainly. "I mean, what the hell, anyway? That's my job. If I didn't do it, someone else would. I— Say, ain't I seen you somewhere be—"

"Would they do it?" I said. "How can you be sure they would, Mr. Krutz? Have you ever thought about the potential in a crusade for not doing the things that someone else would do if you didn't?"

"Say, n-now," he stammered. "Now, l-looky here, mister—"

"I'm afraid you have sinned," I said. "You have violated Section A of Commandment One-minus. Yea, verily, Krutz—"

"Now l-looky. Y-you— you—" He stood shakily. "You c-can't blame me f-for—"

"Yea, verily, sayeth the Lord Lakewood, better the blind man who pisses through a window than the knowing servant who raises it for him."

I smiled and thrust out my hand. He took it automatically.

I jerked him forward—and down. He came down hard on his desk, on its sharp steel paper-spike. It went through his open mouth and poked out the back of his head.

Again Thompson's theory of the shared culpability of man is used by a psychotic to justify a murder. Martin Lakewood has no pity on Mr. Krutz, who is even more of a "sinner" than Carol's ex-husband, since Krutz knows just how shameful his actions are. Ostensibly Krutz has the free choice that so many Thompson characters are denied. Thus Krutz is the "knowing servant," as are all those unwilling to admit the evil implications of their own actions.

Because Marty's plan for Lois might take some time to complete, and they need money right away, Carol is always on the lookout for "some prize chump" they can murder for his bankroll. Marty gets a call at Lois's one evening; Carol has found the chump. She has the john up in a mountain house, and needs Marty's assistance.

Marty has some trouble getting away from Lois, who loudly and explicitly accuses him of having an unnatural love for his sister.

By the time Marty gets up to the mountain house, Carol has killed the john with a poisoned drink. She discovered too late that the chump's huge wad of bills was a Kansas City roll—mostly ones and fives, with a few big bills on the outside. As the twins drive back down to the city, leaving the corpse to be discovered in the cabin, Carol has to stop to vomit. Marty tries to help her the only way he knows how:

I talked to both of us, and for both of us. And if it was rationalization, so be it. Perhaps the power to rationalize is the power to remain sane. Perhaps the insane are so because they cannot escape the truth.

We were culpable, I said, only to the degree that all life, all society, was culpable. We were no more than the pointed instruments of that life, activated symbols in an allegory whose authors were untold billions. And only they, acting in concert, could alter a line of its text. And the alterations could best be impelled by remaining what we were. Innocence outraged, the sacred defiled, the useful made useless. For in universal horror there could be universal hope, in ultimate bestiality the ultimate in beauty and good. The blind should be made to see—so it was written. *They should be made to see!* And, lo, the Lord World was an agonized god, and he looked not kindly upon the bandaging of his belly whilst his innards writhed with cancer.

"Yea, verily," I said. "If thy neighbor's ass pains him, do thou not divert him with bullshit, but rather kick him soundly thereon. Yea, even though it maketh him thine enemy. For it is better that he should howl for a doctor than to drown in dung."

Once again Thompson offers a diagnosis of his upside-down world—both a take on the ungraspable nature of morality/reality and an excuse for its murderous denizens. The Martin and Carol Lakewoods of the world are only the most easily spotted manifestations of a pandemic; a universal disease that can't be cured until all its victims recognize themselves as victims, and victimizers: "the blind should be made to see."

Since only all men acting in unison can "alter a line of its text," the Lakewoods, the Lou Fords, the Charlie Biggers, and the Nick Coreys of the Thompson world are actually hastening the day of reckoning and revolution by their murders. Only when things get so bad that they no longer can be ignored, will men work together to change them.

Like Allen Smith in *Child of Rage,* when society acknowledges the unknowable vacuum at its center—at the center of each of its members—it takes the first step toward a cure. This is the remarkable bit of twisted hope buried in Thompson's fiction, especially those books which seem the bleakest. Acknowledgment, and the resultant personal and societal revolution, is the goal of Jim Thompson's writing career.

In *This World, Then the Fireworks,* Martin's rant has finally opened his own eyes—he now discerns the storyline he's unwittingly been playing out, and the role Lois has played as well. The end closes in on him swiftly.

When they get home Martin and Carol crawl into bed together, trying to comfort one another. Mom discovers them, confirming the dark suspicions of many years. As Martin says, the discovery of their evil has let their mom off the hook, at least in her opinion: "It was justification; it excused everything, the moral cowardice, the silence in the face of wrong, the years of all-absorbing, blindly selfish self-pity."

Marty begins to cry, sealing his mother's fate. Carol puts the mother to bed, slipping her some fatal poison in the guise of a sedative.

Marty's glimpse of his own fate and the death of his mother have driven him over the edge. He is conscious of only some of what is around him, and prone to delusions. His resultant narrative is as confused and frightening as the action of the final few pages of the novella. Carol leaves her brother a note about something she has to do, telling him he doesn't have to go to the funeral if he doesn't want to.

Marty does go to the funeral, wandering away from his mother's grave to visit the final resting places of the other inhabitants of The City of Wonderful People. He marvels at all the good people—the loving daughters, the dutiful sons—and one man in particular:

> . . . there was one guy, for instance, who was only humble. But think of that! Think of its possibilities! Think of what you could do with a guy like that on a world tour. Or if war prevented, as it indubitably would, you could put him on television. A nation-wide hook-up. You could go to the network and say, look, I've got something different here. Something unique. I've got a guy that's— No, I'm afraid he doesn't have big tits, and his ass looks just like yours and mine. What he's got is something different. Something there's a hell of a need for. And if you'll just give him a chance. . . .
>
> They'd never go for it.
> You'd have to nail him to a cross first.
> Only here, only in The City of Wonderful People, was the wonderful wonderful.

Marty knows that the death of his mother has led Lois to cable her "brother" in Japan about her selling the house like Marty wants her to. His phone keeps ringing, but he thinks it's only Lois trying to tell him what he already knows. Then he hears Lois answering the phone—answering his phone.

It's a doctor calling from Mexico—Carol went there for an abortion, but she was five months pregnant. She is dead.

Marty can't accept the truth—he tells the doctor he's reached the wrong party. But the frantic man doesn't know what to do with the body; Carol's been dead four days . . .

> I laughed. I imagined it must be a hell of a mess.
> "What the hell do I care what you do?" I said. "Throw it in the ocean.

Throw it on the garbage dump. Throw it out in the alley for the dogs to piss on."

"But she is—"

"Don't lie to me! I know where my sister is!"

Lois takes Marty back to her house. He's ready for the final act.

Marty already knows the all-too-fitting end, and now, lying in bed with her, he explains it to Lois. His father wasn't stupid, and "must have known that fooling around with another man's wife—and a cop's wife at that—was certain to cost him a lot more than it was worth."

So Marty had never been able to figure out why his dad did what he did—until now. Dad *didn't know* his lover was married to a cop—she made him think she was the *cop's sister*. Just like Lois.

For Lois's "brother," as is now clear to Marty, is actually her husband. And the police department's single-woman policy only one reason for her deception:

"Don't cry, Lois. It can't be changed. There are not enough tears for this sorrow."

"M-Marty! Oh, Marty, Marty! H-how you must hate me!"

She wept uncontrollably. The tears were hot against my chest, and her flesh was icy.

"I've never hated anyone," I said. "Never anyone."

So the riddle of Martin Lakewood's father's death, which scarred Marty and Carol so deeply, is answered only in Martin's own death, a bizarre echo of past events:

"I love you, Lois," I said. "We're going to go away together. We'll all go away together."

A cab stopped in front of the house.

A man in uniform got out.

And, of course, he wasn't her brother.

Thus ends the novel. The man is Lois's husband, and Martin Lakewood is ready to kill all three of them—they'll all "go away together."

The deliberate "confusion" of brother and husband by Lois and Mr. Lakewood's long-ago lover—and the lifelong sexual confusion of brother/sister/husband/wife by Marty and Carol—costs them all their lives.

On this bleak but appropriate note Jim Thompson's writing career came to an end, eleven years after his death.

* * *

Nineteen ninety saw the release of three American films based on Jim Thompson novels—James Foley's *After Dark, My Sweet,* Maggie Greenwald's *The Kill-Off,* and Stephen Frears's *The Grifters.* Reviewer Patrick Goldstein noted in the *Los Angeles Times,* with just a hint of the appropriate irony, that now dead thirteen years, Jim Thompson was the hottest writer in Hollywood.

Though the low-budget, independent film *The Kill-Off* was by far the first film completed, *After Dark, My Sweet* was the first into America's theaters, opening late in August 1990.

The screenplay of *After Dark, My Sweet,* by Foley and Robert Redlin (the co-producer who initially optioned the novel from the Thompson estate), is faithful to Thompson's novel—most of the dialogue is Thompson's own. The film was shot in the Southern California desert, giving it an anti-*noir,* bleached-out look. The dried-up, dead landscape is an appropriate setting for Thompson's desperate, empty characters.

The film captures the three-way dance of mistrust between Kid Collins, Fay, and Uncle Bud through remarkable performances by the actors, especially Jason Patric as Collins and Bruce Dern as Uncle Bud. Most important, the film brought the ending of a Thompson novel essentially unchanged to the screen. Bravely understated and staunchly faithful to Thompson's novel, *After Dark, My Sweet* would have pleased Jim Thompson.

So would Greenwald's *The Kill-Off,* though it takes great liberties with Thompson's plot. The strength of *The Kill-Off* lies in its stunning setting in a dying seaside town and its cast of New York–based actors, who look like they have lived the tough lives of Thompson's characters. Dark, obsessive, and skewed, *The Kill-Off* brought the look of Thompson's diseased environment and people to the screen for the first time.

The Grifters, with a screenplay by Donald Westlake, and John Cusack and Anjelica Huston as Roy and Lily Dillon, was released for a week only in 1990 to qualify for the Academy Awards. Although it captures the strange allure of Thompson's characters, the film's ambiguous direction ultimately declines to identify with them. The script shifts the emphasis from Roy to Lily Dillon, giving Anjelica Huston a star turn—but it is Cusack's Roy who holds the film together, despite having lost much of his "grifter" subplot to updating and streamlining.

The Thompson frenzy in Hollywood reached its peak with the release of the three films and the optioning of most of the other available novels for film; new paperback editions of the best novels were released by Vintage/Black Lizard in the fall of 1990.

Though the Thompson family was immensely pleased that Jim's work was finally receiving some long overdue recognition and praise, much of the Thompson mania seemed just the latest hip trend, which usually quickly devolves into yesterday's fad. "Thompsonesque" began taking the place of "Chandleresque" in everything from restaurant to record reviews when critics needed a description of something bleak, *noir,* or tough.

Thus reduced (elevated?) to a brand name, riding a wave of unprecedented popularity, Jim Thompson's work entered the last decade of the twentieth century. Only time will tell if Thompson's current popularity will serve his fiction well, or, like his undistinguished publishing history and resultant pigeonholing as a pulp writer, only further obscure the murky intentions and subtle ambition of his writing.

Lincoln Fargo, the patriarch of the Fargo clan in Thompson's second novel, *Heed the Thunder,* was the first to pinpoint the plight of Thompson's characters—and all of twentieth-century America. Through science and the industrial revolution, man himself became the last great unknown. The struggle to discover the unknown self, to repair the rift between conscious and unconscious ("the pursuit of happiness")—in a confusing, inverted world is, in thematic and literalized form, the topic of every Jim Thompson novel. Thompson best dramatized this internal struggle through the narrations of his psychotic murderers.

If Chandler and Hammett before him took murder out of the parlor and back out into the streets, Thompson went them one better by taking it back inside. Inside sleazy hotels, cropper's cabins, sheriff's offices, getaway cars, high schools—and, most important, inside the minds of their inhabitants. In doing so he leapt out of the crime genre altogether, landing in terrain very well traveled by modern philosophers and philosophical novelists—man's alienation.

Though Kafka, Dostoevsky, Céline, or Sartre might come to mind, the work of another quintessentially American writer, Christian existentialist novelist Walker Percy, seems an apt comparison. Percy worked the same ground in a much more openly theoretical way than Jim Thompson. Percy's view of the twentieth century as a unique time when all previous codes and beliefs not only no longer apply, but are in fact inverted to the confused, "self-determining" individual, could serve as a good description of the Thompson world. As in Thompson, the vacuum of the "free" self is the ultimate topic of Percy's writing. From Percy's nonfiction work *Lost in the Cosmos:*

> With the passing of the cosmological myths and the fading of Christianity as a guarantor of the identity of the self, the self becomes dislocated . . . both cut loose and imprisoned by its own freedom.

. . . attempts to free itself, e.g., by ever more refined techniques for the pursuit of happiness, only tighten the bondage and distance the self ever farther from the very world it wishes to inhabit as its homeland.

Percy's alienated characters, from Binx Bolling of *The Moviegoer* to Will Barrett of *The Last Gentleman*, enjoy brief periods of internal peace and solace only through second-hand immersion of their selves in grave experience (deadly disease, hurricanes, car crashes) or books and movies about those suffering similar alienation. Thompson characters, much further down the same sliding scale, attempt to reintegrate their selves and discover some meaning in their lives through the ultimate alienated act: murder.

Inherent in both Percy and Thompson is the belief that these alienated, psychotic souls are the natural outcome of a world—twentieth-century America—where the old rules not only no longer apply, but seem upside down or indeterminable. All the dualities—good and evil, success and failure, rich and poor, reward and punishment, guilt and innocence, life and death, love and hate, pleasure and pain, God and the devil—stand in for each other, or are indistinguishable. From *The Killer Inside Me,* as Lou Ford speaks to Johnnie Pappas, whom he soon will kill:

"We're really living in a funny world, kid, a peculiar civilization. The police are playing crooks in it, and the crooks are doing police duty. The politician are preachers, and the preachers politicians. The tax collectors collect for themselves. The Bad People want us to have more dough, and the Good People are fighting to keep it from us . . .

"Yeah, Johnnie, it's a screwed up, bitched up world, and I'm afraid it's going to stay that way. And I'll tell you why. Because no one, almost no one, sees anything wrong with it. They can't see that things are screwed up, so they're not worried about it."

Thompson's murderous narrators—"free" in a disastrous sense never conceived of by the fathers of the Constitution—are the ultimate embodiments of what's "wrong with it." Their hollowed-out psyches are indicative of a larger black hole at the center of society. As Allen Smith muses at the end of *Child of Rage*:

I had tried to do right, when ever and wherever I could. But right and wrong were so intertwined in my mind as to be unidentifiable, and I had to create my own concepts of them.

This is the ultimate warning of Thompson's books. The self-deceit and conceptual confusion of his murderous psychotics are only echoes of the deceit and confusion inherent in a society content with how things appear rather than how they are.

As America enters the final decade of the twentieth century, it is more than ever engaged in cynical self-deception, ignoring the void behind the facade. Jim Thompson would not be surprised that the "leaders" of this country exhibit the same self-denying delusional psychoses as Lou Ford; but he would be greatly disappointed that this state of affairs goes largely unrecognized, or is greeted by the widespread apathy and cynical shrugging of shoulders usually reserved for very old news.

Many people ponder the current vogue of Jim Thompson's vision; the answer seems alternately hopeful and frightening. Perhaps Jim Thompson's pocket-size trips into the abyss are becoming harder to dismiss as America slips deeper into the yawning gap. Or perhaps people finally are ready to comprehend that though Thompson wrote worst-case scenarios, he was writing about all of us:

> All of us that started the game with a crooked cue, that wanted so much and got so little, that meant so good and did so bad. All us folks. . . .
> All of us.
> All of us.

Jim Thompson lived a lonely, marginal life in a near-vacuum, and his life's work seemed to disappear unnoted into the same ironically appropriate cultural void. Yet, like the voice of one of his "dead" narrators, Thompson's voice could not be silenced; it still emanates from the heart of a desolate American, issuing warnings about the desolate heart of America.

Jim Thompson's unyielding books are not just great pieces of genre writing, but powerful, subversive, and yes, diagnostic novels of a people with uncertain vital signs—rotting away from the inside out.

The killer inside me indeed.

APPENDICES

■

APPENDIX I:
Jim Thompson's Novels

First Editions

1. *Now and on Earth*. New York: Modern Age, 1942.
2. *Heed the Thunder*. New York: Greenberg, 1946.
3. *Nothing More Than Murder*. New York: Harper and Brothers, 1949.
4. *The Killer Inside Me*. New York: Lion Books #99, September 1952.
5. *Cropper's Cabin*. New York: Lion Books #108, November 1952.
6. *Recoil*. New York: Lion Books #120, January 1953.
7. *The Alcoholics*. New York: Lion Books #127, February 1953.
8. *Bad Boy*. New York: Lion Books #149, June 1953.
9. *Savage Night*. New York: Lion Books #155, July 1953.
10. *The Criminal*. New York: Lion Books #184, December 1953.
11. *The Golden Gizmo*. New York: Lion Books #192, February 1954.
12. *Roughneck*. New York: Lion Books #201, March 1954.
13. *A Swell-Looking Babe*. New York: Lion Books #212, June 1954.
14. *A Hell of a Woman*. New York: Lion Books #218, July 1954.
15. *The Nothing Man*. New York: Dell First Edition #22, 1954.
16. *After Dark, My Sweet*. New York: Popular Library #716, 1955.
17. *The Kill-Off*. New York: Lion Library #142, January 1957.
18. *Wild Town*. New York: Signet #1461, 1957.
19. *The Getaway*. New York: Signet #1584, January 1959.
20. *The Transgressors*. New York: Signet #S2034, December 1961.
21. *The Grifters*. New York: Regency #Rb322, 1963.
22. *Pop. 1280*. Greenwich, Conn.: Fawcett Gold Medal #K1438, 1964.
23. *Texas By The Tail*. Greenwich, Conn.: Fawcett Gold Medal #K1502, 1965.

24. *South of Heaven*. Greenwich, Conn.: Fawcett Gold Medal #D1793, 1967.
25. *Ironside*. New York: Popular Library #2244, 1967.
26. *The Undefeated*. New York: Popular Library #8104, 1969.
27. *Nothing but a Man*. New York: Popular Library #8116, 1970.
28. *Child of Rage*. New York: Lancer Books #75342, 1972.
29. *King Blood*. London: Sphere Books, 1973.

Posthumous First Editions

1. *This World, Then The Fireworks* (edited). In *Jim Thompson: The Killers Inside Him*, by Max Allan Collins and Ed Gorman. Cedar Rapids, Iowa: Fedora Press, 1983.
2. *This World, Then the Fireworks*. In *Fireworks, The Lost Writings*, ed. Robert Polito and Michael McCauley. New York: Donald I. Fine, 1988.
3. *The Rip-Off*. In *More Hardcore*. New York: Donald I. Fine, 1987.

Lost Novels

1. *Always to Be Blessed*, 1932.
2. *Lunatic at Large*, 1958.

American, British, and Canadian Reprint Editions to 1977

1. *Heed the Thunder* (abridged). Canada: Newsstand Library #54, June 1949.
2. *Heed the Thunder* as *Sins of the Fathers*. Canada: Studio Pocket Books #4, 1952.
3. *Nothing More Than Murder*. Hillman Editions #38.
4. *Nothing More Than Murder*. New York: Dell #738.
5. *The Killer Inside Me*. Greenwich, Conn.: Fawcett Gold Medal #K1522, 1965.
6. *The Killer Inside Me*. London: Sphere Books, 1973.
7. *Cropper's Cabin*. New York: Pyramid #G336, 1958.
8. *Recoil*. New York: Lion Books #124, October 1956.
9. *A Hell of a Woman*. New York: Lion Books #138, December 1956.

10. *A Hell of a Woman*. New York: Pyramid #F739.
11. *The Getaway*. New York: Bantam #N7592, 1972.
12. *The Getaway*. London: Sphere Books, 1973.

French Editions to 1977

1. *Nothing More Than Murder* as *Cent Mètres de Silence*. Gallimard: *Série Noire* #54, April 1950. Gallimard: *Carré Noir* #180, June 1974.
2. *The Killer Inside Me* as *Le Démon Dans Ma Peau*. Gallimard: *Série Noire* #1057, August 1966.
3. *Cropper's Cabin* as *Deuil Dans Le Coton*. Gallimard: *Série Noire* #1319, January 1970.
4. *A Hell of a Woman* as *Des Cliques Et Des Cloaques*. Gallimard: *Série Noire* #1106, February 1967.
5. *The Nothing Man* as *M. Zéro*. Gallimard: *Série Noire* #1009, February 1966.
6. *A Swell-Looking Babe* as *Un Chouette Petit Lot*. Gallimard: *Série Noire* #1199, May 1968.
7. *Wild Town* as *Éliminatoires*. Gallimard: Série Noire #972, September 1965. Gallimard: *Carré Noir* #201, May 1975.
8. *The Getaway* as *Le Lien Conjugal*. Gallimard: *Série Noire* #527, October 1959. *Carré Noir* #93, December 1972.
9. *Pop. 1280* as *1275 Âmes*. Gallimard: *Série Noire* #1000, January 1966.

APPENDIX II:
Jim Thompson's Other Writings

Published Short Work (including True Crime) to 1977

1. "Oil Field Vignettes," in *Texas Monthly,* February 1929.
2. "Thieves of the Field," in *Texas Monthly,* June 1929.
3. "A Road and a Memory" (poem), in *Prairie Schooner,* Winter 1930. Also in *Cap and Gown,* ed. R. L. Paget. Paget and Company, 1931.
4. "Character at Iraan," in *Prairie Schooner,* Spring 1930.
5. "Gentlemen of the Jungle," in *Prairie Schooner,* Fall 1931.
6. "Arnold's Revenge," in *Bandwagon*, February 1935.
7. "The Strange Death of Eugene Kling," in *True Detective,* November 1935.
8. "The Ditch of Doom," in *Master Detective,* April 1936.
9. "A Night With Sally," in *Oklahoma Labor,* September 17, 1936.
10. "The Illicit Lovers and the Walking Corpse," in *Daring Detective,* February 1935 [1936?].
11. "The End of the Book," in *American Stuff: An Anthology of Prose and Verse by Members of the Federal Writers' Project.* New York: Viking, 1937.
12. "Solving Oklahoma's Twin Slayings," in *Master Detective,* March 1938.
13. "Frozen Footprints: Solving the Riddle of Cache Creek," in *True Detective*, March 1939.
14. "The Secret in the Clay," in *Master Detective,* March 1939.
15. "Oklahoma's Conspiring Lovers and the Clue of the Kicking Horse," in *True Detective,* August 1939.

16. "Time Without End," in *Economy of Scarcity: Some Human Footnotes*. Norman, Oklahoma: Cooperative Books, 1939.

17. "Snake Magee's Rotary Boiler," in *A Treasury of Modern Folklore*, ed. B.A. Botkin. New York: Crown, 1944.

18. "The Dark Stair," in *Master Detective*, June 1946.

19. "Mr. Simpson Makes a Sale" (excerpt of chapter Thirteen of *Heed the Thunder*), in *Furrow's End—An Anthology of Great Farm Stories*. New York: Greenburg, 1946.

20. "Four Murders in Four Minutes," in *Master Detective*, April 1949.

21. "Those Amazing Gridiron Indians," in *Saga*, November 1950.

22. "A G.I. Returns From Korea," in *SAGA*, December 1950.

23. "He Supplies Santa Clause" (as Dillon Roberts), in *SAGA*, December 1950.

24. "An Alcoholic Looks at Himself" (as by Anonymous), in *SAGA*, December 1950.

25. "Prowlers in the Pear Trees," in *SAGA*, February 1951.

26. "Two Lives of John Stink," in *SAGA*, March 1951.

27. "Who Is This Man Eisenhower?" in *SAGA*, April 1951.

28. "Death Missed a Bet," in *SAGA*, April 1951.

29. "Blood From a Turnip," in *Collier's*, December 20, 1952.

30. "Time Without End," in *The Damned*, ed. Daniel Talbot. New York: Lion Library #6, 1954.

31. "Bellboy," in *Mercury Mystery Magazine*, February 1956.

32. "Prowlers in the Pear Trees," in *Mercury Mystery Magazine*, March 1956.

33. "The Flaw in the System," in *Ellery Queen's Mystery Magazine*, July 1956.

34. "America's First Murderer," in *For Men Only*, September 1956.

35. "Murder Came on the Mayflower," in *Mercury Mystery Magazine*, November 1956.

36. "The Cellini Chalice," in *Alfred Hitchcock's Mystery Magazine*, December 1956.

37. "The Threesome in Four-C" (as by Dillon Roberts), in *Alfred Hitchcock's Mystery Magazine*, December 1956.

38. "The Frightening Frammis," in *Alfred Hitchcock's Mystery Magazine*, February 1957.

39. "Bert Casey, Wild Gun of the Panhandle," in *Man's World*, September 1957.

40. "Forever After," in *Shock*, May 1960.

41. "Exactly What Happened," in *Ellery Queen's Mystery Magazine*, April 1967.

Posthumously Published Short Stories

(All published in *Fireworks: The Lost Writings*, hardcover edition, ed. Robert Polito and Michael McCauley. New York: Donald I. Fine, 1988.)

1. "Pay as You Exit"
2. "The Slave Girl in the Cellar"
3. "The Tomcat That Was Treetop Tall"

Unpublished Short Stories

1. "The Doe at Twilight"
2. "Lotsa Luck for Lilly"
   The above two are slightly altered chapters from *The Grifters*.
3. "Casey the Killer." An earlier version of "Bert Casey—Wild Gun of the Panhandle," written in the 1930s. Possibly was published at that time in a now-unfindable true-crime magazine.

Realized Screenplays and Teleplays

1. *The Killing* (additional dialogue). Directed by Stanley Kubrick, 1956.
2. *Paths of Glory* (co-credit with Stanley Kubrick and Calder Willingham). Directed by Stanley Kubrick, 1957.
3. *Mackenzie's Raiders* #10b: "Indian Agent," 1958.
4. *Mackenzie's Raiders* #19b: "Death Patrol," 1959.
5. *Mackenzie's Raiders* #28b: "Joe Ironhat," 1959.
6. *Man Without a Gun:* "Satan's Quarter-Section," broadcast as "Devil's Acres," 1960.
7. *Cain's Hundred* #6413: "Five for One," 1961.
8. *Dr. Kildare* #6968: "Pardon Me for Living," 1965.
9. *Convoy:* "Adventure in the North Atlantic," 1965.

Unrealized Treatments, Screenplays, and Teleplays

1. *The Voice of Murder* (original teleplay)
2. *Concrete Pasture* (treatment of *After Dark, My Sweet*)

3. *The Unblessed* (original treatment)
4. *A Scrap of Bread* (original treatment)
5. *Backfire* (original treatment)
6. *Peter Parker* (Private Peeper) (pilot teleplay)
7. *Hard Times* and *'Bo* (first- and second-draft screenplays of *South of Heaven*)
8. *Pop. 1280* (screenplay)
9. *Ready for the Tiger* (first-draft screenplay)
10. *The Getaway* (treatment and first-draft screenplay)

Lost Treatments and Teleplays

1. *Mike Flanagan's Fleet*
2. *Manzi's Millions*
3. *Jeannie*

APPENDIX III:
Jim Thompson's Unpublished/
Unfinished Novels:

Jim Thompson left behind twenty novel manuscripts in various stages of development, from a completed novel, *The Expensive Sky*, to one-page fragments like *The Runaround* and *The Dishonored*. The following list does not include *The Rip-Off* and *This World, Then the Fireworks*, which were published posthumously and in their entirety, but does include other unfinished works from which excerpts were published in *Fireworks: The Lost Writings* (Donald I. Fine, hardcover edition only).

Nearly all of these novel samples were written after 1960; most Thompson manuscripts before then, including all the original Lion Books manuscripts, are lost.

A brief synopsis and an excerpt follow each title.

1. Billington

A novel based on the life of John Billington, one of the *Mayflower* pilgrims, who was eventually accused of and hanged for murder. Although Thompson completed only two chapters, he evidently intended to use multiple first-person narrators, as he had done in *The Criminal* and *The Kill-Off*.

In this excerpt from the second chapter, the narrator is Dick Stryker, a printer's apprentice.

"But it is not my fault!" I insisted. "They blame me for their own sins. Can I help it if being led into the ways of sin, and being young and innocent—"

"Paah!" he said. "Hah! Baah!"

"But that is the way of it," I said. "Who is at fault if, pointed down a certain road, I travel down it beyond the bounds of propriety and discretion? I have sinned," I went on, "but only out of ignorance and innocence. And you will remember what Scripture says of such cases."

Actually being incapable of reading or writing—or little else, save sitting on his fat bottom and swizzling ale—he knew about as much of Scripture as a hog does of pickling. He could not admit this, however, but must on the contrary profess to know all there was to be known. So he scowled and frowned heavily and cleared his throat rumblingly, and declared that he remembered the passage well that I had in mind; but that I was misinterpreting it for my own advantage.

"Let's see, now," he said. "Uh—*hem! haw!*—it is right on the tip of my tongue. How does it go, now, lad?"

"You remember," I said. " 'Tis one of the best known of the Commandments. 'Better the blind man who pisseth out a window, than the knowing servant who guides him thereto.' "

He hesitated, then nodded gravely, saying that it was the very passage he had been thinking of. "But just how it applies to you—"

"There is more to it," I said. " 'Tis really two commandments in one. 'If thy ward be birthed with teeth in his rump, kick him not thereon. For this is but insult added to injury, and thou may loseth a foot.' "

"Hem, ahh-hum . . ." He pursed his lips out with pretended deliberation until one could have hung a pail from them. "Exactly. I mean to say, oh, quite true. Uh—and which of the Commandments would that be, lad?"

My ear paining me as it was, it was a temptation to tell some plausible fib and abandon the joke. Alas, however, it is a failing of mine—and one that has cost me dear—that once caught up in a prank I must carry it on to the end, even though my own neck be in peril. So I identified the Commandments in question as Number One-minus.

"One-minus," he nodded. "Correct. I must admit ye know your Scripture, Dick. And where do you say this One-minus is written?"

"Oh, it wasn't written," I said. "The good God held it unnecessary to do so, since its contents could be expected to be known even to damned fools."

Thompson completed twenty-six typescript pages of *Billington*.

2. The Concrete Pasture

Thompson's cold war novel, concerning Galen "Gay" White, All-American editor/reporter for *Capitol Casebook,* and spy for the Communists.

Gay believed that he missed the talk more than anything else; the wonderful flights of conversation which leaped and sparkled, lightning like, through the cloud-hidden peaks of meaning.

One lazy Sunday afternoon in Staten Island, he and Max got on the subject of the Peloponnesian Wars, which had led inevitably to a political comparison of the warring countries. Max, popular history notwithstanding, could see nothing to admire in Sparta: it was, as he saw it, the ancient counterpart of Nazi Germany. On the other hand, Athens was amazingly liberal, as nearly perfect a democracy as was to exist for more than two thousand years.

Gay went along with the first pronouncement, but scoffed at the second.

"Now, let's take Aristophanes . . ." He paused a moment, baiting the trap.

"Fine!" Max leaped to the bait. "Take *The Acharnians,* for example. Here is a play which severely criticizes Athenian generals and politicians, and argues bitterly against war. And it is produced at a time when Athens is taking a beating from Sparta! Now, if that isn't tolerance—both artistically and governmentally—"

Gay cut in to say that Aristophanes simply happened to be in the mainstream of Athenian thought. An artistic people, they could not object to his attacks upon war and warriors.

"Aristophanes was all for liberty for himself. Where others were concerned—Socrates, to name one of his contemporaries—he advocated the strictest kind of regulation. Or have you forgotten that Socrates was executed on charges of atheism, instigated by your pal Aristophanes?"

Max pointed out that Socrates had lived to the age of seventy, which was about three times the life expectancy of that day. Gay asked him how he could equate democracy with a country whose population of less than a quarter-million included approximately one hundred thousand slaves. Max said that the slaves enjoyed extraordinary liberty, many of them becoming wealthy men. Gay retorted that one had only to consider the popularity of Plato, who proposed severe restrictions on love-making, diet and even laughter, to get the true tempo of Athenian society . . .

It was a very good day. All the days of those days were good. Now . . .

Nowadays . . . the way things were now . . . an eternity of active nothingness. Dostoevsky's kind of eternity: a fly buzzing around an empty privy. But then, always so much . . . meetings . . . lectures . . . rallies . . . the Unemployed Council. The speaker from Texas. Lanky, drawling, shouting the same phrase over and over:

"They gotcha in the concrete pasture, frens. Yessuh. Got y'all in that ol' concrete pasture, an' there ain't ary blade o' grass inside. So whatcha gonna do, frens? Watcha gonna do? Gonna try to bust through that bob-wire, 'r'are you gonna stay inside and starve? Gonna make 'em do it to yuh, 'r'are yuh gonna do the job for 'em . . . ?"

Thompson completed ninety-four typescript pages of *The Concrete Pasture,* plus a two-page plot summary of the rest of the book.

3. Death Is a Living Doll

All that remains of this novel are the first two pages. Here is the first page:

> She stood on a street corner just below the high school, a small delicately boned girl in a jaunty white suit trimmed in red. Now and then a gust of wind teased her wickedly, molding clothes so closely to her body that every crook, curve and cranny of its delectable whole was clearly outlined. And she would blush then, hastily patting and pulling herself until her garb was again as primly decent as she could make it.
>
> An innately shy, insecure girl, she was given easily to blushes. But they were hidden today by her outsize sunglasses and her around-the-head-under-the-chin scarf. Effectively obscured along with most of her face. Anyone could see that she was a very attractive girl, but no one could possibly identify her.
>
> And certainly, most certainly, someone would want to. Someone, given the opportunity, would want to beat her head off . . . or do something equally nasty.
>
> Now, bracing herself, the girl smiled brightly at an oncoming car, then made a small gesture with her thumb. Immediately, the car swerved into the curb and stopped, and the door swung open.

4. The Dishonored

All that remains of this sample is the first half page:

> It was mid-afternoon when the man known as Carl Gavin—which was not the name on his passport—came down out of the mountain road and into the highway to Central City. He had a pockmarked face, hair that was gray-mottled and patched by typhoid, and a lean oblong of a body which had earned him the handle of Poor Boy. The third-hand coupe he drove had a glossy re-paint job and a motor much in need of overhauling.
>
> He stopped to feed it with oil again on the outskirts of Central City, noting the service station attendant's bemused stare as he asked to use the telephone. The Poor Boy had intercepted such looks before, although not in a long time; the look of someone who recognizes or thinks he should recognize a nominal stranger. But that couldn't be in this case, in view of his drastically changed appearance, and he went on into the station, puzzled but unperturbed.

5. The Dog

The adventures of Jug Slurble and his wife Patience Virtue; very likely intended to be a companion piece to *Pop. 1280*. Jug is a no-good loafer waiting for lightning to strike and make him rich; his cousins Plinkplank Plunk and Chastity May arrive in town to make sure his dream doesn't come true.

> They'd all just hike themselves out of Wheeler Junction, and go somewheres else. And he [Jug] would buy a pool hall of his own, and have a lunch-counter in it, and he'd holler at other people an' make 'em eat shit to earn their daily bread. An—
> *Was it really possible? Could he ack-shly do it when the chips was down?*
> Well he'd already did a lot to improve hisself. Sort of become a real leader of men, some men, anyways. An' most everyone liked him—he'd made 'em like him—even if they sort of poked fun at him.
> But he'd had to start out life from such a way-down place. Way, way down in the cellar. So far down that he could still sniff must and the stink of toads an' dead things. An' his father . . . his own father, denied his wife's bed . . . crawling onto the pallet where he, Jug, the family's youngest, lay . . .
> *And he'd liked it. HE'D LIKED IT!*
> And when you had a memory like that clinging to you, an' you couldn't no ways never wash it away . . .
> It was a awful big load to carry. Because if someone treated you like dirt, you might get irked but you couldn't really fault 'em. You couldn't fault 'em for getting sick to their stummicks. You made yourself sick to your own stomach.
> Didn't watch out, you got sicker and *sicker* an' SICKER AN'—
> Jug abruptly opened his mouth and leaned forward. A roily mass rolled up through his throat and gushed past his lips. Solid chunks of food, undigested or partially so, mixed with a thick, stinking slime.
> He finished vomiting.
> He rose from his knees, and walked homeward. Occasionally wobbling with weakness; repeatedly spitting, then wiping his mouth with a sleeve.

Thompson completed forty-three typescript pages of *The Dog*.

6. Exit Screaming

"Turk" Leone thinks he's finished up his twenty-year hitch with the Los Angeles Police Department, but his last case is dragged into the station house on his last night, in the form of crazy, hysterical, beautiful Celia Rowland. After nine years of peace, the "Holders" had appeared again, tonight, in Celia's office. Celia tells Turk the Holders have been after her for years, ever since her parents died in a shotgun double suicide. They follow her around, grabbing her in movie theaters, on the street, in her office; she screams and struggles, but there's always some plausible explanation for the Holders. Still, she says they're after her, and that she isn't crazy.

Fascinated by the disturbed woman, Turk takes her home and cooks her dinner, more and more drawn to her, aware he'll have to solve the riddle of Celia and the Holders before they can be together.

"And what about those men grabbing me in my office? Turning off the lights, and hanging on to me? What about all those other people grabbing me when I was trying to get away? What about—"

"Please," said Captain Leone. "We don't have to go through that again, do we?"

But he saw that he did have to; and he did.

No one had turned out the lights. There had simply been a power failure. As for the men who supposedly had grabbed her in her office, they hadn't; not in the context she implied. One was a window-washer, a poor deaf-and-dumb guy working late. The other was the elevator operator, who checked all the offices every night to make sure they were locked. They had bumped into her in the dark, and they were as startled as she when she started struggling and screaming.

"Oh, sure. Of course," said Miss Rowland, wearily sarcastic. "There's always an innocent explanation. I'm sure all those people on the street had one, too."

"For trying to save you from yourself when you were apparently throwing a fit? For keeping you from running out into traffic?"

"Oh, what's the use talking?" Celia Rowland sighed. "I'm in the wrong and everyone else is in the right. It's always the same way."

"It's a plot," Turk declared, having had about enough of this crapola. "Just like in the movies. Any minute now, a shadowy hand will come out of nowhere and drop a net over you."

She sat up abruptly, slamming her feet to the floor. Face flaming furiously, she said she wasn't crazy no matter what he thought. Turk said he wasn't crazy, either, so why was she packing a gun?

"This one," he said, taking a small automatic from his pocket. "It was stuffed down inside your suit jacket."

"But—but—" She shrank away from the evil little weapon. "I never saw it before, Captain. I've never owned a gun in my life, and I never will! Guns scare me to death!"

Thompson completed forty typescript pages of *Exit Screaming*, plus this development note:

The book will have an upbeat ending, and the answer to the riddle of the girl is nothing so stupid or simple as making her a psycho or providing her with a look-alike sister.

It's intended to be an offbeat, scarily humorous crime story which builds to a hair-raising climax.

The author having been a newspaperman in Hollywood, with first-hand police and criminal contacts, and having worked extensively in motion pictures and television, thinks he is uniquely qualified to tell a story which is itself unique.

7. The Expensive Sky

Thompson's one completed, extant novel that has not seen publication. Though it is wonderful to have such a completed work, one wishes he had completed another of the fragments on this list.

The 194-typescript-page novel chronicles the last days of New York's Hotel Van Anstruther (which has been owned and operated by the Van Anstruther family since 1901) and the fate of its assorted (and sordid) owners and employees.

An uninspired outing, it was written in the lean months after Thompson's dismissal from the *New York Daily News* and before he met Kubrick and Harris. The novel does offer a good death scene, that of Chester Van Anstruther, the insane, alcoholic shame of the family:

Clark started to take out his passkey. Then, letting it drop back into his pocket, he tested the doorknob.

It wouldn't turn. It should have, regardless of whether the door was locked, but it wouldn't. It was as though someone was gripping it from the other side.

And someone was.

And in one wild, sickening moment Clark was:

hurtling into the room, hurtled in by the suddenly jerked-open door, tripping and turning sideways as he caromed and skidded along the floor on his knees and chest. he turned over on his haunches, and started to push himself up with his hands, laugh-scolding Chester, the silly bastard, more irritated than angry or frightened: and his eyes were full of the light outside, and in here in the shade-drawn darkness, he could hardly see at all. there was just a great gray-white blur coming toward him, wobbling through the areaway between wall and bed; and he blinked his eyes and his throat-cords tightened; and he gasped, Chester, it's me, you stupid son-of-a-bitch, goddammit, I'm goin' to kick the. and he didn't have time to get to his feet and he couldn't skid away any further, and Chester was sagging down over him, face contorted, his outstretched hands two great fat claws. and he couldn't get away and jesus he didn't dare call for help, and it wouldn't have done any good anyhow. and he said it's Pete, for Christ's sake, Pete Clark. no. no, no, no, no, no, Chester. nothing to be afraid not going to hurt Mr. Clark, the manager, I'm your friend I'm

*smiling see remember remember Jesus you never been this bad just like the
wind son come to play friendgoddamitfriend remember the stars that night
the stars and the lights all winkinanblinkin smiling at you because don't
Chester don't no n—*

*and he was squeezed back as far as he could go, down on his shoulders,
and Chester was coming down on him like a ton of flabby brick. and he
drew his feet back and kicked, God, he had to do something didn't he, and
Chester grunted and there was a kind of dull cracking sound and Jesus
Jesus he sat up and Chester was sitting right across from him, butt flat on
the floor, back braced against the side of the bed, and he panted, now that
made a lot of goddamned sense, didn't it. that was a nice thing to do. I look
after you like you were a baby, and you you're just like the rest of the
family. not really giving a damn for anyone but yourself. letting people
knock themselves out for you, playing with them and then pissing on them.
and if I wasn't a nice guy I'd have killed you long ago. I'd have killed every
goddamned one of you . . . and Chester's head kind of vibrated, jerked
this way and that, and then it flopped backwards, drooped down on his
neck like a knot in a wet towel, until it was touching the bed.*

Because he was dead, of course.

The stars had killed Chester Van Anstruther.

8. The Glass Whirlpool

Johnny Blair, an inveterate ne'er-do-well, currently an office building
window-washer, runs into two sirens on the same day: Carol Ashton,
whom he spies in the nude in a doctor's office whose window he's
washing, and the stunning Lana Lee, whom he meets while having an
after-dinner drink. Before Johnny knows what's happening, he's visited
by a knife-wielding, five-foot-tall "confidential investigator" named
Harry the Jock, inquiring about Miss Ashton.

He had cried easily as a child. He had been easily saddened by the
world's minutest tragedies and wrongs. As far back as he could remember,
Mom and Dad and Betty—Mom and Betty in particular—had had to shield
him from emotional upsets. Once when he was about eight, he had gone
"hunting" with some other boys. And he didn't have a B-B gun like the
others did—Mom hated any kind of gun, and he didn't really want one,
anyway. But one of the boys had insisted he take a shot with his rifle.
"*Come on, sissy, I dare ya to!*" So he had closed his eyes and shot blindly
at the brash, telephone-pole-perched sparrow which all the other boys had
missed. And it plunged to the ground, dead.

He fled home in hysterics. A doctor was called and gave him sedation,
but he was again wild with remorse as soon as it wore off. Finally, Mom
and Betty had told him what had *really* happened; they'd convinced him of

it. And after that he was all right. He hadn't shot the bird, you see. It had been one of the other boys—after all, they'd fired at it a dozen times, hadn't they?—and the bird had just happened to fall at the time he shot. He wasn't guilty of killing it. In fact, looking back on the days of his youth, he could find himself guilty of none of the sins normally peculiar to nonage.

There was the time when he had dated up his best friend's steady girlfriend. The friend had been bitterly nasty about it, and he, Johnny, had been terribly upset—briefly. Until Betty and Mom made him see that he was entirely blameless. It had been the girl's fault, not his. She had taken his simple courtesy and friendliness for something else—for flirtation. And not knowing how to set her straight without hurting her feelings, he had taken her on a date.

For a youngster as conscientious and sensitive as he was, he was blamed with surprising frequency for things of which he was completely blameless. Once, for example, there had been a fire in the high school gym—inspired by forbidden cigarettes—and the other guys had accused him of squealing to save his own neck. (And it wasn't that way: he had simply wanted to do what was right, to make a clean breast of things.) On another occasion—

But let it go. Let all the occasions of seeming guilt and actual innocence go. The point was that, regardless of appearances, he was really very sensitive and unselfish.

Thompson completed forty-five typescript pages of *The Glass Whirlpool*.

9. A Horse in the Baby's Bathtub

The adventures of a super-intellectual psychotic teenager named Herbie, who has previously killed his parents and is now torturing Carol, his nanny, whom he desires and who desires him.

A variation of *Child of Rage*, with which it shares many plot elements.

"You've got to admit one thing, ladies," I said, drawing them conspiratorially close. "When the chips are up and the chickens go to the neighbors to roost and earth's last picture is painted, you got to admit one thing . . ."

"Yes, Herbie?" Their eyes gleamed with piggish anticipation. "What is it, Herbie?"

"When everybody puts his shoulder to the wheel and stands up to be counted, you got to admit that Hitler put the people to work."

They all nodded in wise agreement. It had been a very long time, I suspected, since they had listened to these puerilities of mine; merely nodding to whatever I said, since they were sure of what it would be. I am certain they would have agreed with me if I had said that crap smelled like clover.

I have had the same thought sometimes when listening to the wild laughter which ensues when a popular comedian makes a completely non-humorous remark. Or the thunderous applause when a political candidate proves himself an oratoric imbecile. *("We can only advance by going forward.")* Or to the preposterous delight of a soap-opera husband when his wife tells him she is going to have a baby. (What he would actually do is kick her in the stomach.)

What I mean to say is that there is only the most tenuous, if any, connection, between remark and reply, action and reaction. Strength has become the parent of pusillanimity. Virtue is treated as vice. Wisdom as wackiness. Blessed are those who are deprived of what they need (it says here). Suffer little children period. Genocide is better than vanilla, and you can't hardly get ovens like that no more.

Dr. Barsdall, my psychiatrist, insists that things are not as I view them. He says (and I quote) that I look at an acorn and see a forest—a most inaccurate statement of the case. Reality is in the object beheld, not in the eye of the beholder, and he cannot see what does not exist. What he sees, of course, may be disguised. The facade of a church may mask a den of devil worshippers, its labyrinthine chambers muffling the shrieks of unbelievers who are put to the question. Or a school may actually be a kind of Procrustean bedchamber—an elaborate complex of equipment which fits every student to the same pattern, and cruelly shears away any protruding parts. Similarly, what is nominally a home is often a whorehouse, a hospital is a butcher shop and a bank a bandit's lair. And finally, to cite a common phenomenon, who will deny that the seemingly intelligent physiognomy of a man is frequently a disguised horse's ass?

Thompson completed 105 typescript pages of *A Horse in the Baby's Bathtub*.

10. I Hear You Calling

All we have of this sample is the first three typescript pages, which relates this curious phone call:

With a grim smile, Mr. Tillotson replaced the receiver of his telephone and consulted the ledger upon his desk. There was page after page of names, many of them suffixed by a neat check mark. Mr. Tillotson checked off another name, then reached for the telephone, and his hand trembled with insane glee.

To most people Mr. Tillotson was a mild, even-tempered little man who would go to any length to avoid an argument. But there were those who knew another Tillotson, a Tillotson who was a fiend incarnate, pitiless, cunning, deadly. It was that Tillotson who now spoke into the telephone, masking his voice with a prim lilt:

"Dr. Warfield's office? I'd like to speak to the doctor, please."

"Who is calling, please?" came an answering lilt.

"This is Mr. Tillotson's office. Mr. Tillotson would like to speak to Dr. Warfield."

"Oh . . . uh . . . Mr. Tillotson, you said?"

"Mr. Tillotson's office," corrected Mr. Tillotson. "This is his office calling for Mr. Tillotson."

"Well, why doesn't . . . ?" *Why not, indeed, thought Mr. Tillotson.* "I'll see if the doctor's available."

Mr. Tillotson waited, smiling. When he heard the doctor's restrainedly impatient voice, he banged the transmitter briskly against the desk before replying.

"Dr. Warfield?"

"How are you, Tillotson? What's—"

"This is Mr. Tillotson's office. Hold the line, please."

Mr. Tillotson took out his pipe, filled it, tamped down the tobacco, and leisurely applied a match to the bowl. When it was going good he again picked up the phone.

"Is this Dr. Warfield?"

"Yes."

"I wanted to speak to Dr. Warfield," said Mr. Tillotson. "This is Mr. Tillotson's office calling Dr. Warfield."

"Warfield speaking," snapped the doctor.

"Mr. Tillotson wished to speak to you Dr. Warfield. Will you hold the line, please?"

"Well, look, now. I'm rather bus—"

"Here's Mr. Tillotson now, Doctor. Go ahead please."

Mr. Tillotson puffed contentedly at his pipe while the sounds from the receiver grew louder and louder. A full two minutes passed before he spoke again:

"Mr. Tillotson's office," he trilled. "Who is calling, please?"

"I'm—this is Dr. Warfield! I've been—"

"Did you wish to speak to Mr. Tillotson?"

"Confound it, he called me! I've been waiting to—"

"Oh, I'm sorry," cooed Mr. Tillotson. "Mr. Tillotson is busy on another line, right now. Could I help you, Mr.—uh—Wharfrat?"

"WARFIELD!"

"How do you spell it, please?"

"W-A-R-F-I-E-L-D, WARFIELD!"

"Thank you, sir," said Mr. Tillotson, stiffly. "I'll connect you with Mr. Tillotson immediately."

Taking a ruler from his desk, he slapped it loudly against the transmitter. "Wharfrat?" he boomed. "What's on your mind?"

"This is Dr. Warfield," said Dr. Warfield, icily.

"Oh, how are you, Doctor?"

"I believe you called me."

"Why, yes, I did. I was calling for Mr. Tillotson. Will you hold the line, please?"

Mr. Tillotson hugged the phone against his chest, listening, shuddering with silent laughter. At last he said:

"I'm sorry to keep you waiting, Doctor. Mr. Tillotson will talk to you in a moment."

"W-who—who is this talking?"

"This is Mr. Tillotson's office."

"Now, you listen to me"—sounds of heavy breathing. "Can you hear me?"

"Certainly, sir."

"Well, you tell that boss of yours the next time he wants to talk to me to call me himself. Tell him I think it's blamed rotten manners to have a subordinate call me. Besides that, it wastes time. It wastes my time and the subordinate's time. D'yu get that?"

"Yes, sir. I'll type it up and send a copy to your office for your files."

"Well . . . you don't need to do that."

"I disagree with you, Doctor."

"What do you . . ."

There was a long moment of silence.

"I see," said Dr. Warfield, heavily. "I see."

"I'm so glad you do," said Mr. Tillotson.

11. The Jesus Machine

Hotel detective Bascom "Bunk" Hascom is getting along quite well, thank you, till the night he rapes Mona, the Negro hotel maid. And when the hotel owner, Mister Jack, covers up for Bunk the episode seems over. Over, until Mona tells Buck that she is pregnant, and expects him to do the right thing.

He yawned, lighted a cigarette and glanced about for an ashtray. There was one on the desk. It sat on top of the looseleaf notebook in which the doctor was always writing. Bunk dropped his burned match into the tray, and flipped the book open.

He was completely incurious about it. It was just there and so was he, so he opened it. He began to read, lips moving slightly as his mind fumbled over the words.

His first reaction to them was that they were funny. Doctor Sam was writing kind of a funny story. Then, his smile faded and he began to feel an unaccountable uneasiness. Once on a Friday afternoon in school, the teacher had read from a book, Golliper's Travels or something like that. Bunk had snickered along with the other kids, and then the teacher had explained that it wasn't really a funny book at all. It was—what was the word she used? Well, no mind. But it meant that the guy was saying one thing but meaning something else. He was a very bitter man, and Bunk couldn't really see why he was, because he had things a lot tougher himself. But, anyway . . .

The story had made him awful uneasy. It opened a dark door for him, a door into a bewildering world where no white-trash dumb-bell could ever make out (He couldn't even do it here, for Christ's sake!). And this thing, the story Doctor Sam was writing, affected him the same way. He didn't understand it—but yet he sort of did. He started to close the book, then opened it again and began reading from the top of the page:

    . . . *it came to pass that the woolly lambs summoned the lions together, yea, and the tigers and elephants, and all the other noble and kingly beasts of the Garden. Now, it should be said that the lambs had departed their obvious physiological destiny; inferior and fearful though they were, fainting even at the sound of a large fart and the tinkling of their own piss, they had through intolerable and incessant bleating and generally pesky behavior, acquired dominance over their superiors. So having summoned them together this fateful day, the lambs made an edict, as follows: You, they said, indicating a certain animal family, you shall do the dirty work, henceforth, and be sure to keep your balls tucked up tightly, for we shall undoubtedly want to kick you. You, they said, pointing to still another group. We shall want to use your brains, so hand them over and then get the hell off the earth. You—again pointing—kindly instruct your females to take one step forward, for*

Doctor Sam took the notebook from Bunk's hands.

Thompson completed seventy-five typescript pages of *The Jesus Machine*, plus a four-page letter to Robert Mills detailing the rest of the novel.

12. Kingdom Come

"Crazy Frank" Barrow is the governor of Oklahoma, sometime around 1920. He gives the people what they want, abiding the corrupt system but trying to change it if he can. Beneath the gruff, cynical exterior is a man with a vision of a better Oklahoma, if he can stay in office long enough to effect some change. His main problem is the pardoning of Junior Saul, a convicted murderer on death row; Barrow is caught in the middle, facing severe consequences if he pardons Junior, and worse if he doesn't. But he does have a plan in mind.

He drove on toward Tulsa, musing that Original Sin must be man's will to turn truth to cliche. Where, oh, where was the Populists' audience? Where the legions who would not be crucified on a cross of gold?

Gone with the wind, that was where. A wind doubtless created by their own bored yawning.

Tell people that the soil in great sections of the state had been ruined, and you were making speeches. Tell them that the state was being wastefully stripped of its natural resources, and your statement was "the same old political propaganda." Tell them of the state's shameful contradictions, starvation neighbored with fabulous wealth, and you were guilty of divisive tactics—and damned tiresome ones at that.

Oil money had generally gone to join older money, the financial sources from which the wildcatters and independents got their backing. Barrow knew of a man, now dependent on rag-picking for sustenance, who had made oil discoveries worth more than $50,000,000. But when he talked to him of the system which had produced his plight, and was producing it for others, the man's attention wandered. What really concerned and worried him was the danger of Bolshevism.

A fighting chance, a rough evening of the odds—that was about the best you could do for anyone. Whatever else was done would not be *for* them but *by* them.

Bred and circuses, thought Barrow. That's what the people want, and the people are always right.

Vox populi, vox Dei. The voice of the people is the voice of God.

He caught himself yawning, and chuckled sadly.

Thompson completed fifty-four typescript pages of *Kingdom Come*.

13. Mitch Allison

Another episode in the career of the eponymous con man, hero of the short stories "The Cellini Chalice" and "The Frightening Frammis." This time Mitch escapes from his arresters on a speeding train, but in the process unknowingly crosses a very dangerous woman.

She was just opening the door of the toilet as he came in. Mitch pushed her on inside, slammed the door, whipped her over his knee and jerked up her dress. He waited, then, her mouth pressed tightly against his thigh, her near-nude bottom in line with the door jamb.

She twitched and fidgeted, struggled weakly to break free. She made smothering, gasping sounds. Mitch gave her a reassuring pat. For a kid that was a way-out square, he thought absently, she had a very well-stuffed pair of panties. There were definitely no corners on them that he could see, and he had an exceedingly sharp eye for such things. She stopped struggling. Mitch gave her a pat of appreciation. Then, since it was really no trouble for him and they had a little time to kill, he gave her a few more pats.

Thompson completed forty-eight typescript pages of *Mitch Allison*.

14. A Penny in the Dust

Inspired by Thompson's high school years, when he worked the night bellboy job at the Texas Hotel, Fort Worth. Here our first-person narrator is Robert Hightower, whose family moved to Texas three years previous. Since then his father has managed to lose the family fortune, and Robert has to work nights and go to school days. He can't afford to lose the job, and fooling around with a co-worker is the surest way to lose it.

I opened the door at fifteen. Rosie, my only other friend in the hotel, stepped into the elevator. Rosie liked me. Rosie more than liked me.

Rosie was the night mezzanine maid; she worked a split- or dog-watch, from six in the evening until two in the morning. She kept the ashtrays clean, disposed of any discarded newspapers or other litter, and did a little light dusting or wiping up as needed. Primarily, she served as the attendant in the ladies' restroom (which was on the mezz') keeping it clean and seeing to the needs of any ladies who required them.

Generally, then, she had very little supervision; and she could always cite some errand, germane to her restroom attendant's duties, as her reason for being absent from the mezz'. She could—but she almost never had to. For Rosie with her look of wide-eyed innocence, her readily dimpling, creamed-coffee face was a great favorite among the well-to-do white women she served. They said she was really a little darling and a dear; and it was just too bad that such a sweet little thing had to be a nigger. So the hotel, knowing of her popularity, was anxious to keep her, and let her do pretty much as she pleased.

She gave me a pouting look as she got into the car, and announced that she was very mad at me. "I mean it, Mis' Bobbie! You really tore your ass wif me this time!"

I was already chortling and giggling, as always the ready and willing victim for her shocking, endearingly hilarious coquetry. I stopped the car between floors, where no one could look in on us, and turned around to her.

"Why, Rosie?" I grinned. "Why are you mad at me?"

"Well . . ." She leaned into me, pressing the fluffy warmth of her breast against me. "Well. You pet my ass, I tell you."

"All right," I said, squeezing and patting her bottom, fingering the cleft between her buttocks. "Why, Rosie?"

"Because . . ." she shivered with incipient laughter. I shivered with her, choking with held-in gales of mirth. " 'Cause you been tellin folks m-my my p-p-pussy's no good!"

And then we both gave way to an insane, uncontrollable paroxysm of laughter. Two naughty children, clinging to each other, hugging each other with shared delight and amusement.

"Ahh, Rosie, Rosie," I said at last, all laughter spent. "What am I ever going to do with you, Rosie?"

"Shuh, now. I done tol' you, Mis' Bobbie. I *been* tellin' you. You come up on the mezz'nine 'bout two t'night an' give me some jazzin'."

"Now, Rosie," I said, laughing and blushing. "You know you're just teasing. Why you want to jazz me?"

" 'Cause you're nice, that's why. Cause you one real, real pretty white boy." She shuddered enthusiastically. "First time I see you I think, *mmmph, mmmph!* I gots to have 'at white boy in my puss!"

Thompson completed forty-eight typescript pages of *A Penny in the Dust*.

15. The Red Kitten

Black "Blackie" White is caught in a loveless marriage with Myra; caught, because Myra's substantial inheritance is to be shared equally between them, except in the case of death or divorce. In the event of death, all the money would, of course, go to the surviving partner. But in the case of divorce or desertion, then all the money goes to the spouse deserted or divorced.

This setup destroys any love they once had for each other, and we come upon Blackie, a private detective and our narrator, as he tries to ponder a way out of his marriage. He doesn't know that Joyce Ives and the terrible Red Kitten will solve the problem for him.

Planting that kitten here had been a nut's job. What his motives were, I didn't know, and in all likelihood neither did he. But one thing was certain. A kitten couldn't hurt me, regardless of its color and my unreasoning dread of the cat family.

I had wound up my search in the kitchen. I dropped the poker to the floor, and went over to the sink. Drew a glass of water, staring down through the black void of the canyon to the twinkling maze that was a city . . . the mingling cities of Hollywood and Beverly Hills, of Los Angeles, Long Beach and waypoints. They seemed a billion miles away, a billion-billion miles. It was as though I were on another planet, lonely eons removed from the warmth and friendship of my own kind.

"I wish Myra was here," I said aloud. "I wish just . . . just anyone was here."

And then, absently, for no reason that I knew of, "He must have hated me. You'd have to hate a kid to give him a name like . . ."

I left the sentence unfinished, turned moodily away from the sink. I took a final look around the room, looking for what I don't know; merely delaying, perhaps, my return to the bedroom. And so at last I saw the tracks—the tiny pawprints that went up the white enamel side of the deep-freeze.

It stood in a far corner of the room, in shadow except when the lights were on full as they were now. I rubbed my eyes, not sure that I saw what I saw. Unwilling to admit that I did.

But they were there, all right. The claw-paw marks of a cat. And they were etched in red. And—

I crossed the room.

I raised the lid of the deep-freeze.

Myra's body was inside.

Thompson completed forty typescript pages of *The Red Kitten*.

16. The Runaround

Only the title and a half page of text was among Thompson's papers:

Poor Boy Murphy, otherwise Wash (Washington) Murphy, came up out of the subway in the Wall Street district, a lanky rawboned man with ever-so-slightly protuding teeth and a stubborn stoop to his shoulders. Even that nominally irresistible force, the Corps, which had had its own way, the uncontestably *right* way, with the Poor Boy in all else, had been unable to correct his stoop. As frustrated as were the Navy psychiatrists who battled his seeming inability to distinguish between killing and murder. Now, catching a glimpse of himself in a gleaming plate-glass window, he conscientiously straightened and walked erect . . . for almost a block or two. Which was about his limit except when wearing the shoulder braces Maybelle had bought for him. Then . . .

Then he remembered the wrathful chidings of the Navy doctors, and he grinned inwardly with sour grimness. Caressing the photographer's leather plate-holder he carried, patting the professional-type camera suspended by a strap from his shoulder.

17. Snake Magee and Johnny Too Late

Concerning the title characters, the former a grizzled old oil field hand, the latter an Indian born "too late" to share in the apportioning of the

Territory. A big oil company intends to drill the nominally worthless land upon which Snake has been squatting for years, and he realizes he probably has a hell of a claim to the land, and what's underneath it. He risks his claim to help out the battered Indian, only to find that he is actually Johnny On-Time, and owner of the land to which he wants to lay claim.

> Magee smiled upon him with strange gentleness. No matter what happened he was glad Johnny was there. A lot of people might think twice about taking in an Indian they'd never seen before—one that'd been mixed up in some kind of brawl. Might be afraid he'd take advantage of the favor to hit 'em over the head, an' take what they had.
>
> He squirmed, uneasily, a sickening thought crossing his mind. Was—could that be the way that Johnny had got hurt: trying to hold someone up or break away from the law? Loyally, he tried to banish the idea, snorting—or, rather, belching—his utter disbelief in it. Johnny wasn't that kind of a boy; one look at him an' you could tell that. Of course, he did need money, and he hadn't seemed much interested in the talk about going into business. Acted kind of like he had plans of his own—like, maybe, he didn't intend to stick around very long.

Thompson completed twenty-six typescript pages of *Snake Magee and Johnny Too Late*.

18. Sunrise at Midnight

Brad Maxwell, a typical Thompson psychotic narrator, is an ex-newspaperman living off the earnings of his prostitute girlfriend, Johnnie. He blames Narz, a crooked city detective, for getting Johnnie into whoring, but knows deep-down that he's just as responsible. Eventually he beats Nartz to death.

> When you grow up as I did, when the only parent you remember having is a tramp newspaperman and a dipso, when you are out of school as much as you're in, in your almost incessant traveling from city to city, when you are always ill-fed, ill-housed, ill-clothed: when that is the way things are, you make a lot of mistakes.
>
> Then, Someone comes to you during the night, God or the Devil—both like to latch on to you when you're young—and He says, Jesus Christ, kid, what the hell *is* the matter with you? You don't have time to study books, even if you do feel like it. Anyway, you'll have different books next month—a different school, different teachers—and studying won't make you any more than it did in the last town you were in and all the towns

before that. So let's get it all together, baby, grab that ring for a free ride. (I remember now; it was the Devil talking. God was conferring that night with the Four Horsemen.)

I wasn't any smarter (not academically) after the Old Fellow's lecture; but my grades proclaimed me a budding genius. And my rise to that status was both swiftly and simply accomplished. Being the cleanest kid that ever was, was a big part of the miracle. Being the neatest kid that ever was—and, this despite my runover shoes and frayed garments. *(The poor, brave little man! Practically nothing to do with, but doing so much with it. Oh, I think I'm going to cry! Sniffle-sniffle.)*

Met with general admiration and approval, I lost my shyness and the curse of mumbling and bumbling, and became eagerly vocal and fluid of speech. My hand was the first to shoot up when a question was asked—regardless of my ignorance of the answer. For I could talk interminably—by turns smiling or serious, but always with a mystically charming air of brightness—about nothing whatsoever.

Virtually the only studying I did was that of popular public figures— picture stars to politicians; people who were overwhelmingly attractive to others. I studied their mannerisms: the way they spoke, and smiled, and gestured, and used their eyes—the multitudinous elements of personality with a capital P. And I aped those mannerisms until they became mine, and I could use them as naturally as had their original owners.

So, ultimately, along with being the cleanest, neatest and smartest, I became the most popular kid in whatever class, or classes, I attended. Regretfully, I was not popular among the brooding, overgrown element who were detained in the same grade year after year. Regretfully, since any of them could whip a spindling sprout like me in a fair fight, with one hand tied behind him, and were increasingly insistent upon demonstrating the fact.

As always, however, when I was in need and cried out to Him, my Mentor popped up with the answer to the problem:

Fight, schmite (he jeered), and forget about that fair stuff. You don't fight *period*. Fighting can make your clothes lousier than they already are. It can spoil your looks—and you got none to spare, kid. It can hurt your snow-white reputation, no matter whose fault it is. It is *o-u-t-*, and I'm shitting you not. What you do is get the guy alone (a cinch since he thinks you're a pushover). Then, jump on his back, and scratch and claw and bite and make with your heels, until he's crying for Momma. Contingency plan: Butt him in the belly, or give it to him in the nuts, and when he goes down, *stomp him!*

Clobber the guy: that's what you want to do, baby. Clobber the living crap out of him. And if he's stupid enough to whine about not fighting fair, why join the crowd that laughs at him. A loser is a loser is a loser—that's all that matters, in the end—and no one will want what he got. And he won't want a rematch. Because, baby, when you really give it to a guy, when you really clobber the crap out of him, you fill the void with something very special. The stuff that won the world for all the smart boys, from the first Fascists, the Syrians, on up to modern times. The good stuff. The stuff that makes men into mites . . .

Terror, baby. Terror.

Thompson finished forty-nine typescript pages of *Sunrise at Midnight*.

19. Sunset and Cienega

Sanderson Blake is an alcoholic, washed-up writer of bad television shows. Once a moderately successful novelist on the East Coast, Sanderson was lured to Hollywood by the promise of a lucrative screenwriting career, only to be repeatedly swindled and fall on very hard times. His wife has left him, and his son was killed. Now, he's at the end of his rope.

It was a few minutes before seven when Sanderson Blake arrived at the studio gate, and he still wore the expression of terrifying illness with which he had arisen some two hours earlier. It was his normal early-morning expression, one that had its beginnings about a year ago when his wife had left him and his already wavering career had gone into an abrupt nosedive. He looked hung over, very badly so, but he was not. He was simply sickened and horrified by the necessity of facing another day; a day that, despite his best efforts, was certain to be maddeningly frustrating and bitterly disappointing, and to perform the most hideous tortures on the little that remained of his ego. And at this hour of the morning, after a too-brief respite of sleep, he could not mask his inner terror and illness.

Thompson finished forty-four typescript pages of *Sunset and Cienega*.

20. Very Nice for Framing.

Police Captain Corey, a man of bad reputation and uncertain character, recruits rookie Jill Sanders for a most dangerous undercover assignment: baiting a serial killer into attempting to make her his latest victim. The man has already killed three times, according to Corey, but there is no real proof against him. The most recent victim was Dolly Banion, a woman with knowledge of most of the corrupt goings-on in town; in fact, Corey probably had a good reason for killing Dolly himself.

"Yes, Miss Sanders? You're wondering if there were any other suspects besides Parton?"

"Well, yes, I was."

"I don't think so. None that's even half as hot as Parton. Unless you think I am."

"Now, Captain," Jill laughed uneasily. "I—"

"Maybe I did kill her, Miss Sanders. Not hard for you to believe, is it? I was at the scene of the murder. I had plenty of motive. Put opportunity and motive together, and it gives you your criminal. Isn't that right, Miss Sanders? Isn't that what they've been teaching you, Miss Sanders?"

"I think I'd better leave," Jill said. "Shall I report to you tomorrow night?"

Corey said she'd damned well better report, and he'd tell her when she could leave. "Now, about my question, Miss Sanders? I was jealous of Dolly, and I was sore at Parton for taking over for me. So I kill her and frame him for the job. Couldn't find a better chump for framing, could I, Miss Sanders? No holes in that, is there?"

"Yes," said Jill quietly. "A very large hole, Captain." She felt guiltily responsible for his anger, and she was trying hard to be reasonable. "You didn't know that Mr. Parton would make such a perfect chump, as you put it, until after Miss Bannion's death. You didn't check on his background until then."

"What makes you so sure? You've only got my word for it. You're not going to take my word for anything, are you?"

Thompson completed forty-six typescript pages of *Very Nice for Framing*.

INDEX

"Adventure in the North Atlantic" (*Convoy*), 244
After Dark, My Sweet, 188–89
The Alcoholics, 149–50
Alsberg, Henry G., 58, 66, 67, 69–80
Always to Be Blessed, 7, 40–42, 63–66
American Stuff, 63
"An Alcoholic Looks at Himself," 101, 103, 123–24, 131–32
"Arnold's Revenge," 51–54

Bad Boy, 23, 24, 26–7, 144–47
Bandwagon, 51
"Bellboy," 196
"Bert Casey, Wild Gun of the Panhandle," 198
Bick, Jerry, 249–50, 281–85, 289
Big Spring, Texas, 27–30
Bill, Tony, 273
  involvement with *Getaway* film, 276–77
  on *South of Heaven* contract, 275
  Thompson's visit to Utah, 275
Billington, 197, 316–17
"Blood From a Turnip," 138
Bo, 274–75
Bogdanovich, Peter, 277
Boomer, Lucille
  meeting with Thompson, 36
  lost to another man, 39–40
  on relationship with Thompson, 39
Boomer, Russell, 33, 42, 48
Bootlegging scam, 34–35
Bryans, Jim, 135, 141, 256
Burwell, Nebraska, 19–20

Cain's Hundred, 226
"A Calendar of Annual Events in Oklahoma," 71, 81
Cassill, R.V., 249
"The Cellini Chalice," 197, 226
"Character at Iraan," 17, 38
Child of Rage, 262–70
Clean Break, 198, 204
"The Clue of the Kicking Horse," 80
The Concrete Pasture, 317–18
Convoy, 244
Coup de Torchon, 293
The Criminal, 154–57, 159
Cropper's Cabin, 152–54
Cunningham, William, 57–69
  leaves Oklahoma project, 67

Daring Detective, 55
"The Dark Stair," 105
Death Is a Living Doll, 319
"Death Missed a Bet, 132–33
DeWitt, Ned, 58, 59, 61, 67–8, 73, 77, 80, 285
The Dishonored, 319
"Ditch of Doom," 55–56
The Dog, 320
Dr. Kildare, 226, 244

"The Economy of Scarcity," 61
"The End of the Book," (*Always to Be Blessed*), 7, 40–42
"Exactly What Happened," 256

Exit Screaming, 320–22
The Expensive Sky, 322

Farewell, My Lovely, 282
Fireworks: The Lost Writing, 294
"The Flaw in the System," 196–97
"Forever After," 226
Fort Worth Press, 23
Foster, David, 276–78
   corrections to T's screenplay, 278
"Four Murders in Four Minutes," 130
"The Frightening Frammis," 197
"Frozen Footprints, 80

"A G.I. Returns From Korea," 131
"Gentlemen of the Jungle," 39
The Getaway, 216–24, 276–82
The Getaway (film), 276–82
The Glass Whirlpool, 323–24
Godard, Jean-Luc, 290, 293
The Golden Gizmo, 148
Goldfarb, Robert, 198–200, 285
   on meeting Thompson, 200
The Grifters, 231–32, 302

Hallen, Ingrid,
   introduces Thompson to Hano and Bryans,
   134
Hamon, Jake, 22, 49
Hano, Arnold, 134–43
   on unfinished manuscripts, 270–71
   on Thompson's drinking, 190–91
   on editing Thompson, 141–42
   on meeting Thompson, 135, 138–39
   on reading *Killer Inside Me*, 139
   on *Savage Night*, 179
   on Thompson's loss of New York job, 190
   on Thompson's work habits, 143
   "synopsis" controversy, 140–41
   on origin of Lion Books, 142–43
   on Thompson's funeral, 285
Hardcore, 294
"Hard Times," 274
Harris, James
   on *The Killing* credit dispute, 199
   on script of *The Killing*, 199
   on Thompson's drinking, 200
"He Supplies Santa Claus," 132
Heed The Thunder
   analyzed, 105–20
   writing of, 105
A Hell of a Woman, 176–78

Hill, Walter, 279–81
   on *The Getaway* screen credit, 279
A Horse in the Baby's Bathtub, 261, 324–25

"The Illicit Lovers and the Walking Corpse,"
   55–56
I Hear You Calling, 325–26
Ironside, 256–59

The Jesus Machine, 271–72
Judge, 23

Keach, Stacy, 282
Kennedy, Burt, 282
The Killer Inside Me,
   analyzed, 158–76
   film version, 282
The Kill-Off, 205–9, 302
The Killing, 198–204
King Blood, 195, 272–73
Kingdom Come, 328–29
Kouba, Maxine Thompson, 33, 40, 103, 104,
   137–38
   on Jim's visits to her house, 255–56
Kubrick, Stanley, 198–205, 211–16

"A Labor History of Oklahoma," 70–80, 81–83
L'Amour, Louis, 71–72
Los Angeles Mirror, 130
Lunatic at Large, 215

Mackenzie's Raiders, 217–18
Man Without a Gun, 225
Man's World, 198
Master Detective, 55, 56
McQueen, Steve, 276
Medavoy, Mike, 276–79
Miller, Patricia Thompson, 48
Mills, Robert, 251, 271–72, 289–94
Mitch Allison, 329
Modern Age, 10, 101–2
More Hardcore, 294
"Murder Came on the Mayflower," 197
Musso and Frank Grill, 254
Myers, "Pa," 20

"A Night With Sally," 60
Nothing but a Man, 259

The Nothing Man, 186–88
Nothing More Than Murder,
    analyzed, 126–30
    newspaper interview on, 125
Now and on Earth, 11–16, 85, 86, 101
    analyzed, 87–98
    family reaction to, 102

"Oil Field Vignettes," 31–33
Oil fields, 26–31
Oklahoma Labor, 60
The Oklahoma State Guide, 7, 79, 83
Oklahoma Writers' Project, 7, 57–80

"Pardon Me for Living" (*Dr. Kildare*), 226, 244
Paths of Glory, 211–16
    Thompson's contract, 204
Peckinpah, Sam, 250, 277
A Penny in the Dust, 24–5, 330–31
The Police Gazette, 134
Pop. 1280, 233–42
The Prairie Schooner, 37–39
"Prowlers in the Pear Trees," 132

Quantico, Virginia, 137

"Ready for the Tiger," 250
Recoil, 150–51
The Red Kitten, 331–32
Redford, Robert, 273–75
Reed, Sharon Thompson, 60
    on *South of Heaven* contract, 275
    on Thompson's strokes, 283–84
The Rip-Off, 294–95
Rissient, Pierre,
    on Michael Thompson suicide threat, 262
    on Thompson's trip to Paris, 262
"A Road and a Memory," 37
Roberts, Dillon (Thompson pseudonym), 131,
    198
Rockefeller Foundation, 7, 83
Roughneck, 10–12, 144
The Runaround, 332–33
Ryan Aeronautical, 8, 84

SAGA magazine, 131–33
San Diego Journal, 124
"Satan's Quarter-Section," 224
Savage Night, 179–84

Schulberg, Ad, 216
"The Secret in the Clay," 80
Série Noire (line of paperbacks), 251
Série Noire (film version of *A Hell of a Woman*),
    290
Snake Magee and Johnny Too Late, 333
"Solving Oklahoma's Twin Slayings," 68, 81
South of Heaven, 251–54
    film option, Redford-Bill, 275
"The Strange Death of Eugene Kling," 55
Sunrise at Midnight, 333–35
Sunset and Cienega, 226–28
A Swell-Looking Babe, 184–86

Texas by the Tail, 27, 247–49
Texas Hotel, 24
    bellboy job, 24–26, 33
    doorman job, 50, 57
Texas Monthly, 31
"Thieves of the Field," 32
This World, Then the Fireworks, 195, 272, 295–
    301
Thompson, Alberta Hesse,
    first meeting with Thompson, 42
    recalls wedding to Thompson, 44
    on *South of Heaven* contract, 275
Thompson, Birdie Myers, 7, 19–20, 104
Thompson, Freddie. *See* Townsend, Freddie
    Thompson
Thompson, James Sherman,
    left in rest home, 8
    janitor's job, 61
    oilfield letter, 49
    congressional run, 19–20
    death of, 8–16
    losing fortune, 27, 30
Thompson, Harry, 19
Thompson, Maxine. *See* Kouba, Maxine
    Thompson
Thompson, Michael, 246–47
    on Thompson in nursing home, 284
Thompson, Patricia. *See* Miller, Patricia
Thompson, Sharon. *See* Reed, Sharon Thompson
"Those Amazing Gridiron Indians," 131
"The Threesome in Four-C," 198
"Time Without End," 61–63
Townsend, Freddie (Winifred) Thompson, 21
    on Jim and Communist Party, 71
    on true-crime stories," 51
    runs for state senate, 83
    on Hollywood, 226
    Thompson's letter to, 218–19
    on Thompson's strokes, 283
    on Thompson's alcoholism, 123

The Transgressors, 228–30
True Detective, 23, 55
Tulsa, A Guide to the Oil Capital, 8, 71, 81
"Two Lives of John Stink," 132
Tyrrell, Susan, 282

The Undefeated, 259
University of Nebraska, 36, 48

Very Nice for Framing, 335–36

Western World, 23–24
White, Lionel, 198, 204
"Who Is This Man Eisenhower?" 132
Wild Town, 209–11
Writers' Guild of America, 201, 279
Writers' Project
    accused of Communism, 59–60
    Thompson assumes directorship, 67
    Thompson resigns, 75–76

Zimmerman, Vern, 273